Here, Kitty

Hays Blinckmann

Here, Kitty

Copyright © 2023 Hays Blinckmann
ISBN: 979-8-9934292-2-9
Cover design by Irene de Bruijn
Author photograph by Bert J. Budde, Sr.

For my friends
who want something to read.

Forever and always,
Jan, Hugo, and Max
- my fraternity.

"The Truth must dazzle gradually
Or every man be blind—"

Emily Dickinson

As of 2020, the top ten reasons books
were challenged or banned, according to the
American Library Association, included:

1. sexual content (92.5% of books on the list)
2. offensive language (61.5%)
3. unsuited to age group (49%)
4. religious viewpoint (26%)
5. LGBTQIA+ content (23.5%)
6. violence (19%)
7. racism (16.5%)
8. use of illegal substances (12.5%)
9. "anti-family" content (7%)
10. political viewpoint (6.5%)

Here, Kitty gladly took that as a challenge
to incorporate most of those issues as content.

Chapter 1
Dancing With the Stars

No one knows the day things will change—the moment when one's life will get pushed in a different direction. We wake up, open our eyes, and expect nothing more, nothing less, than the day before. It's not until we look back and remember the details. Was the sun shining? Did the coffee spill on the floor? Was it a bad hair day? The ominous little signs that foreshadow life was about to alter irreversibly. In hindsight, events, colors, and feelings come back clear as day. But seeing the empty toilet paper roll doesn't exactly scream, "Go back to bed!"

But then again, while change can be difficult and unpleasant sometimes, in the long run it can be good. As Peter Wise was about to discover, getting to the good part could be a little strenuous, weird, and unpredictable.

That September day, Peter woke, as usual, noted the crispness of the fall air, and scratched his head like a dog with fleas. He couldn't help it, he always had a dry scalp, and when the summer humidity abandoned him, his skin shriveled and flaked with a vengeance. Why he still lived in Massachusetts and not the Bahamas was a needling conundrum. It sounded nice in theory— beaches, beer, and perpetual summer. But that would require motivation for change, which Peter decidedly did not have.

At 25, Peter wasn't unhappy with his life. If anything, he was complacent with it, which was good enough for him. His day was a scheduled monotony, and unlike his older brother, Charlie, Peter was okay with the lack of highs and lows. He wasn't looking for a better job, more income, or even an adventuresome existence. He preferred vacations on the couch watching old Westerns versus throwing himself off a mountain on skis or driving a fast car. That would be his older brother, an investment banker who worked 80 hours a week in Boston only to abuse dating apps and drugs on the weekends. Charlie liked fine wines and oysters Rockefeller, and Peter enjoyed Sal's Meat-a-palooza pizza and Miller High Life, the champagne of beers. To each his own, Peter always mused.

But by Peter's barometer, he had his shit together. Just enough to keep his parents, Bob and Edie Wise, at bay, although they wouldn't let go of the wasted tuition they had spent on his first two years at Yale. Yes, he had gone to Yale, and by the third year, he didn't return. He didn't fill out the paperwork, didn't register for classes, didn't say goodbye to his handful of friends. He just didn't go back. Peter couldn't precisely tell anyone why. Unexpectedly, he said yes to Mr. Dins, the Hillsdale Tennis Club owner, when asked to stay for the winter. He had coached juniors all summer and thought, *Why not?* Then, upon having said yes, at that moment, he made the decision not to return to college. Peter was not good at much forethought.

"GODDAMMIT!" Peter heard through his cracked bathroom window. It was Coach Clark, his landlord, downstairs. Peter peeked through the glass and saw garbage strewn all over the driveway. A bevy of greasy pizza boxes, various Styrofoam take-out containers, and Gatorade bottles created an abstract portrayal of modern life on the driveway. Peter had forgotten to secure his trash can lid from the raccoons. Shit.

"I'll clean it up, Coach Clark, don't worry!" Peter shouted from the window.

"You better, you little pissant." This was a term of affection from Coach Clark, and Peter didn't take offense. Coach Clark had been his high school tennis coach and Geometry teacher, and had called his students pissants since the '80s when no one gave a damn. Coach Clark and his wife, Lois, both retired, rented Peter the apartment over their garage.

With tufts of cottony gray hair coming from his head and the top of his flannel bathrobe and bare legs, Coach Clark began to pick up the garbage. He couldn't help but clean up the trash. That was who he was. A short, stout little man with the backhand equal to a Grand Slam winner. He was perpetually grumpy with a sweet side underneath all the grousing.

Peter looked out the window again to see Mrs. Clark holding a handgun in her bathrobe and slippers.

"No, Lois, goddammit, put that away," Coach Clark said, annoyed but unfrightened by the firearm.

"I can get him!" Lois shouted shrilly and aimed at a deer chewing her tomato plants. But as soon as the deer heard the commotion, he jumped the fence out of their yard. Peter smiled and watched.

"No, Lois, look, he's gone already!" Coach Clark waved his arms.

Lois lowered the weapon and shook her head, her hair still in curlers.

"Stevie, you are no fun. What's the point of having a garden if I can't have a little target practice now and again?" Lois put the gun, which was only a pellet gun, in her fuzzy pink pocket and returned inside. Originally from Minnesota, Lois Clark enjoyed shooting the deer, who ritually ate her vegetable garden, in the ass. Peter stopped flinching at the *"pop pop"* sounds heard in the early morning hours.

"I am fun, old woman!" Coach Clark shouted at her backside and continued picking up Peter's garbage.

Peter thought about how much he liked the Clarks. They were way more interesting than his parents, who, right now, would be sitting in their breakfast nook eating egg-white omelets and discussing retirement packages.

He smelled a supposedly clean, white-collared shirt, put it on, and combed his straight brown hair that he kept neat and trimmed. Peter had a tennis body, long, lean arms and legs, and stood a good 6'3". People liked to compare him to a young Roger Federer, which wasn't so bad. His face was boyish, with a slightly crooked nose covered in freckles and wide green eyes. At work, the women and teenage girls flirted with him just for kicks. It made his tips better if he flirted back. His last girlfriend was Susanne, an engineering student at Yale. She was pretty but, unfortunately, incredibly motivated. She had a one-year plan, a five-year plan, and a whole life plan. Peter had no plan, which was a point of annoyance for her that blossomed into a mushroom cloud one night when he did not want to see Bill Clinton lecture in the student hall. *Once Upon a Time in The West* was playing on TBS, and even though he had seen the movie a dozen times, it still sounded better than listening to a former leader of the free world talk about his vegan diet and the downfall of democracy. Suzanne dumped him immediately and said he would never get anywhere in life on a couch. He retorted, "But there isn't anywhere I want to go." Suzanne told any and every other female to avoid him. For Yalies, a lack of drive was like not having a pulse.

Peter threw some Gatorade in his Adidas bag and was ready for work. The simplicity of it made him happy.

Downstairs, he apologized again for the garbage. "Hey, Coach, sorry about that. Thanks for cleaning up."

"Listen, you little moron, I would have kicked you out for this, but Lois has a soft spot for you. God knows why," Coach Clark huffed.

"And you don't?" Peter gave him a bump on the shoulder.

Coach Clark ignored the remark. "Who have you got today?"

"You know, Mrs. Cantor, who thinks she's Steffi Graf but can't serve, and the new juniors."

"Anybody any good?" The coach couldn't help but ask. He would only ever admit to Lois how much he missed teaching tennis.

"Not up to your standards. Except me, I will always be the best."

"Ha! You couldn't hit water if you fell off a boat, sonny boy. You're late. Now get going." Coach Clark turned and shouted, "Lois! Put that GD gun away!" Lois was in the window practicing her aim.

Peter grabbed his bike and headed down the tree-lined streets of Hillsdale. He liked his hometown for its quaintness. He never felt compelled to try city life. The term "hustle and bustle" sounded like a bad porn movie to him. Peter had grown up in quaint Hillsdale, 40 minutes outside of Boston. It was a small enclave, less put together than Belmont or Brookline, towns closer to the city. It was "out of the fray," his parents said. Peter liked being out of the fray if the fray meant traffic and too many people on the sidewalks.

Hillsdale was precisely the type of town movies glorified. It had one main street with useless shops selling candles and Etsy-type crafts. The hardware store still sold dollar items, and the barber shop's special was Kennedy-era crew cuts. There were old fashioned parking meters that required quarters, and the streetlamps were adorned with whatever holiday was looming. Even though neighboring strip malls enticed with the Gap and a Panera, Hillsdale residents still got their brick oven pizza from Spaggio's and homemade ice cream from Scoop Du Jour. The movie theater had old, creaky seats where almost every teenager had attempted or received a first kiss. The streets wound outward in a random pattern carved by horse buggies and cattle drives in the 1800s. Current GPS still confused Harbour Lane with Harbor Way, and if you didn't know the stoplight on Elm was called the "punishment light" for taking too long, you didn't live in Hillsdale.

Someone played pickleball with your mother, dated your sister, or was coached in little league by your dad. There were two degrees of separation, not six, by the very nature of existence in Hillsdale. And no one minded. Hillsdale didn't embrace modernization, although Uber had arrived unbeknownst to many. But that was a delightful convenience during the Christmas season with all the cocktail parties. It wasn't a tourist town, no antiquing for urbanites or hocking of "Hillsdale Strong" t-shirts, because nothing had ever really happened in Hillsdale. Aside from a blizzard or two, Hillsdale remained humble, not looking for attention or accolades from the outside world, much like its residents.

By mid-afternoon, the tennis club had already dealt with the morning ladies. Mothers and semi-retired middle-agers who booked their lessons before a boozy lunch or school pick-up. There were male retirees who thought they still had "it." They preferred single lessons to strut in shorts left over from the nineties. Afternoons were mostly kids forced to get off their devices and exercise. The club had always been popular in their little town. Especially in the winter with their indoor courts for those who wanted to work on their game to beat their summer neighbors on

Martha's Vineyard or Nantucket. Peter's clients were pleasant, if not a little gossipy. He quickly learned not to take up not-so-subtle offers of seduction from the women. Word would get around.

In the beginning, just once, he had stupidly accepted Mrs. Cami Tinsdale's offer of an after-lesson lemonade. They ended up having sex standing up in her kitchen, which lasted all of 60 seconds. Peter liked the smell of her expensive perfume, but her manicured hands scratched his arms. After her make-up rubbed off, Peter just saw the sadness and desperation in her eyes. Mr. Tinsdale was 20 years her senior, and Cami was clinging to what was left of her youth. That wasn't Peter's problem. Never again, he vowed.

It was around 4 o'clock when Peter spotted the maroon minivan. It wasn't unlike the others lined up dropping off pimple-faced teens. But it was parked off to the side, and Peter swore he could see smoke inside. He squinted and made out two figures laughing. The driver got out, and Peter was momentarily mesmerized.

The driver was a teenage girl who looked around sixteen. She was extremely tall and stout, and her shoulders were too broad for her body. Her build reminded Peter of a swimmer. Her legs were thick like tree stumps, rock solid and straight. He wondered how someone could have been born without ankles. The unfortunate pink velour shorts were too small for her behind, and her floppy t-shirt printed with "In Your Dreams" on it made Peter laugh. The girl approached him. Her thick round glasses came into view, and messy blonde hair amassed around her face as if a lion sat on her head. The girl was not attractive but not unattractive, more odd-looking in a fascinating way. Her body proportions were off, and it was a point of interest for Peter. She kept approaching, and Peter watched as she pushed her glasses up over enormous blue eyes. Her nose was piggish, a little too small for her face, probably why the glasses fell.

She stopped short of Peter and put her hand on one hip as if already annoyed. But he was used to that attitude from people.

"You a tennis coach?" Again, she pushed her glasses up, and Peter noted she must have been about 5' 10", model tall. He thought of Maria Sharapova, his childhood crush. But this girl was no Maria Sharapova.

"Yes, can I help you?" Peter used his pleasing client voice.

"Yeah, teach me how to play." It was a demand, not a question. Peter liked her sassiness already.

"Okay, have you played before?"

"No, why would that matter?" She stared hard at him.

"Dunno, just wondering if you're a beginner or not. Kind of helps with the whole teaching thing."

"I'll be good, don't worry. So can we hit, or do we talk or something?" She kept staring at him without blinking.

"Well, you have to sign up and pay inside," offered Peter.

"I'll pay with a credit card, okay? But can I hit now? I don't like waiting."

Peter was supposed to coach the under-twelve boys, who were obnoxious and spent the lesson making farting noises and hitting each other with their rackets. He'd let one of the assistant coaches take over; in other words, the high school kids who got ten dollars an hour for standing around.

"Yeah, I don't see why not. Meet me on court three." Peter pointed to the court.

Without a word, the girl turned toward the office.

"Hey, what's your name?" Peter had to shout behind her.

The girl stopped and looked back. "Kitty." She said it like he was the stupidest person in the world for not knowing. Peter shook his head. His day just got more interesting.

Kitty returned to court three, and Peter noticed she had procured a racket from the pro shop, an expensive one too. His buddy Dave must have made the sale.

"My name's Peter, by the way." Kitty just stared at him.

"Okay." She exaggerated the *kay* sound, like how could she be bothered to retain this new information? Peter walked with her onto the court, chuckling, and began the basics. Swing from low to high, move your feet with your right foot forward, grip low on the racket, etc. Kitty listened intently, then said, "Got it." She stood staring, waiting for him to go to the other side of the court, and Peter oddly obeyed.

He tossed her some easy lobs, and she hit them perfectly. Inches above the net, the balls came full force back to him. She began alternating corners and deftly hit the ball cart for fun.

After forty-five minutes, Peter liked what he saw. Kitty had talent.

"You're pretty good," he encouraged.

Kitty was gulping from a Coke bottle and let out a belch. "Yeah, I thought I would be. So, again? Tomorrow? Pet...errrr." She smirked at him and marched toward her minivan. She didn't wait to hear him say, "Absolutely."

"Did you see that?" Peter asked as he walked into the pro shop.

"Did I see what? You mean the girl who looked like Meg Ryan and Seth Rogan had a baby?" Dave didn't look up from the register as he was sorting receipts.

David Dins, pro shop extraordinaire and boss's son, was never Peter's high school buddy. They were the same age and grew up in Hillsdale, but rarely saw each other during their formative years. The Dinses owned the Hillsdale Tennis Club, and Dave was their fourth child. He was slightly, but not overtly, autistic. Without wanting to acknowledge Dave's Autism Spectrum Disorder or ASD in elementary school, his parents home-schooled him. He was low on the spectrum, they liked to whisper behind his back to others. Like when Dave asked Mrs. Tinsdale why she married a man who looked like Gandolf, or questioned Bunny Ryan where the wrinkles on her face had gone because they had been there the month before. When they had to use his autism as an excuse for his quirks was the only time it was acknowledged. Dave knew he was different and was unapologetic about it. His parents could do all the apologizing, he told Peter. If anything, Dave had a self-deprecating manner which, like many other awkward young adults, ASD or not, suited him just fine. It was his choice to call out his eccentricities but not necessarily the right of others. And like Peter, Dave was equally unmotivated with solving life's problems, which had nothing to do with his ASD.

Mr. Dins forced Dave to work at the pro shop to get him out of the house. But secretly, Dave confessed to Peter he liked his job. Otherwise, he would watch movies or play video games all day. His parents didn't pay Dave, but he didn't care because he dealt weed on the side for money. Then Massachusetts made weed legal, so Dave just stole the petty cash from the pro shop.

It didn't take long for Peter to get used to Dave's oddities and grow to appreciate them. Dave rarely made eye contact and repeated questions often, but he was great with math and had done Peter's taxes the past two years. He had extensive trivia knowledge about old movies, which they both had an affection for, and marijuana. When stoned, Dave's pop culture knowledge was highly entertaining. "Peter, did you know Elvis was blonde as a child?" No, Peter did not. Also, Peter and Dave were both disappointments to their fathers, so there was that.

"She had a credit card, the number was number 4235-6754-2009, expiration 1/22, but I can't say the secret code. Kitty is only sixteen. I'm 25, and I still don't have a credit card."

"So her name is Kitty Kittrick? Sounds weird. Wait, is being a Kitty better than being a Bunny? Like Bunny Ryan, who plays doubles?" Peter mused.

"Cats live longer than bunnies because they have fewer predators. To be a Kitty is better than a Bunny," Dave deadpanned and began re-sorting the receipts. Pete knew he would review them at least five times before putting them away.

Peter smiled and waited patiently, watching his buddy, who was absurdly fit for spending most of his time at an Xbox. Dave's muscles were chiseled, and he had that glowing platinum blond hair like his parents, former tennis stars on the B circuit. His face was lean and angular, and he had radiant light blue eyes. Peter thought the Dinses must have descended from Vikings. How cool. His fitness had to be genetic because Dave ate like a rat behind a Denny's. Peter loved watching the girls flirt with Dave until they realized something was off. Which also didn't have anything to do with his ASD, because Dave was gay. Peter knew it, but Dave's parents didn't. Information like that might send them over the edge, Dave explained. Dave had revealed this fact when they were discussing porn sites. He liked HotMathMen.com and GamerGods.com because his kind turned him on. But then again, he went on Tinder because who was he to be so picky?

"Well, Miss Kitty Kittrick has piqued my interest," Peter told him. "She's a good player. Do you know anything about her family?" Everyone knew everyone in Hillsdale or someone who knew everyone in Hillsdale.

"Do I know anything about her family? Her name is Kittrick, so I assume her older sister is Nina Kittrick? Nina is our age and graduated from Hillsdale Prep with you in 2015. Nina invited me to her thirteenth birthday party because her grandmother felt sorry for me. It was well known I had no friends." Peter always admired Dave's honesty and lack of embarrassment.

Dave continued, "They live at 22 Oakland Drive, and I live at 44 Oakland Drive. Their parents were deceased before she and her sister moved here to live with their grandparents. The grandparents are now deceased. My mother made them three lasagna casseroles and then stopped when they didn't return the Tupperware."

"That's sad…about the parents, not the Tupperware," Peter replied.

"That's how it goes, I suppose. Wanna smoke? Everyone is gone." Dave held up a joint.

Peter followed Dave out the shop's back door, and they lit up the blunt.

"Mmm, Nina," Peter pondered out loud, never knowing if Dave was listening. "She was a shy girl who didn't talk much in high school. Kind of nerdy. She had glasses and blonde hair like her sister, but not as big or tall. And she had a lot of acne. The kind of acne that makes you feel really bad for someone. She would have been pretty without all the acne."

"I didn't have acne because the autism was enough. God didn't want to pile it on too hard. That's what I heard my mom tell my dad." Peter coughed with laughter. Dave was the best.

When Peter got home, he was greeted by Coach Clark raking fall leaves in the yard. "You got a visitor," Coach Clark grumbled and nodded toward the driveway. Peter, pleasantly high, rolled his bike on the front lawn. He checked to ensure he was still wearing his sunglasses so Coach Clark wouldn't see his red eyes.

Peter looked toward the driveway and let out an audible groan.

"He never stopped being a little prick, eh?" Coach Clark offered. Coach Clark had once taught the visitor as well.

"Wish me luck," Peter said as he walked his bike up to the yellow Porsche revving in the driveway.

"Hey, Chuck," Peter said to his brother, who was scrolling through his iPhone in the driver's seat.

"Don't call me that," Charlie said without looking up. His

brother also had neatly cut hair; they got that from their father. Charlie wasn't as handsome as Peter, which made Peter a little too happy. Charlie had a round, soft face from their mother's side and a stumpy nose. Shorter than Peter, Charlie's gut toppled over his khakis from the fine dining and sitting at his computer all day. At 28, his youth was fleeting, along with his good manners.

"Why are you here, Charles?" Peter asked.

"Get in. We gotta go." Charlie's stubby fingers poked at the phone like it was an ATM.

"Where?"

"The hospital, numb nuts."

"What? Wait, why?" Peter was confused. Did he forget something, like his mother having brain surgery?

"Dad and Mom, you little turd, we have to get them." Peter hated when Charlie spoke to him without any greeting, subject matter, or words that somehow explained the situation. Charlie rolled his eyes. "Mom's waiting for us, so toss your Hot Wheels and get in."

"Not until you use actual words to tell me what the hell is going on. Are they okay?" Peter was getting anxious.

Charlie dramatically lowered his phone, audibly sighed with irritation, and said, "Yeah, well, you know, the bleeding stopped."

"What..." Peter sucked in his breath to withhold his anger and fear for his parents. "Bleeding?"

"The cut on Dad's face."

Peter realized Charlie wasn't panicking, so it couldn't be too bad. Slowly, he said, "Cut from what?"

"When he fell down the stairs. Do you need a dissertation? Get the fuck in, I gotta be somewhere later." Charlie revved the engine for no reason...again.

"When did he fall down the stairs?"

"Today, you idiot, and now Mom can't drive them home."

"Why?"

"Because of her twisted ankle..."

"And her ankle is twisted because...?"

"Because Dad fell on her at the bottom of the stairs."

The thought of Lois's pellet gun popped into Peter's head. Maybe he should get one.

"Are they okay?"

"What do you think?"

"Well, I don't know because you haven't told me anything."

"They are old, Peter. Shit like this happens."

Peter gave up and got in the yellow penis mobile. He thought about the leftover pizza he would now have to wait to eat and groaned.

"BOYS!" His mother cried when she saw them. As if her children had just saved her from a cave mining accident.

Charlie strode over to her, all business in his three-piece suit. Peter looked like a twelve-year-old in his tennis shorts. Tennis outfits weren't really hospital attire, he noted.

"Take off your glasses, darling," Edie said. Peter forgot he was still wearing them inside, but they helped with the fluorescent lights. Damn, they were bright! He wanted to retort, but kept his mouth shut. His mother, Edie, looked perfectly together with her neat graying hair in a pink ribbon, her signature Lily Pulitzer sweater, her pink lipstick perfectly applied, and an actual pink Ace bandage around her foot. How did she get that? Were there rainbow options in the ER? That was something he would need to discuss with Dave later. His mother was sitting in a wheelchair next to Peter's father, Bob, atop a hospital gurney.

His father looked stoic in his dark blue crew sweater, gray hair perfectly combed, and tall, angular face like Peter's except for the bandage neatly taped over his right eye. He reminded Peter of the naval officer he once was, about to give a command. Like Sean

Connery in *The Hunt for Red October*, if his dad had a Scottish accent. "Re-verify our range to target...one ping only." Gosh, he was stoned.

"Dad, what happened?" Peter asked, trying to appear normal. He resisted the urge to salute him and ask him if he was going to defect. Naturally, his father turned toward Charlie to respond.

"Tripped over the damn cat and flew down the stairs like Superman into your mother. Don't know why she was there," Bob grumbled.

"I was coming up the stairs, darling!" his mother shouted like it was an inquisition. Their father always did have a passive-aggressive way of blaming everyone. Already Peter noted the accident was caused by one: the cat, and two: his wife for being in the house.

"Damn glass cut my eye." Three: a glass. Trifecta.

"What glass?" Peter asked, but was pretty sure he knew the answer already.

"You know, a glass..." His father looked at the window as if physically turning away was equivalent to answering the question.

"Perhaps a martini glass in your hand?" Peter started to giggle, now able to imagine the scenario fully. His father was going downstairs for maybe his second or third cocktail and tripped over nothing, or perhaps the cat, and his mother happened to be coming up the stairs. There was an Abbott and Costello feel to it.

"Now, Dad," Charlie interrupted. "Don't bother with the details. I'm glad you are all right." And right on cue, Charlie absolved their father of any responsibility, the great enabler and kiss-ass.

"So, is everyone okey-dokey, or should I call Great Willow and have the presidential suite made up?" Peter chirped. He was still a bit high. Great Willow was the local old folks' home.

"Peter, your humor isn't very welcome," his father warned.

"Ohh, tsk..." his mother blurted. "We are fine. Just need a ride home, darling." She had her Kate Spade handbag on her lap, the sure sign it was now someone else's duty to get her from A to B.

Peter asked, "Mom, how did you get here?"

"Well, I drove, of course." His mind struggled with how she got there with a twisted ankle, but he didn't want any more information at this point.

"Well, Mom, Dad, chin up. All's well that ends well," Charlie again chimed. "I'll leave Peter to get you back to the house. I'd drive, but my car only fits two, and I have to get back to Boston. Tonight we have a thing with Citibank."

Bob brightened. "Oh, Citibank. Are they going to merge with —" Peter knew they'd be trapped there if his father and Charlie began discussing business. He was still thinking about pizza.

"Right!" he interrupted. "Let's get your things and get going! *Dancing With the Stars* awaits!" Peter had no idea why he said that. It was a fun non-sequitur that made his dad squirm.

A nurse walked in. "Mr. and Mrs. Wise..." She was looking down at her chart. "You can go home now, and here are your prescriptions for pain relief. Mrs. Wise, please keep icing your ankle and be careful on the stairs. And Mr. Wise, I suggest you don't walk into any walls tonight." She chuckled a little at her joke, but no one else did. The nurse was pretty and petite, with her blonde hair in braids. She looked about Peter's age and wore gold-rimmed glasses highlighting her heart-shaped face. Peter saw Charlie eye her like prey and felt automatically protective of the stranger. He thought about a fuzzy bunny and sighed. Yep, still high. Got bunnies on the brain again.

"Now, Mr. and Mrs. Wise, do you have a ride home?" The nurse looked at Charlie and Peter, and Peter saw her faintly sniff the air between the two brothers. She could smell the pot on him. He knew it. He held his breath like that would take away any odor.

Then he reminded himself he hadn't been drinking. She kept her face down and didn't look at the brothers. Yeah, he wouldn't want to bother with them either.

"Right, O! Jolly, best be going now," Peter shouted too loudly. Somehow he had affected an English accent in his paranoia, grabbed his mother's wheelchair, and started swiveling her around. Time to get out of there.

Peter drove his parents' Mercedes sedan home slowly, grateful it was still light out. His sunglasses had returned. His father grumbled to let him drive, but Peter gripped the wheel and deposited them safely back at his childhood home. "Mission accomplished," he shouted. Again, his father gave him the side-eye. Bob never was amused by his son's antics.

"Dear, come in and have some dinner with us," his mother cooed as she limped to the kitchen.

"No dinner for me," his father griped. "Just going to watch Shark Week and go to bed." But Bob headed to the pantry where he kept his martini fixings.

"No, Mom, that's okay," Peter said. "Do you want me to make you something? You really should get your foot up."

Edie looked gratefully at her son and raised her hand to his face. "You are such a love when you want to be," she said sweetly, without sarcasm. "Go home. I'll be all right. Can you grab me an ice bag and a glass of cabernet?" And she hobbled to the staircase. Peter got her settled in bed while his dad sipped a martini in the downstairs den with sharks swarming his TV.

Peter left, closing the front door quietly. No one said thank you or goodbye, and Peter knew everything was okay. But life would change soon, and Peter had no idea, the clueless bastard.

Chapter 2
Eco-Friendly Water Bottles

"I'll be fine, Mom," Adam said without looking away from his Xbox. He was playing *Minecraft*, as usual. Mia was somewhat obsessed with watching it. What would this future generation create, knowing how to build a fantasy world on a screen? When she was a child, she read books and watched copious amounts of TV. But also, she had no friends and grew up on a farm in Vermont. Her parents, former hippies, talked about cows and cheese, and Judy Blume seemed the only person who understood her.

"Adam, you are ten. I can't in good conscience leave you alone in the house at night."

"What's 'conscious,' Mom?" Again, he didn't look away from the screen, but kept tap-tap-tapping until there was a boat with a hamster steering it toward a palm tree.

"It's your mental abilities. If you don't have a good conscience, it means you are doing something wrong." She thought immediately of her ex-husband, Adam's father.

"Okay," he responded. Mia had no idea if Adam understood. But she loved explaining things to him, her only son. He was on the small side, *like his father's penis*, Mia joked in her head. Adam had wiry arms and legs, cute grayish eyes, and floppy red hair that she loved to run her hands through. She was glad he was ginger because he looked more like her than his father, Eric the prick. Eric was now in the Bahamas with Camila, her younger sister, whom he'd had a two-year affair with before they, in "good conscience," came clean with Mia. Now, they all have to pretend everything is "okay" for Adam and Camila's twins from her previous marriage. Her nieces, Luna and Aria, were named after goddamn mystics. Camila was a yoga teacher, of course.

Nowadays, one didn't have a bitter divorce, but consciously uncoupled, co-parented, and pretended to get along because some idiotic podcaster said so. Every time Mia saw Eric and Camila, she imagined taking one of their eco-friendly water bottles and slamming it into her sister's kneecap. Admittedly, she was angrier at her sister for the affair than her husband. How could someone who shared her DNA be so dumb? Eric, on the other hand, was an incredible imbecile. He hadn't noticed since the divorce that Adam had grown into a recluse. Mia constantly badgered Adam about having friends over, but he was hibernating, licking his wounds from their shattered family. Worse, Mia suspected Adam was embarrassed that his cousins would now be his stepsisters. It's not beyond the scope of a ten-year-old to understand that's messed up. Mia hoped Adam's quietness was a phase, and maybe this school year he would start socializing again. But she didn't push it, still feeling guilty about the divorce, although she didn't regret it.

Eric was the reason they lived in Hillsdale. Mia had met Eric in Boston through friends after college. He was working at a software company outside the city and commuting. He made a decent living pushing paper, but it wasn't an exciting career choice.

That should have been a red flag for Mia, but she got pregnant on their fourth date. Wanting to keep the baby, she settled for Eric, and they moved to Hillsdale. He could be closer to work, and she could get a teaching job. It all sounded good, but the reality was far different.

Mia shouldn't have married Eric. She knew it while standing in a white satin dress in front of 100 people, but she was seven months pregnant with Adam. Adam had not been an easy pregnancy, and there were complications. She became weak and willing, terrified for her baby, not strong enough to say no to someone promising to care for them. Mia assumed she couldn't raise Adam alone if he had health complications, or something worse. But Adam came out perfect—premature and small, but perfect—and she was more in love with him than her husband. Probably because Adam was healthy, the marriage didn't last. But she preferred that scenario to any other.

Mia shook the thought of her ex and her sister out of her head. Her therapist kept saying to move on, but she still dreamed of setting their Prius on fire. Hell hath no fury like a woman scorned.

She had to find a sitter. Mia Golding was an English teacher at the local private school, Hillsdale Prep. She wanted to be head of the department and tonight was the teacher's social, where she needed to schmooze everyone. Mia could be charming when she wasn't being an asshole in her mind. She loved English literature. She related to the nerdy kids who took solace in books from the social prison of high school. To be head of the department felt like an achievement, and the fifteen percent pay raise was appealing. Over the years, people likened her to the icon Kathryn Hepburn, tall and slim, with neat red hair and pale, freckled skin. Her face had that same angular shape as Hepburn's, and at 40, Mia was one of those rare women who got better looking with age.

Her last sitter had moved away, so she was in a pickle. Mia hated using any of her students, not wanting to cross the line between personal and professional life. But she had no choice, and a junior Hillsdale Prep girl lived across the street. She looked out the window at the house. Mia had never been neighborhood-friendly and didn't know the family. The teenage girl looked a little odd, always dressed in tight-fitting colorful clothes, and she parked her minivan at an angle in the driveway, which disturbed Mia's sense of order. The girl wasn't one of Mia's students, so she didn't know much about her.

What was she to do? Oh, hell, all the girl had to do was cook some pizza rolls and make sure Adam got to bed, right? And not do drugs in front of her kid, so there was that.

Mia had no choice but to march across the elm-lined street and knock on the small cottage-style house door. It was a pretty house, painted buttery yellow with blue trim. Most of the homes on the road were either cottage or shingle-style. It was a typical New England suburb. The houses had lawns with big hydrangea bushes that bloomed in the summer and bumpy sidewalks full of weeds. The neighborhood was quiet and close to Adam's elementary school, so he could walk back and forth. Hillsdale Prep started in 9th grade, and Mia couldn't wait to see him in the halls every day.

A young woman in hospital scrubs answered while eating an ice cream sandwich.

"Hi, can I help you?" the pretty blonde said brightly.

"Hello, I'm Mia from across the street. Sorry, I've never introduced myself."

"That's okay. Need some help or something?" The girl continued eating. Mia envied how breezily she reacted.

"There is a teenage girl who lives here, right? I was wondering if she babysat?"

"Kitty? That's my little sister. I'm Nina, by the way." Nina kept eating even though the ice cream was dripping down her arm.

"Nina, that's a lovely name. I have a son named Adam, who is ten, and I am desperate to have someone watch him tonight so I can go to a work thing."

"KITTTTYYYY!" the girl yelled. Then in a lower tone, she said, "My sister is a little weird, I have to warn you, but she is a good kid. She comes off a little strange."

"I'm a high school teacher, so I know all about teenagers. Is she responsible? Can she microwave things and call 911?"

The girl laughed. "Yeah, she can do that, but she is not the most predictable, so fair warning. KITTTYYYYYY!"

"Jesus, Nina, will you get laid or something?" Kitty said, bounding down the stairs. She saw Mia and pushed her glasses up on her face. She recognized Mia as a Hillsdale teacher and said quickly, "What? I didn't do it."

Nina laughed at her sister's paranoia. "No, Kitty, this is our neighbor Mia, and she wants to know if you can babysit across the street tonight. She has a boy."

Mia closed her eyes and breathed. This felt like a bad idea already. "Adam, he's pretty easygoing, and I won't be gone long."

"He doesn't cry, does he?" Kitty asked bluntly.

"Not unless he's hurt..." Mia said.

"Does he watch TV?"

"Yes." Now Mia felt like she was being interviewed.

"You have Wi-Fi?"

"Yes, and pizza rolls if you like."

"Can we order pizza? I'm on a certain diet."

Nina rolled her eyes and said, "Kitty, pizza is not a diet."

Kitty looked at her sister like an idiot. "If you eat certain kinds of food all the time, that is your diet. You're a nurse. You should know that." Nina rolled her eyes again.

"Yes, yes, Adam would always prefer pizza." Mia nodded,

submitting to Kitty's demand.

"Okay, what time and how long? I watch Jimmy Fallon every night." Kitty made it sound like she had to perform surgery at exactly 11:30 pm.

"I have to go at 6, and I should be back by 9-9:30. Ten dollars an hour okay?" Mia thought it should have been less, but wanted to make the job appealing.

"Yeah, see you at 6." Kitty returned up the stairs.

Nina offered, "Sorry, as they say at the hospital, her bedside manner is atrocious." Mia liked the way Nina used the word atrocious.

"That's okay, thank you, thank you both." Mia was visibly relieved.

"Can I ask? You had a husband? Short guy, wore blazers? What happened? I'm nosy, I know." Nina licked the ice cream from her arm.

"Ran off with my sister, and they are at a Sandals resort right now, pretending to care about sea turtles, sucking on cheap drinks." The sentence flew out of Mia's mouth.

"All right, gotcha." Nina laughed. "Living the cliché dream." Mia smiled gratefully.

"And your parents? I don't see anyone but you and your sister," Mia asked brightly.

"Oh, that's right, you never met my grandparents. This is, or was, their house. Now it's ours. My parents passed away a long time ago. I care for Kitty, but no worries, we're good." It struck Mia that Nina probably had spent a great deal of time deflecting the pity, but there wasn't a trace of bitterness in her voice. This generation was so different from hers. Nina wiped the ice-creamed fingers on her scrubs.

"If you need anything, just knock." Nina smiled.

"Thanks, you too," Mia said meekly and returned home.

Promptly at 5:50 pm, Mia opened her door for Kitty. The girl was shockingly on time. "I'm here," Kitty announced, and walked into the house without being asked. She was dressed in a sky-blue tracksuit, and her unruly hair was in a high pony. Mia watched her stop and look around, seemingly finding her home agreeable. Mia did have a homey house filled with plants and books, or so she thought.

"I ordered both a cheese and pepperoni pizza and paid for it. It should be here soon. Adam is upstairs." Again, without waiting for a go-ahead, Kitty went straight up the stairs and found Adam's room.

Before Mia could get there to introduce Adam, she heard the girl say, "I'm Kitty. What are you playing?"

"*Minecraft*," Adam responded.

And Kitty said, "Get me a controller. I want in. I built the Titanic in less than an hour the other day."

"Cool," Adam replied. And that was that. Mia loved Kitty. Adam had a friend!

Chapter 3
The Multitasker

The crash occurred at Oakland and Seminary at 9:33 pm. It wasn't a big crash. No one heard it because the only sound was a dull thud. That happens when a bike veers at five mph into a telephone pole, and the cyclist falls sideways to the ground in slow motion.

Dave lay there clutching the wrist he had used to break his fall, and he was laughing (or crying?) without making a sound. His head bobbed up and down as he tried to untangle himself from the chain and pedals.

"I'm such an asshole," Dave said out loud, still laughing.

"Why are you an asshole?" The girl, Kitty Kittrick, approached. She, too, was on the street, but didn't offer help.

Dave squirmed on the ground, still trying to get, at the very least, on his hands and knees.

"Why am I an asshole? I had 10 more miles to bicycle home, and I fell," he replied flatly.

"That would make you more of an idiot than an asshole. An asshole would do something to hurt another person. You were just stupid."

"Fair point. But I wouldn't say I like referring to myself as stupid, because it triggers me. After all, I am autistic. I am not stupid." Dave had made it to his knees and was half-standing while Kitty looked down at him with her own hands resting on her hips. She pushed her glasses up her nose.

"Are you all right?" she asked. "Are you hurt? Do you need some sort of emergency service?"

"Am I all right? Am I hurt? Physically, mmm," Dave checked his body, "no. But I lost my Taco Bell beef and cheese burrito somewhere, so mentally, I am hurt. I'm hungry, and that beef and cheese burrito would have hit the spot."

He smiled, so Kitty smiled and finally extended her hand to help him. She was remarkably strong, and Dave flew to his feet. He was shorter than her and swayed unsteadily. He was little for a guy.

"Are you drunk?" Kitty asked, surprisingly without judgment. Dave knew what judgment sounded like because his mother would have asked, "Are you drunk?" with a hefty emphasis on "ARE YOU drunk?", like "HAVE YOU drowned a kitten?"

"Am I drunk? Yes, I am. I would suspect my blood alcohol level to be above a .08, the state limit for intoxication."

"Why?" Kitty crossed her arms, genuinely interested.

"Why am I drunk? Because I asked a boy out, and he said no. I was at a bar, so I ordered three more drinks after that." He didn't look her in the eyes. "I don't take rejection well. It causes embarrassment, which is my least favorite emotion. I like rum and Cokes because they taste sweet."

"Why did he say no?"

"Why did he say no? Because I am an asshole, like I said." And Dave started laughing again.

"Did you hurt him?"

"Did I hurt him? No, I hurt his feelings because, as they say, he was a ten, and I am a five, and fives don't ask out tens. They get offended."

Kitty scratched her arm and stared hard at Dave.

"You look like a short model, so why aren't you a ten?"

"I am not a ten because bluntness can annoy some people, or so my mother tells me."

"You don't annoy me, and I'm a twelve," Kitty said while pulling at her underwear bunched up in her tracksuit.

Dave had a hard time looking at her. Instead, he focused on her scratching and pulling at her undergarment.

"You are the girl from tennis today. Kitty Kittrick, Nina Kittrick's little sister, and my neighbor."

"You helped me buy a very expensive tennis racket," she replied, smiling.

"It cost 225 dollars, but with sales tax, it came to $237.73," Dave said and picked up his bicycle.

"I think you are a ten because a five wouldn't talk to me." Kitty winked conspiratorially and turned to walk away.

"I'll see you at 3:15 tomorrow for your appointment with my friend Peter on court number three. He likes you, by the way," Dave said, but added, "I have to charge your card 85 dollars for a private lesson, no sales tax."

"Yes, you will." Kitty blew him a kiss and walked away. "Toodles, ten." Kitty made Dave laugh. Dave hated to admit when people hurt his feelings, like the guy at the bar. He wasn't entirely sure the guy at the bar was gay, so that also might have been the cause for his rejection. Dave tried hard to remain closed off from the world to avoid others' dismissal or disapproval. It was easier to spend Saturday nights at the computer than to "put yourself out there," as his mother urged him. He knew people like Kitty

Kittrick were rare. She was bold, confident, and unfazed by him. But then again, maybe she was just young and naive.

Dave tried to slip into his house unnoticed. But his mother was firmly planted in front of the TV in the living room. She was precisely the type to watch *Dancing With the Stars*.

"David, where have you been? You didn't come home after work. How was the club today? I was worried. You didn't tell me that you wouldn't be home for dinner. I mean, a simple text would have been nice. If you don't want to talk to me, say so, but you live here, so we have expectations like knowing where you are." Her mouth rocketed questions at him.

Dave hated how he was the spitting image of her. Small, muscular, and platinum blonde, Mrs. Dins dressed constantly in athleisure wear made by celebrities. Unlike Kitty, she didn't look goofy, but like an advertisement for Depends undergarments.

"I am 25 years old, and it is normal for me to be out past dinnertime," he stated defiantly.

"Well, when you live under my roof, young man..."

Dave, still tipsy, stopped listening and rummaged for leftovers in the fridge. Not as good as Taco Bell, but they may still be warm from dinnertime. Aha! Her spinach lasagna was cut evenly in some Tupperware. He stabbed it with a fork, and sauce dribbled on his chin.

"David, please, use a plate. And a napkin... Jesus," she huffed.

"Mom, Jesus doesn't live here. I do." His mother chuckled.

"Asshole," she muttered.

"That's right." He smiled back, spinach in his teeth.

Dave went up to his room and settled in at his computer. Truth be told, his childhood bedroom was his favorite place in the world. By and large, it was where he spent the majority of his life.

Everything was exactly where he wanted it, and it never changed. The bedspread was the same red and green checked monstrosity he had picked from the sale box at Bloomingdale's when he was eleven. His mother hated it, which gave Dave more of a thrill. He had forced his parents to paint his walls a deep emerald color that reminded him of a room he had seen in Giovanni Versace's Miami mansion. Unlike Versace, there was absolutely nothing on his walls, bedside tables, or floor. He liked it clean and tidy. His older siblings remarked that it was the room of a serial killer. He replied by saying, "No one has died...yet."

Dave wasn't close to his older siblings because they were older and, yes, more culturally stereotypical than he was. They had social media accounts adorned with selfies and the latest achievements, like going to a party or their baby spitting up. Dave hated social media. His siblings had left home long ago, gotten married, had children, and were mostly imprisoned with mortgages and cases of sciatica and tennis elbow. Dave wished them well but really was too selfish to care. He liked his autonomy in the family.

The first person he had remotely become close to was Peter. For almost five years, they had worked together at the club. They shared as much as any two young Hillsdale guys could: movies, alcohol, drugs, and work. But really, it was the fact that Peter didn't care much about life's hindrances. Peter didn't pester him about where he had been or where he was going. He just accepted Dave without any questions at all. They were like a modern, comical version of *Easy Rider* without the bikes or the coolness. They lacked self-awareness, and that was their freedom. Dave didn't want that to change.

The most important part of Dave's room was his desk. It was a long, thick-wooded antique. On it was his computer with not one, but three monitors. It had hard drives that gently hummed and enough memory to store part of the Pentagon. There, Dave could play video games and watch his old movies at the same time. He was a multitasker.

Still chewing on his pasta, Dave turned on his computer and checked today's scores. He had many secrets, not just the fact that he was gay. Dave was a gambler. He was probably an addict because he gambled daily. He bet online on most sporting events, even women's volleyball and curling. He loved going over the stats. The more numbers, the better. And in sports, every stat was recorded and available immediately on the internet. He could have cared less if Tom Brady played for the Buccaneers or if he divorced a model; it was all about the numbers.

And then there was online poker. He loved how his brain could count cards, and the thrill of winning and losing. Losing only meant he had to try harder, focus more, and learn how to win next time. It felt like he was playing against himself. He bet small amounts because it wasn't about the money. It was about the action. When his brain was calculating, he was at peace, at home in the world. Gambling was an endless Rubik's Cube to solve. He loved it.

Dave knew he had to keep his hobby a secret because people had nefarious opinions about gambling. If an intervention forced him to admit his shortcomings, he was an autistic, gay gambler with a penchant for drugs and alcohol. When you say it out loud, it doesn't sound so good, so Dave kept his proclivities to himself.

Someone like Kitty or Peter wouldn't care, but his parents would. It wasn't that he was afraid of disappointing them. Dave knew that ship had sailed. He was fearful of the power it would give them. They would feel the need to seek help for him, like the doctors he saw when he was young. His parents would want to fix him. Each time his parents had hoped for a different result, that Dave wasn't Dave. He knew they wanted an average child. But come on, who is normal nowadays? He didn't want them to try and change him and see that fail again. They had such a hard time accepting who he was 20 years ago. How would they accept him now?

Finishing off the lasagna, he logged in to one of his many sites. Tonight, he wanted to play blackjack. Keep it simple. After all, he had been drinking and didn't want to bet everything accidentally. But he laughed and thought, *What do I have to lose?*

Chapter 4
Pflaumenkuchen

A long time ago, Nina decided to lie to Kitty. She had gotten the idea while watching *General Hospital* when she was fourteen. No one told the truth in soap operas. Granted, the truth always came out, but at the time, young Nina thought it was a quick fix to a bad problem. When she concocted the lie, she went to her grandparents, who shockingly approved. Adults weren't supposed to champion lies from a fourteen-year-old and partake in them. But the three of them looked at little Kitty, only five years old, with her big blue eyes and ringlet curls, and thought it was an excellent idea.

Nina reflected on that long-ago decision as she cleaned Kitty's dirty dishes. Would Kitty be different today if she hadn't lied?

Would her habits still be the same? At least Kitty brought the dishes to the sink instead of scattering them throughout the house like other teenagers. Nina wasn't a very good disciplinarian regarding Kitty's habits. Her nurturing side won out, and she acted as Kitty's handmaid, folding her laundry. She was only a step away from calling Kitty *M'lady*. Maybe Nina did it because she felt guilty for lying to Kitty all these years about their family, or maybe she just liked taking care of her. She had done it since the day she was born.

Nina hummed as she scrubbed the old soda glasses and caked-on orange juice pulp. Cleaning relaxed her in the way that her grandmother found joy in keeping a tidy house. At the end of each day, Nina's grandmother would hug them and say, "Job well done." Either she was referring to all the life chores accomplished or the fact that they were living a relatively normal life. Either was good.

Nina missed her grandmother, who was also named Nina, but they had called her Oma, the German term for grandma. Oma was a force in a way her mother never was. She was second-generation German, and you didn't mess with her. Her portly body loved hard work, and her disposition was sunny but assiduous. Her gray hair was kept in a neat bun, and her hands were coarse from housework. Oma made fresh jam and bread, eyed every grocery store receipt to ensure it was correct, and kissed them goodnight at bedtime with a firm tuck of the sheet. After Nina and Kitty lost their parents and moved in with their grandparents, Oma watched over them like baby chicks, never leaving their side.

Her grandfather was Irish, and they called him Pop. Pop was gentler than Oma, but that was probably due to his pints throughout the day. Like his wife, he was a stout man with a belly and thick, strong arms. He laughed a lot and tried never to take things too seriously. Pop was a second-generation immigrant too. Oma and Pop had met in Boston, where their parents had landed from their homelands. But they moved to Hillsdale so Pop could open an auto body shop for specialty cars. He specialized in anything European—Ferrari, Porsche, Mercedes—and customers came from Boston to service their vehicles. He did well and bought the house that Nina and Kitty lived in without a mortgage.

Oma and Pop passed away two years ago, within weeks of each other. Nina missed them terribly, but thanks to them, she and Kitty would always be okay, financially and emotionally…as long as Nina kept it that way.

Nina had been in nursing school when her grandparents' health declined. She got more training at home than at the hospital. She used Medicaid to outfit the house with all the hospital beds and toilet seats they needed. Nina had her grandmother's economic savvy and genuinely loved caring for them. It felt like repayment for the years of love they had given her and Kitty.

When Oma and Pop became bedridden, they were irritable, hating being old and useless. They had spent years getting up at dawn, and working hard, and they rarely fell to illness. They were the type of people who thought they could go on forever just by willing it to be. Never had they crossed a hurdle they hadn't managed to find some way over. But old age and death come for everyone, even the best of people. Nina watched over them the same way they had tended to her as a child. She switched TV channels, made them comfortable with fuzzy blankets from TJ Maxx, and read to them from *People* magazine because Oma had a thing for Brad Pitt.

All three of them worried about Kitty. How would Kitty handle the loss of them? It was natural to worry about the youngest in the herd. Those who know about grief don't want those who don't know to know. Kitty had been too young to remember losing their parents. Silly but true, if they could all keep Kitty in the dark, they might live a little in the dark too.

Nina and Kitty's mother, Lily, was the only daughter of Oma and Pop. They had adored their daughter. When she died, a part of them died too. Nina was twelve and Kitty three when it happened. Nina spent the better part of that time in shock. She clung to Kitty as a security blanket. Kitty was all she had left in the world. But Oma and Pop stepped in and managed Nina's grief and confusion the best they could. Oma would reassure her. "Kids bounce, but don't break," she would say. She did not want Nina to feel broken, and oddly, with time, she didn't.

After Lily died was also when Nina learned about real love, the true kind that could exist in a marriage. In her grandparents' grief, she watched them love each other harder and stronger. Pop would bring Oma strong coffee in the morning in bed. He'd set the alarm early to make it before the girls were awake so Oma could have time to herself before taking care of two children all day. He often put his hand to her cheek, looked into her teary eyes, and whispered, "I know." Because he was grieving too, Oma would bake him his favorite *pflaumenkuchen* cake, a German recipe made with fresh plums, when he was having a bad day. They often held her mother's picture, and then they would hold each other.

Nina wanted that kind of love, she thought, as she continued scrubbing the leftover pots. She daydreamed about a husband beside her who would dry and put away the dishes without being told. Right now, a doctor at the hospital was pursuing her, but she had no interest. His name was Stan, and he liked to get too close to her when tending to a patient. She watched how curt he was with patients, unlike her, who lingered until they felt comfortable. She had rejected his dinner offers, imagining him vainly lecturing her about his career or his BMW. Nope, that kind of love wasn't for her. Besides, she had Kitty to keep her occupied. Kitty was more important.

Oma taught Nina, not with specific words, the ability to get out of bed each day and do what needed to be done. Germans were known for fortitude, pulling up their lederhosen and all that. So Nina did what needed to be done and got on with it. She kept the house, went to work, and made sure everything was okay for Kitty. Daydreams were fun, but they could be foolish.

After her grandparents passed away, Nina finished her nursing degree and enjoyed the structure of the hospital. People came in, needed comfort, care, and attention, and left better for it. They were grateful to have survived, which is how Nina felt deep down in her soul. She got it. She and Kitty had survived the loss of their parents and grandparents and felt eternally thankful for what they had, not what they didn't.

Caring for Kitty evolved so naturally that it never felt like a burden. It was just an extension of her. The house had to be maintained and the bills paid; luckily, Nina was left with enough money to do just that even on her meager nurse's salary. It reminded her of when Oma used to pull bread from the oven, smell and tap it, and smile every time. She was always unsure whether the bread would be good, but it always was. Nina appreciated her grandmother's humility and her doubt. It felt appropriate. Nina liked to think she had that humility and questioned herself enough to keep doing a good job and not slack off.

Don't take things for granted, Oma warned the girls. Nina couldn't tell if Kitty understood this concept. The way Kitty acted, Nina had no clue. Was her sister appreciative of the sacrifices she and her grandparents had made? Would Kitty ever know that they came from abnormal circumstances made to appear normal? How could she if Nina never told her what really happened to their parents? Kitty was like a one-pot stew that Nina kept feeding ingredients into, hoping, wishing, it would all turn out okay.

Her little sister was odd in so many ways. The physicality of Kitty seemed destined to cause her problems. But strangely, Kitty didn't care about her bottle-thick glasses and tree-trunk legs. She didn't suffer self-consciousness like the average teenage girl. Poor Nina, at sixteen, wanted to hide every day under the high school tables, wishing never to be seen. Her acne was horrible, and her thick glasses made her obsolete in the teenage hierarchy. Unlike her at that age, Kitty commanded a room, and when she laughed, it boomed in a way that caused others to join in. Nina never had that power of confidence. Kitty didn't worry about the details of life. She certainly didn't fret over the credit card bills or the overflowing recycle bins. Because she was a teenager? Or because these life tribulations were meager and trivial to her? Someday, opening a can of tuna in her apartment, would Kitty know to drain the water out? Had Nina sheltered her too much, or just enough that she came out more normal than she would have been?

Nina's brain could go around and around about it, but she still would say nothing about their past to her little sister. Why? Because Nina was terrified of the truth and what it might do to her.

So Nina gave Kitty the minivan to use, let her stay up late watching TV, and didn't ask when she smelled like an ashtray coming in at night. Again, Nina was not her parent. She was her older sister, official guardian, and she loved her more than anything on the planet. Her job was to protect Kitty and not mess her up too badly. If Kitty did mess up, then that was Kitty's fault.

Nina finished the dishes and was startled by the knock at the door.

"Oh, hi, Mia!" she said, surprised to see her neighbor again.

"Hi, Nina. My, you look nice today!" Mia said with genuine interest. Of course, Nina never managed to see that she had grown into a beautiful young woman. Her face was clear now, and her blonde hair was straight and long. She had traded her thick glasses for thin ones lined in gold that made her big blue eyes shine.

"What can I do for you?" Nina passed over the compliment.

"I was wondering if Kitty was here. I want to hire her on a more permanent basis. Like a set schedule with Adam, if possible?"

Nina turned and yelled, "KITTTYYY!" making Mia jump.

"Oh my god, Nina, just use a bullhorn, why dontcha?" Kitty

came tromping down the stairs in a purple tracksuit this time and her hair in braids. Nina thought she looked like a Teletubby but didn't say anything.

"Mia wants to hire you."

"As long as it doesn't interfere with tennis," Kitty responded nonchalantly.

"Tennis? What tennis?" Nina looked confused.

"Duh, my tennis lessons are three days a week." Kitty pushed up her glasses.

"You never told me," Nina said. Mia's head bobbed back and forth like at a tennis match.

"You never asked." Typical Kitty remark, and Nina sighed.

Mia jumped in, "Well, any time you aren't doing tennis, I'd love to have you babysit. Adam had fun the other night. And I just got the promotion as head of the English department, so I need to spend a couple afternoons doing extra work."

"Okay. Sounds good. How about Tuesday and Friday? He didn't cry last time, so he's cool." Kitty looked bored with the conversation already.

"Three to six on those days?"

"Yeah, sure. And nights if you need me. I'm saving up for some tennis clothes. Have to look sharp on the court, like the Williams sisters. Apparently, I hit like Venus." Then Kitty tromped equally as loud back up the stairs without a goodbye.

Nina's mouth dropped open. "I had no idea she played tennis," she said to Mia.

Mia laughed. "I'm terrified of Adam being a teenager. But it seems like you are doing a good job. I deal with teenagers daily, and some of them, frankly, I want to throat punch."

Nina burst out laughing. "You can't say that!"

"I suppose I can't, but as long as it's not on social media or in an email, I should be safe."

"Where do you think she is taking tennis lessons?" Nina mused.

"Hillsdale Club is open. They have indoor courts," Mia offered. She knew too many Hillsdale Prep mothers who had nothing better to do with their day than exercise and drink white wine laden with ice afterward.

"Nina, if you need anything, please knock on my door. I've been a bit of a hermit since the divorce, so if I'm not at work, I'm here."

"Thanks, Mia. You too!"

Nina promptly went upstairs to confront Kitty. "Tennis? Since when?"

"A couple weeks. I'm good too. That's what Peter says." Kitty was tapping at her computer without looking up.

"Peter? Peter who? Does he coach you?"

"Yeah."

"Is he okay?" Nina had read all about male gymnast coaches who preyed on young girls. The articles freaked her out. "He's not some creepy old dude? He won't…you know…take advantage of you?"

"Jesus, Nina, he's your age. Get your mind out of the gutter. He reminds me of a stray kitten or something, cute but harmless and a little hyper. But he's okay. Don't be all weird."

Nina didn't want to be all weird, but she would investigate this tennis thing. She started cleaning Kitty's room. Kitty did nothing to help or stop her, but kept tap-tap-tapping on her computer.

Chapter 5
Farmer Ted

Peter couldn't believe someone was pounding on his door. It was Sunday morning, his only morning to sleep in. *POUND, POUND. POUND*. He hoped it wasn't Coach Clark. He didn't want him to see the state of his apartment. Last night, Peter had a party of one with a six-pack and a pizza, and somehow his living room looked like Alpha Delta Phi after a kegger.

POUND.

Peter opened his door and groaned.

"Need a shower, bro..." Charlie stormed into his tiny apartment and started taking off his clothes.

"Chuck, what the hell? It's 7 am on a freaking Sunday."

"Sorry, bro. I had a hook-up last night and had to sleep in Hillsdale. I can't go to Mom and Dad's like this."

Charlie was unshaven and looked a little hungover.

"Mom and Dad?" Peter questioned.

"Brunch, you idiot."

"We have brunch? With them? Today?"

"Christ on the cross, Peter, I texted you days ago."

Oh… Peter usually ignored Charlie's texts. He switched topics. "Who did you hook up with?"

"No one, never mind. It was just a thing from an app."

"I don't think you should refer to people as things."

Charlie ignored him and began yelling from the shower. "You know, you should get laid more often. Join Tinder or something." He just wanted Peter down on his level of human connection. No way was Peter interested in random sex. Except for that time with Mrs. Tinsdale, which wasn't so bad but still left him feeling shallow. Sex wasn't the problem. The idea of not knowing someone and then physically touching them grossed Peter out. How can you meet a person for five minutes and then grope them? What if they have horrible breath or long toenails? Are you allowed to run away? Can you get up and go without apology? Or would you get a bad review on Tinder? He certainly did not want to get into one of those situations.

Peter was just about to ask what time brunch was when the fire alarm went off. It was similar to a submarine whistle. They could go deaf from the screeching.

"JESUS!" Charlie shouted from the shower, and Peter looked frantically around like he was trying to find a bat in the room. He ran outside in his boxers and saw Lois smoking a cigarette in her fuzzy pink bathrobe.

Peter could hear Coach Clark swearing from his kitchen.

"Goddammit, Lois! I told you not to smoke in the house! The new fire codes have this place wired to the hilt." *Wee woo, wee woo.* The sound was waking up the neighborhood, and people were opening their front doors, more annoyed than willing to help. Where there was no smoke, there was no fire, they presumed. A fire truck arrived, and Lois calmly explained that she had lit a cigarette while cooking Stevie's morning bacon. She thought the fan over the stove would take care of the bacon burning and her Parliament. She told the fireman it was her husband's fault because he did not splurge for the GE model fan; that would have done the trick, because GE's worked like a jet engine. Instead, Stevie bought the cheap version of a stovetop fan, and now everyone was put out. Clearly, it was Coach Clark's fault.

The firefighters turned off the alarm and removed the pan of burnt, smoky bacon to the outdoors.

"WOMAN!" Coach Clark glared at her. "You told me you were quitting smoking!"

"I also told you we had potatoes last night, but it was mashed cauliflower. I am not above lying." She stood her ground and tightened her robe. "And was it me who had a third scotch last night? No."

Coach Clark pursed his lips at her. He was clearly trying to hold in another remark. They had been married forty years, and arguing was more for sport and entertainment at this point. Lois went over and kissed Stevie on his bald forehead. "Let's go to the diner for breakfast. I'll change." And she went inside.

Peter felt self-conscious and chilly in his boxers, but didn't want to leave Coach Clark, who still looked like he had something to say.

"Peter, what can I tell you? She has been great in bed for forty years, but not in the kitchen." Coach Clark tossed up his hands and went inside.

Peter didn't quite know what to say to that. This was life in Hillsdale. Happy Sunday.

"Now she is very nice," his mother, Edie, said while pouring most likely her second mimosa. "She's just darling," she kept going. "Graduated from Sarah Lawrence and is interning at her father's law firm. Very bright girl, you will love her." His mother wore a neat silk blouse and wool pants as if hosting a gathering at a yacht club. His father was standing off to the side in khakis and a dark blue blazer. Peter wore an old Pink Floyd t-shirt and jeans. They obviously had different standards for brunch.

"Why will I love her, Mother?" Peter didn't know what was happening. His father and Charlie were consumed in financial talk, and his day had already been ruined when he was so rudely awakened. He grabbed a flute.

"Oh, they will be here any second!" Edie was nervously arranging food on the buffet table. Peter wasn't savvy enough to realize that the spread of fresh croissants and quiche wasn't lovingly made for him. They were for guests.

"No, Mom, you didn't," Peter whined. "You set me up on a date here...at home?"

"Well, how else was I going to do it?" Edie looked at her son like he was an idiot. "You clearly have not been pursuing any girls lately. 'Sweat sock' is not an ode de cologne, by the way. And forgive me, I would like grandchildren at some point." Edie said this like it was his duty to provide said grandchildren.

Peter looked at Bob Wise. "Dad, did you know about this?" He thought maybe his father would rescue him.

"Know about what? What's wrong now?" Peter caught the irritation in his father's voice. Ever since Peter didn't return to Yale, Bob had no patience for his son. Written him off, so to speak, and focused solely on Charlie's accomplishments. Feeling like he was in competition with his brother, Peter wanted to tattle on Charlie for having random sex last night and using some mind-altering drug to do it. But he kept quiet.

"Mom, how come you don't set Charlie up? He's..." Peter waved a finger at his brother, shoving a raspberry danish in his mouth like an ape, "you know...older."

"Oh, Charlie, well, he is so focused on his career right now.

So much like your father, and your father found me. It will all work out for him when the time's right. Charlie is so particular, and the right one will come along who can understand him better." Edie said this with a sympathetic head tilt. "And besides, you have all the time in the world to fall in love!"

Peter didn't know how to take that last bit.

The doorbell rang. *Crap*, Peter thought.

Then Cami Tinsdale walked into their house with old Fred Tinsdale and their daughter Ashley. She looked vaguely familiar to him; he guessed she was about his age.

No, no, no, Peter's head screamed, and he tipped a full mimosa into his mouth in one gulp.

Not one to miss a moment, Charlie whispered to Peter, "Hey, bro, looks like you got some tail you can chase around the brunch table."

"God, Chuck, do you have to be so gross?" Peter said back.

Peter could not look at Cami when he shook Mr. Tinsdale's hand. He waited for the room to explode, but it did not.

"Hi, Peter," said Ashley, equally annoyed by the set-up. "I'm sorry, I found out in the car on the way over. I thought we were going to a restaurant. Mom didn't tell me brunch meant blind date."

"It's okay. Alcohol?" He tipped his head at her. Ashley laughed.

"Why do people mess up a good mimosa with OJ?" she asked. Ashley was a roundish girl, short, with auburn hair in a messy bun. She looked like she preferred books to exercise and had a toothy smile. Peter couldn't help but compare Cami's boobs and her daughter's; same double-Ds, he guessed. At the club, most of the boobs were too pert, having been surgically altered. But the Tinsdale women, he could tell, were all natural. He didn't want to meet Cami's gaze, embarrassed by their tryst, but she approached him anyway.

"Hello, Peter. So good to see you off the court!" she said a little too loudly. Fred wasn't listening if she was trying to make him jealous. Peter felt her hand run a little up his spine, and he shivered.

"When Edie thought of this brunch, I said perfect! Only the best for my daughter, if you know what I mean!" She winked at Peter. He wanted to fold into an origami swan and hide under the table.

"Mom, cool it," Ashley said. "This set-up is beyond juvenile. It's not 1950 anymore, and I do not need this." To Peter's relief, Ashley was clearly annoyed, which meant he was off the hook.

"Oh, you two are darling! Peter is exactly the boy I would have imagined myself with back then," Cami said brightly and winked again at Peter. Peter just looked into his empty mimosa and wished this would stop. He observed poor Fred Tinsdale, short like his daughter with too much nose hair, dribble some strawberry jam on his chest. He was just one hip fracture away from a wheelchair. It was a cruel twist of fate that his bank account was big enough to attract someone like Cami. Money cannot buy you class.

Edie shooed Cami away from Peter so he could be alone with Ashley.

"You don't remember me, do you?" Ashley asked, grabbing a croissant and putting extra butter on it.

"Huh, yeah?" Peter tilted his head and tried to think.

"I was a sophomore when you were a senior at Prep. It's okay if you don't remember. We only talked once at a party. You were pretty messed up and told me if you had tits, you would stay home and play with them all day." Peter couldn't help but laugh. Sounded like him.

"God, I wasn't being some sleazy asshole, was I? Was I trying to hook up with you?" He made a face, scared of the answer, not remembering much from his old party days.

"Oh god, no. Honestly, name a horny teen who wasn't looking at boobs? Hell, even I admired Francesca D'Amato's. Remember her? All the girls wanted her tits, perfect sweater tits. You were pretty good-looking, in a cute way, but man, you were an idiot. We nicknamed you Farmer Ted. You know, the geek from the movie *Sixteen Candles*."

"The guy who held up the underwear and got trapped under the table?"

"Bingo. You were no Jake Ryan."

"Thanks," Peter said, a little hurt. He had no idea he had a nickname back then. Was he some sort of loser and didn't know it?

"Mom says you teach tennis now. Dropped out of Yale or something?" Ashley continued to plow through the croissants.

"Yeah, I thought it would be pretty glamorous." Peter couldn't help his sarcasm. It was sinking in. He was Farmer Ted.

"Mom hit on you yet?" Ashley asked, noticing Cami cooing over Charlie, who looked fairly nonplussed. "She's certainly eyeing you." Peter choked on his drink. Ashley continued, "You think I don't know my mother? I am 100 percent sure she slept with Mr. Potter, my Ancient Civ teacher. He was only 26." Peter's mouth opened in shock, but he quickly tried to cover up his look of surprise.

"Oh my god, she did!" Ashley said and burst out laughing.

"She... Your mother... I did not!" Peter lied badly.

"It's okay. Poor old Dad hasn't a clue, nor does he care. He'd fuck a *Wall Street Journal* if he could. He should have married someone like Ruth Bader Ginsberg, not a cocktail waitress named Cami with an i." Peter was speechless. How does one respond to that?

"Listen," Ashley whispered. "Play along, and I will get us out of here. Okay?"

Ashley turned to the adults. "Mr. and Mrs. Wise, thank you so much for the lovely food. I was wondering if it would be okay if Peter and I stepped out? He mentioned a movie playing, and we thought we could catch the matinee." Now Ashley winked at him.

Edie and Cami bobbed their heads with great enthusiasm, and the other men didn't break a note talking about the Dow futures.

Outside, Ashley said, "So, Farmer Ted, ground rules. I have a boyfriend. His name is Ravi, and he is an engineer in Boston. My parents cannot know about him, nor will they. This partnership is completely platonic and will serve to get our parents off our backs. Capiche?"

"Sounds good to me." Peter nodded. Things were looking up. "So, you wanna get a drink?"

Ashley and Peter were able to walk to the local Irish pub, Flanigan's, and he was surprised to run into Kitty.

"Hey, Kitty." He approached her table. "Happy Sunday."

"Oh, hi Pe...terrrr." She was wiping bits of a Rueben sandwich off her face. Her hair was tied up in colorful ribbons, and her t-shirt said "Haters Gonna Hate" with a unicorn. "What are you doing here?" Like Peter wasn't allowed to be in a bar at midday on a Sunday.

"Getting a drink," Peter said dumbly. There was a guy with Kitty who looked like a young Cheech Marin. He had long black curly hair, a beard, and a bandanna. In fact, he looked precisely like Cheech Marin and was nibbling on some fries.

Peter introduced himself but had no idea why. "Hi, I'm Kitty's coach." Ashley was waving him to the bar.

"Dude, I know. I watch Kitty play," Cheech said. This would explain the cigarette smoke emanating from the minivan.

"Is Ashley your date?" Kitty asked, squinting behind her glasses.

"No, well, kind of, it's weird. You know her?" Peter responded.

"She's not your type." Kitty took a slug of soda and burped.

"How would you know my type?" Peter wondered.

"I don't, but I'll know when I see it."

Peter couldn't handle any more ridicule that day and switched topics. "You ready for tennis this week?"

"Duh, I got my carbs and protein right here…" Kitty pointed to the pool of grease that used to be pastrami.

"Well, you know, fruits and vegetables work too." Peter blurted it out, but Kitty retaliated with a deadpan stare.

Peter continued, "Your body is a machine now, and you gotta feed it the right things."

"I recall I kicked your ass the other day." It was a valid response. Kitty's serve was better than his.

"Man, I keep telling her to eat better," said Cheech. "But my little pussycat knows what's best for her." Kitty smiled at him, a piece of sauerkraut in her teeth. Cheech smiled back.

Peter, mortified, escaped back to Ashley.

"You know Kitty?" asked Ashley.

"She's one of my students."

"Really? Wow, that's interesting." Ashley squinted her eyes, trying to imagine Kitty on the court.

"And get this, she is really good. What do you know about her?" Peter asked over shots of chilled tequila that appeared from nowhere.

"I babysat her a couple times for her sister, Nina, when the grandparents were ill. Kitty was weird but funny. She always wanted to watch a comedy like *Animal House* or *The Jerk*, the old stuff, and she would laugh hard. She's a good kid. She'll probably end up some Hollywood star, and we'll be like, 'No shit,' when she marries a hottie and has like a billion dollars."

"You know, I can see that." Peter looked over at Kitty. She was wiping some mud pie off her t-shirt. Peter and Ashley did more shots and compared notes from high school. Ashley had been way more popular than Peter.

Sometime later, Kitty approached them. "Hey, Ashley. How's it being back at home?"

"Sucks, but hanging with Farmer Ted takes the sting out." Ashley hiccuped.

Kitty eyed them. "Okay, so who is ready for a ride home?" They both giggled. Kitty's voice got firmer. "Not a question. You two smell like you showered in booze. So I'll rephrase, Jerry and I are going to drive you home now." Kitty pushed up her glasses.

"Who's Jerry...?" Peter asked, then hit his head. "Cheech?" Kitty stood still while Peter started snorting like an eight-year-old.

"Yep, come on now. The bus is leaving the station." Kitty got their check and expertly put Ashley's credit card on it.

Jerry/Cheech started smoking and riding shotgun when they were all in Kitty's minivan. Ashley and Peter swayed in the back.

"TOURNAMENTS!" Peter shouted all of a sudden. "Kitty, you will be a tennis star, and I will sign you up for tournaments! I will be your coach! That's what I want to do! Ashley, I figured out what I want to do!" He started snorting again.

"Okay, cowboy," Ashley said, patting his leg. But Peter saw Kitty smile in the rearview mirror. Finally that day he had said something right.

Chapter 6
Subversive Deeds

Adam had a secret box he kept from his mother. It wasn't hard, because she was preoccupied with work most of the time. Also, he was smart enough to keep his room clean, so she didn't fuss around in it. The box held old photos of his parents, a secret wish list about what he wanted in life (to be 1. a YouTube star, and 2. someone in a Marvel movie), and a list of all his father's computer passwords.

He liked the photos of his parents because there was a time when they were a family. An actual family, not a stressed-out single mom he worried about and a dad he was pissed off at. That's why he started compiling the passwords. Adam just wanted to know more about him. His mother's computer wasn't password-protected, and they shared the Amazon account, so there was nothing new. She liked to shop for "loungewear" and books on bestsellers lists.

His father was a different story. Adam could learn loads about him because Eric never cleared his search history. Usually, his father and Camila were so wrapped up processing vegetables into Slurpees or meditating that Adam was unsupervised using his dad's computer. He could log into Eric's Keychain command and procure the passwords to snoop from his computer at his mom's house. Adam wasn't always playing *Minecraft* or *Fortnite*. He regularly checked his father's credit cards and bank account and used his Aunt Camila's Amex to buy video games. Either Camila wouldn't notice, or if Adam spent too much, she'd complain to Amex and get a new number. Adam inevitably got the updated number from her wallet or their Amazon account. Identity theft wasn't that hard, Adam thought.

To offset his greed, Adam sometimes made donations in Camila's name to the local food bank or the Boys and Girls Club of Hillsdale. His mother had made him read *Robin Hood* as a child (he loved the Disney movie version), so he thought the good deeds outweighed the bad. Adam usually got the urge to donate when he saw Camila's shopping bags from the mall. How many yoga outfits and expensive purses does one woman need? His mother never spent that amount of money on herself, unlike her sister, his aunt, or now just his dad's girlfriend. Adam would also send his cousins, Luna and Aria, gifts. He chose self-help books titled *How To Deal With Bad Parents* and *My Mother is a Narcissist*, messing with everyone's heads because he used their Amazon account.

Adam hadn't planned on telling Kitty about his subversive deeds, but one afternoon, his dad called to cancel their weekend plans, and Adam got upset.

"What's up, little person? You seem off." Kitty was astute. She had brought him a bowl of Oreo ice cream. He didn't touch it, which is pretty telling when a kid doesn't eat ice cream.

Adam explained how he felt he wasn't important to his dad. Kitty listened intently and didn't interrupt or try to hug him. He appreciated the lack of emotion. His mother would have started crying.

Kitty offered, "My parents are dead, but my grandparents made me feel special. So I agree, it's not cool of him to cancel on you. Every kid should be made to feel special."

Once Adam opened up, he desperately wanted to share his Robin Hood activities. Again, Kitty listened.

"Okay, first off, I have to admire your genius. I appreciate that in a person." (Kitty never referred to him as a kid, which he appreciated) "But smart can get you in trouble, so you have to be careful. Secondly, I'm not sure I approve. While they deserve the karma, karma can come back atcha."

"What's karma?" Adam asked, and Kitty explained.

"It's like if you do something bad, something bad will happen to you. I mean, there's no science behind it. It's the idea that if you do good things, good things will happen too. So your dad did a bad thing by cheating on your mom, so maybe the universe will do something bad to him. Like maybe someday, Camila will cheat on him. Karma. Sometimes people wait on karma instead of taking revenge. What you are doing—albeit making donations is a good deed—is revenge. I'm not a big believer in an eye for an eye. That's Hammurabi's code from ancient Egypt. You shouldn't just hurt someone because they hurt you. That would only make you the same as them, not better."

Adam nodded and hung his head. "I didn't wait for karma."

"No, you didn't, so we have to ask ourselves, does this fall under the category of lying? You see, little person, the one thing I will absolutely not do is lie. It's my golden rule. You ask me a question, I will, hands down, tell you the truth. The truth is more important than anyone or anything."

"But they haven't asked me if I'm the one doing these things, so I haven't lied!" Adam cried out.

"Yes, but then there is lying by omission. That's when you only tell someone part of the story but not the whole story. But also, you are spending their money without their permission, and that's stealing." Kitty scratched her arm in thought. "You got yourself in a pickle. I can't say you are acting like a truthful person."

"Mom calls that a gray area. She often uses that term when talking about my dad and aunt."

"Correct. We are in a gray area. So, what if they ask if you are the one spending their money? What will you say?"

Adam thought about it. What would Robin Hood say?

"I will tell them the truth," Adam said solemnly as his red hair flopped on his bobbing head.

"You swear? And what about confessing? Think you could do that?"

Adam scratched his chin, and his red hair flopped again. "Can I get back to you on that?"

"Sure, you'll know when you are ready." Kitty smiled at him. "Because next to telling the truth, you better do what you say you will do. When you swear you will do something, you must be a person of your word. Otherwise, people won't respect you. And without people's respect, you got nothing. God's honest truth, nothing."

"Who told you that?"

"Pop, my grandfather. He said that's how he built his business, getting people's respect and never lying to them. And he said 'God's honest truth' a lot."

"Snooping makes me feel like a private detective. Kitty, what's Viagra? Dad buys a lot of it. I googled it, but I don't understand. It seems like something I can't ask my mom."

"Right-o! Don't ask her about that! It helps him to have sex with her sister. Not the conversation a mother wants to have with her son." They both laughed.

Chapter 7
Wonderfully Preposterous

Mia rubbed her eyebrows. She often did this when frustrated at a meeting. Her English department comprised four other teachers, and she only liked two. Probably because they were older and little fazed them. The younger teachers caused endless frustration by listening to parents' demands and bringing politics into every conversation. They were sensitive to everything. Now she was sitting here, again, arguing over the junior class reading *The Handmaid's Tale* by Margaret Atwood. The younger two thought it was inappropriate.

Mia remembered reading it for school back when dystopian fiction was more of a novelty than mainstream actuality. Her personal opinion was that the book was more relevant to read now since the American climate had turned against women's rights. And the TV show was phenomenal, but that was beside the point.

Mr. Tyler Dunning and his cohort, Miss Jules Hamel, were causing Mia to go browless.

"Mr. Dunning, I appreciate your, mmm…thoughtful consideration about dismissing *The Handmaid's Tale* from the curriculum, but…"

Mia watched Tyler's face contort. He was a 28-year-old white male and undoubtedly Republican. Even though profiling had become a dirty word, Mia wasn't above profiling him. She doubted he had ever been discriminated against or suffered in his life. He seemed like the type who had been in a fraternity and most likely date-raped a girl and blamed it on her drinking. Tyler talked too much about the moral compass of America, and Mia didn't trust him. He thought his duty as an educator was to bring values to the classroom. *No, it's to teach literature, you twit.* But she wondered why he chose to be a teacher, especially English lit. He seemed better suited to running someone's political campaign or selling timeshares. Tyler was an anomaly to the stereotypical liberal arts-loving academic. But nowadays, some doctors didn't believe in vaccines, and schools didn't teach the Holocaust, so who was she to question? Everyone had their own agenda, and she couldn't be bothered to investigate why perfectly sane people fell off cliffs for a picture on Instagram.

"The book, to say the least, is anti-Christian and makes the church look like some sort of cult run by men," Tyler argued. He had slammed his hand on the table like he was making a Supreme Court argument. Mia hated his scrawny body and pale, manicured hands. He resembled a weasel with dark black hair and acne scars from childhood. "Furthermore, the sex scenes are preposterous. They are far too graphic and unreal to teach kids."

Old Mr. Baxter coughed and laughed simultaneously at Tyler's remark. He was Mia's favorite colleague. In his 60s, Mr. Baxter talked about Shakespeare like he was in love. He smelled of stale coffee, and his saggy jowls made her think of the old movie actor Jason Robards. And the kids thought he was funny. Mia gave

Mr. Baxter a look like, *Yes, I know, but we can't laugh…*

"It's not anti-Christian, Mr. Dunning," she responded. "It's anti-fundamentalism, which is a pretty important lesson for kids today."

"It's all about the mistreatment of women by men!" Tyler shouted. Again Mr. Baxter's head started bobbing as he looked down, trying desperately not to laugh.

Mia inhaled calmly. "Yes, yes, it is, Mr. Dunning. Are you trying to say that women are not or cannot be mistreated by men? Have women not been used as slaves for their sexuality? Have women never been mistreated by men, so thus writing a fictional story about such a thing is unteachable?"

"No, Mrs. Golding, I am saying that we should not perpetuate the notion that men are evil toward women as a society. We don't use them as breeders. We aren't a cult! The story is ridiculous!"

Mr. Baxter interrupted. "'Many a true word hath been spoken in jest,' old Willie Shakespeare wrote."

"Mr. Baxter…" Mia shook her head, *Not now*. She continued. "That's the thing about fiction, Mr. Dunning. It's wonderfully preposterous and honest at the same time. Stories are allowed to be excessive to broaden our imagination. Correct?" Mia had no clue how this guy became an English teacher. What did he grow up reading? Just the Bible? Trump pamphlets?

Mrs. Wills sat silent. She was in her late fifties and had let her hair go gray for the hell of it. Mia knew she had an opinion on the subject but chose to remain quiet. Mrs. Wills had rejected the offer of the department head for years. Her children had grown, and she jetted out of school faster than the kids at the end of the day. She liked to go home, pour a bottle of wine into a glass, and watch old shows with her retired husband. Mrs. Wills was what Mia wanted to be: old, content, and living a simple life with a man who puttered around the house.

"Tyler's right," Jules Hamel piped up. "It's just too controversial. I've had parents complain. I mean, like, why can't we teach Jane Austen?" Jules, only 29, was desperate to have everyone like her, parents more than students. Mr. Baxter groaned. All things Jane Austen had been exhausted to death by Hollywood. Jules, with her prep school name, long glossy brown hair, and Ann Taylor suit, was a wannabe heroine in her head. She had read romantic fiction and thought the safest course in life was teaching until Mr. Darcy arrived to swoop her away from the workforce.

"It's after 5, and I need to get home, so let's table this discussion," Mia interrupted. "For now, it remains on the syllabus, and I am teaching it, so Mr. Dunning, you're off the hook if the story makes you uncomfortable."

Mr. Baxter let out a little, "Aye!"

"The Christmas party should be fun this year, don't you think?" Mrs. Wills giggled and quickly grabbed her purse, running for the door.

Mia slammed her folder shut. She wasn't going to let a kid who had been teaching for two years bulldoze her.

"I'm not the only one with this opinion..." Tyler whined as he left the room.

How had the world come to this? Banning books, thoughts, and enlightenment, for god's sake. Sure, reading Toni Morrison's tales of sex and children is not easy. But that was the point: good literature is uncomfortable and would make these privileged Hillsdale Prep kids realize there is a big bad world out there. One where Mia's white male husband screwed her sister on her expensive linen sheets.

Mia had already heard the grumblings amongst school parents. The more radical parents fell into two camps. Those like Mr. Dunning, who saw no separation of church and state, thought religion was a life requirement and denied the existence of bigotry or misogyny in America. Then the other camp wanted more LGBTQ literature, to ban peanuts, and thought the Third Reich created homework. But all the radicals on both sides had one thing in common. They wanted their brilliant, perfect-in-every-way kid to get into an Ivy League school…no matter what.

As a parent, Mia just wanted Adam to be happy. How come she didn't care so much about hand sanitizer stations? She got Adam vaccinated and told him not to eat unwashed vegetables. All the rest was too exhausting to worry about. What his clothes were made from, or if he said the pledge of allegiance daily? None of that mattered to her. Talking about a cult, pledging to your country every morning, sounded absurd in this day and age. How about pledging to grow up and be kind and not shoot anyone you don't like in high school?

And who could have ever predicted pronouns would become controversial? People did not want to be he or she anymore. She understood and respected it, but couldn't wrap her mind around it. It felt like half the world had decided to change its name overnight. She didn't know who was who, what was what, or how to keep up without hurting someone's feelings. Or worse, making a child feel uncomfortable or unloved. Why was being a teacher and a parent so bloody complicated?

Mia got into teaching to talk about great books and inspire the next generation. When she read *Their Eyes Were Watching God* by Zora Neale Hurston, Mia was awed. She could never write anything as beautiful or moving with all her education and privilege. Shakespeare's sonnets were masterful, and he wrote with a quill. Hell, even Stephen King lit her on fire with his imagination. Where did the passion go for the written word? Why was the world becoming resistant to new and old ideas and so sensitive to learning about both? Yikes, she hated to think the world was becoming so short-sighted.

Kitty popped into her head. Kitty, in her straightforwardness, somehow came off unaffected by these modern conundrums. Maybe being younger, she was more acclimated to change, or was she unhardened by change? The girl plowed through life like a sunflower field and reveled in its beauty. Was Mia that unaware as a teenager, or was that the nature of being a teenager? Regardless, she was glad Kitty hung out with Adam. He needed that innocence in his life. She laughed, thinking how Kitty had handled Adam's father the other day when he came by unannounced.

Mia had just gotten home from work, and Kitty was finishing a backgammon game with Adam. She had taught Adam how to play on a whim because she missed playing with her grandfather. *Go for it*, Mia thought. At least Adam was off the computer.

Eric didn't even knock. He barged through the door and shouted, "Hey, kiddo. Wanna go out for pizza?"

Mia was in the kitchen when she heard Kitty say, "Hey, pervert, you can't just walk in here and ask to take a kid out. It's not 1980."

"Who are you?" Eric asked, stunned at the backlash.

"Hey, Dad," Adam chimed. "This is Kitty, my babysitter. Kitty, this is my dad."

"What are you doing here?" Mia interrupted.

"Thought I'd take the kid out for dinner," Eric said nonchalantly.

Mia sighed like she had to explain to a toddler. "It doesn't work like that, Eric. We have set times, and if you want to do something spontaneously, you need to call first and ask me; because it's my time, and this is my home."

"Where's Camila? She dump you or something?" Kitty asked, pushing her glasses up on her face to inspect him. Adam giggled.

"No, she's teaching tonight...and what business is it of yours?" Eric said sternly, but Mia could see his face redden and start to sweat. It did that when he got flustered. Mia smiled and thought, *Go, Kitty, go.*

"It's not my business." Kitty also shrugged nonchalantly. "Just asking."

"Adam." Eric tried to ignore the stares of both Kitty and Mia. "Do you want to go for pizza with your ol' dad?"

This is what pissed Mia off. She knew Adam wouldn't mind going and wanted him to have quality time with his father. But barging in here, entitled? *Camila can have him*, she thought.

"Hey, little person, whatever you want to do is cool." Kitty looked at Adam. She probably sensed that this situation made him uncomfortable, being stuck between his mother and father. "Don't worry about your mom. I'm going to make her hang out with my weirdo sister. They need some girl time." Kitty winked at Mia.

"Yeah, honey, do what you want." Mia never wanted to put Adam in the middle.

"Okay, sure, Dad. But none of that veggie pizza crap that Camila orders. I am gluten tolerant, and pizza dough should not be made out of cauliflower," Adam said sternly.

Kitty laughed and high-fived Adam, then looked at Eric. "Now, what do you say?" He returned a confused stare. She continued, "Seriously, Mr. Golding, we practice manners. You came in without permission, got what you wanted, so… What… do…you…say?" The words came out slowly, filling the room. Kitty stood on one leg, her muscular arm on her hip, posing like an unbreakable wall. Mia was enthralled watching this teenage girl with a *My Little Pony* t-shirt and her blonde hair in a high pony— because she liked to be ironic like that—put Eric in his place.

"Um, thank you?" Eric said meekly.

"Atta boy," Kitty said with a smile. "Now, you two get out of here so we girls can have some fun. Have him back by nine, okay? Adam needs his sleep." Mia almost lost it at that point, smirking absurdly, but Eric didn't respond.

"And Mr. Golding?" Kitty called after him. "Call first next time, kay?" Eric visibly began walking faster toward his car.

Later that night, Mia had a glass of wine in her hand and replayed the story for Nina.

"I swear, my sister has no boundaries." Nina laughed.

"But it's so oddly fantastic. I wish I could be like that sometimes. My generation was raised to be seen and not heard. Does she get that from your parents?" Mia was curious about their background, which she knew very little of but didn't know how to pry.

"We don't remember them," Nina told her. "I would guess it was Oma. Oma never put up with anyone rude or pushy. I remember little Kitty throwing a fit in a store, and some man commented, 'Like, if you can't keep your child under control, you should stay at home.' Oma looked right at him and said, 'Did people speak to your mother like that when you were a brat?' He huffed away. Oma never let anyone say a cross word without putting them in their place."

"She sounds amazing. You girls were lucky to have had your grandparents." Mia hoped Nina would say more about her family.

But Nina changed subjects and asked, "So, you seeing anyone?" The women switched to the universal language of love and the typical lack thereof. Regardless of age, talking about one's dismal love life could bring any two women together. And with that, Nina and Mia became friends.

Packing her bag at the office, Nina's Oma popped into Mia's mind. She would have liked to have met her. Mia could have learned a thing or two about not backing down from an argument or having just the right thing to say to put Mr. Dunning in his place.

Chapter 8
Pros and Cons

Dave was in a bad mood. That night at home, the Dinses had summoned their youngest to the dining room. Dave hated the dining room because that was where his mother hung her inspirational sayings painted on cheap Hardie board, like "It's Wine O'Clock Somewhere" and "Glitter is the Sparkle in Everyone." The room resembled a back-alley tourist shop. There, his parents sat with matching martinis. His father, like David, was short and athletic, but had let his hair go gray and referred to himself as a silver fox. Dave didn't understand why, because foxes weren't silver but red.

The Dinses then announced they were retiring.

"What?" Dave was confused.

"We want to move to Florida, which means selling the club and possibly the house…" Mr. Dins began. His father said it in a tone reminiscent of a bank teller telling someone their loan was denied.

"What?" Dave repeated, his mouth open in shock.

"We thought a lot about it. And you are right! You're 25. You can handle yourself now, son. You don't need us coddling you anymore!" Mr. Dins continued. His mother just nodded her head in agreement.

"What?" said Dave.

"Now, son, don't be like this. You have said it yourself many times, you are an adult, and your mother and I should start treating you like one! Time to get a real job! Get an apartment! Be free from us!"

"What?" repeated Dave.

"It's everything you ever wanted. Now, don't worry. We are not going to toss in the towel just yet. We have only rented a place in Florida for the winter to start, and we'll see how it goes. Your mother and I can play tennis in the sun! In the winter! Isn't that wonderful?" Mrs. Dins' head continued to bob.

"What?"

"Now just calm down, David. You can stay in the house until summer. We won't sell it until we get back, or the Club, so you will have plenty of time to figure out your next move this winter! Isn't this exciting?"

"What?" Per usual, Dave couldn't look at either one of them.

Later, hiding in his room, Dave replayed the conversation in his head. His parents did, as they say, a complete 180 on him. From babying him for 25 years to literally shoving him out of the nest, expecting him to fly. Of course, he wanted to be an adult, but didn't actually want to pay for things. Clean his apartment? Buy food? God, it all sounded awful.

Dave was feeling pretty off from the news from his parents. Pot and video games calmed him, but he needed something more. He needed his ideal distraction: sex. Dave had learned over time and a lot of trial and error that sex was an incredible high. He didn't have to think about anything but pleasure for a brief time. Dave had a weird relationship to touch. Whether it was his ASD or his germaphobia (he would never, ever touch a kitchen sponge) or that most people annoyed him in general with bad breath and body odor, he wasn't keen on physically mingling with anyone. He thought personal space was sacred, and usually kept a good two feet from other people to ensure maximum isolation. He didn't like shaking hands or the casual hug. Physical touch had to be out of necessity. It took a while, but Dave had managed to do the unmanageable and put sex in the necessity category.

Dave's introduction to sex was through the movies. At first, the hugging and kissing on the screen made him uncomfortable. Not because it aroused him, but because he didn't understand why someone would actually want to caress, cuddle, rub, or fondle— words that set Dave on edge—someone else. But as he grew older and the movies became more "adult" in nature, the anatomy of the human body became a point of interest. Boobs came in all shapes and sizes and created a multitude of questions. How did it feel to have lumpy sacks of fat attached to one's chest? Why were bigger ones better than smaller ones, according to men? But according to women, smaller certainly was preferred for comfort. And men, what was with all the chest hair, and why would a woman want to run their hands through it? Chest hair contained sweat, which was an odd thing to want to place one's hand on. (Since Dave was a true genetic blond, he had very little hair on his own body). Just watching sex created more questions than answers for him.

Arousal finally happened for Dave when he found some dirty magazines in his dad's underwear drawer. They, of course, were full of naked women. He had seen boobs and a vagina or two onscreen, but pale purple labia stared at him like a third eye. Again, it didn't click for Dave. What was the big deal? But when he came across photos with naked men usually inside—or, say, halfway inside those labia—that spoke to Dave. Penises, usually of a magnified size, hard and protruding from other hairless men like a triton... Now *that* got Dave all tingly. He could look at his penis and relate. Curious, he did what any teenage boy would do. Not go to his father, but to the internet to answer all his questions. And that's how Dave found YouPorn, and, well, it's not hard to imagine what happened after that. He shook that monkey like his life depended on it and loved it.

But it gnawed at him why having another human jerking him off could be pleasurable. Would it be better than his hand? Like a video game, was there a next level he wasn't getting to? Was he missing something? The idea of having someone else's hands on him was frightening. And kissing? A hard no on that point. But Dave grew out of the magazines and exhausted his supply of hand cream—damn his parents for circumcising him. Finally, his curiosity got the best of him.

By the time Dave was 18, he was ready, or so he thought, to have actual sex.

His name was Rocky, that's what he told Dave. Rocky was a hired prostitute Dave found online in Boston. Long ago, his dad had told him you get what you pay for, so Dave saved up as much as possible for the best. Rocky was slightly older than Dave, in his twenties, and met him in a high-priced Boston hotel room. He looked like Mark Wahlberg from the Calvin Klein ad, beefy and hairless, and Dave was pleased with his purchase.

It started easy. Rocky asked what Dave wanted, and Dave had compiled an exact list of where and how he should be touched—down to the exact speed. There was even a pie chart.

Rocky, a veteran of strange requests, was a pro. He took the list and asked a few questions about logistics. You know, lying down, standing up, things Dave hadn't thought about.

Dave, in true Dave fashion, explained he was a virgin with

autism spectrum disorder, and if this didn't go well, he might never have sex again.

"Well, we can't have that happen!" Rocky exclaimed because, of course, sexual pleasure meant a great deal to him—giving and receiving. And Rocky did take pride in his customer satisfaction rating of 4.5.

But the first time wasn't so great, not that it was Rocky's fault. Dave couldn't help but be shy and uncomfortable. He was attracted to Rocky, and as soon as his shirt was off, Dave got an erection. But no one had touched him since he was a child. And after he got naked, he freaked out a little and locked himself in the bathroom. Dave had yet to have a crush or an emotional connection with another person, which would have caused the desire to override his fears. Dave and Rocky had yet to share even a meal, let alone the heralded first kiss.

Rocky soothingly gave him a rum and Coke and convinced him to watch porn on the hotel TV for a while.

"We're going to get you through this, buddy. There just has got to be a way," Rocky reassured him. Dave thanked him and cried a little.

Rocky explained that he had three younger brothers, and he hoped that if one of them had problems like Dave, someone would help. While the TV blared two men having a go on a velvet couch, Rocky slipped his hand under the sheet without touching any part of Dave's body except his very engorged member, and gave him sweet relief.

"You did it!" Rocky encouraged, and Dave yelled, "I did it!" back at him. He was immensely proud he had conquered a fear and had a great orgasm.

Rocky offered they try again at half-off. He was really dedicated to his craft. Dave knew a deal when he saw one. The following weekend they met again, and Rocky had him smoke some mild pot and have a drink beforehand, which totally helped. With some more instruction, both seemed to figure out what Dave needed and liked. They met once more, and Dave found the supposed sweet spot of sex and was eternally grateful to experience physical bliss.

Rocky's final advice to Dave was that since he knew what he liked and how it should be done, he should try online dating. It was free. So, after their last sexual escapade, they poured some drinks and had a lot of fun putting together Dave's online profile. Rocky came up with "minimal physical contact and maximum pleasure" as Dave's tagline. It was the correct tease that would clearly state his intentions up front. As a tip, Dave paid for another night in the hotel just for Rocky because he had nicked his father's credit card. Mr. Dins would never ask why his 18-year-old son had stayed at a Boston hotel. Mr. Dins wasn't stupid…or *that* stupid.

Now, seven years later, Dave was a pro at random hookups. He had recurring regulars from his Mathmen site, and when he felt adventurous, he went mainstream. He swiped and was surprised at how many people were in his area. But later, Dave learned that many of them were from Boston and used the rural suburbs for anonymity. No one wanted to enter a corporate meeting and see the guy or gal they banged the night before dressed in a three-piece suit and wielding a lucrative deal over their heads.

This particular night, Dave was wheeling from his parents' news. It was like a data dump in his head. Where would he live? How would he make money? Who would keep pulp-free orange juice in the fridge and fold his underwear in quarters in his drawer? But then again, no one would ask him where he had been, when he would be home, or why he smelled like a bar mat. His list of pros and cons grew to such an enormous length that he felt his brain would short-circuit.

He needed a release. Sex would do.

Dave anxiously went on Tinder and swiped a guy who said he was "all business in the front and party in the back." Wasn't that a mullet?

They met in a bar outside town, and Dave splurged for an Uber to get there. Well, not really, since he charged it to the company Amex. The guy wasn't unattractive. Dave would say a seven because he was being generous. But since he considered himself a 10 in looks and 5 in personality, the numbers matched.

The guy was brusque and said his name was Ken but didn't like small talk. Ken had booked a hotel far outside of Hillsdale for one night. After smoking his one joint, Dave downed two rum and Cokes and thought that if someone found him headless in a ditch tomorrow, that would solve most of his pressing issues. What the hell? He wanted sex.

Ken talked about business and finance the whole time. It turned Dave on. Numbers were a great distraction, so he responded by figuring out the commission percentage on specific stocks. Ken was impressed, and they both found common ground: math. They also had exceptionally good sex, as both liked it relatively fast and hard, without an ounce of sentimentality or what some people called "passion." They were there merely for physical pleasure and release and to forget all the other nonsense in their lives. Dave and Ken drank from the mini bar and continued evaluating stock projections and interest rates until the sun came up. When Dave caught an Uber home, he realized he was smiling. He'd had fun despite the mental aerobics going on in his life. He would swipe Ken again.

"David, I really don't like this disappearing act," his mother chided him when he walked in the door.

"What act? I didn't disappear. I was technically gone from the house," Dave muttered and drank straight from the OJ container.

"Really, David? Is this how you are going to talk to me?"

"Really, Mom? It is how I am talking to you."

"You're just mad about having to grow up. And it is time, David. No need to overreact about it. You just blame us for everything. You think we didn't do enough for you, but your father thinks we have done plenty, and I agree. But really, you do need to call if you aren't coming home. And what will the neighbors think? Coming in at 7 am on the front lawn; you could use the back door at least…" But Dave had tuned her out and had begun climbing the stairs to his bedroom. Pro: no more Gestapo when he returned home from partying. Con: someone had cleaned his sheets, and his bed felt soooo good.

Chapter 9
Don't Get All Theatrical

Although hungover after getting bombed with Ashley, Peter did not forget his declaration. In fact, the week after, he pushed Dave away from the pro shop computer and began researching junior tennis tournaments for Kitty. Dave got on board with the idea and felt compelled to make a color-coded chart on the dry-erase board for Peter. "There has to be some organization, Peter," Dave quipped. "We aren't animals."

"Dave, is there any way your parents would sponsor Kitty? I mean, Hillsdale Tennis Club? I don't have a dime, and we need to get her to these tournaments and hotels and whatnot."

"Can we sponsor her? I don't see why not. Sure, I'm saying yes. I have access to the bank account and can make withdrawals." While all this was true, it did not mean Dave had permission to play with the club's money. But he had crossed that line a long time ago.

"Maybe we can get another sponsor?" Peter asked. "Dave? Are you paying attention?"

"My parents want to sell the club and move to a place called Boca Raton. Do you know what Boca Raton means? It comes from the Spanish saying, *Boca de Ratones*, which is translated as rat's mouth. They are leaving me for a rat's mouth in Florida."

Peter was stunned. Sell the club? But then there would be a new owner. He hoped he wouldn't lose his job.

"What about you, Dave? Don't you live with them?"

"Yes, what about me? I will be homeless, without a home," Dave mused. Peter could see Dave's anxiety grip him and gave him a bunch of receipts to sort so he would calm down.

"Dave, don't worry, you can always crash with me. We'll figure this out. I got your back, buddy. Let's focus on getting Kitty to a tournament."

They set their goal for Kitty to compete in the November Indoor Junior Invitational in Hartford, Connecticut.

Kitty arrived promptly for her lesson, which relieved Peter from Dave's melancholic sorting and arranging.

The tournament took place over Thanksgiving. "Does it matter if you miss Thanksgiving?" Peter asked Kitty while she was practicing her serve. Every single time, she threw it straight up and slammed it with her racket. It was goddamn beautiful, he thought.

"Why?"

"Dunno, it's a holiday, Kitty. Don't you spend holidays with your family?"

"I eat with my sister daily, so it's no biggie. She'll probably be working anyway."

"I remember your sister from high school," Peter mused.

"Why? Most people don't." Slam.

"Yeah, we were in the same class, but not really friends."

"She doesn't have many friends. But I hooked her up with the divorced lady across the street so they could drink wine and talk. Both of them are a little sad, if you ask me."

"That's not nice, Kitty," Peter chided.

"No, I mean literally sad, not like losers. They are both really cool. But sad, sad. Nina still misses our grandparents, and Mia got dicked over by her husband. He left her for her sister."

"Ouch," said Peter. "Well, that is sad. Nice of you to make them friends."

"Yeah, well, somebody had to," Kitty said without irony. "So, I just win my matches at this tournament, right?"

"Yeah, I guess it's that simple. But these girls will have trained for years, and it's not going to be that easy. Have you ever competed in anything before?"

"A spelling bee in the 6th-grade count?"

"How'd you do?"

"I won. The prize was a gift certificate to Dairy Queen."

"Well, there you go. So let me ask you, have you ever failed at anything?"

Kitty thought.

"Oh yeah. Big time."

Now Peter was curious. "Do tell."

"Last year, I auditioned for the high school musical, *Grease*. I watch a lot of TV and wanted to know what acting was like. I mean, Eddie Murphy makes it seem really easy. So I wanted the starring role, of course."

"You wanted to play Sandy?" Peter started mentally comparing Kitty and Olivia Newton-John, and his brain couldn't quite grasp the image.

"Yeah, duh. So I get up there, and I say some lines. It's not that hard. But then Mr. Peterson, the drama teacher, says I gotta sing too. Well, I did. I had sung Madonna's 'Papa Don't Preach' like a million times at home." Again, Peter was still having difficulty mentally visualizing all this information.

"There I am singing...those summer niiiiiights..." she

imitated for Peter. And Peter's eardrum had a visceral reaction. Kitty literally sounded like a cat, caterwauling. She was awful.

"I was awful. Even I could hear it. So I started laughing. I laughed so hard I had tears coming out of my eyes. And then Mr. Peterson couldn't help himself and started laughing along with everyone else. I bombed big time."

"How'd it make you feel?"

"Not bad, really. Like I could check acting off my list."

"You weren't embarrassed?"

"Why?" Kitty gave him her signature stare like he was an idiot.

"Kitty, people get embarrassed when they are bad at something."

"That's stupid. Don't do it if you are bad at it, duh."

"So you'll be okay if you lose at the tennis tournament?"

"Of course, then I just won't play anymore." Slam, she hit an ace. And Peter was more excited than he had been in a long time.

Peter went home, cracked a beer, and sat numbly on the couch. Kitty's words were echoing in his head. *If you are bad at something, don't do it.* And that is precisely what Peter had done. But unlike Kitty, he was embarrassed and couldn't laugh it off. His embarrassment had become a secret, ruining his relationship with his father. Any Oprah addict could see that.

Peter had the annoying habit of just being Peter. He had gotten straight A's in high school, was in advanced classes, and got early acceptance into Yale. But the catch was…Peter didn't care. He had only done as he was told, but without enthusiasm or motivation. The other kids resented the ease with which he strode through the corridors unencumbered by teenage stress. Peter succeeded not because he wanted to or even tried. It just came to him, and he enjoyed it.

But that ease came to a crashing end when he began to fail at Yale. That was his secret. Peter didn't just walk away as he led others to believe, but failed his classes so spectacularly by the end of his second year that they threatened to expel him. He told no one and left college when offered the coaching job. It should have been his wake-up call to work harder and stop skating through life. Life wasn't just going to work itself out in his favor without him doing something, anything, to get it there. Sitting in his little apartment, scratching at the label on his beer bottle, Peter felt shame about what he had done. Failing wasn't the worst of it; it was his unwillingness to confess and own up to his father.

Enough people had paved his childhood with adoration for his "natural" athletic abilities as the captain of both the soccer and tennis teams, and also his academic abilities. High school had been pretty straightforward: do the work, get an A, and move on. When applying to colleges, it was his father who had pushed him toward Yale. At eighteen, maybe he knew it wasn't right for him, but then again, he wasn't one to argue a whole lot either. His great-grandfather and grandfather had gone to Yale. His dad had gone into the Navy and then went to Yale Business School. The only reason Charlie hadn't was that Charlie had no willingness to excel in anything other than economics. Humanities were a waste of time, he said. But Charlie knew what he wanted and achieved it without an Ivy League degree. Peter, on the other hand, accepted the glowing recommendations from Bob's Yale alumni friends, and apparently a legacy still had clout. It had made his father happy. And it had been easy.

But Peter had no idea how hard Yale would be. The other students were so dedicated and absurdly intellectual. Peter didn't study coding in his spare time or dream of a start-up company. Instead, he enjoyed the freedom of bong hits and pizza late at night. But there was only so long he could fake it. Sure, Peter could have worked harder and applied himself, but it wasn't in him.

When something wasn't uncomplicated, effortless, or straightforward, that was Peter's Achilles heel. His ego got in the way, and instead of owning up to it, he ran like his ass was on fire. Now, five years later, what had changed? Watching Kitty, Peter was amazed at how the girl knew what she wanted. She accepted her faults and kept rising to the challenge. Her honesty struck him and mirrored the fraud he felt like. That's what irritated his father, because Bob couldn't pinpoint the dishonesty. It was in the air between them like a smell.

Peter drained his beer and said out loud to no one, "I'm such an idiot."

Later, Peter knocked on Coach Clark's door.

He was greeted with, "What now, moron?"

"I need your help."

"You didn't get a girl knocked up, did ya?"

"Eew, Coach Clark. Coaching, I need your help coaching this girl in tennis."

Lois walked over. "Oh yes, please! He needs to get out of the house! He's following me around like the police. Peter, he hid my gun!"

"Woman, you are going to shoot someone with that thing!" Coach Clark shouted back.

"Am not," Lois pouted.

Peter interjected, "Yeah, just a couple hours in the afternoon. This girl Kitty has got real talent, and I want her to compete."

Coach Clark eyed him suspiciously.

"Well, son, don't be embarrassed that you are out of your league. I can come and help."

"No, that's not what I am saying..." Peter shook his head.

"Now, son, of course, you need me. I'll do it once as a favor."

75

"Just do it, Stevie, don't get all theatrical," Lois scolded him.

Peter let it go but did say sarcastically, "Thank you, Coach Clark. I am ever so indebted."

"Little pissant." And Coach Clark slammed the door.

Chapter 10
Teaching Pornography

"Mr. Dunning, I'd prefer if you kept politics out of department meetings," Mia said, already exasperated. They had gone over the usual list. Kids who needed help, a timeline of tests for the next month, etc. Unfortunately, Mia learned she was obligated as department head to ask if anyone had anything further to discuss, and this opened the proverbial can of worms.

They were in the teachers' lounge of Hillsdale Prep. The walls were dark and lined with molding from a century ago. Usually, Mia found the room a sanctuary. Books lined the walls, and the smell of coffee was like a second home to her. Mia stared down at the personalized mug Adam had given to her one birthday —"Best Teacher, Better Mom"—trying not to look at Tyler. She loved that mug and did not like him.

"This is Florida's list approved by their governor, Ron DeSantis," Tyler Dunning said while passing out the list around the table. "He went to Yale, and these are the books they say absolutely should not be read in school by children."

Mrs. Wills asked to see it and began to chuckle. Half the titles she didn't know, and the other half were novels she had read as a kid. "Mr. Dunning, am I crazy?"

"What?" Tyler looked confused.

"I mean, let me clarify, do I come across as a sex-crazed maniac? Did I change my gender since birth? Do I use swear words prolifically?" Mrs. Wills reminded Mia of Olympia Dukakis in *Moonstruck*. She had a slight Italian accent and wore a buttoned-up white silk shirt daily.

"No, but I haven't known you very long." Tyler cleared his throat uncomfortably. Mia liked how older people unnerved him.

"No, Mr. Dunning," Mrs. Wills continued. "I have read quite a few of these books. Well, the ones written before 2000. And never, not once, have I cheated on my husband or had sex with the same gender. Not that there is anything wrong with homosexuality, I imagine it quite interesting having the same parts to play with. I had copious amounts of teenage and premarital sex because I am not a religious woman. And I didn't do it because I read a book. I did it because it is human nature. The body is designed to crave sex from puberty, which is natural. It is not like voting or joining the army with an age limit. Do you know why I am telling you all this?"

"No, ma'am, but I don't think it's relevant." Tyler was trying to stand his ground.

"But it is, Mr. Dunning. These books are not 'gateways' to nefarious behavior. Reading them will not lead to a life of degradation. Think about it." Mrs. Wills, forever a teacher, attempted to school Tyler Dunning that reading these supposedly illicit books would not change anyone from who they were. She then began to shuffle the papers in front of her, clearly the end of what she had to say. Mrs. Wills was annoyed that she was missing the latest episode of *The Great British Baking Show* with a glass of chardonnay.

Mia had never had to deal with a confrontation like this. When she became a teacher, people liked to talk about their favorite books they had read, not books that shouldn't be read. This was a subject she wasn't prepared to handle, and now she felt in over her head. Eric had bulldozed her for the last decade at home, and now a different man was doing it at work. Why did men like this feel they could intimidate her? It didn't help that Mia didn't enjoy arguing. She felt out of her depth, like she wasn't smart enough. Typical for a woman to feel like that, she thought. She longed to be one of those lawyers on TV, so intelligent and sassy. What would that feeling be like? Able to put someone in their place as Kitty did with Eric. Mia needed to be more like Kitty. Direct, confident, honest.

"Mr. Dunning. It's hard to give credence to a list that includes Judy Blume. She was the first writer who talked about girls' menstruation, which happens to girls. Blume helped millions of women understand their bodies when parents and teachers wouldn't discuss such a subject. Now, book banners go after her for everything. And why? Because her books talk about teenage sex and birth control? Blume wrote *Blubber*, for god's sake. Mr. Dunning, open any newspaper in the country, any movie, any TV show, and somewhere there is sex, birth control, and ooooh…four-letter words." She couldn't help the sarcasm.

Mr. Baxter had been intently listening and said, "Peckerheads," giggling.

"Mr. Baxter, that doesn't help." Mia shook her head at him. "Mr. Dunning, none of this is relevant to the curriculum at Hillsdale Prep. The overall goal of these kids is to have a higher education, not a lesser one. Don't you remember those ads on NBC with the slogan 'The more you know'? That is the essence of education, is it not? To teach more? Not less?"

"But it is not our job to teach sex! These books contain pornography."

"Does Judy Blume arouse you?" Mr. Baxter asked slyly.

"No, but the children!" Tyler whined.

"So you read your father's *Playboys* for the articles?" Mr. Baxter smiled. Mia ignored the remark, although it was funny.

Instead, she continued, "Now that's a bit dramatic, Mr. Dunning. Let's save the drama for literature. Books that contain sex or sexuality cannot always be labeled pornography."

"Son," Mr. Baxter asked, "I'm curious. How do you think you were born? How did the twinkle in your parents' eyes come about? The stork?" Mr. Baxter couldn't stop. To him, this was a game.

"Mr. Baxter..." Mia was losing control of the meeting.

Jules chimed in, "The parents are talking, and quite a few agree that some of these books are inappropriate."

"*Catcher in the Rye* is about a teenage boy lusting after women and using vulgar language. Several school districts have removed it," Tyler added.

"Bollocks," said Mr. Baxter firmly. "Name one teenage boy who isn't lusting after someone. If they can do it, they can read about it."

"How many parents, Jules? Have you taken a poll? Do you have names, a percentage?" Mia hated vague references.

"Well, no, but they certainly are talking, and for the sake of Hillsdale, I don't think we should ignore them." Jules would jump off a bridge if a parent asked her.

"'For the sake of Hillsdale,' what does that mean?" Mia asked while using her pointer finger to tap the table. "This is for the sake of education. Are we losing the concept that to be uneducated is to be ill-informed? Unknowing? Thus, these kids will not be competent to make the right decisions, especially if they become doctors, lawyers, teachers, or even politicians. What if we label Biology class too graphic? How would that affect all future doctors and scientists? What if Calculus is too symbolic? What if some politician claims those symbols could be misconstrued about a certain culture, race, or country, so we stop teaching it, and your little iPhone is never again updated? This is preposterous, the idea of taking away knowledge instead of giving it. We are teachers!" Mia was frustrated, but tried to keep her cool.

"Well, I don't feel comfortable teaching pornography," Tyler said, having not listened to a word.

"Yeah, and, like, the parents don't want that either," Jules chimed in.

Mr. Baxter whispered, "Fuck nuggets," and left.

Left alone, Mia rubbed her eyebrows and felt defeated. She already knew this problem wouldn't go away, but would only get bigger. Dammit.

Chapter 11
Wise Men Say Only Fools Rush In...

"Peter!" Ashley was calling his name and rushing toward the tennis court. She was dressed in work clothes, a women's suit, and speed-walking toward Peter, trying to draw his attention. Her chest bounced in a way that Peter couldn't help but notice.

"Hey, Ashley, what's up?" Pete was surprised to see her.

"Okay, forgive me, but I got to do this," and before Peter could respond, quick as a flash, Ashley's hand got the back of his head and pulled him into a throaty kiss. Not that the kiss was terrible, and Peter admittedly returned it a little out of his confusion.

When she pulled back, Peter stood stunned.

"I'm sorry about that," she said, looking across three courts, "But I had to do it. Mom thinks we are officially dating." Ashley used air quotes for "dating."

"What? Why?"

"Well, she caught me texting with Ravi, and I said it was you.

I hope you don't mind?" Ashley scrunched up her shoulders, *Oops?* She looked over to make sure her mother on court six was watching. She was with Bunny and a couple other spray-tanned ladies.

"Ashley, why don't you just tell her the truth about Ravi?" Peter looked at her.

"What? No, she would want to meet him, and that will not happen."

"Why? What could be so bad?"

Ashley pulled out her phone and showed him a picture of Ravi. Oh. The guy had more tattoos than the skin area would allow, and he was wearing a ladies' pink mesh tank top. His lip, nose, and ears were pierced, and was that a mohawk?

"Ravi is the bad boy phase I am going through before I become a lawyer, so it's just best to keep this kind of ammunition against me secret. Daddy might have a heart attack before I pass the bar." Peter was still trying to compute this plump girl in her ill-fitting work blazer and low heels dating a goth metalhead.

"Ashley, I want to help you, but…"

"This helps you too, right? I mean, how many of them…" Ashley nodded to court six, "want to get their gel manicures into you? And seriously, Peter, it won't affect your life," she said with a raised eyebrow.

"What?" Peter got defensive. "I've got a life, you know, things going on."

"Okay, Farmer Ted." Again, the single eyebrow went up farther.

"I'll take you out for drinks this weekend. Okay?" Ashley offered.

"You're buying, right?"

"Somebody has to." Ashley walked away but turned around to give him a little wave so her mother could see. Now Peter rolled his eyes.

"So, you and Ashley?" Kitty said, approaching. "Not the right call, dude." Kitty pushed up her glasses. Somehow she found the only pink fluorescent tennis skirt on the internet with a matching rainbow top.

"It's complicated," Peter muttered.

"Whatevs," Kitty responded.

"Okay, let's get to work!" Coach Clark shouted and blew a whistle.

"Coach Clark, you can't use a whistle here. It will annoy everyone."

"My boy, that's what you lack, the ability to show power and strength!" He blew it again, and Peter winced.

"Who are you?" Kitty asked, arms crossed, eyeing the old man in a nylon tracksuit that came from *The Sopranos* collection at Dillard's.

"My dear, I am the best tennis coach in town and will help you win."

"In that outfit?" Kitty said.

"Kitty, play nice. Coach Clark is very good and willing to help us for free."

"Who's your favorite singer?" Kitty demanded.

Coach Clark didn't miss a beat and looked her straight in the eye. "Taylor Swift. You got a problem with that?"

Kitty and Peter both burst into silly smiles and tried not to laugh. "Nope, no problem at all, Coach Clark," Kitty said, holding up her hands. "I guess you're feeling 22."

Coach Clark winked at Peter, and Peter remembered why he was such a good teacher. He connected with kids in a way only great teachers do.

"Now, let's get going, you little pissants."

Peter forgot about Ashley and played tennis with Kitty. Coach

Clark shouted changes and orders to Kitty's swing, which did help her overall game. Kitty was a quick learner. They only had weeks until the tournament, and Peter was more nervous than Kitty.

Afterward, Kitty and Coach Clark chatted about Swiftie songs, and Peter let them bond and moseyed back to the pro shop. He needed some Dave time.

"Was that Ashley Tinsdale kissing you?" Dave said without looking at him.

"Don't start, and it's not what you think."

"How would you know what I think? But when a boy and girl are kissing in public, yes, one would directly correlate that to being together. That's why I don't kiss anyone."

"You don't kiss anyone because you don't like it, a wholly different thing."

"I don't kiss anyone because they might have eaten tuna fish salad. I do not like tuna fish salad."

Dave was now sorting tennis rackets on the walls. He ignored the sizes and brands, but liked to designate them by color and prove the theory that men mainly bought ones with red or blue and ladies liked yellow. He kept a running tab in his drawer every time someone picked one.

"Let me ask you something, Dave."

"You are implying I don't have a choice. You said *let me*, not *can I*."

Peter ignored him. "Where do you see yourself in the future?"

"Where do I see myself in the future? That is quite possibly the worst question to ask me. First, I am neither a fortune teller nor do I have psychic capabilities."

"No, what do you want for your future?"

"What do I want for my future? A bedroom with fresh sheets and someone else to go to the grocery store. I dislike grocery stores because I can see what people eat by looking into their carts."

"Fair point. But do you have any dreams or goals?"

"I just told you I do not want to go to the grocery store. Weren't you listening, Peter?"

"So how will you make money to have someone go to the grocery store and pay for groceries?"

"Are you trying to give me nightmares, Peter?"

"No, I am trying to figure out a future. Something you and I, regardless of your ASD, have actively avoided. But I feel like it is becoming unavoidable."

"MMMMmm?" Dave dug out a little pot pipe. "Really? Is it unavoidable?" Peter smiled. Maybe it was for another day. Dave started singing Elvis: "Wise men say, only fools rush in…"

But Peter's phone rang. Dammit.

"Hey, Chuck," he said, seeing the caller ID.

"Hey, numbnuts, we gotta get to the hospital." This time Peter didn't react.

"Dad fall again?"

"No, you are such an idiot. He had a heart attack." Oh shit.

"Is he still alive?" Peter whelped.

But Charlie had hung up. Thanks. Thanks a lot.

Peter was pretty fast on his bike. The hospital was close to the club, and he made it there in minutes. Peter noted that when one is panicking, one can pretty much double their speed on a bike.

While his parents annoyed him, he still wasn't prepared to live without them. His father was one of those types of fathers who believed that if he had a son, they would be a replica of him. That a son would be a better version of him. Peter had failed, while Charlie made the cut. Charlie had done exactly what Bob had wanted and finished Boston University and got a degree in finance. He was definitely on track to be a chip off the old block. But then there was Peter.

For his father, the fact that Peter didn't discover a great ego or pride in his academic abilities unsettled him. Bob was immensely proud of his son on paper, but when sitting around the dinner table discussing possibilities of Peter's future, Peter checked out. He didn't give his father the emotional response he wanted.

Questions like, "Son, have you considered law school?"

Peter met with, "Why? I don't like to argue with people."

"What about medical school?"

"Nah. Too gory. Yuck."

"A business degree?"

"I thought Charlie was doing that?"

"Engineering?"

"Too much math."

Around and around the father and son would go, and Peter couldn't commit to a single subject. Nothing inspired him, and he knew it infuriated his father, who couldn't understand being so nonchalant about life.

His mother, forever the placater, would respond, "Bob, don't worry. Right, Peter dear? You will figure out what you want to do in good time." She reassured them like someone with all the hope of winning *American Idol*.

Peter destroyed his parents' lingering hope when he dropped the bomb that he would not return to Yale.

The announcement made Bob Wise so upset that he threw his empty martini class in the trash before making a new one. Edie fished it out because it cost $150 from Tiffany's. Bob used the timeless platitude and told Peter he was "throwing away his life." It didn't help when Peter retorted, "Okay, boomer." But Bob didn't get the reference to his generation and continued, berating Peter that he had been given every opportunity to make a life for himself, thanks to them. Bob declared he was proverbially washing his hands of the situation. Peter was on his own from now on.

Peter retorted, "Good, because you spilled some gin on them."

Peter moved out the next day to the Clarks', and things had not been the same.

Five years had passed, and the chasm of resentment between the two felt like an uncrossable river. But neither had been willing to try. If Peter had been able to reject the free ticket to Yale, or even just confessed it was too hard for him, where would they be now? Would it be better between them?

Biking through the streets of Hillsdale, his heart racing, Peter did not want his dad to die, not like this. Bob was supposed to grow old in a wheelchair that Peter could push around and laugh when his father made remarks like, "Back in my day, women were women!" But not now, not while Peter was in tennis shorts parading as an adult.

What would life look like if he couldn't have his father there to disappoint? To get angry at him for not being a better person? He was the yin to Peter's downward spiral yang. People needed opposites in life, especially family. Without having a counterpart, what would he bitch about? Who would Peter measure himself by? He needed his dad to challenge him, but also, he needed to do something to make him proud. To make himself proud. But what?

Pounding through the hospital's doors, he raced to the elevator, and by the time he got to his father's room, Peter was in such a panic that he pushed the door open with full force.

"OOOW! Dammit." A nurse stood on the other side with her hand on her head. "Ugh." She was clearly annoyed and rubbing the bump.

"Oh my god, I am so sorry!" Peter cried.

Edie Wise blurted, "Peter, for heaven's sake, control yourself!"

"It's okay, I'm all right," the nurse said. When she looked up and saw Peter, she clearly looked agitated and raced from the room. Peter remembered her as the same nurse that smelled pot on him. Oops.

"Sorry, Mom. Dad, are you okay?" Bob Wise was lying flat, and this time in a hospital gown. Wires were hooked to his chest, and there was the steady beeping of a machine. He looked pale and a little sweaty, and his eyes were closed.

"Honey, they gave him something to rest," Edie assured him. "I asked for something too, but they wouldn't give me anything. I don't see why not. I am very upset."

"Mom, really?"

Edie ignored the tone in his voice and explained, "It was just a mild cardiac infarction, or that's what they said. He'll be okay. It was just a scare. They are testing to see if he needs a stint in a heart valve or something."

"A stent, Mom," Peter replied.

"What?"

"It's called a stent, not a stint. It means Dad may have mild heart disease, and a stent is a tube that would open up his arteries and allow the blood to flow better."

Edie looked at her son, perplexed. "How in the world do you know that?"

"I'm lazy, Mom, not dumb. Learned it at college."

"Well, see, education is a good thing." Edie nodded at him, making a point.

"Not now, Mom," said Peter, annoyed at the little jab. "What did the doctor say? Is Dad in any danger now?"

"No, thank goodness, darling. As Charlie always keeps telling us, we are getting old."

"Mom, don't listen to him." Peter looked at her in her pink sweater and her greying blonde hair pulled back. In moments like this, he saw her fragility. The last thing Peter wanted was for his mom to lose her husband.

"It will be okay. Doctors know all about this stuff. But, Mom, Dad may have to quit drinking."

"Oh, dearie me, I hadn't thought of that." Edie's face physically twisted as if in pain. "He is not going to like that one bit."

The door opened again, and Charlie strode in loudly on the phone. "Dr. Klose, next week," he announced.

Peter and Edie just stared at him.

"Dr. Klose," Charlie repeated, then sighed exasperatedly. "He's the head cardiologist at Mass General?"

Peter held up his hands. *So?*

"He will see Dad tomorrow. I got him past the waiting list. I play squash with his son." *Ohhh*, Edie and Peter nodded.

"Of course you do, Charles," Peter said, irked. Then he leaned down and kissed the top of his mother's head. "See, Mom, Charlie came to save the day." The sarcasm was lost on them.

Peter had convinced Charlie to drive their mother home so that he could stay with their father. Like all his monumental decisions, Peter didn't really have any forethought, just that his mom looked tired and Charlie was being obnoxious to the local doctor. It was enough to send them away.

A different nurse came and adjusted his father's tubes and wires while Peter sat there and waited patiently. He thought about Kitty, and it comforted him. Hoping she would win filled him with anxiety, but also a thrill. If he could make something out of her, if he could have an effect on her, was motivating him in a way he had never felt. There was something there he couldn't put his finger on.

"Son, what are you doing here?" Bob Wise was coming to and moving about, irritated by the needles and wires in his skin.

"Hey, Dad. I sent Mom home to get some rest. How are you feeling?"

His father fiddled with the plastic tubing coming out of his arm. Then, resigning to the situation, he let his head sink back into the pillow, taking a deep breath.

"Old and knocked down." There was a tinge of sadness in his voice. It was an unusual display of emotion from his father.

"Well, they will fix it, and you'll be fine." Peter tried to sound cheerful.

"You look like you did when you were twelve, and I picked you up for tennis." There it was, the subtle dig at Peter wearing play clothes. That's the Bob he knew.

"Hey, Dad. I'm sorry," Peter blurted while picking at his tennis shorts.

"Sorry for what?"

"You know, Yale, disappointing you. I didn't mean to make you so angry."

"You lied. I am dying, aren't I? People only get sentimental when they think it's their last shot." Bob groaned.

"No, Dad, you're going to be fine. I'm just apologizing for being an ass these past few years."

Bob remained quiet. Peter continued. "I get it. I walked away from all that opportunity, as you said. But the thing is, I want other opportunities." Peter surprised himself. He hadn't realized he wanted other opportunities.

"Like what, son?" Bob was genuinely interested.

"I don't know." Peter searched for a way to explain. "Like, you and Charlie, you guys like finance stuff, business, and figuring it all out. You look at spreadsheets and newspapers and see what's before you to work with. I like that. I like looking at what's in front of me and working with that. It's why I like tennis so much. The ball comes at me, and at that moment, all I have to do is think about hitting it the way I want, where I want, and it's nobody else but me making that decision."

"Interesting," Bob agreed. "But what does that mean, son?"

"Don't hate me for saying this, but I don't know yet. It will all mean something, but I don't know yet, and I can't force it. It just has to happen."

"Okay," Bob said.

"Okay?"

"Yeah, but figure it out before I kick it. I'd hate not to know the end of this story. Shit," Bob almost shouted. "Tonight, I'm missing the end of my Ken Burns documentary on TV. Your mother still doesn't understand how to work the DVR."

Peter chuckled. "Okay, Dad, don't worry. They replay that stuff all the time." Bob closed his eyes and drifted off pretty fast. But Peter sat there and felt better than he had in a long time. He let his mind wander to his father, referring to his life as a story. That would make him the main character. So what was his agency? He asked himself what he would need to do to change his life. What would make him grow up? What would make him happy?

Chapter 12
A Fly in the Car

Nina rubbed her head and muttered, "Twit," after she got hit by the hospital room door. She knew exactly who Peter Wise was, the boy she stupidly had a crush on in high school. But he never looked at her back then, with her stringy hair, braces, glasses, and acne. Who did?

Nina was too embarrassed to out herself. She knew she looked different now and tried to hide from Peter. Nina didn't want that awkward first recognition. "Oh! Nina Kittrick, weren't you the one who lived with your grandparents and liked dissecting frogs in biology?" It was true she did like dead, gross things, and she had no problem with blood and guts in the ER.

Once in senior English class, Peter had written a paper about Scout, the young character from *To Kill a Mockingbird*. The teacher had asked them to pick any character from any novel, and Peter had chosen Scout, a girl. He reasoned that Scout represented the difference between what people appear to be and who they are.

Nina wanted to cry behind her thick glasses because that was how she felt. She wanted someone to realize who she was, and for that to be Peter Wise. Nina imagined Peter being the one guy in high school who got to know her and might date her. At the time, Nina thought he was intelligent, cool, and attractive. And now, Nina was utterly mortified just looking at him. The high school girl will forever live in every woman, deep in their soul. Those insecurities never vanish, but get deftly put aside, like unfolded laundry.

That first time the Wises were in the hospital, it was a shock to see Peter. She had forgotten all about him until then. But he smelled the same, precisely like a bong. Peter used to come to class stoned and still aced his tests. It was an unusual earthy smell that Nina recognized immediately. Especially on her ER patients who came in after cutting their hands on a knife trying to make a triple grilled cheese. It happened not once, but twice. Or the teenager who thought if he duct-taped bubble wrap to his body and threw himself down the stairs, it wouldn't hurt. That was only a mild concussion, and the kid ate three pudding cups while she bandaged the cut on his head. She liked stoner patients because they were always apologetic and partially sedated, unlike drunks.

So, yes, Nina knew Peter was stoned when she first saw him. The sunglasses inside also gave it away. It was like she had gone back in time, and they were teenagers again. And that was the last feeling Nina wanted.

"Hey, Nina bo-bina!" Oh god, it was Dr. Stan. "So, Friday night? How about it? Let me take you out for a steak dinner. Oh man, nothing is better than that! It just ends the week on a high note, a T-bone. Maybe you're one of those veggie people? I'm down. I'm cool." He was so not cool. Stan's hair was already thinning in his thirties. Nina guessed he would be bald in a decade. He wasn't a bad guy. Just no one had taught him how to act around women.

Nina thought about Mia. Dammit. They had promised each other to "get out there" more. As in, they needed to go on dates. And Dr. Stan was now offering her a date. Shit.

Luckily, they were interrupted.

"Hello, Nina." It was Dr. Matthew Mayfield. Nina thought he came from the set of *General Hospital,* and most nurses swooned over him. Tall, rugged, with high cheekbones, thick brown hair, and divorced. The only problem was that he was too old for Nina. He may have already been 50, which just was a no-go for her.

"Did you finish up with Mr. Wise?" he asked. Nina went over the details, and Dr. Mayfield nodded and sauntered away because that's what dreamy hospital doctors do down the corridor. If all doctors were like him, everyone would work in hospitals.

"Nina!" Stan, who had waited patiently, blurted at her. "Whatcha say? Me, you, and a little meat... Oooh, oh, god, that came out wrong. I am so sorry." Stan was turning bright red, and Nina, being Nina, felt sorry for him.

"Okay, yes, Stan. Friday night."

She thought she heard him say "Yippee," and he left shouting, "I'll text you the deets!"

"Don't say 'deets,' Stan," she muttered under her breath.

That Friday night was crisp and clear, and all Nina wanted to do was curl up on the couch and watch *Terms of Endearment* and cry. She always thought she would be the type of mother who would scream, "Give my daughter the shot!" She was already so fiercely protective of Kitty. Sometimes Nina just stood outside Kitty's bedroom door and listened to her gentle snoring. If Kitty was okay at the end of the day, then Nina was okay. Nina had a stack of baby Kitty pictures on her dresser that sometimes she would flip through to cheer her up. Her baby face had been so round, with a high forehead and those curls circling her face. Even back then, her clothes were always bright colors. When she had to get glasses by age five, Nina thought she looked like a little Dalai Lama but with hair.

Nina was nine when Kitty was born. She would stare for hours at Kitty swaddled in the bassinet, sucking on her toes. From that moment, Kitty was like the pet Nina asked for but never got. She would take Kitty from her mother and hold her for hours while her mother was busy with their father. The arguments were terrible between her parents, shouting and throwing things. So Nina would take Kitty to her room and read *Harry Potter* to her. Kitty was a baby. What did it matter? But Nina could go on for pages and pages, ignoring the family tempest.

Nina figured out her parents hadn't "planned" Kitty. Words like "accident" were often used. But to Nina, Kitty was a gift, not an accident, and something she could hold and love when things got bad at home.

Now, in the present, Nina pushed that time in their lives out of her head. The time with their parents. The night Oma and Pop came to get them, Nina was hiding in a closet with three-year-old Kitty, wrapped in a blanket and covered in blood. Nina was never going to let anything happen to Kitty ever again.

But they were older now. The past was in the past. Nina had been moving on since they left their parents' apartment that one last time. But had she been moving on? Kitty was so independent now and didn't need Nina fussing over her. And wasn't it time she thought about men, marriage, and kids like other women her age? Work at the hospital fulfilled her. She could simultaneously care for people and earn a decent living. Everyone said she was a natural, and she always met new people. Patients were so vulnerable, and Nina had infinite empathy for them. Even the rude ones, who bitched about hospital food and complained that doctors were incompetent. She tucked them in and gave them extra ginger ale.

That night, while sitting in a hot bath, Nina asked herself what she wanted. She wanted that feeling of holding a baby again. That joy a tiny human could give looking up at her and smiling. That sense that the baby needed her just as much as she needed them. Nina wanted a pack of children who would be loud, demanding, funny, and fill her life with noise and purpose.

When she was dying, Oma confessed to Nina that she had wanted many children. But after Lily, there were miscarriages, and she and Pop gave up.

"When you and Kitty moved in, I felt twenty years younger. Never were you two a burden. You were the children I was meant to raise," Oma assured Nina.

Nina also wanted the kind of relationship her grandparents had. It was hard to pinpoint, but they were meant for each other. Oma's German tenacity and Pop's Irish joviality complemented each other. Nina would sometimes catch them in the kitchen, drinking pints, playing music, and dancing all alone. Pop would make Oma laugh, and Oma made him clean shirts and *currywurst*, German sausage. They argued, of course, but it was never serious, unlike her parents. When Oma got mad, she quietly scrubbed dishes like she was going to break them. And when Pop was angry, he went out to the garage and worked on a car. Then, like that, whatever had angered them disappeared, and they'd have a quick kiss.

Oma died first, and it broke Pop's heart. The old man was frail, and his spirit left with her. Oma went in her sleep, which shocked everyone. But it was just like her to go without a big fuss. Pop only lasted three more weeks. Kitty swore it was from a broken heart. Nina was with him, and thankful Kitty didn't see that last look in his eyes. Nina recognized his fear.

"Don't worry, Pop," she whispered in his ear. "Kitty and I will be okay. We got this. Go be with Oma." And as Nina laid a kiss on his forehead, he went.

It was the first time Nina watched Kitty suffer as a real person. Kitty locked herself in her room and blared music for two days. She crawled into Nina's bed at night, and they held each other and cried. They had a quiet funeral, and Kitty wore her brightest outfit and hair ties. She said Pop and Oma wouldn't have appreciated all that black clothes nonsense.

Kitty brought Nina coffee in bed for a month after because Pop had done that for Oma whenever she was sad.

Kitty refused to clean out their grandparents' clothes for years, and often wore one of Oma's old dresses to school, or Pop's old fedora on a rainy day. They worked through their grief in their own way. But Nina had been right: they were going to be okay.

Now, Nina looked in the mirror at her 25-year-old self and began to apply makeup for her date with Stan. She wasn't hopeful it would go well, but like Oma would say, "At least you tried." So she was going to at least try to be happy.

Kitty stormed into the room. "Here, you will look like a Kardashian if I let you do this."

Kitty loved to play with makeup—like blue and green eyeshadow. Nina looked scared.

"Oh c'mon, Nina, you have to trust me." Kitty started applying some powder to her older sister's face. "You are one of those '70s Ivory girls, and I am more like an '80s Madonna. So just a little makeup will do." Kitty pushed Nina's chin side to side and applied mascara inches from her face. Nina could smell Kitty's Fruit Stripe gum.

"Look," Kitty demanded. And Nina had to admit, she did a great job. Nina could hardly notice the makeup, but she looked better and prettier.

"Thanks, Kitty."

"So, who's the guy?" Kitty shoved her glasses up her face. Nina loved it.

"A doctor... I don't know about him. But Mia says I should try dating, and well, I'm trying." Nina rolled her eyes.

"Nina, one shouldn't have to try at love. Love happens. It's a belief, not a school project. It will happen if you believe in it, and for Mia too. She just forgot to believe because her ex is an asshole."

Nina blinked at her little sister. How did she know all this?

Kitty continued, "Oma said, love is like air. You need it to stay alive, so don't be an idiot and hold your breath." Nina burst out laughing. That sounded like Oma.

"Thanks, Kitty. Wish me luck."

"Damn, girl, it ain't about luck. Express yourself, don't repress yourself."

"Who said that?"

"Madonna, duh." And Kitty looked at her like she was an idiot.

The date was excruciating. Stan had knocked over his glass of water on her and ordered dinner for them both—which she hated. He kept talking badly about her co-workers at the hospital. She thought he was exactly the type who would become head of the hospital one day and make everyone's life miserable. Plus, he talked while he chewed, which was gross.

Stan took a phone call, and Nina was left alone with a slab of rare meat in front of her. It reminded her of the ER accident victims. Car metal could rip a body to shreds. Stan had gone outside, so she walked up to the bar and asked for a shot of tequila. Rarely did Nina turn to alcohol, but desperate times called for desperate measures. She asked for the most expensive shot and told the bartender to put it on Stan's tab. As Nina sipped the drink—she never could take a shot—someone bumped her from behind, and the tequila dribbled down her chin. "Jesus," she muttered. It was probably Stan.

"Oh, sorry! I didn't mean to… Hey, you're the nurse!" Nina turned to look and went still. It was Peter.

Her face flushed. Peter looked nice. His hair was cut just right, and he wore a relaxed blue button-down shirt. He smelled good too, some kind of shaving cream. Nina liked it. Oh god, it was the same feeling as in high school again.

"Oh, hi," she blurted while trying to look away.

"I keep hitting you." He laughed. "I'm really sorry." Peter attempted to rub the spot of tequila from her shirt, but he was touching her boob, and she jerked back.

"Oh shit, I'm sorry." Peter now was embarrassed himself. "Can I buy you a drink? You know, for helping out Mom and Dad?"

"No. No, thank you, Peter." And she fled back to her table. Peter was left standing perplexed.

When Stan returned, Nina feigned a headache and asked to go home. All the while, she eyed Peter at the end of the bar. He looked comfortable sitting there sipping a drink. He didn't play with a cell phone, but chatted with the bartender. Peter still had the cool breeziness from ten years ago. Like he didn't have a care. She envied his ease, while she wanted to crawl under the table.

Then in walked Ashley Tinsdale. Surprised, Nina watched Ashley barrel through the bar in a pantsuit and heels, waving at Peter. Nina thought Ashley still looked like a teenager, just dressed up. Ashley kissed Peter on the cheek, and he smiled at her. Nina's cheeks flushed again, embarrassed to realize they were together. And here she sat with balding Stan, arguing with the waiter over the surcharge for butter and demanding to know who drank a tequila. This was her life. Shit, she did need a change.

Stan dropped her off and went in for a kiss, but Nina began waving her hands like there was a fly in the car. She couldn't get out fast enough while muttering sorry and thank you for dinner.

Relief flooded her when she saw Kitty sitting on the couch with a giant bag of M & M's, watching TV.

"How was your date?" Kitty asked.

"Shit." Nina flopped down and grabbed some candy.

"I could have told you that. You are not supposed to be with a doctor." Kitty munched and kept her eyes on the re-run of *The Golden Girls*. Bea Arthur was her favorite.

Nina was used to Kitty's declarations and decided to ignore them. Maybe she *was* supposed to be with a doctor, which would prove one of Kitty's many theories about her wrong.

"I saw Ashley Tinsdale tonight. Didn't know she was back in town."

"Yeah, she's a lawyer or something. She's dating Peter Wise, I think." Kitty wasn't looking at her sister and missed her visibly stiffen.

"How'd you know that?" Nina asked.

"Cause it's Peter."

"What do you mean? How do you know Peter?"

"Duh, Pet...errr... My tennis coach?"

Nina took in a deep breath. Well, this was going to be awkward, and she shoved more candy in her mouth.

Chapter 13
Eat This

Peter was happy to be sitting at the bar holding a stiff martini in his hand. It had been a helluva week. The weather was turning colder, and things were progressing with Kitty. He had begun coaching in earnest with her. Dave was banned from selling her soda or candy from the pro shop, and he was working on her diet. It didn't help that Coach Clark snuck her away to Dairy Queen after practice. He was a handful. Even off the court, Peter couldn't slip inside his apartment without the coach wanting to go over Kitty's stats.

Coach Clark jotted down Kitty's daily serve, agility, and mistakes. Peter admitted it was helpful, but he reviewed his clipboard endlessly when all Peter wanted to do was watch TV.

Lois had assured him Stevie would calm down, but Peter doubted that. Then yesterday was a doozy.

Around five o'clock, Peter got a frantic call from his mother.

"Peter, I just can't. I don't know what to do!" Peter, holding his cell phone, had no idea what catastrophe had struck the Wises this time. Of course, there was little information to go on.

"Mom, slow down. Is Dad okay?"

"He's an asshole," Edie declared. Peter stopped walking while on the phone. Edie Wise never cursed. Her frustration consisted of "Dang it" and "Oh Lordy."

"Mom?"

"He is a right, old asshole. I mean, that son of a bitch…"

"Whoa, Mom. What's going on?"

"Can you come over now, please? Or else, I don't know what I will do."

"On my way."

When Peter opened the door, he found his mother slumped on a chair in the kitchen. Her makeup had faded, and her hair was messy, unlike Edie. There was a coffee stain on her lime green sweater. She had been crying and held a glass of chardonnay in her hands.

"Mom, what is it?" Peter rubbed her shoulders.

"He is fucking sober." And she took a big swig of her drink. Bob had been out of the hospital for a couple weeks and hadn't had a drop of alcohol. They had put a stent in his heart, a relatively simple procedure, and he was back home in no time. As far as Peter could tell, it had been years since his father hadn't had his one, two, most likelythree nightly martinis. Oh jeez.

"What is your mother telling you?" he heard his father scream from the other room. The voice was a low growl, the same one Peter had been scared of most of his life.

Bob marched into the room. "I am fine and don't need you two conspiring against me!" Bob's own hair was disheveled, and his collared shirt looked wrinkled. His eyes glared at Peter as if he had sided with Putin.

"Peter, he has been like this for two days, just yelling at me. He called me the c-word," she whispered.

"He called you a…" Peter was flabbergasted.

"Yes, he called me a clown! Said I wasted my whole life dressing myself up, and for who, the grocer?! Just because I choose to look nice!" Edie's eyes brimmed with tears.

Peter knew that wasn't it. His dad was facing a lifestyle change —getting old and sick, and now he couldn't drink away the days. Oh boy.

"Well, all this nonsense!" Bob screamed. "Putting on airs, we always have to be nice to people. Why, Peter? Why do we have to be nice all the time? She wanted to have the Tinsdales over again, and what the hell do I care? Fred is an old fart, and Cami is just a…"

Peter breathed in and out. Okay, this situation was not going well.

"Dad, can you go to the other room?"

"Don't you come into my home and tell me what to do, young man. You don't have any rights here!"

"Bob, stop!" Edie whined.

"Dad." Peter went right up to his father. "GO IN THE OTHER ROOM."

Bob, taken aback, shouted, "FINE! This family is so ungrateful. I might as well have died, and you two could have thrown a brunch!" And then he stormed out.

Peter, really not knowing what to do, thought for a minute. Looking at his mother, his heart wrenched a little. Then an idea came to him, and he grabbed his backpack.

"Wait here, Mom. It's going to be okay," he assured.

Peter entered the den and found his father using the TV remote like an assault rifle. The poor TV was a blur of channels.

"Eat this." Peter held his hand out.

"What the hell is that?" Bob demanded.

"A brownie."

"Seriously, you want me to eat a brownie?" Bob looked at his son like he was a complete buffoon.

"Yes, it will be the only thing I ask of you. It's chocolate, your favorite." Peter and Bob began a stare-off.

"I promise to leave if you do." Peter tried to entice him. Bob didn't budge. "Dad, it's sugar, chocolate…" Peter gave the baked good a little wag in front of his father's face.

Bob grabbed it and shoved it in his mouth. Peter had never thought someone could eat a brownie with so much rage. Who gets angry at a brownie?

"Fine."

"Fine," Peter replied and went back to his mother.

"What happened?" she asked.

"We wait twenty minutes."

"Huh?"

"Don't worry, Mom."

Thirty minutes went by while Edie and Peter sat in the kitchen. When Peter heard his dad laughing, he went back into the den.

"Whatcha watching, Dad?"

"Have you heard of this show, *The Office*? It's hilarious."

"Yep, and there are a lot of episodes. Here." Peter showed him how to stream all the seasons.

"That's him! That's my old boss," Bob started howling. "I had this boss, Donald Sultan, a real dipshit."

"Dad, you hungry?" Peter asked slyly.

"Yeah, I am, but I don't know what I want." Bob looked at Peter, confused.

"How about I order a pizza, and we watch TV for a while?"

"I haven't had pizza in years!" Bob cried with glee. Then he asked, "What are you wearing?" Peter was in his tennis tracksuit. "You look like Grandma Nona when she started wearing wigs and elastic pants." Bob chuckled.

"Okay, Dad." Peter was smiling. "Very funny."

"Can you get those round, spicy things on the pizza?" Bob looked confused.

"Pepperoni?" Peter offered. His mother stood at the door watching, her mouth agape.

"That's the ticket!" Bob snapped his fingers and pointed at Peter. Then he returned to *The Office* and muttered, "That's what she said." Peter almost died with delight.

In the kitchen, Edie asked, "What did you do to your father, Peter?"

"Don't worry, Mom. I gave him a pot brownie to ease his tension. It's great for withdrawal from alcohol."

"You gave your father marijuana?" She was in disbelief.

"He'll be like a kitten tonight."

Edie put her hand up to his face. "I know I should be mad, I suppose, but thank you, Peter."

"No problem. Everyone should have one screwed-up kid around the house. We have alternative ways of solving problems." He gave her his charming smile and called Sal's for a pizza.

"So, if I asked for more brownies?"

"No problem, Mom."

Peter decided to hang around and eat with his father. No way he would miss Bob Wise stoned out of his mind. They watched *The Office* and talked about nothing and everything. It was the best night he had ever had with his dad.

At the bar, Peter felt tired, but a good tired. Like he had accomplished something. And this was an unusual feeling. He found himself sneaking peeks at the nurse. He didn't even know her name, and he was disappointed when she ran away from him at the bar. Granted, how many times could he slam into her? She probably thought he was a loser like everyone else did.

The nurse certainly was pretty outside of her scrubs and with her hair down. She had one crooked tooth in her smile that he liked. It made her less perfect. But that guy she was with, he didn't look like any fun. The nurse kept putting her head down and hiding behind her hair. Even Peter could tell she was unhappy. He was relieved to see Ashley, because sitting alone at a bar was only fun for about three minutes. Much longer, and Peter felt creepy eyeing other people and their dinner orders.

"Hey, Farmer Ted!" Ashley kissed him on the cheek.

"I don't have a dumb nickname for you. It feels unfair." Peter smiled. Ashley wasn't so bad to hang out with.

"Life is unfair, my friend," Ashley said. "Oh hey, there's Nina. Did you say hi?"

"Nina who?" Peter asked dumbly.

Ashley stared at him like he was a moron. "Nina Kittrick, from high school? In your class?"

"Where?"

"Seriously, Peter? Do you even know who the president is? Right there." Ashley subtly pointed. "With that toady-looking fellow. The blonde."

"Oh shit!" Peter blurted. "That's Kitty's older sister? She looks completely different." Before Peter could say anything else, Nina and her date were already leaving.

"Is Kitty's sister a nurse?" He wanted to double-check.

"Yeah, and by the looks, a hot one." Ashley swirled her drink. "But I guess she's taken, Farmer Ted. Too late again."

Peter watched the couple leave, and his only real thought was about why Nina didn't say anything to him. She must have recognized him. He hadn't changed all that much since high school. Peter realized she probably didn't want to. Maybe he was the loser Farmer Ted after all. Then he remembered that Nina had called him by his name; weirdly, he felt better.

Chapter 14
Insolent Teenager

Mia wanted to get off the phone, scream, and hit something. But none of that would do any good.

"No, Eric," she tried to tell her ex-husband calmly. "I do not think a big family Thanksgiving is a good idea." Eric had proposed they all get together—Camila, her nieces, Adam, and her.

"But psychologically it would benefit us to move on together. Accept what has happened." Mia thought he was doing it for appearances, not really for the benefit of anyone, only the benefit of their guilt.

"Are you Gwyneth Paltrow now? Did you read a brochure or something? Eric, you and Camila can lead a long, happy life together, but how about this? I choose not to be a part of it. And I will not pretend I want to in front of Adam."

She had barely spoken to her sister in over a year since the break-up and divorce. The idea of watching Camila and Eric play house nauseated her. And the thing was, she wasn't in love with Eric. She didn't even have a broken heart—if anything, now she felt relief—but it was the betrayal and the lies. Mia's ego was bruised and humiliated. How could she not have been smart enough to see the deception? Admittedly, she assumed she was more intelligent than that, more intelligent than them.

Camila had always been her flighty little sister. She was taller and bustier than Mia, but had the same chiseled face and red hair. She was a beautiful woman on the outside. But Camila had no regard for anyone's feelings. She would charge hundreds of dollars to their parents' credit cards for clothes and stupid things and shrug when she was caught. Sincerity wasn't in her vocabulary. Instead of college, Camila went to Bali, wore thongs, and discovered Yoga. In her own words, she was a "free spirit," just as long as someone else footed the tab. She and Eric were perfect together: both of them remora fish on each other's backs.

Mia and her sister never had much in common. Camila was obsessed with her 1200-calorie-a-day diet, and Mia was with her books. Eric was the only thing they ever really shared in their life. But did Mia want to watch them firsthand and up close? Hell no. She had already been thinking they would share the holiday with Kitty and Nina, which would be more fun for her and Adam.

"We have plans," Mia announced.

"With whom?" Eric demanded as if she had offended him.

"Not that it is your business, but the neighbors."

"Not that babysitter? I don't like her. She is an insolent teenager. That's not a good influence for Adam, Mia."

"Oh, get over it. You barged into my house, and a sixteen-year-old called you out. It certainly wasn't her with the bad manners that day." Mia rubbed her eyebrows.

All Eric could say was, "I don't like her."

"I don't care," Mia retorted. "We are busy on Thanksgiving."

"He's my son."

"Not this Thanksgiving." Mia knew the exchange was petty,

but she was done fighting with people for the day.

Tyler Dunning was stirring up trouble about the curriculum again. He was talking to his students about the dangers of particular literature. Mia had her spies. Some students adored her and wanted to be writers, so they tattled avidly on him. Mia also knew the end game. If he talked about it enough, maybe those poor kids would relay the message to the parents and get them riled up.

She hadn't gone to Principal Jenkins yet because, as the new head of the department, she wanted to handle the situation herself. But she was getting nowhere. Unfortunately, she couldn't speak to Tyler as she spoke to Eric. If only she could call him an asshole.

There was a knock on her office door, and Mia thought, *What now?*

"Oh, Kitty!" Mia was pleasantly surprised.

"Hi, Mrs. Golding," Kitty plopped down in the chair without being offered.

"What's up, Kitty? Everything okay?" Mia felt herself getting a little paranoid. What if Kitty didn't want to babysit anymore? Adam truly loved her, and Mia had come to rely on her. "Everything good with Adam?"

"Oh, yeah, sure, little guy and I are fine. But I agree with you. He needs less screen time. I will work on that." Mia was relieved and allowed herself to chuckle at Kitty's t-shirt. It had a poop emoji and said in bubble letters, "That's Life!" It was spot on.

"Thanks, Kitty, I'd appreciate that. It's been a rough couple years for him, and I appreciate you being his friend."

Kitty nodded.

"It's Nina."

"Oh, is she okay?"

"Yes and no. Well, you know about our family. I mean, it's just her and me. But what if I leave? Everyone is always talking about college, and now I got this tennis stuff going on, and what if I have to move out later? I can't leave her alone. I mean, she will watch TV and think about our grandparents for the rest of her life. I think she is too sad."

Mia wanted to reach across her desk and hold Kitty in her arms. What a sweet girl.

"Kitty," Mia began slowly. She knew she had to choose her words carefully. "I know Nina a little bit now, and I know about life. It won't always be this way for her. Nina is so wonderful and special and young. There is more for her—we have to wait and see. But that does not mean you can't leave her side. Nina would never want you to stay behind just to stay with her. Everything she does for you is so that you go out in the world and be the best version of yourself. That is what would make her happy. For all of us parents, we want the people we love to be happy, which is our happiness."

Kitty sat there and scratched her arms, thinking.

"Can I tell you a secret?"

"I'd be honored."

"I don't want to let her down. She's never let me down." Kitty hung her head, and Mia thought about the weight of being a teenager. Thoughts and feelings were so big back then. As if the world was insurmountable. The irony was that the world had so many possibilities for the young.

"No, Kitty. I doubt that you could ever let your sister down."

And with that, Kitty smiled brightly. "Thanks, Mrs. G!"

Kitty got up, but said, "Mrs. G, Mr. Dunning handed out a list of books we should avoid because of," Kitty made air quotes, "their content. So I'm reading all of them one by one."

Mia asked, silently fuming about Tyler's crusade, "Why are you doing that?"

"Because he told us not to. Duh. Never tell a teenager not to do something, because that guarantees we will do it!" Kitty laughed.

"Atta girl, Kitty."

"Back 'atcha, Mrs. G." Kitty left, and Mia felt infinitely better. Kitty just had a way about her.

Mia felt like lying down and sleeping forever, as the kids say. Making decisions was hard, but worrying about what decision to make was even harder. It felt better knowing Kitty worried about something other than what t-shirt slogan she would choose for the day. Everyone had real problems, not just her. She couldn't mire her thoughts in self-pity. Women often did that, unfortunately. So many books and movies were devoted to the sad woman with a pint of ice cream lamenting their lack of happiness. Mia often tried to remind herself that it was about perspective. If life weren't hard, then it would have no soul. Books have soul, she thought, and jotted that down for her next run-in with Tyler Dunning. As limited as his perspective was on life, somewhere, he had to have a soul.

Chapter 15
Bathed in Poison Ivy

Nina got off work early and veered her old 2002 BMW toward Hillsdale Tennis Club without much thought. Kitty should be at her lesson, and Nina needed to face this situation with Peter.

Nina rubbed the steering wheel, which calmed her. The car was her best friend in many ways, and served as an oasis from the world. Pop had gotten it for her when she graduated high school. He had taken Nina to a car auction, and the boxy gray-blue thing spoke to her. Pop had sold his shop long ago to his protege, a young kid named Arnie, who serviced her car and kept it running at no charge. Every time Nina was in it, she thought of Pop's kindness and love for her. He had said, "Lass, you can always sell it if you're in a pinch." But she never would. Like Kitty driving Oma's old minivan, they had to hang on to whatever was left of them.

Nina practiced deep breaths. She tended to get rashes when she was nervous, and didn't want to see Peter looking like she had bathed in poison ivy.

Entering the pro shop first, she exclaimed with surprise, "David Dins!"

"Nina Kittrick!" he shouted back without looking.

"I can't believe we are still in the same neighborhood and never see each other," Nina said politely. Oma had worried about David as a child because he was home-schooled—*Kids need to be around other kids, outside and playing!* Oma invited Dave to their house parties, but Mrs. Dins always declined.

"I can believe it. I am either here or at home. You are a nurse now, and I do not go to hospitals. I hate hospitals."

Nina laughed. Dave had always been frank.

"Well," she said, "let's hope you can avoid them."

"Are you looking for Kitty? She is on court six today."

"Thanks, Dave. Hey, everything good with you?" Nina was stalling by making conversation.

"Is everything good with me? No, my parents are selling my house and the club, and I will be homeless and jobless. But I sold three blue rackets today."

"I'm sorry, Dave. That's too bad. You know where to find me if you need help with anything."

"22 Oakland Drive. Thank you, Nina Kittrick. You have always been nice. And now you are pretty too. I'm glad the acne went away."

Nina laughed, not embarrassed. "Me too, Dave. Me too."

Nina was surprised at how many courts there were inside. Groups of kids of all ages were hitting balls. It felt very professional, and seeing her sister in such a setting was odd. She leaned on the back wall and watched.

There was her old teacher, Coach Clark, shouting at Kitty. "Have you got cotton in your ears? Add top spin to the volley and put it away!" Pacing along the net, he looked like a hefty bag in his black tracksuit.

Peter was opposite Kitty, lobbing her balls. She pounded one after the other, and Nina was impressed. Her awkward little sister looked at home, focused on the ball. And Peter hit it so naturally, smiling and cheering Kitty on. Nina felt like the odd one out of her sister's life and had a twinge of jealousy.

"Nina, watch this!" Kitty aced the ball past Peter, who had turned to look at Nina. Of course Kitty had seen her hiding in the corner. That girl didn't miss a thing.

Kitty ran up to her. "See... Did you see? I'm good, big sis." Kitty had an I-told-you-so smile.

"I did, love." Nina smiled back. Seeing Kitty happy filled her with satisfaction. She wished Oma and Pop could have seen it. But Nina let her eyes wander over to Peter, who had a goofy grin staring at her. He gave her a little wave and went to lob the ball in his hand off the court. But he looked at her when he hit the ball, and it went sideways and smacked Nina on the shoulder.

"Oweee!" she shouted and rubbed her arm.

"Shit!" Peter yelled and ran over to her.

"Peter, you are such a dork," said Kitty, rolling her eyes. "Nina, you okay?"

"Yeah, fine." But somehow, seeing Peter with her sister, remembering Peter with Ashley, getting embarrassingly hit—Nina instantly became annoyed.

"Can I speak to you for a moment?" Nina said sternly to Peter.

"Hey, I'm so sorry. It seems like every time I'm around you..." He held his hands like, *Oops*, and his casualness fueled Nina's frustration.

"So, Nina Kittrick, long time no see. I can't believe you didn't say anything at the hospital..."

Off to the side, so Kitty couldn't hear, "Peter Wise, you haven't changed, have you? Still floating through life in a waft of pot smoke?" Her voice was filled with sarcasm.

"Hey, yeah, about that…" Peter made another sad face.

"Let me stop you. This is a warning. That's my sister and her life you are messing with, and thus, my life. You can't do drugs around her, you can't make her promises you won't keep, you can't lead her down this tennis path and then give up like she's an Ivy League school. This is becoming a dream for Kitty, and if you are the one to give it to her and then take it away? Well, I know how to remove body parts. DO YOU UNDERSTAND?" Nina felt like a mother bear. Peter stood stunned.

"I won't. I mean, I'm in this too…" he stammered.

"Really? Because from where I'm standing, you haven't followed through on much except graduating high school."

Peter started to get offended. "Hey, enough with the jabs at me. You haven't seen me in seven years! Ease up. I'm just as serious as Kitty is about this."

Nina pushed her glasses up on her face, just like Kitty, and let her blue eyes bore into him.

"I mean it, Peter."

"Okay, I hear you." Peter held up his hands and then joked, "I mean, look at old Coach Clark there." Coach Clark was madly taking notes on his clipboard. "This is like Geritol for the old man. We all want this, Nina."

Nina wanted to chuckle at the joke but didn't allow herself. The best she could do was turn and storm out. She didn't really understand why she wanted to be so angry with Peter. Just because he ignored her in high school was a bit extreme. But it was like she couldn't help herself.

"Hey, pissant!" Coach Clark shouted at Peter. "Stop flirting and get back to work!"

Kitty was standing on the court watching her sister rush out and smiling.

"What are you smiling at?" Peter growled.

"Oh, this just got way more interesting. Nina doesn't get mad at just anyone." Kitty snickered.

Nina slammed her car door and sat in the parking lot. Why did he get to her? Peter stupid Wise. As she pulled out of the club's lot, a black Toyota with tinted windows pulled out too. She remembered the vehicle pulling in at the same time as her because Hillsdale wasn't the tinted window kind of place. The car had low wheels and looked like a drug dealer's. Weird. Now it was following her, or so she thought. Unnervingly, the vehicle trailed her almost home but veered away before she turned onto Oakland Drive. Like any modern woman, Nina questioned the nagging sense of being watched. She and Kitty were young and lived alone. After Pop died, Nina had a locksmith come and put extra locks on all the windows and doors. It just made her feel better at night.

A couple years ago, a woman had gone jogging early morning near Hillsdale and was raped. Nina was on the night shift at the hospital and treated her. She stayed with her all the next day because the woman was comfortable with her. Nina remembered her stoicism. The victim looked pale and depleted, but turned to Nina and said, "Bad shit happens in this world. None of us are immune. Even here." The woman meant Hillsdale, which had always felt so secure. Her words sent shivers down Nina's spine, knowing all too well the violence that a man could cause. And dammit, she would do everything she could to protect Kitty and herself. Good thing Pop had left a gun for her hidden in his closet.

Chapter 16
Eggplant

Adam didn't feel well. His side hurt all day at school, and he felt cold and feverish. But didn't want to tell the teacher. He didn't like attention being drawn to himself at school. The other kids had already teased him for being small, and he didn't want to appear weak either.

It took everything out of him to walk home the few blocks from Hillsdale Elementary. When he reached the house, he texted his mom that he was home because he did every day. She sent a heart emoji back. But he didn't call Mia because she had been complaining about the meetings after school that day, and he didn't want to bother her. Today Kitty had tennis and wasn't coming over. He was on his own.

But Adam was getting more feverish by the second, and the pain doubled. Suddenly, he had to throw up and ran to the bathroom. He started to cry. Adam was scared but thought if he just waited on the bathroom floor, his mom would come home soon.

But the pain got worse.

He texted his mom again: "When will you be home?" But no response. She had turned off her phone for the meeting. She had told him she did this as an example to the other teachers to do the same. If anything was wrong, he should call his dad.

Adam never told his parents that he knew about his father and Camila. He was only seven; back then, his weekends were filled with soccer practice and playdates. His mom accepted any invitation from another parent, whether to go to a movie or get ice cream. She always stressed the importance of friends to him. She explained that she spent too much time alone as a child and wanted Adam to be different. One Saturday, his buddy Tim's parents took them out for pizza after their morning soccer match. His mom was at his game but went back home to grade papers. His father didn't make it because he wanted to take a morning yoga class. Adam was happily gnawing on his pizza when he saw his aunt Camila and Eric emerging from the yoga studio. He waved through the window, but they didn't see him. Instead, he saw his father walk Camila to her car, then lean down and give her a quick kiss on the lips.

It wasn't right to Adam. That was how his father said goodbye to his mother, not his aunt.

The image bothered Adam, but he said nothing. Instead, he started paying closer attention to his father. He started a little notebook charting how many times his father went to this yoga class. Four times a week seemed an awful lot, since soccer only had one practice and one game a week. Adam checked his father's phone. It was the first password he stole from his father. 1234 was the code to his iPhone. Not very clever, Adam thought.

Then, when his dad was occupied in the shower or watching TV, Adam scrolled through his texts and phone calls. Why was he texting Camila daily? The texts had strange emojis that Adam didn't understand. Did Camila want to eat eggplant all the time?

It wasn't all his father's fault that they didn't have a good relationship. Once Adam guessed his father's secret, he withdrew from him. He declined whenever his dad asked if he wanted to go to the movies or play a game. He felt bad for his mom and unknowingly chose sides. His dad was a liar, lying to both of them. Then one day, Adam used his father's phone to text his mother to meet him at home before Adam got home from school. He knew Camila would be there because he had read a text from her that morning.

Adam had lingered returning from school, not knowing if his plan had worked.

"Mom, Dad," he said, slowly entering the house that day. He didn't know if there would be screaming or grown-ups fighting each other. He found his mother sitting in the kitchen, wiping away tears. Adam immediately felt guilty.

Without telling Adam about the affair, his mother just stated that his father had moved out and, most likely, they would get a divorce. Adam said nothing but offered that they should have ice cream for dinner and skip school the next day. He was no dummy, and his mother quickly agreed to both. But his lack of emotion was testimony to his first instincts. He had known all along where his family was headed.

And now he was ten and alone on a bathroom floor, wondering what was wrong with him and what to do.

He didn't want to, but he called his dad. Eric didn't answer either.

Adam felt worse and started to really cry. *Kitty*, he thought. *I need Kitty.*

He texted her, "Kitty, I don't feel." And that was it. Adam passed out from the pain without finishing the text.

When he woke up later, he was in the back seat of a car. It

smelled like cigarette smoke and was going fast. The seat belt was weirdly wrapped around him, and he could hear cars honking outside. He saw a stop sign, but the car didn't stop. He moaned.

"Adam!" He heard Kitty's voice from the driver's seat. "Hold on, little man, we will be at the hospital in two minutes." Then the car swerved around the corner at top speed, and Adam barely stayed on the seat.

He closed his eyes and groaned again.

The car screeched when it stopped, and Kitty shouted, "He's in the back seat!" Adam kept his eyes closed as large hands enveloped him and laid him on a gurney.

He heard Nina. "Find Mia, Kitty!"

Nina held his hand and said calmly, "Adam, you will be fine. We got you. Nothing is going to happen to you. I'll be with you the whole time." Then Adam felt a stab of pain and was out again.

Chapter 17
Karma

Mia was mid-sentence when Kitty burst through the library doors. Everyone looked up, but when Mia saw the fear on Kitty's face, her heart stopped.

Kitty shouted, "It's Adam. He's at the hospital."

Mia didn't miss a beat and grabbed her bag. Kitty was steps ahead of her. Mia followed to the running minivan by the front door, and they both jumped in.

"What happened?" Mia cried. Her mind raced to Adam getting hit by a car or cutting his hand at home. Kitty already had her foot on the gas pedal and turned corners like Max Verstappen. Mia didn't scold her.

"Nina has him. He texted me a weird text, and I knew something wasn't right. So I went to your house and found him in the bathroom. He has a bad fever. That's all I know. I got him to the hospital and came to get you." Mia grabbed her phone, saw Adam's missed calls, and panicked. Guilt flooded her like a coldness.

Kitty ran a red light, and a series of horns honked. The minivan ran well at high speeds.

Mia texted Eric's number and tried to calm herself. "Eric, Adam is at the hospital. I'm not sure what's wrong. Get there as soon as you can."

Kitty made it to the hospital in record time. Mia ran to reception and started shouting Adam's name at the receptionist. *Terms of Endearment* much? Luckily, Nina came out the double doors. "Whoa, it's okay, Mia. I got him." Nina nodded at the receptionist and led Mia and Kitty through the doors.

"Mia, we think it's his appendix. We will know after one more test. Adam is sedated and fine, but we will need to operate." Mia took some deep breaths. The appendix wasn't so bad, right?

A doctor came around the corner. "Mrs. Golding?" Mia could only nod.

The doctor was very tall and leaned down to talk to her. He put a warm hand on her shoulder, and she could feel herself relax. "Nina has told me all about Adam, and we are going to make him better as fast as possible. Take a deep breath, okay?" Mia found herself responding to his voice and friendly smile with clean white teeth. He had a faint smell of aftershave and gray hairs around his temples.

"Mia, this is Dr. Mayfield, and he has done this operation many times. He's the best, I promise." Mia looked between them and let tears come to her eyes.

"Adam… He's everything to me," she whimpered.

"And then he's everything to me." Dr. Mayfield squeezed her shoulder again and walked away.

"I'll be out when it's over," Nina assured. "Kitty, you'll stay with Mia?"

"Duh," Kitty said.

There was a particular room they could wait in with a TV blaring CNN and a vending machine. Kitty badgered the receptionist for the remote and found reruns of *The Golden Girls*. She emptied Mia's wallet of change and purchased a haul of M & M's, potato chips, and soda.

"Gotta have sweet and salty," she explained to Mia, popping the candy and potato chips simultaneously in her mouth.

Mia had calmed down but was on edge. The guilt she felt for turning off her phone was overwhelming. As a single mom, she felt like the only one truly there for Adam. And she had to be 24/7. It was a crushing feeling, the idea that she could turn off her phone for only an hour, and Adam was lying alone on a bathroom floor, in pain and needing her. Mia reached out her hand and placed it on Kitty's arm for reassurance.

"I can't thank you enough for being there for him, for us." Tears came to Mia's eyes. "You and your sister are...just so great. I'm lucky. How did you know to get him?"

"Mrs. G, no biggie. The clue was that Adam always finishes a text. Such a teacher's son, texts in complete sentences, including punctuation." Kitty put a bag of Skittles in Mia's hand and patted it a little. Mia marveled how this teenage girl could have such an old soul.

The waiting room door burst open, and Eric stood there like he just walked out of a Yurt. He was wearing spandex leggings and a tank top. Mia couldn't believe he was wearing Birkenstocks. Then Camila strode in like a model for Lululemon yoga wear. Kitty turned away from the TV, knowing this would be far more interesting.

Mia took a deep breath and explained the situation.

"Wait." Eric stood there in a pompous stance, his arms crossed and legs planted in Jesus's shoes. "You turned off your phone? That's not very responsible, Mia. He's only ten, and you leave him alone so you can work? And then you have to be saved by…" Eric nodded in Kitty's direction, "this girl? I mean, can I trust you to watch him?"

Mia stood flabbergasted at the tone of Eric's voice.

"Are you serious right now?" Mia's hands flew to her hips, and her face contorted with anger. "You are somehow finding a way to blame me? For going to work? TO TAKE CARE OF OUR CHILD WHILE YOU DO…" Mia's hands flew up and she screamed, "YOGA?"

"Gaslighting," Kitty offered nonchalantly while digging around a bag of Doritos.

Mia and Eric looked at her. Kitty continued, "You know, gaslighting. Mrs. Wills said it's psychological manipulation to make someone doubt themselves so the person can blame them. It's really messed up."

Mia looked at Kitty and then at Eric. "Thank you, Kitty. It's amazing how this girl is ten times smarter than you, Eric. You haven't been there for Adam in years. Did you get a missed call that you ignored? Or did Adam not call you because he knew you wouldn't answer?" Mia was screaming. But before Eric could respond, Nina and Dr. Mayfield walked through the door.

"Mhm, mmm," Dr. Mayfield cleared his throat. "Hope we are not interrupting?" Mia's face flushed with embarrassment, and Eric switched gears.

"How is he, Doc? How is my boy?" Mia scoffed at Eric.

"Fine. Excellent. Down an appendix, but stable and good to go in a couple days." Nina eyed Eric and Camila and looked at Mia with sympathy.

"Was it his diet, Doctor? I mostly keep only vegan and gluten-free foods in our home. I have told my sister for years that supplements are the key to a healthy body," Camila said, giving Mia a side-eye and looking conspiratorially at the doctor.

Mia barked, "Oh, give a rest, Camila. Being on a diet doesn't make you a medical professional. It just makes you shallow."

"Mia, you can be a real bitch," Camila barked back. "Maybe if you spent less time on your career and focused on mental wellness like Eric, he might still be with you."

"Camila, you think you won some prize? A cheating narcissist whose ego is larger than his IQ?" Mia shouted at her sister.

"Hey, you can't talk to her like that!" Eric's face was getting red.

"Why, Eric? Because she's my sister or because she is your fuc —"

"OKAY! Mrs. Golding, come with me..." Dr. Mayfield grabbed Mia's elbow and gently led her from the room.

Mia kicked the hospital wall outside and yelled, "That son of a bitch."

Dr. Mayfield said, "Divorce is fun, isn't it?" He smiled without mocking her.

"I'm so sorry, Doctor, I just... I..."

"Matthew. Please, call me Matthew. Nina filled me in a little about the situation. I'm divorced too, and I have kids. It's not easy."

"He left me for my sister, but that's not the worst part. He left Adam and barely is around for him."

"My wife left me for our neighbor," he offered. "So not only did I have to move, but my kids now have two mommies."

Mia stared, and Matthew nodded. "My neighbor was a former beauty pageant queen, internet 'influencer,' whatever the hell that means, and a woman. So I wasn't pretty, cool, or woman enough for my wife." He smiled, and Mia couldn't help but laugh.

"Really?"

"Really."

"Well, aren't we a pair."

Eric and Camila waited until Adam woke, but only spent a

few minutes reassuring him everything would be fine. Mia managed to hold her tongue when they said goodbye. Unlike them, she wasn't going anywhere. Nina made sure they had a single room so she could spend the night with Adam.

Mia didn't sleep, of course, but just stared at her son. His innocence was what she wanted to protect the most. She didn't want his father to break his heart. She didn't want him to feel less important in the world or let down by adults, having seen too many kids with chips on their shoulders before they even graduated high school. Mia wanted Adam to feel loved and worshipped because that's what every child deserved. But she would have to do the heavy lifting for Eric. Mia knew deep in her heart that Eric loved his son, but his ability to prove it was lacking. Yelling at him didn't help. She would have to find another way to get Eric to step up to the plate. But how?

"Mom," Adam groaned from the bed.

"I'm here, honey." She rested her hand on his cheek.

"Mom, karma got me." Adam's little face scrunched up.

"What in the world? What do you mean?"

"Karma. You know when bad things happen because you did a bad thing."

Mia was confused.

"No, your appendix had nothing to do with karma. Who told you such a thing?"

Then Adam confessed what he had done to Eric and Camila. Mia sat and listened patiently as he told her about the credit card charges and the self-help books for his nieces. Afterward, Mia, not knowing how to navigate the situation, just said they would talk about it in the morning and that she was glad he had told her. On the one hand, no, he shouldn't have stolen from his father, but on the other, he was hurt and acting out. Mia understood totally. After his confession, he fell asleep, and Mia slipped out of the room.

Outside the door, she started laughing. Laughing so hard, tears began to flow, and she clutched her side.

"Mrs. Golding, are you okay?" Dr. Mayfield rushed to her but saw she was laughing.

"Doctor. Matthew. Call me Mia. Yes, I'm fine, and my son is normal and brilliant." Mathew looked confused.

Mia exclaimed, "Karma is a wonderful thing!" Mathew asked if she wanted some coffee, and she explained what Adam had done to his father. They both laughed. Maybe it was wrong, but it felt good. They decided that Adam would have to confess to his dad as punishment, but Mia saw it as the opportunity she needed to show Eric that he needed to do better because there was karma, after all.

Chapter 18
Beanie Babies

Dave rolled over in bed and stared at Ken. Dave didn't often stare at people because he didn't want them to look back at him. But Ken didn't. Instead, Ken's eyes darted back and forth, reading the laptop resting on his protruding naked belly.

They had gotten into a rhythm and met Thursday nights at the hotel. Not that they actively planned it. It just happened. Both of them enjoyed structure and schedules, and Thursday worked for them. They rarely talked about their personal lives, but David had a lot weighing on him and wanted Ken's financial opinion.

"If I wanted to buy a business, how would I do that?"

"You need a plan. You need numbers. How much does it cost, loan requirements, and down payment. Then factor in monthly expenses, insurance, and profit margins. Will you need advertising?" Ken started listing information, and Dave whined.

"That's a lot."

"Yep. Why? What do you want to buy?"

"My parents are selling their business, and I might lose my job. It's a dumb job, but I like it. I don't like change."

"Wouldn't it be easier to get a new job?"

"Would it be easier to get a new job? Yes. But I don't want a new job. Everyone knows me at my job, and I work with my best friend. And he might lose his job if they sell the business. So that would make two of us not doing what we want."

"How noble," Ken tittered.

"And I want to buy their house."

"Your parents' house?" Ken asked, his interest peaked.

"Yes, my parents' house. I live there and have never lived anywhere else, so I don't want to change that too."

"You live with your parents?" Ken asked. Dave detected judgment.

"Yes, why not live with my parents? It's free, and they do everything for me. Why wouldn't someone like that? It's very economical."

"Well, most people want independence and freedom. I'd murder myself if I still lived with my parents."

"Why murder yourself? Wouldn't it be more beneficial to murder them?" Dave pondered.

"You know, you can be strange sometimes," Ken said, undisturbed.

"Yes, I can be. But I want to buy the house I live in and the business I work for. How do I do that?"

Ken opened a new tab and wrote a detailed list for Dave.

"These are the numbers you will need." Ken was pounding on the computer. The list looked long to Dave. Honestly, he didn't even know how much Hillsdale Club was worth, or the house. He knew how much he had, but he would need a lot more.

"Maybe this is a dumb idea," Dave said out loud.

"Beanie Babies were a dumb idea," Ken offered. "Stupid

cheap stuffed animals that people bought for thousands of dollars on the internet. They made Ty. Inc hundreds of millions and, in truth, are worthless. They are an example of a dumb idea executed by a good business plan. The idea is never dumb, but people can be. You're smart, Dave." Ken's voice betrayed him. Dave could tell Ken liked him, and it made him smile.

"So do you think if I had a business plan, there's a chance?"

"Beanie Babies, Dave. Beanie Babies." And Ken went back to his list.

The next day at work, Dave had a lot to think about. So he smoked a joint and reorganized the storage room. He started calculating the costs of things: inventory, lessons, client payments. His father assumed Dave never went into his files on his computer, but he could if he wanted. So Dave did, and started following Ken's list, researching the monthly bills: electricity, insurance, and payroll. Dave meticulously wrote down every number and calculated profit, overhead, etc. It thrilled him a little, because knowing he could share this information with Ken, it would give them more to talk about. While Dave appreciated Ken's reservedness and lack of sentimentality, he still wanted to get closer to him. He didn't know why, but he felt a bond with Ken. It was an attraction that he wanted more of. Was this what love was? Dave didn't have a clue. He just knew he liked his life better with Ken than without Ken, and it scared him like losing his childhood bedroom.

"Peter, have you ever been in love?" Dave said while sorting the apparel section of the store. Naturally, he color-coded it. Men's and women's clothing was separated by white, black, and pastels.

"Can't say I have. Is that weird?" Peter responded. He was bouncing a tennis ball nervously, and it annoyed Dave. Peter had strangely been abstaining from drugs at work recently.

"Is that weird? You are asking me, is that weird? Think about whom you are asking."

Peter laughed.

"Well, I guess that makes two of us." *Bounce, bounce, bounce.*

"Stop that."

"I can't help it. I keep thinking about Kitty's tournament."

"Why? Is it important?" Dave asked. He knew it was, but he liked to trick Peter.

Peter rolled his eyes. "If Kitty can win, then we can work toward the junior circuit, you know? Then I won't be teaching bored retirees. Maybe we can attract other tennis wannabe stars. It would be good for the club's reputation."

Dave perked up. "Reputation?"

"Yeah, the better club we are, the better clientele, and we will be important...like one of those places where we make tennis stars." Peter waved his hands up in the air for effect.

"Better clientele would mean more money, right?" Dave's brain was lighting up.

"Yeah, Dave. That's how it works."

"Then Kitty has to win, Peter. She has to win."

"Okay, no pressure or anything."

"No, that's a lot of pressure, Peter. Beanie Babies, Peter, Beanie Babies!" Dave danced on his toes and pointed at Peter.

"What the hell?" Peter said, confused, and left the shop.

"Where were you last night? I made dinner. Did you even consider that? No, David, you don't consider us anymore. You do what you want when you want. It must be nice to have such freedom." Mrs. Dins barraged Dave with questions the moment he got home from work.

Dave didn't look at her but looked around the house and began to inspect it.

"What are you doing, David?" His mother watched him.

"Shopping."

"You make no sense, David. Now sit down. Your father and I have something to tell you."

David noticed the boxes. They were moving boxes.

"What is going on?" he asked, concerned.

"David, don't get all emotional," Mr. Dins chided. "We are heading to Florida a bit earlier. Decided no time like the present."

"Okay…" David said skeptically.

"Now, just calm down."

David was confused. He was calm.

"We figure no time like the present! Have to make haste and stop wasting time. I mean, why wait, right? Go for the sun!"

"What your father is trying to say is that we found a house already! I know it's sudden, but we found it on the internet, and it's perfect. It's in a gated community called Flagler Village. Isn't that adorable? It has ten tennis courts, three swimming pools, and a golf course. Also, a clubhouse and gym! I can do Zumba with other ladies. What more could we want? But the realtor was adamant that we had to act now. The units are just selling themselves, and we don't want to miss the opportunity."

Mr. Dins nodded along. "We just can't be those people who missed a great deal, that's what the realtor said, and he should know."

"He called us 'snowbirds,' isn't that darling? Because we come from the snow!" Mrs. Dins' eyes were alight.

"What are you talking about? Don't birds migrate south for the winter and then go back north?" Dave asked.

Mrs. Dins wouldn't look at him, but said, "Pish, posh, David. We are going to list the house and the business a bit earlier than we planned. Your father, well, he is so excited to move to Boca Raton."

"The rat mouth place?"

His parents looked confused but moved on.

"So we will list the house and the business for sale sooner than we thought," his mother repeated.

"You told me this spring," David retorted.

"Potato, patatoe," his father responded.

David's pulse raced. He thought he had months; now he had weeks, maybe even days. He didn't have a business plan yet. He did not have all the information for Ken. His breathing started getting harder.

"Oh dear, now, David, it's going to be all right," his mother said with just an inkling of sympathy. "You are never home anyway. You won't miss us." Right! He wouldn't miss them, but he would miss his room and the fresh orange juice in the fridge.

"How much?" Dave shouted at his parents without looking at them.

"How much time? Well, I don't know, it could take a while to sell…"

"No," said David sternly. "How much money for everything?"

And his parents told him.

Dave marched upstairs and turned on his computer. He sat there for the next eight hours playing online poker. Dave only got up to pee and didn't answer the door when his mother knocked. All he could hear were numbers in his head. The zeros sounded like a drumbeat. He needed one million dollars to keep his life the way he wanted. One, *boom*, zero, *boom*, zero, *boom*, zero, *boom*, zero, *boom*, zero, *boom*, zero, *boom*.

That night, Dave also needed a straight flush, blackjack, and the Canadian curling team to win in Lake Placid.

Chapter 19
Raw Tendons

Nina was at the kitchen window facing the street when she saw the car again. She was exhausted from the hospital and worried for Mia and Adam. Not that she needed to be, but she had grown so fond of them that it was hard not to feel for her friend. It was unusual for her, because she was so good at compartmentalizing her feelings.

She learned it as a child. Nina created boxes in her mind. One would have been labeled "parents," another "Oma and Pop," and another "dorky teenager." It's what made Nina an excellent nurse. Once on duty, she wholly forgot herself and any of her problems. When a patient came through the trauma doors, she had a list of procedures she could start: administering an IV, checking their pulse, speaking to them, finding out their name, using the name repeatedly to comfort them, stopping the blood from flowing out of various body parts, etc. Trauma was a step-by-step procedure; it all felt natural to her. Why? Because she compartmentalized. It was formulaic to her, and by the time a doctor arrived, she had basic answers to their questions. Nina was excellent at being prepared.

Blood did not scare her like some people. Raw tendons and bones poking through the skin were natural. Once a man came in with a knife sticking straight up from his scalp. He had ducked when his wife threw it at him. The steel blade jutted from his head like an antenna, but he was fully cognizant. Nina didn't flinch. She compartmentalized.

It wasn't until the patient was stitched and bandaged or off to surgery that Nina would retreat to the bathroom and inspect the damage done to her scrubs. Blood squirts were akin to paint splatters. Often she found it in her hair, her ears, or decorating her arms in intricate patterns that she scrubbed away. Every six months, she threw out her black sneakers (always black, never white) because she knew the blood residue was there even though she couldn't see it. Saving people wasn't a pretty business, but Nina reveled in it. Oma was in her head, proud of Nina's attention to cleanliness. It was in those moments when she left the ER, when she was alone, that she found herself again. "From soldier to human," her old nursing school teacher had said.

Needless to say, she didn't like being unprepared. In her personal life, Nina hated surprises. Surprise parties and surprise gifts unnerved her. Order and knowledge helped her feel centered. Learning Peter was Kitty's tennis coach surprised her, and she did not react well. *Why had I been so angry at him?* she asked herself a million times after she left the club.

And now this, the black Toyota with tinted windows on her street, slowly driving by her house. Nina knew it was the same car she had seen the other day. She told herself it was nothing, but the car didn't fit in with their suburb of minivans and sensible SUVs. Nina met all sorts of people at the hospital and knew no neighborhood was genuinely safe in Hillsdale, as much as people wanted to believe it was.

Then there was a knock at the door, and Nina jumped. Mia was at the hospital and was bringing Adam home later. The knock came again. Someone for Kitty? Her sister was upstairs napping after having spent almost two days playing with Adam at the hospital. Nina admired how devoted Kitty could be to people. She got that from their grandparents.

Nina had had the night shift and the day off, so she was in her favorite sweatpants and a Hillsdale Prep t-shirt. She opened the door and was surprised. She hated surprises.

"Nina, you're here," Peter said, leaning casually against the door.

"Yes, well, I live here." Her heart fluttered, and she could feel a rash blossom by her neck.

"Of course. Sorry to bother you, but Kitty missed two practices and didn't answer my texts."

Nina nodded.

"We had an emergency with our neighbor, and Kitty was helping out," she said, realizing she looked destitute, and closed the door slightly, embarrassed.

"So she's okay? Do you mind if I come in and talk about the tournament?" Peter was too relaxed for Nina.

"What about it?" Nina did not want Peter Wise in her house.

"Well, it's in a couple weeks, and there are things to go over."

"Kitty is asleep. I'm sure you can handle it later. Now's not a good time."

"But…" Peter stammered, and Nina closed the door in his face. Why did she do that? She could handle a gunshot victim, but couldn't manage Peter Wise at her door? What was wrong with her?

She waited and could hear him stand there for an achingly

long minute. Nina went to the kitchen window and watched him grab his bike from a tree, thus why she hadn't seen him approach. *Good job, Nina,* she thought, *you handled that supremely well.*

"Who was that?" Kitty came clomping down the stairs. She was wearing fuzzy UGG slippers that were loud on the old staircase.

"Oh, I thought you were asleep. It was your coach, Peter."

"Oh, was it now?" Kitty pushed her glasses up her face and crossed her arms. "Why didn't you let him in?"

"You were asleep." Nina stared at her sister.

"You'd let in a squirrel if you thought it would talk to you." Kitty tilted her head.

"What? What do I need to talk to your coach about?" Nina shrugged nonchalantly.

"Mmm, mmm," Kitty grunted.

"WHAT, Kitty?" Nina said with too much emphasis.

"Ohh, nothing. It'll come to you."

"What? What will come to me?" Nina practically shouted. She deflected. "Tennis is your thing, not mine."

"We will see about that," Kitty said and tromped back up the stairs.

Chapter 20

Bare Assets

What does Nina Kittrick have against me? Peter thought as he biked away from her house. He wasn't used to girls, especially pretty ones, being so put off by him. He tried to think back to high school. Did he do something horrible to her, like make fun of her? He'd have to bounce that idea off Ashley. She was good at deciphering things. He enjoyed having a girl as a friend—Ashley counter-balanced Dave's quirkiness. The only people he saw lately were Kitty, Dave, and Coach Clark, who became more animated daily. He was taking this tournament thing even more seriously than Peter.

His phone rang. Looking at the caller ID, he answered.

"Bare Assets Strip Club. Hold for Peter."

"Very funny, asshat." It was Charlie. "Get over here."

"Annnnd where would you be?" Peter said slowly.

"Home with Mom and Dad. "

"And why should I get over there?"

"There's something wrong," Charlie said, irritated. "I don't know what is happening."

"Is it an emergency?" But Charlie had hung up, and Peter had no choice but to head to his parents' house.

"Mom? Charlie? Dad?" Peter shouted as he walked into the house. Nothing was broken or turned over, and there wasn't an ambulance in the driveway. These were all positive signs. Peter did hear music and found all three of them in the back yard.

The sun was setting, and it was crisp out. The stars were beginning to shine, and his parents were bundled up and standing around a fire. Why was there a fire in the back yard?

"Hey, guys, what's up?" Peter saw his dad loading firewood into... Was that a fire pit? He didn't know his parents had a fire pit. Edie was in her fur coat and had a stick in her hand. At the very tip of the stick was a marshmallow. His father, wearing an old ski jacket circa 1972 with rainbow stripes, stood beside her. Charlie was next to them, poking his phone and texting someone.

"There you are!" Charlie shouted at him with disapproval.

"There you are!" his father said jovially.

"Hi, honey! Want a s'more?" his mother shouted brightly.

"What did you do to them?" Charlie interrogated Peter.

"Umm, don't know, Chuck. They seem fine to me. Hey, Mom, Dad, having a party?"

Charlie glared at him. "Really? Does this look normal to you?"

Peter watched his parents. They were happy and giggling. They were feeding each other. Bob smashed some burnt marshmallows into her mouth, and she smeared chocolate on his lips. No, this was not normal. Peter had to agree with Charlie.

"They are high as kites, Peter. Dad can't be doing drugs with his heart condition."

Peter began to laugh. His parents looked so happy.

"It seems pretty medicinal to me," Peter offered.

"Yeah, Charlie. Medicinal," Bob echoed. "Thank you, son. That's just the right word. I have been searching for that." His father searched the ground as if the word might be lying in the grass.

Edie giggled. "Oh, don't be such a drip, Charlie. They sell the stuff next to Costco. Everyone's doing it." She turned to his father. "Bob, this s'more thing is heaven. I haven't had a graham cracker in years." She went back to eating. "Oh, sorry, boys, do you want one?"

"Dad, where did you get the pit?" Peter asked.

"COSTCO! And sweatpants, did you know they sell them for less than ten dollars? Look at my new pair!" His father stuck out his leg and twisted it back and forth.

"That's great, Dad." Peter smiled at Charlie. "Happy you have discovered buying in bulk."

"Bulky buying!" Bob shouted with a goofy grin.

"Peter, do you see this?!" Charlie yelled at him. "I've called the doctor. He should call me back shortly. Did you do this to them? Did you hook our parents on weed?"

"Ummm." Peter shrugged. "Maybe..."

"Oh, Charles, it's fine. We're fine," Edie giggled. "I haven't felt this good in years. And look, no wine! Your father and I are both off the sauce and feel fantastic. Don't we, honey?" His mother looked great. There was a rosiness in her cheeks, and her hair was down.

"Yes, indeed," Bob said, equally relaxed.

Charlie's phone rang, and after a few "Yeses" and "Nos," he hung up.

"The doctor?" Peter asked.

"Yes," Charlie said stonily. "He said they are fine."

"Charles, dear, you need to relax. I bought gummy

marijuana. Maybe you should have one? You seem a little wound up." His mother snickered.

"Yeah, Chuck, maybe you should go have one?" Peter smiled smugly. He liked this new family.

"Bite me," Charlie said and stormed off.

Peter stayed a while, but he was tired and wanted to get home. It was strange to call his tiny apartment home, but it was for now. Kitty had recommended he reread *Of Mice and Men*, which was a wholly different read as an adult. Peter didn't know if she was correlating him and Dave with the main characters, George and Lennie. Not that they had much in common. Let's face it, Peter and Dave were two upper-middle-class dudes with all the privileges in the world, not migrants in the Great Depression. But he did grasp the idea of searching for a better life, and that humans are all pretty lonely. Loneliness is the catalyst for most decisions people make, and the same rings true in the modern world. Steinbeck was on point.

Peter would never admit that loneliness sometimes overwhelmed him. Who was he to complain? He had a decent life, a family, and a little money in his pocket. But as the years passed, staying home alone with an old movie and pizza, and drinking beer until he passed out was no longer as satisfying. He would have felt lonely in high school, but there was always too much to think about: grades, college, sports. Back then, he wanted to escape everyone who expected so much from him, especially his father. When you are young, you are constantly surrounded by people, but you want to be alone. And now he was, in a way he hadn't expected. And he was lonely.

Peter had never shared his life with anyone except his family. He and Charlie weren't the closest brothers. Charlie was just Charlie, and not much had changed over the years except that he was more severe and anxious than ever. Even though he could be overzealous, Peter still liked his brother. Peter appreciated how much he worried for their parents. He was there for them. And Peter knew his mother called Charlie first when they were in trouble because he was the responsible one. What was Peter? The entertainer? He couldn't help that he wasn't obsessive or a go-getter. Like he told his dad, Peter wanted to see how his life would unfold. But by waiting, would he miss it? Would it fly right past him? Would he wake up in a garage apartment twenty years from now?

Peter hated getting broody like this. Usually, when deep life thoughts struck him, he smoked some weed and let it go. But lately, he hadn't wanted to do that. He wanted to get a good night's sleep and be prepared for Kitty and the club. He actively wanted to be a more responsible adult. What was happening? Peter thought about all this biking home through the quiet streets of Hillsdale. At least he had this town and wasn't unhappy here; with himself, maybe, but not here.

Back at the Clarks', Peter opened his apartment door and screamed.

Lois Clark screamed back. "Peter, goodness, you scream like a girl!"

"Mrs. Clark?" Why was she in his apartment?

"I made too much lasagna tonight and wanted to leave you some in the fridge. Hope you don't mind."

"That's really nice of you." Peter smiled. He loved lasagna.

"And it's a thank you. Stevie has been so happy these past few weeks coaching again. That Kitty must be something. And well, you made him happy, including him in this venture."

"Well, he is a great coach, and I admit, I like having the help. This level is all sort of new to me."

"When I met Stevie, he wanted to be a tennis star, not a high school teacher. He was magnificent back then. He was small and sturdy but so handsome on the court. All the girls had a crush on him, but he picked me." Lois smiled with a faraway look. The kind that went through time and saw the past. "But then he tore his shoulder. Stevie tried to keep playing but only did more damage to it. And that was that. Back then, people were more practical and gave up on dreams faster. Teaching was a steady option. Not that he didn't love it, but I know he missed putting those trophies on his mantel."

"Well, maybe we can get him another one."

"I do hope so, but, Peter, I have something serious to tell you. Stevie would kill me for telling you, so it's our secret." She paused, so Peter nodded yes. He would keep her secret. "He's got a touch of cancer."

Peter's heart fell. Lois quickly said, "It's not serious, not yet. It's his prostate, which is fairly common with men his age. But for old folks like us, the mere mention of the big C is terrifying. We have good doctors and are going to start treatment soon. Stevie has it all worked out to do everything in the morning and be on the court in the afternoon. He doesn't want to let you down."

"Mrs. Clark, if it's too much for him... I don't want his health compromised." Peter didn't want to cause them any harm.

"No, no. I think, mentally, coaching is good for him. We can't sit around thinking about dying all day. But if he seems tired, can you ensure he doesn't overdo it?"

"This is Coach Clark we're talking about. Have you seen the clipboard?"

Mrs. Clark chuckled.

"Peter, don't worry. Coach Clark is like an old battleship. It will take a lot more to sink him."

"I hope so, Mrs. Clark. I kind of like the old guy."

"I do too. Now eat up before it gets cold."

"Thanks, Mrs. Clark." Before she left, she eyed his dirty

laundry basket and picked it up. He didn't know what to say when she marched out the door with his smelly clothes.

Peter sat down on his couch and felt overwhelmed. His dad's heart, and now Coach Clark's cancer? He grabbed his phone and thought about calling someone, but who? He could only think of Dave, but Dave had been so preoccupied with work that he didn't want to talk about work. And now he thought Dave had an actual boyfriend, which was good for him, but that made him feel more alone. Ashley? But it was the weekend, and she might be with Ravi at a club doing fun drugs without a care in the world. He thought about Kitty and Nina and what they do on a Saturday night. Nina probably was with that doctor guy, and Kitty had her good old Cheech/Jerry boyfriend, who was now showing up after practices with cold Gatorade for his "pussycat." Man, he *was* Farmer Ted.

Chapter 21
Not Pleasant

If Bunny Ryan hadn't said yes to lunch at Spaggio's with Cami Tinsdale, things could have gone differently that day. They had played two sets at the club, and Bunny had lost to Cami 6-4, 6-3. It wasn't her day. Her backhand volley was shit, and she double-faulted on her serve several times. She had run out of Ambien and hadn't slept the previous night. She was on edge and didn't want to play, but Bunny was never one to cancel. That would have been impolite.

Bunny said yes not because Cami was great company or even sympathetic to Bunny's horrible menopause symptoms, but because Spaggio's meant white wine with lunch. Bunny had long ago promised her husband Rick that she would never be the kind of wife or mother who drank alone at home. Because that was what Rick's mother had done to get through the monotonous days of his childhood. Rick's mother was overbearing and rude, and no one was safe when she fueled herself with alcohol. Not even her children.

So Bunny, for 23 years of marriage, had checked her drinking habit along with her steady diet of salads and exercise. The result was that she was still pretty and thin at 52. She got her nails done weekly, and her hair was highlighted every six weeks. She was a model wife and mother, some would say. The waiter at Spaggio's might differ when he watched her teeter from those lunches and lurch her Mercedes coupe out of the parking lot at two in the afternoon.

If Cami drank at lunch, it would have also been rude not to join her. And today, of all days, Bunny wanted a pinot grigio. Her hormones were raging, and she felt like putting her tennis racket through the net once or twice. She envied how John McEnroe and Serena Williams could vent their frustrations on the court. Smashed rackets and waving a fist shouting at an opponent would feel pretty good right about now. Bunny hadn't slept in weeks, waking with night sweats or insomnia. She had taken to roaming the house, plotting ways to murder Rick because he warned that hormone replacement therapy would be too dangerous. Rick was an orthopedist and thought all areas of the medical profession were his expertise.

She had quietly asked her ob-gyn for some Ambien after confessing to taking Advil PM too often. Menopause lasted for years; at this point, it had felt like an eternity. Rick was unaware of her prescription as he touted vitamins and exercise as a cure for something he would never have. Bunny had already found his stash of Cialis and knew he was a hypocrite. Imagine if women doctors stopped prescribing for erectile dysfunction and just said have some black tree root from Hungary, and you'll be riding a mare like a stallion. HA! But no, women's bodies are "complicated," the internet said, and there wasn't enough research on HRT. Bullshit.

How, after centuries of ovaries shutting down, had no one come up with a pill to fix the glandular waterfalls she slept in at night? Bunny would personally award them a Nobel Prize if anyone could stop the decisive rage she felt when Rick left his dirty coffee cup on the counter every morning. She barely kept it together in line at the Stop n' Shop, watching the cashier slowly beep every item over the X-ray machine. It felt like a portal to hell, watching whatever new hire they had figure out where a bar code was located or ask her what kind of bell pepper a green pepper was... It's a goddam green pepper! Or the barista at Starbucks who couldn't be bothered to take cash simply because they couldn't figure out the exact change. The world was full of idiots.

Bunny Ryan was in a mood that morning. Hormones, lack of sleep, and a general annoyance with people set the tone. So when she nearly got hit by a black Toyota in the club parking lot, she threw up her hands and shouted, "Watch it!"

The car was out of the ordinary. Bunny generally knew everyone's station wagon or SUV.

It stopped, and a man Bunny knew she didn't care for slowly got out of the car. He hadn't even parked the car. He just stopped and got out. Again, the blatant rudeness of people offended her.

"Good morning, sorry about that," a large man with bulky shoulders said. His longish gray hair was slicked back, and he had a menacing posture. He could have been from one of Rick's shows that highlighted gangs and police ad nauseam. The man's face loomed over Bunny, staring at her with slitted gray eyes. He wasn't sincere in his apology, she noted.

Bunny had been a flight attendant before meeting Rick in his first-class seat. From age 19 to 29, she flew the friendly skies back and forth from New York to LA. Seeing so many people throughout the day, she became adept at summing them up. It was the ultimate job in profiling. She knew the jerks, con artists, businesspeople, or "pleasants"—her code word for the easy passengers who barely asked for a glass of water or slept the whole flight.

This man was not pleasant.

"Can I help you?" Bunny said, feeling like he was not where he was supposed to be.

"Yeah." He licked his lips, and Bunny took a step back, holding her racket in her hand, ready to strike if needed. "You wouldn't happen to know a Kitty Kittrick, would ya?"

Of course she knew Kitty. At this point, the whole club was talking about Kitty's talent. She didn't know her personally, but everyone knew about the tragic loss of their grandparents and her older sister raising her. Bunny immediately felt protective. Kitty was an odd girl, but that didn't stop Bunny from remembering she was only 16, a child in her eyes.

"Why are you asking?" Bunny stood her ground.

"Just looking for her, that's all. I'm an old friend, you might say."

"Well, sir, this a private club, and anyone who doesn't belong cannot enter." This was untrue, but Bunny felt this man wouldn't know the difference between a salad fork and a regular fork.

"Thought she was playing tennis here?" he ventured again.

"Again, this is a private club, and it's not for me to disclose that information." Bunny was standing her ground, not so much afraid, but annoyed with the stupidity of humanity. Honestly, if he lunged at her, she wouldn't have minded taking a whack at him.

"I hear ya. Okay, I'll find her somewhere else." The man slowly got back into his car and revved the engine. Bunny stood there, not moving. Not on her watch was this guy getting away with any funny business.

The Toyota drove away slowly, and Bunny felt smug with satisfaction. Now, about that pinot grigio; she thought it was well-earned.

Chapter 22

For Dummies

"Mom, stop. You're doing it again," Adam said from his bed with one eye open and one closed.

"What?" Mia stepped into his room and gathered the ice cream bowl from last night. "I wasn't doing anything."

"I'm fine. You don't need to watch me sleep." It was true that since she had brought Adam home, she couldn't stop checking on him.

He sat up and shook out his hair like it had gathered snow while he slept. "Can Kitty come over today? It's boring just sitting here."

"Sure, if she wants, but your father will be here shortly. It's time you two talked."

After Adam's confession, she had given him a few days, but now he had to tell Eric what he had done.

"What if I just stopped stealing from them? And we forgot the whole thing?" Adam pleaded.

"Nope, Mr. Smarty." Mia went to sit on his bed. It was hard not to touch him like when he was a toddler. Brushing his hair out of his eyes or squeezing his arm calmed her anxiety. Nothing like one's child gives the simple joys of love. She had wanted more children, maybe just one more, but it had not worked out.

Two years after Adam was born, she and Eric had tried. Mia had wanted it more than Eric. She remembered that clearly. Eric wasn't a hands-on dad. Rarely had he done the diapering, the feedings, or the relentless filling of sippy cups. For Eric, fatherhood existed at the dinner table, telling Adam not to throw his peas at the wall. He was not a natural parent. Mia wondered if he had carried Adam in his body for nine months if it would have been different. Her anxiety skyrocketed when the doctors warned of pre-eclampsia. Adam was barely the size of a melon in her stomach, and although she hadn't met him yet, she was terrified of losing him. Eric brushed everything off like it would all work out fine, which, he smugly noted later, it had. But Mia didn't like his inability or his unwillingness to be scared. Fear was a good thing. People acted better for it. Pregnancy had finally caused her to quit smoking; it was easy knowing the harm it might do to the baby. That was a reasonable fear. She never drank a drop, she took all her vitamins and did everything she could to have a healthy child.

But Adam was born one month too early. The birth, because Adam was so small, was relatively easy. But she barely had a chance to hold him before he had to be incubated. Mia didn't leave his side, but the days passed, and he grew healthy. Almost as if Adam had sensed his mother's worry back then and willed himself to get better for her sake. She never felt like her attachment to him was abnormal. She was a mother, and good mothers love their children with everything they have.

Then she couldn't get pregnant again. The disappointment was overwhelming, and Mia fell into a depression. Eric wasn't a source of comfort. Again, his attitude was that it would all somehow work out. Probably because, mentally, he was moving away from her. He was distancing himself and making way for his affair with Camila that would come eventually.

If Eric had the capacity for fear, he would have feared for his wife's mental health, his marriage, or losing his family. He did not, because it all worked out for him, not her.

Unfortunately, for Adam's sake, Mia was complacent with their dysfunctional family. She wanted him to have a loving home with a father and mother. If anything, she should have thanked Eric when she returned home that fateful day and saw smoothie cups on her counter. But when you have been living with someone for years, you know when they are lying. When you don't, it's simply a matter of not wanting to acknowledge the lies.

Eric moved out, and divorce proceedings began immediately. He didn't fight the end of their marriage or beg for her forgiveness. A sure sign they were through. Adam had been young and confused, and she tried to temper the hurt. A father was still a father, after all. But she had to recognize that Adam was still hurting and needed Eric's help—no, cooperation—in changing that.

"I want you to list everything you bought or donated from their credit cards. This will be a full confession, young man. It's the only way to get past this."

"How mad do you think Dad will be?" Adam looked scared. Mia knew how mad he would be: furious. His son had hoodwinked him, and his ego wouldn't like that one bit.

"Don't worry," Mia lied. "He will understand."

An hour later, Eric came fuming down the stairs.

"Did you know about this?"

"Yes, Eric, I helped him," she said sarcastically. "No, I didn't know about this."

"He didn't do this to you, did he?" Ah, there it was. The bruised ego was speaking.

"No, but…"

"Do you know he sent me a copy of *How to Be a Dad for Dummies*?!" Eric barked.

Mia's hand flew up to her mouth to hide her laughter. *Well done, Adam*, she thought.

"Mia, it's not funny. He has donated over $3000 of my money to charities!"

"Better than buying heroin…" She knew she shouldn't have said that. "But how come you didn't notice, Eric? I mean, don't you look at your credit card statements?"

Mia knew he didn't because she had done all their finances without even a thank you.

"Don't be trite," he warned. "I want him to pay me back."

"Oh, for god's sake, Eric, he's ten. Don't you even see the bigger picture here?"

"I see that this environment, with his mother all the time, may not be good for him. I see that he has a pompous babysitter who might be teaching him all these dirty tricks. I see that maybe this shouldn't be joint custody!"

"Don't you dare threaten to take away my child, Eric Golding. The same child I cared for while you had your dick in my sister's pretzel."

"Well, he didn't learn to steal from me!"

"Oh, of course not, because he hasn't learned *anything* from you. You haven't been around long enough! Don't you see? This is a cry for your attention!"

"I give him attention! He comes to my house."

"Yeah, and he started doing this at your house because you ignored him."

Eric was huffing now. Score, she had made a point.

"Are you implying I taught him how to be a thief?"

"No, I am not implying. I am telling you that Adam is doing it to get some emotion out of you that will indicate that he matters to you."

"Of course he matters to me. He's my son!"

"Being a father doesn't mean the occasional slice of pizza because Camila is busy or having him over so he can play video games all day. It means talking to him, being with him, taking him to a goddam ball game."

"How about you, Mia? Ever think about how you had to control us all the time? Act this way and act that way, I was never good enough for you, never played the part you wanted me to. Maybe you were the reason I left. I'm not all to blame."

"Hey, whoa!" The front door opened, and Kitty walked in. "What's with the shouting?" Kitty stood there with her hands on her hips and poked her glasses up on her nose.

"I thought we didn't just barge into 'this' house," Eric clapped back at her.

"Touché, Mr. Golding. But you didn't hear me knocking over your screaming, did you?"

"Kitty, I'm sorry, you're right." Mia calmed down.

"Why are you apologizing to her?" Eric was fuming. "Apologize to me!"

"For what?" Kitty asked.

Eric turned to her and yelled, "This is none of your business, tennis Barbie!" Kitty was in a hot-pink tennis outfit, and her blonde hair was in pigtails.

"Eric, please don't call her names. It's childish."

"This place is a nuthouse. No wonder Adam is screwed up. Seriously, Mia, I might reconsider custody." Mia knew he was bluffing, but it hurt her deeply.

Kitty heard this and took an offensive step toward him, but

Mia shook her head no at Kitty.

"Eric, go home, cool off, and think about spending more time with your son than money at a lawyer's. Okay? Go have a fruit smoothie with Camila, and we will discuss this later."

"You." Eric pointed at Mia and then at Kitty. "And you too. This isn't the end."

As he stormed out, Kitty called back, "Is it the beginning or the middle? Not sure what we are talking about here?"

Mia slumped down on the couch and started to cry.

"Oh, Mrs. G, don't do that." Kitty stood over her.

"It wasn't supposed to be this way, none of it," Mia said. "Promise me, if you ever get married, make absolutely sure it's the right one. Don't ever do it because you have to or for someone else."

Then there was a knock at the door. "Oh, for Christ's sake." Mia was at her wit's end.

She pulled open the door in a fury before seeing who it was and shouted, "Just GO AWAY!"

"Okay," the man's voice said. "But might I ask why first?" He stood there in a nice polo shirt and jeans. His hands held a Star Wars Lego set and some flowers. It was Dr. Mayfield.

"Oh, Matthew! Oh my god, I am so sorry. Eric was just here and…"

"Hey, Doc!" Kitty said brightly. "Mrs. G was just about to have a meltdown, good timing."

"Kitty!" Mia hissed and began nervously smoothing out her hair.

"A meltdown, huh? Let me guess, Mr. Golding found out about Adam's online activities?"

"Yes," Mia sighed with relief. He understood.

"Well, I was in the neighborhood…" He held out the gifts. "Thought you guys could use some cheering up."

"No, you weren't in the neighborhood, Doc." Kitty smiled brightly and winked at him.

Mia grabbed the Lego. "Take this to Adam, Kitty. Now." Kitty gave Mia a goofy smile and left.

Mia asked Matthew in, but he declined, which disappointed her. His visit felt gallant and old-fashioned. She liked it.

"I thought since you were home with Adam, maybe I could bring you some dinner later? Maybe a bottle of wine as well?" Was this a date? Was this a date with a man who didn't want to exclude her son?

"Would you be joining us? I mean, only if you join us, of course."

"Are you asking me to have dinner with you?" Matthew leaned against the door in that dreamy James Dean way. *This cannot be real*, she thought. Something had to be wrong with him. She was blushing. My god, she hadn't blushed since high school.

"I'd be happy to, thanks for asking," Matthew said, and then he turned, and what had Nina told her before? Yes, he sauntered to his car. It was a sensible Audi station wagon, which relieved Mia to no end.

She heard Kitty upstairs. "Nina! Doc Mayfield just asked Mrs. G out."

"Seriously, KITTY!" Mia shouted up the stairwell. That girl had no boundaries.

Chapter 23
Whole Kit-n-Caboodle

"Dave, man, you look like shit," Peter said, staring straight at him.

"That's not a nice thing to say, Peter." But it was true. Dave was pale and a little shaky. His blond hair was limp and unwashed, and dark circles were under his eyes. It was a chilly, rainy November day, and Dave was madly taking notes on his father's computer.

"Have you been partying too hard? You look like a nerdy crack addict," Peter asked, concerned. "Is it the new boyfriend?"

"Have I been partying too hard? No, I have been working and haven't gotten much sleep." Dave didn't look away from the computer. "And Ken is not my boyfriend. Or I do not think he is my boyfriend, because we have not said those words. It is my understanding that people in relationships clearly state that one is a boyfriend out loud before being a boyfriend."

"Well, are you still seeing him a lot? Weekly?"

"Yes, we saw each other twice last week." Dave was surprised that Ken had texted on Saturday night after seeing one another on Thursday night. It was out of the ordinary for Ken to veer from their schedule. Ken had been upset by something. He said his work had irritated him, and he needed an escape. Dave asked him if he was Ken's escape, and he replied, *Yes, that is what you are.* And Ken also hoped it could stay that way. Dave agreed.

"So what's got your knickers in a wad? You have been squirrelly around here lately."

Dave knew he had been acting more manic than usual, but he had been waiting for his plan to come together before springing it on Peter. Because he was a big part of the plan, and Peter could act squirrelly too.

"Will you come into the office and take a seat, please?" David asked with his hands folded before him. He wanted to project seriousness. That's what Ken advised him, to quote "project seriousness."

"Peter, I have informed you that my parents are selling this business, correct?"

"Yes, correct."

"I have become worried about my future. I like my job here at the pro shop. I do not like change or wish to find a new job. I also like working with you. I consider you to be my best friend."

Peter sat with a curious face. "Go on." He didn't argue.

"Well, not wanting to lose my job, and not liking change, and not wanting you to lose your job…"

"Why would I lose my job?"

"Why would you lose your job? Because some developers could come in here, buy the place, and level it for condos. Think, Peter."

"You just sounded like my brother Charlie," Peter said, a little annoyed.

"Nothing is for certain, Peter, unless…"

"Unless what?"

"We own the club. The whole kit 'n caboodle, as they say."

Peter sat stunned.

"I take it this idea never occurred to you?" Dave implored.

Peter nodded stupidly. "But how can we own this place?"

"That's a stupid question, Peter. We buy it."

"Dave, I like your initiative here, but we don't have any money. I buy pizza with coupons."

"Well, Peter, according to my Tinder-ship…"

"Wait, what?"

"The relationship I made on Tinder… Ken? He's a finance guy and will help me map it all out once I get him the numbers."

"Dave, I mean, this all sounds great… But own the club?"

"As you said, if Kitty wins, we can attract better clientele."

"That's a BIG if, cowboy. But how would we ever buy the club? With what money?"

"Well, that's what I am working on, and now, I want you to work on it too." Dave looked at Peter sternly. Dave thought that he had given him an assignment he couldn't refuse.

"I didn't even finish college," Peter said stupidly.

"I didn't even go to college," Dave countered.

"So…we've got nothing to lose?"

"We've got nothing to lose."

Peter left, and Dave knew he would think about it. Peter was like a good lovable dog that had to have the scent of a trail to know where to go. Peter could be the face of the business, and Dave could be the behind-the-scenes guy who kept it running. It was perfect, at least to Dave.

Bunny Ryan came into the shop. She always wanted something.

"David, how do I put this… Have any strange men been in

here?" Did she know he was gay? Dave's life had been filled with strange men. She continued, "A big guy, rather unsavory, asking for Kitty Kittrick?" She tapped her painted nails on the glass countertop.

"Not that I know of, Mrs. Ryan. May I ask what would quantify as strange? I am strange, so my perspective on the situation may not be the same as yours."

"Oh, yes, right." David let the remark pass. Like Bunny Ryan was normal in her tennis visor? She played indoors, so the visor was unnecessary. "A tall, menacing fellow with a big face and greasy hair? Not the Hillsdale sort, I'm afraid. He nearly ran me over in the parking lot. He drives a black Toyota with tinted windows and a license plate from New Jersey."

"No, ma'am."

"Well…" Tap-tap-tap went her fingernails. "I did not like the looks of him, and I didn't like him asking about a sixteen-year-old girl. People like him do not belong in tennis clubs asking about young women. Do you hear me, David?" People often said that to him because he didn't look straight at them. He wasn't deaf, just bored.

"Yes, ma'am. Unsavory sort asking after Kitty. I will keep an eye out, don't worry." Dave, any other day, would have ignored her, but if he were going to be the club owner, the customer would be right. He saw that knitted on a pillow once.

"Thank you, David. I don't care what your mother said about you years ago. You are a good boy." Bunny waved her nails and exited.

What had his mother said?

Dave didn't think twice about Bunny and got back to work. He had compiled enough data to send to Ken, which was also an excuse to contact him. He sent him an email and felt accomplished. His phone rang thirty seconds later.

"You want to buy THE Hillsdale Tennis Club?" It was Ken, and he sounded slightly upset.

"Yes, I want to buy THE Hillsdale Tennis Club," Dave parroted.

"Your last name is Dins?" Ken asked. Guess they had avoided the most basic personal information.

"Yes, my last name is Dins. My parents are Donna and Derek Dins. I have three siblings named Deborah, Dina, and Douglas." The names of his sisters and brothers were unnecessary, but since he had revealed his identity, why not reveal them all? Ken was quiet, which made Dave nervous.

"Why? Do you know the club?" Dave asked. Ken cleared his throat, and there was more silence. "What, Ken, is this a terrible idea? I just sent you the numbers. You couldn't have read them that fast." Dave was sure Ken had not read the numbers because, from what Dave could tell, the club was somewhat lucrative. His father had run a tight ship, and the business had grown by 1.5% yearly.

"No, sorry, I didn't realize you were into tennis."

"I'm not. I play like shit, and I hate exercise. I told you, I don't want to lose my job."

"Yes, yes, yes." Ken sounded irritated. "Give me a few days, and I will look at all this. I promise." But then Ken hung up, and Dave was hurt. Ken's reaction wasn't what he expected. Dave hoped he would be impressed by his due diligence and attention to detail. He had even written down the cost of toilet paper as an expense. Dave thought that it would be insightful to list every detail. What had he done wrong?

Chapter 24
Horse Hockey

"Good morning, Mr. Baxter," Mia said cheerily, entering her office. It wasn't unusual to find the older man there. He needed a quiet space sometimes to finish his *New York Times* crossword.

"Taylor Swift sees what color?" Mr. Baxter said without looking up. His ballpoint pen was poised for the answer.

"Red," Mia responded with a smile.

"Why can't they just stick to real questions like names of African rivers?" Mr. Baxter grumbled.

"Because they are trying to market to a younger crowd." Mia was moving papers about. Mr. Baxter was like having a crotchety grandfather around, and she liked it.

"You got trouble brewing," he offered, his pen deftly filling in little blocks.

Mia's mind wasn't on trouble. After Adam's scare, she stayed home and recuperated with him for a few days. Dr. Mayfield had brought dinner, and Mia had allowed herself to relax for the first time in a long while. Aside from a drink with Nina, Mia hadn't had any fun lately. Adam had come from his room for dinner when he smelled Spaggio's chicken, and her first date was enjoyable with her son in attendance. Matthew had a way with Adam, and the two began joking and laughing about Mia. Adam told funny stories, and Matthew patiently listened, learning more than Mia would have revealed if she had been alone with him. A ten-year-old was actually a good wingman.

By the end of dinner, the two were fist-bumping and promising to get the Lego Millennium Falcon regardless of Mia's permission to buy a $400 toy.

Mia learned Matthew had two teenage daughters that spent most of their time frightening him with crop-top shirts and boys with tattoos. Legos would be a reprieve for him. They had talked until it was late, and he excused himself like a gentleman. He promptly called the next day for another date, and Mia quickly agreed.

"How so?" She was casually interested in Mr. Baxter. The thought of touching Matthew's hair had begun to consume her. Would it be soft? She already knew it smelled great.

"Mr. Dunning is circulating a petition about the curriculum," Mr. Baxter warned.

Mia looked up, shaken from her daydream. "How come I don't know about this?"

"Because he excluded all of us from the email."

"Little rat. How did you find out?"

"Because I am an old rat and make it my business to know. And a few of my students hate him, so that helps."

"Always the wiser one, aren't you?" Mia could feel the tension return to her shoulders.

"Been in this game a long time," Mr. Baxter offered. "I saw Martin Luther King Junior on TV. I remember Nixon as president and saw a golf ball fly off the moon. I don't take kindly to young pompous know-it-alls who know nothing."

"Maybe it's what people want, books with unicorns, rainbows, and married parents?" Mia countered sarcastically.

"Horse hockey. I've taught for 40 years, and you know what kids want? They want to learn. I've seen them say they don't, but that's just because they hate to work. Don't we all? But when I see someone like the freshman Abel Miller, dyslexic and struggling, choosing to read Faulkner... Faulkner! Why? Because he relates to it. The companionship, the story, the connection, that's what these kids desire. They want to see a version of themselves in print."

"Now they get that from technology. Why do students even need books anymore?" Mia liked these back-and-forths with Mr. Baxter.

"Because books are human. They are written by humans and about humans. No app or video game can replace that," he grumbled.

"I like the theory, but what about morality? Isn't that what Mr. Dunning is arguing? That we are messing with the kids' values?"

"That's the problem. They aren't kids by the time we get them. They know right and wrong, if they prefer girls or boys, or if they believe in God or Thor, God of Thunder. Their parents must have been morons if the foundation wasn't already there."

"But they are just teenagers. Maybe they don't know all this stuff yet, and we are pushing them too far in one direction," she mused.

"No, we are giving them choices. It's simple. We are opening up their worlds, not narrowing them. We are putting them on the plane. Mr. Dunning is shutting down the airport."

"Mr. Baxter, of course I agree with you. But what do I do if he starts anarchy with the parents?"

"Let the kids decide. Do they want to broaden their horizons or stay home forever?"

"Mmmm." Mia thought and went back to shuffling her papers.

Baxter sent her a copy of the email:

Dear Hillsdale Parents,

At Hillsdale Prep, all consideration is taken when choosing the literature curriculum, and your opinion is most valued! These are your children, and we intend to ensure that the values instilled at home are carried out within these hallowed walls.

Hillsdale Prep would never want to be the arbiters of moral complacency. Several historical and recent novels have a high percentage of material categorized as inappropriate for young minds. Three general categories apply when deeming works unsuitable. Books that contain 1: Offensive Language 2. Are Sexually Explicit, and 3. Unsuited for the age group.

It is time for Hillsdale to re-evaluate and re-configure the English Department's choices in educational materials. And again, we value your thoughts on the past curriculum (see enclosed list) and welcome the elimination and/or addition of material more suitable for our young minds.

Please email me with any concerns,

Best. Mr. Tyler Dunning.

"That snake," Mia said out loud at her desk. They weren't teaching Q'Anon. They were teaching fiction. Wait, Q'Anon was fiction… Oh, never mind. She emailed Tyler for a meeting that day.

Three hours later, Tyler was sitting in Mr. Baxter's chair with a holier-than-thou look. His black hair had too much gel, and his suit looked trim and expensive.

"Mr. Dunning. I am curious, what is your aim in involving parents?" Mia asked slowly. "They pay us a lot of money to teach their children what they cannot. That is the entire point of education."

"I think parents should have the right to decide what we teach. These are their children, after all."

"This is not a public school. They are well-aware of the type of education Hillsdale offers when they enroll their children. They are choosing this particular curriculum and paying for it."

"They may not be aware of the dangers of some of these books." He casually picked some lint from his jacket with a pale effeminate hand.

"And I suppose you will be the hero in pointing out those dangers?"

"Someone has to." Again, he smiled in that sanctimonious way. He didn't break eye contact with Mia.

"Mr. Dunning, unless you have become the head of this department overnight, I am cautiously warning you to stay in your lane. The curriculum is not a public forum, and reaching out to parents to promote your agenda blatantly disregards how we operate."

"I have received several responses from parents to have a meeting on the matter. I think it's a great idea." He was gathering troops, she thought.

"Then I need to involve Principal Jenkins in your actions. This may be dangerously close to overstepping your role as a teacher at Hillsdale." It was a veiled threat. Mia was trying to remember the teaching contract she signed years ago and if there was anything that might remotely mean job dismissal.

"I am just advocating for the parents." Tyler held up his hands. "I don't see anything wrong with that." His beady eyes twinkled.

Mia stared at him with incredulity. Was this what everyone meant by millennials having no respect for authority? She didn't have the right to fire him, or she would have on the spot.

"Dangerously close, Mr. Dunning," Mia repeated. "I believe you have a class to teach." It was her way of dismissing him. He left, and, goddammit, he whistled as he walked away. He thought he had won! Ooh, her blood boiled. His arrogance was unreal.

Chapter 25
Onyx or Sable

The man in the black Toyota drove slowly around Hillsdale. He was disgusted by how people lived, worrying about pumpkins on their doorstep! How they piled the dead leaves in neat piles and stacked wood by the side of their homes. He had been there a few days, and as far as he was concerned, this sleepy little town was what the problem was with this world. It wasn't reality; far from it. Privileged people getting lattes and filling their houses with Amazon boxes wasn't close to how the world worked. At least it didn't go that way in Jimmy Kittrick's world.

He pulled up to a Starbucks drive-thru and shouted, "A large coffee, black."

The cheery female voice said, "Large? Do you mean Venti?"

"What the hell is a Venti? I said large, as in size," the man shouted like she was deaf.

"Okay, sir, did you want French Roast, Cafe Verona, or a blend?"

"A blend of what? I WANT COFFEE! Is this America?"

"Milk? Cream? Oat milk? Soy milk?"

"Oats don't make milk, for Christ's sake. BLACK, or is it now called onyx or sable?" Couldn't people take the most basic instruction anymore?

"Come around," she said meekly.

The barista/young girl shakily handed him a steaming cup.

"That'll be $6.95."

"What the hell?" he shouted back at her. His large eyes narrowed with defiance, and his tone growled, "It's COFFEE."

She smiled and waited. This wasn't her first angry customer at Starbucks.

He handed her a ten and drove away. He hated Hillsdale. At least coffee was free in prison.

James Kittrick had been out of prison for three weeks and was relishing his freedom. Gone were the smells of stale bed sheets and sweaty men, and now he had fresh air. Granted, he preferred to be in the city, but he was laying low right now. Jimmy, in fact, was taking his time and planning for his future, something maybe he should have done two decades ago, but live and learn. He thought about his wife, Lily, and how she was never supposed to be his wife.

When he went into that club and heard her sing, he thought Lily had a great ass and liked her enormous blue eyes. Probably because she was on stage, she had more allure. Off stage, Lily was needy and an easy mark. Jimmy's dad taught him never to get attached to a woman because it wasn't worth the trouble. His own mother had run off when Jimmy was a child, and his dad, a drunk gambler, pretty much left Jimmy on his own. But that was okay. Jimmy hooked up with the O'Malleys, who ran Boston's south end, and got himself jobs as an errand boy. He learned to grift for cash, and life was pretty easy as long as he didn't rip off anyone associated with the O'Malleys.

As soon as he talked to Lily, he knew she was out of his league in the sweet-hometown-girl way. But she was naive, and that made it more appealing to sleep with her. It was easy after he promised Lily he'd help with her singing career. Ha, he had no such intentions, but it worked. Women could be so gullible. His dad taught him they were the easiest targets. But he hadn't planned on knocking her up. Most girls would have taken care of the situation, but not Lily, that bitch. She had to go and ruin both their lives with kids because she was a Catholic girl at heart. The O'Malley brothers laughed at him and told him to get a woman he could control. So that's what he did. If she was going to punish him by having the kid, he would punish her right back. Hey, she asked for it. Again, that's what his dad always said.

Now Jimmy was in this stupid town. He thought about knocking on Nina's door but then reminded himself he was Jimmy Kittrick and smarter than that. Scope out your mark, do a little research, and get to know your game. He hadn't seen his daughters in over twelve years, so why not take his time? He'd get what he wanted. He just had to have a little patience.

Chapter 26
Business of Living

Nina ignored the text from Stan. Couldn't this guy take a hint? She had just worked a double, and whenever she saw him in the hospital corridors, she quickly turned around or hid in a hospital room. Once, she ran into Dr. Mayfield and promptly started smiling. Mia had told her about their wonderful evening together, and Nina fully supported the union. But Mia kept asking her, "What is wrong with him?" There had to be something wrong with the guy. Was he unnaturally involved in men's self-help groups, or did he want to play dress-up in the bedroom...with other people? There were all sorts of scenarios that women could imagine, thanks to the internet and movies that made the handsome husband the pedo-serial-rapist-pro-lifer with a secret family in Utah. The imagination could run wild.

So Nina just asked, "Dr. Mayfield? May I talk to you as a person?"

"I am nothing but that, Nina." He looked at her with a sly grin.

"About Mia. You know, she and I are good friends, and she doesn't need any more, let's say, bullshit in her life. Divorced, single, middle-aged women can get *Dear John*-ed. You know the documentary?"

"Not really, but I get what you are saying." He eyed her. "You don't want me to take advantage of your friend."

"Well, that, but… What's wrong with you? I mean, you look too good to be true." Nina's Kitty-ness was coming out. She could be just as blunt as her sister sometimes.

"Okay, I see." Dr. Mayfield was used to this interrogation by patients. They said he was too handsome to be a doctor. Was this gene discrimination?

"My deepest fault, according to my ex-wife, was that I worked too much. I put more effort into being a doctor than being a husband. Granted, she had to live through my residency. But she also preferred the ladies, so I think I was at a disadvantage from the start. I can be far too serious, which is good for the job, but not necessarily for the home life, but I am taking steps to counteract that by rewatching all the *Saturday Night Live* that I've missed in the past two decades. I immensely dislike loud concerts and amusement parks, much to the chagrin of my teenage girls. And I am a stickler for making my bed. It has been remarked that I am too fastidious. In other words, Nina, I can be a bore sometimes. I am not very exciting and prefer mojitos on a quiet beach to anything too taxing, like sports or, to be frank, watching sports."

Nina started laughing, "Carry on, Dr. Mayfield. You and Mia will have a wonderful life sitting on the couch reading old books and sharing charcuterie."

"Ah, Miss Kittrick, a guy can only dream." And Matthew sauntered away, whistling.

Now Nina was home cleaning up Kitty's room. Kitty's tennis

clothes had begun to smell, and Nina couldn't stand it. Kitty's solution was to buy more clothes rather than wash the old ones, which were also new. Picking up a sports bra, Nina bumped into Kitty's desk, and a portrait of their mother fell over. She lightly brushed the dust from the frame. "Oh, Mom," she said to no one.

Nina tried not to imagine how different their life would have been if their mother were still alive. No matter what scenario she replayed in her head, life with Lily most likely would have been worse, not better. Not that she didn't want her mother back; for years, she desperately did, because losing a parent never feels right.

Nina remembered her mother's perfume; it was woody and flowery, but she didn't know its name. When her mother held her tight, she could smell it on her skin and in her clothes. Sometimes her whole room smelled like that. Once, Nina was in a store and caught a whiff of it on someone, but it was there and then gone. Like her mother, who had been there, then just as quickly had gone from her life. Lily had become a page in her memory from the past, and as years went on, she may end up a footnote.

Even though Nina had twelve whole years with her mother before she died, she never really got to know her. When you are young, your parents are just parents, not actual personalities with needs and desires. She could only remember snippets of her. Lily sang old Billie Holiday songs when she cooked. She wore dresses instead of pants, and had a lipstick collection in the bathroom. These details lingered, but she didn't remember any conversations or explanations of why her mother cried more than she laughed.

After Lily passed, Nina badgered Oma with questions about her mother. How could she have guessed how many questions would remain unanswered by the dead? No one warns a child that people take significant events and details with them when they die. And that is precisely when answers are needed.

Oma tried to describe Lily to Nina the best she could. Lily, as a teenager, had always been ambitious. Not in school—she couldn't have cared less about her marks—but in life. Oma partially blamed herself for always going on about the American dream to Lily. They invoked the sense that anything was possible, they were the children of immigrants with a business and a home. Lily wanted to be a singer. Unlike Oma, who had no talent whatsoever, Lily had a lovely voice. She had always loved to sing, it made her the happiest, but at eighteen, the only jobs she could get were in late-night clubs and sometimes as a backup singer. She didn't realize how many people had had professional training before entering the city. But she was determined.

After a couple years of scraping by, she met James Kittrick, or "Jimmy." Jimmy promised her a contract and a recording studio. He wanted to be her agent. He said he would protect her. All the things a naive girl from Hillsdale with two loving parents would fall for. She had no idea that he was full of shit. Jimmy was a hustler. He was large, brawny, with big gray eyes and curly blond hair. He wasn't bad-looking, but when he got angry, he could terrify anyone. Jimmy lived from hustle to hustle, but Lily ignored his proclivities because she wanted to sing.

She was pregnant within a year of knowing him. The last time she sang in public was two days before Nina was born. And then her whole life changed.

Oma and Pop were devastated when they met Jimmy. He wasn't the kind of man they would choose for Lily. Oma regretted not raising her daughter with more street smarts. Pop didn't like Jimmy's shady businesses, and Oma didn't like how he bossed Lily around. She thought she had raised Lily to be stronger than that and was disappointed in herself and Lily.

Lily and James rarely visited Hillsdale, both feeling unwanted. Occasionally, Lily would call her parents and ask them for money, and they would send more than enough. They offered her a place back home for her and Nina, but Lily refused. But really, Lily was holding onto the hope that she would sing again.

Days turned into years, and Lily had a couple miscarriages before she eventually had Kitty. Oma had wanted to be more part of their lives, but Lily had kept them at bay.

That's what Oma knew. Nina could fill in the rest of the story.

For Nina, her memories of living with both her parents lacked sequence. They were a hurricane in her mind. Thoughts swirled of her mother drunk, her father drunk, arguing. How often did she crawl into her mother's bed to find her weeping and distant? Her mother's sorrow cascaded through the dingy apartment like the air they all had to breathe. An unbridled sadness in Lily blocked out the sun of Nina's childhood. She now understood it was her mother mourning a singing career. Her life would never find the spotlight she had longed for all those years. Her dream was never to be a wife or a mother. These things happened to her, they were chosen for her by fate.

Her mother wasn't a bad person. There were hot meals and clean clothes, but Nina knew from the start that she was not the center of her parents' attention. She was the supporting actress, not the main character. Her mother's turbulent emotions easily angered Nina's father. When her mother cried, her father got angry. Her father lacked patience for both of them. He often stormed out, not to be seen for days.

And then Kitty came and cut through the loneliness that Nina hadn't been able to identify. The innocent, fatty baby brought her so much joy. When Kitty first smiled, it was at Nina, and when she laughed, Nina laughed with her. Kitty was so unblemished by their parents' dysfunction that Nina held to her as hope for herself. They could love each other the way their parents couldn't love them.

After Kitty came, her parents fought more, especially over money. Nina was frightened to leave Kitty alone in the house. She didn't trust her parents to rush to Kitty when she needed changing or a bottle.

The worry consumed young Nina, but she told no one. She grew quieter and more removed at school. She rushed home, relieved to find Kitty giggling and cooing in her crib, and Lily relied on Nina's devotion to her baby sister. What Lily lacked, Nina was expected to make up, and she did so willingly because she knew nothing except love for the child.

Now that Nina was older, she pitied her mother. She knew that if her father had been a decent man, a loving husband and father, maybe everything would have turned out differently. But things didn't because he wasn't, and that was now a fact that could never be changed or altered. If Lily and Jimmy hadn't failed, hadn't allowed tragedy to fall upon themselves like ash from a volcano, then she and Kitty would have never ended up in Hillsdale. They would have never found the loving embrace of Pop and Oma. And there would have never been the secrets.

Nina pushed Kitty's clothes into the wash and tried to clear her mind. Maybe someday she would tell Kitty the whole story. But for now, it was best to get on with the business of living. That's what Pop used to say.

Chapter 27
Full Tuition

Peter hadn't slept well. For the first time in his life, he felt anxious. It was odd to feel so unsettled, like he was wearing someone else's shoes. The weather had turned cold, and his apartment had a distinct chill. Mrs. Clark had started sneaking in regularly and dropping off food and laundry, which comforted him. Admittedly, it was nice to have someone looking out for him. Lately, his thoughts swirled around his parents, Coach Clark's cancer, buying the business, and mainly Kitty. Could Kitty improve her splice? Get lobs faster? Have a harder groundstroke? What if all this was a joke? What if Kitty got out there and tanked the match? What if the club was sold to someone else, and he and Dave lost their jobs? What would they do then? Peter thought maybe he needed one of his parents' gummies.

He heard a noise outside his front door. Charlie again? Could he ask him about buying the club? Perhaps for once, his brother could be helpful.

He swung open the door and was surprised. "Ashley? It's 8 am."

"Yeah, I spent the night here last night," she said, barging past him. She was dressed in a sparkly dress and had crusted makeup on her face. With raccoon eyes, she was drinking a super-sized coffee.

"Did we have fun?" Peter asked sarcastically.

"Shut up. I was with Ravi and didn't make it back home, so Mom's going to wonder. I gotta clean myself up for work." And, like Charlie, she overtook Peter's bathroom. When she emerged, smartly dressed and wet hair slicked in a work bun, Peter marveled at how some people had two personalities. He could barely keep up with one.

"Ash, let me ask you a couple questions, if you got the time?"

"Anything for you, Farmer Ted." She looked around his sparce apartment with a sad little shake of her head.

"Okay," he began, "would it be foolish to buy the Hillsdale Club? I don't have any money, so I don't see how it's possible. What would you do if you were in my position?"

"No, I don't believe it's entirely stupid. A bit far-fetched, but not stupid. The place has been around forever, and the Dins seem to have done well. But you have no money, right?"

Peter held out his hands.

"Mmm." Ashley looked intensely serious. "How many years of Yale did you do?"

"Two," Peter dumbly replied.

"So you didn't do two?" She pondered.

"Generally, four is the requirement for the piece of paper." Peter had no idea where she was going.

"Your parents pay full tuition?" she asked.

"Yeah, and they were pissed. Dad, quote, 'threw good money after bad' at me."

"But they only paid for two years. What happened to the money for the other two?" Ashley pondered. Peter still looked blank. "Peter, you really are daft. If they only paid half, there must be half leftover, earmarked for you." The realization was slow, but Peter began to get it and started nodding.

Ashley continued, "Yale is like, what, $75,000 a year? So that would leave $150,000 your parents never spent."

"Yeah, but Dad…"

"But your dad paid for Charlie's school, right? And what about Charlie's graduate school? Maybe they could invest in your future this way." She sipped her coffee like the answer had been so obvious.

"Oh my god, Ashley, you will make a great lawyer." Peter couldn't help but plant a huge kiss on Ashley's head.

"I know, I know," she laughed.

"Hey, also, I need another sponsor for Kitty's tennis tournament. Would your dad's law firm do it?"

"Are you kidding? It would give Cami every excuse to think we are dating. Nice one, Farmer Ted! Done and done!"

"Last question. Do you know Nina Kittrick well? I think she hates me. She's giving me a 'you're a creep' vibe."

"Thought you would be used to that by now." Ashley chuckled. "Maybe you did something to Nina back in high school? Women can really hold a grudge. Okay, I have to jet, Peter. Someone has to earn a living around here."

"Ashley, thanks. I appreciate the help."

"Oh, you owe me!" And she was gone.

What the hell had he done to Nina Kittrick?

Peter ran into Coach Clark downstairs.

"Coach, you know, if you don't feel up to practice for any reason, you don't always have to come." Peter was eyeing him to see if he looked the same. Coach Clark ogled him right back.

"GODDAMMIT, LOIS!" he turned and shouted into their house. "She told you, didn't she? Peter, it's just cancer, not ebola. I'll be fine, and we will have no further discussion about it."

Peter thought Coach Clark looked cartoonish, huffing and puffing, throwing trash can lids around.

"I meant no offense, Coach." Peter waved his hands a little.

"Listen to me, you little pissant. We have only two weeks to get that kid ready, do you hear me? That's what you focus on, nothing else. I'll see you at three today. We gotta work on her volley."

"Yes, sir." Peter gave a little salute and got on his bike to leave.

"And, Peter," Coach Clark said quietly. "Don't tell Kitty I'm sick. I don't want to worry her."

Peter nodded. What a softy.

Peter got to work and found Dave at the computer. He told him Ashley's idea about confronting their parents about their forgone tuition.

"You had three siblings who went to college, right? So they got something you didn't get?" Peter urged.

"Peter, I'm impressed. You have made a very valid and fair point. I will consider that in my negotiations. But we still don't have enough."

"Maybe your parents will let us pay them in installments?"

"I don't know. Dad's pretty keen on cashing out and riding off into the sunset. He said he wants to buy a Corvette to drive in the rat place. A hideous car, if you ask me, but I do not have to drive it."

"What did your boyfriend Ken say? Did he look at the numbers?" Peter asked hopefully. He needed some good news.

"He has ghosted me," Dave said dully.

"What? What happened?" Peter was surprised.

"I sent him the numbers, and he has canceled our date this

week. I texted him, but no response. I assume ghosting is the correct term." Peter looked at Dave and felt terrible for him. Dave didn't deserve to be dumped.

"Maybe he's just busy or something?" Peter lied, trying to be hopeful.

"Peter, let's face it. I'm too much for some people." Dave was looking away, but he always looked away. Peter could hear the sadness in his voice.

"You're not too much for me. Fuck Ken if he can't see how great you are. So we are going to buy this business and show them all." Peter attempted to sound confident.

"That's the problem, Peter. I only want to fuck Ken."

"I know, buddy, I know." Peter would have hugged him, but Dave would have hated that.

Later, like clockwork, Peter found Kitty lounging over the glass case, talking to Dave at three o'clock. Before each session, the two seemed to have endless things to chat about, forcing Peter to retrieve Kitty.

"Guy's a loser," Kitty was telling Dave.

"But he's not. This isn't like him to go silent on me," Dave confided to Kitty about Ken.

"Then he's lying about something. He's got a secret... Ooh, maybe he has another boyfriend." Kitty pushed up her glasses, and her blue eyes got wider.

"KITTY," Peter shouted. "That isn't helping. Time to get to work."

"Dave, something's up here, and the sooner you know, the better." Then Kitty turned to Peter. "Okay...ayyy. Pe...teeeerr."

"I hate when you say that. You need to focus, get your head in the game."

"I was just helping Dave get head in the game," Kitty deadpanned, and Dave laughed.

"You both are not funny. Let's go."

"I love it when he tries to sound like he has authority!" Kitty winked at Dave. "Yes, sir. Coach Wise, sir!"

Kitty proceeded onto the court where Coach Clark was waiting to clock her serve. It was 76 mph, which was truly impressive. Peter played a set with her and barely won 7-5. By the time they finished, everyone at the club had halted playing and was watching. Cheers rose whenever either one of them won a point. No one knew whom to root for, but secretly it was Kitty because, if she could beat Peter, she could win the tournament.

A boy with red hair and a small frame bounded up to Kitty and hugged her. Peter was again mesmerized by the effect Kitty had on people.

"Hey, Pet…eerrr," Kitty yelled over to him. "Meet Adam. You are going to start coaching him."

"Am I?" Peter looked the scrawny kid over. He had arms like twigs and little to no potential at sports.

"Hi, Peter," Adam said shyly. "Kitty says I need less screen time and to be involved more with humanity."

"Oh, does she now?" Peter shook his head.

"Kid will be good, I promise." Kitty slugged some Gatorade and wiped her mouth with the back of her hand.

"Kitty, does the kid have parents? Or is he yours?"

Adam giggled.

"Mia, his mom, teaches at Hillsdale. He's cool. Just sign him up."

"Kitty, I don't take orders from you. He can join the boys' clinic after school."

"That's cool," Adam said, but Peter watched Kitty wink at Adam like whatever Peter said was nonsense.

But Peter was distracted. He had seen Nina in the corner watching them. Oddly, he felt he had to prove himself to her. He had to prove he was worthy enough to coach and even be around her sister. The intensity with which Nina watched him was worse than his father's. He never felt the need to make his father happy. That task was too hard. But he realized he wanted Nina's approval. Peter had watched her watch Kitty with pleasure and admiration. Her smile was brilliant. And Peter, more than anything, wanted to be the recipient of that smile too.

Chapter 28
Shakedown

Edie Wise knew she was a terrible driver. She exemplified the stereotype that women drivers were worse than men. She tended to get distracted easily by the radio, her phone, or even just by her thoughts. The car was the one place that offered solitude and reflection for Edie. Bob was always home now, so the respite of her Mercedes was a haven for her thoughts. Sometimes it was as simple as what she would buy for dinner. Other times, she imagined herself a widow. There was quite a range of scenarios Edie would cultivate in her head. And once lost in those thoughts, the car could drift into another lane or forego a stop sign altogether. She could admit she was haphazard at times, but that didn't do much to alter the situation. At her age, it was what it was.

So when Edie got hit from behind, she hadn't a clue whether it was her fault. She had been thinking about Charlie, worried about him lately. Recently, he had become more manic with work, and his general demeanor was erratic. He still was her more reliable son, always had been. But Charlie, unlike Peter, had natural anxiety, and bless him, now that she and Bob were getting older, Charlie was more alert. He had taken to calling or texting her almost every day. It was sweet and annoying simultaneously, because if she didn't respond immediately, he repeatedly called back in a panic. She figured she and Bob still had a good 20-30 years left, and if Charlie was this way now, she might want to kill him further down the road.

She respected that Charlie loved his work, similar to Bob's fanaticism. But Bob had Edie and the boys at home, and Edie couldn't remember the last time Charlie had a proper girlfriend. He would be thirty soon, and should at least be dating more than working. Like any mother, she wanted someone to love and care for her sons as she did. And she wanted them to have someone to love. But Charlie was so high-strung, pounding on his phone and driving that stupid sports car. It was unattractive. Even she, his mother, was put off by his frenzied behavior.

This is where her thoughts ended when she felt a sharp push on the back of her driver's seat and lurched slightly forward. What the hell?

Edie turned around and saw a low black vehicle behind her. Did he hit her?

She watched the driver exit the vehicle in the rearview mirror and thought, *Oh dear, something must have happened.* She used her hand to brush her hair off her face and got out.

The large man was not wearing an appropriate jacket for November weather. It was too thin. He was slicking back his gray hair with his hands and licking his lips. The car was a black Toyota, Edie noted, with tinted windows. Who needed tinted windows? Edie Wise had no idea Jimmy Kittrick was short of cash.

"Why did you stop so suddenly?" Jimmy's gravelly voice conveyed annoyance, which unsettled Edie. As he approached her, she felt small. She was petite naturally, but this man could pound the top of her head with his fist. Edie took a step back.

"I'm sorry. What happened?" she responded politely, trying to remain calm.

"Well, you stopped short, and I ran into you because of that. It was your fault." Now, Edie would fully admit, but not to Bob, that she wasn't a great driver, but all she had done was stop at the stop sign that day. How could that have been her fault?

"Ma'am, look at my bumper and what your car did." He pointed to his front bumper, but Edie didn't see a scratch on either vehicle.

"I'm gonna need some insurance, please," he said forcefully. "Or we'll have to get the police involved." He took another step toward her, and Edie's heart raced. She didn't like him and wanted him to go away.

"But there's nothing wrong…" she stammered. She wished Bob was there to handle the situation. He was tall and stern and would have put this man in his place.

"Well, give me $500 and we'll call it even," Jimmy demanded, and his gray eyes bore into her. He kept licking his lips.

"I don't have $500." Edie didn't know what to do. She never thought of jumping into her car and driving away. She was not a runner.

"I've already got your license number. I can find you," Jimmy said with a steeliness that rattled her further.

Oh dear, she thought, just wanting him to go away. She reached back into her car and grabbed her purse.

Opening her pink wallet, she said, "I only have $128. Would that be okay?"

He stared at her, and Edie's hand shook as she held it out to him.

"Fine. But remember, I know your car, lady. You can't go

around causing traffic accidents and getting away with it. Entitled bitches like you think you can get away with anything." He lurched forward and grabbed the money.

Edie got back into her car and was shaking all over, barely able to grip the steering wheel. Jimmy followed her for a couple blocks, but finally turned away. Edie, close to tears, saw she was passing the Hillsdale Tennis Club and pulled in. Thank god she could find Peter.

Edie took a minute and thought about what had just happened. Was that a shake-down? Who was that awful man? She felt vulnerable and stupid. Nothing like that ever happened in Hillsdale. Nothing like that had ever happened to her.

Edie went into the club and heard a big commotion by the courts. She investigated, hoping to find Peter to make her feel better.

Ever since Peter was little, Edie felt a calmness wash over her when he was around. His natural, relaxed personality never demanded much of her. Unlike Bob and Charlie, he lacked judgment and the need for her approval. Peter had an uncanny knack for mimicking her, but he did it with kindness. He'd rifle through her handbag, saying, "Oh dear, where are my glasses?" in exactly her voice while they were perched on top of his head. He teased her to make her laugh. Peter was a light in their family that they needed. Someone who could be less severe than more. Edie likened him to a cat, and never worried he wouldn't land on his feet somehow, someway.

When she entered the arena, her son was surrounded by a cheering crowd as he served the ball to a tall girl. They were in a heated match, Edie could tell. She stood back on the wall, and all thoughts of the previous incident left her while watching her son revel in the game. His face registered concentration and seriousness, which was so rare for him. And as his mother, one who held him and wished the world for him 25 years ago, she saw what Bob had not seen. Edie Wise could see that her son was happy.

The crowd was cheering for both players, and it was hard not to get wrapped up in the enthusiasm.

Edie said to the woman next to her, "Who's winning?"

"Kind of even. It's been back and forth, a real nailbiter," the girl said without taking her eyes off the court.

Edie recognized her from the hospital, the darling blonde. "Oh, you're the nurse!" The girl had been marvelous with Bob. After his heart attack, he treated all the nurses terribly. But this one managed to get him to relax and ease up.

The woman turned to her and said, "Oh, Mrs. Wise! How is your husband doing?"

"Very well, and thank you again for putting up with him. Bob can be rude when he is sick, but overall he is getting better."

"Oh, he wasn't that bad. I've seen worse. He just had a scare, is all."

"Who are you rooting for?"

"That's my baby sister, Kitty."

Edie marveled at Kitty. The girl, with her long arms, modeled strength and power, things Edie wished she had more of. "She's fantastic. Wow. Peter has his hands full. But he loves it, I can tell." Edie started cheering herself, proud to watch her son.

Nina smiled at her. "I'm Nina. I went to school with Peter. He seems to be good at coaching her."

"Really? What a small town." Edie gave Nina a closer look. Why hadn't Peter brought someone like her home from high school?

"I hope they're ready for the tournament," Nina mused.

"What tournament?" Edie asked, confused.

"Peter wants Kitty in the junior circuit, and they have their first tournament in a couple weeks."

Edie had no idea. Why hadn't he told his parents? Well, they had been so distracted by Bob's health. Edie felt a tinge of disappointment. She didn't know what was going on in Peter's life. She made a mental note to get more involved. Just look at him, he looked like such a professional out there, and all these people were watching him. Maybe these past few years hadn't been the waste that Bob thought.

Edie stayed for a while. Watching the match washed away all her troubles. Another boy, who looked Peter's age, came over to Nina. He was very handsome, if short, chatting with Nina, and Edie longed to be that young again. The business of getting old was terrifying, and standing next to twenty-somethings didn't help but exacerbate the feeling that time was fleeting. Life was too fast, and her children were moving on without her.

Chapter 29
Sitting Duck

Mia just looked at Adam, dumbfounded. He stood there in the kitchen and looked at her with interest. His eyes had both pleasure and apprehension. They were at a standoff reading each other's emotions.

"Mom, you okay?"

Mia just nodded. But she turned around, pulled a wine bottle from the fridge, and poured herself a big glass.

"Mom, you sure you're okay?" Adam asked again.

Mia looked at him and asked, "Are you okay?"

He nodded.

"Mom, I'm okay. I promise. Kitty told me it would be cool. Like her and Nina, they have each other."

In the span of one run-on sentence, Adam had told her that he had joined a tennis clinic. Hoorah! Her heart had soared thinking of him playing with other boys again and getting out of the house. Kitty was going to help get him there in the afternoons.

Mia was counting her blessings that Kitty had not only taken such an interest in Adam, but was making progress with him. He was a newer version of his old self, a boy with interests other than being alone. He was getting a life again. But then, Adam dropped the bomb.

Blah, blah, blah, tennis, clinic…Camila was pregnant. *What?*

"Adam, how do you know Camila is pregnant?" Adam's face flushed, and he turned away.

"You were snooping through their emails, weren't you?" While side-swiped by this new information, Mia couldn't ignore the fact that what Adam was doing was wrong. "Adam, you have to stop going through their stuff," Mia admonished.

"I know, Mom. But I can't help it. It's so…easy," he whined.

"No computer or Xbox for a whole week," she said firmly.

Luckily, Adam agreed without a fight. Phew, at least he wasn't one of those kids who threw a full-throttle tantrum when being punished. He accepted it. "Okay, Mom," he said. "But are you okay with them having a baby?"

"I suppose it's normal. My sister is five years younger than me, and they are in love. I wasn't expecting it, I guess. How did you find out?"

"Her email password is YogaUnicorn." They both moaned and laughed. "She emailed Grandma about it." Mia sipped her wine and nodded, still ingesting the information. So her mother knew but not her. Sometimes Mia felt like the world was trying to deceive her.

"How does it make you feel?" she asked Adam.

"Well, Kitty said having a baby brother or sister is fun. I can create my relationship with them, and it won't have anything to do with you guys. Like he or she will be mine, and that's cool. I've been alone, and now I won't be."

"You know you always have me!" Mia blurted because she

didn't like hearing Adam feel alone. She wanted to tell him how she tried to have more children to give him a sibling. Now, her sister was doing that for her, and Mia felt a raw disappointment. Like life had cheated her of that ability.

"I know, but you are my mom. I mean, a baby brother or sister I can teach *Minecraft* to and play with, you know, someone more MY age." Mia had to agree that it was good for Adam.

"You won't feel jealous if your dad gives him or her more attention?"

"Nah, Dad is Dad. Maybe I'll have someone to joke about him with."

"That's very optimistic of you."

"Kitty says make lemons into lemonade."

"Well, what would we do without Kitty?" Mia smiled and pulled Adam close to her. They hugged, and she was grateful he didn't squirm away. Maybe he had grown up too fast during the divorce, but he would always be her baby.

Mia couldn't tell if this was the worst news of her day. Earlier, rumors had been circulating that Mr. Dunning was calling a parent meeting to discuss the curriculum. When she confronted Principal Jenkins, he was non-committal about it. Mia knew well enough that a maybe was most likely a yes. When parents pay thousands of dollars for education, that usually affords them the self-appointed right to bully the principal. And vice versa, the principal caves due to the thousands of dollars they spend. Why couldn't people leave well enough alone? Instead of grading papers tonight, she would be googling counterarguments to banning books and reading Stephen King memes against the whole situation. Mia felt like she would have to become a lawyer overnight only to argue in a court of idiots.

The bright spot in her day was Matthew, who had taken to texting funny anecdotes and checking in with her. Every time her phone pinged, she couldn't help but get giddy. They were taking it slow, getting to know each other, but he made her feel less lonely. They loved their work, but there were a million pitfalls in the teaching and medical professions. They commiserated over the lack of common sense that pervaded the country, why TikTok was so addictive, and what episode of Ina Garten was their favorite. Their budding relationship was calming, unlike the rest of her world.

Luckily, her night was interrupted by Nina and Kitty arriving with pizza and more wine. While eating, Kitty asked Adam what color outfits she should wear to the tournament, and Adam wondered if a baby brother or sister would be better.

Mia was able to question Kitty about Mr. Dunning.

"Some kids like him, and some kids don't. He is what you would call polarizing," Kitty said nonchalantly as she stacked extra pepperoni on a slice.

"Well, that's a good term," Mia said, impressed by her choice of vocabulary. "Let me ask you, as a student, how do you feel about this argument? Whether parents have the right to reject books because they have too much sex or talk about race or gender too much?" Mia asked.

"That would mean they don't talk about any of that stuff at home. They don't want you as a teacher to discuss those topics with their kids because they can't or are unwilling to. It's the parents who are repressed. They want to keep us children, which we are not. It's the parents who can't handle the hard stuff. Let me tell you, Mrs. G, we have gay students, and I know of one girl who had an abortion this year, and she was terrified to tell her parents. There are a couple kids who have chlamydia too." Kitty rolled her eyes. "It's pretty much a soap opera at school. Drama, drama, drama."

"What's clam…eda?" Adam asked, his green eyes glistening. He knew it was something his mom wouldn't want to answer.

"Chlamydia," Nina stepped in, "is when it hurts when you pee."

Adam looked down, and his eyes got wide. "Can I get it?"

"No," Mia said quickly. "Not unless you are having sexual activity. Do you want to talk about sexual activity?"

"NO, eewww, Mom, I'm ten." Adam swallowed his last piece of food and ran upstairs, shouting, "Ewwwww."

"Well, I would if he wanted." Mia laughed. "I don't want to be a repressed parent."

Kitty laughed too. "I mean, whether we read about sex or not, whether we talk to teachers or our parents, it's happening. Sex is happening." Nina eyed her sister. They'd had many discussions about every male and female body part, thanks to Nina's extensive medical knowledge. Nina put condoms in Kitty's room just so they were available, but had let Kitty make her own decisions on the matter.

"And, no, not yet, Nina." Kitty pushed her glasses up and looked at Nina. "I know what you are thinking, but Jerry and I are just partners, and my mind is on other things. Thank you very much."

Both Mia and Nina averted their gazes but secretly sighed with relief. They didn't have to worry about Kitty yet.

Kitty continued, "We are going to grow up sooner rather than later, and reading the word 'fuck' isn't going to change that." Kitty wiped the grease from her mouth and left to play video games with Adam.

"Why does it seem so easy for her?" Mia asked Nina.

"I know, right? At that age, I was so bent out of shape," Nina agreed. "Girls in general were so insecure. My insecurities rendered me mute. But then, even the most popular girls were always asking, *Do you like my hair? Do you like my outfit?* Desperate to be accepted."

"That was Camila. God, I couldn't have cared less whether or not she had bangs, but she could go on and on about it. I bet she is asking everyone whether to tell her sister that she is pregnant with her sister's ex-husband's baby." Mia shook her head in annoyance. It wasn't that Camila was pregnant so much that bothered her; it's that she was keeping it a secret. Did they think she was that stupid again?

"And now," Nina started waving her hands, "women need advice on everything. *Should I date him? Should I break up with him? Should I get implants?* Then you say yes or no, and they ignore you anyway. Then stop asking me!" Nina laughed.

"Oh, I have always hated those types. At my age, they go around asking the grocery store clerk if they should get a divorce. Like it will be decided by a poll! If you need people's advice, something is wrong with you. I didn't talk to anyone about Eric, not even my parents. He lied, he cheated, and he was out of here!" Mia pointed to her front door for effect.

"But, Mia, why is standing up for yourself, or just being okay with yourself, so isolating? I mean, I'm still home alone in sweatpants. Maybe if I could be more shallow, wear ridiculous outfits, and worry about Kardashian lip gloss, then maybe…"

"No, no, shut your face." Mia shook her red locks back and forth. "You are beautiful and perfect, and your time will come. Don't change one damn thing."

"Thanks, Mia." And as if on cue, Mia's phone pinged, and Mathew's name appeared. Nina eyed it and smiled.

"Well, you are certainly giving me hope," Nina said.

But still, there was a nagging sense that everything wasn't right for Mia. Would Matthew disappoint and deceive her like Eric and Camila? Could Eric and Camila ever be able to show her a modicum of respect? Speaking of respect, would a whiny millennial like Tyler Dunning best her at work? Mia knew if she kept quiet, she would be a sitting duck, *quack quack*. She needed to figure out what she wanted.

Chapter 30
That's Sports

Dave was beside himself. Ken had only been texting back one-word answers like yes and no. About buying the tennis club, Ken had just said, "Yes. Will be profitable." And that was it. No plans were being made to meet up. When Dave asked, he got from Ken, "Busy. I will try soon."

That kind of vague text Dave was unable to decipher. He liked clear answers. Were they over? Was that it? He didn't have the heart to pursue anyone else and ignored his apps. Ken had been so easy to be with and fun. Well, at least for Dave, maybe not delightful for others. Ken was just as emotionally distant as Dave, but that appealed to him. He liked how Ken smelled, which was a dealbreaker for Dave. The German company Nivea made Ken's aftershave, so Dave bought himself some to smell like Ken. Also, he liked how Ken assumed things. If Dave got up to get something from the mini bar in their standard hotel room, Ken presumed Dave would get him something.

Sometimes Ken snapped his fingers like hurry up now. But the gesture made Dave laugh. He knew women would find that kind of command gesture de-moralizing, but it was non-verbal efficiency for Dave. In fairness, Ken put up with Dave sleeping atop the bed sheets like a weirdo. Dave constantly tidied their hotel room because everything had a place and needed to stay there. Ken had not argued. How was Dave supposed to find another weirdo equal to Ken and himself? The thought made him feel empty and sad in a way he had never felt before. Dave had never remotely sensed anything close to love for another. His parents, sure, but that was a dull, distant love that he could detach from. He wouldn't miss them when they left for the rat place, but he already missed Ken.

So Dave got high and went to his favorite bar, Flanigan's. It was his preferred bar because the bartenders knew him and never bothered to ask him a question. They just placed drinks before him, and he could watch sports on the eight TVs they had strategically placed throughout the place. Not that Dave was interested in the actual games, but in the outcomes and his bets.

Right now, he was happy because the Bundesliga, the German soccer league, was playing on TV number four. Bayern Munich against Borussia Dortmund, two excellent rival teams. Dave, for the most part, enjoyed soccer because they didn't stop except for fouls and injuries in two 45-minute halves. And Germans weren't the kind who fell faking a kick to the shin, so usual play went as planned. He had money on the game, which should have made him nervous. But he was too depressed about Ken and didn't celebrate when Mueller got a penalty. The penalty was in his favor because he picked Bayern to win. Also, soccer was easier to watch because the players were more attractive than most sports. They were lean and athletic, and badass. For instance, Mats Hummels, Dormund's defensive player, was a twenty in Dave's mind. And soccer players didn't have tobacco in their mouths or pants that made their asses resemble J-Lo's. So Dave settled at the bar and didn't notice the large man sitting next to him.

Dave didn't ever initiate contact or, god forbid, small talk in public places. But the man's odor offended Dave. It was meaty and musty, as if he had been walking uphill with a dead animal on his back.

"What's that shit? Some Euro trash nonsense?" Jimmy shouted to no one. "Those pussies over there don't know how to play real sports. They call it football. That shit ain't football. Football is when you strike a man. That's sports." Jimmy had a Bud Light bottle in front of him.

Dave had a stiff gin and tonic, maybe one too many, and responded, "Well, that's a pussy beer." He hadn't looked at the man directly, just at the soccer game.

"What'd you say?" Jimmy turned his sizable shoulders toward Dave and poked him in the arm.

"I said that's a pussy beer. Real men, in your terms, like to get hit, so I'd assume they would like something stronger to drink than watered-down piss." Dave still didn't turn away from the TV. Bayern was headed for another goal; if he turned away, he would miss it. This goal would win the game, at least in terms of his money on it.

"Hey, I wouldn't talk like that to me. Not a good idea." Dave had no idea he was sitting next to an ex -con who once used his fork to stab an inmate over a piece of french toast. Jimmy said slowly, "Are you even American? Americans don't watch that shit. Go back to your own fucking country to watch that shit."

"Am I American? Yes. That's a stupid question unless Hillsdale is in Germany. And, in fact, 3.5 billion people watch soccer each year, and 32% of Americans watch it. So Americans do watch this 'shit,' in your vernacular." Dave was sipping his gin and tonic when a hand slammed down his wrist on the bar, spilling his drink.

Jimmy leaned in close, and Dave could smell something of a fast-food nature and cigarettes on his breath. Dave didn't get a good look at him because he kept watching the game. But the paw on his wrist was large and had a tattoo running up its side. It looked like a malnourished dragon.

"Don't fuck with me, asshole," Jimmy growled.

"I wouldn't fuck you. You are not my type." And then Dave only felt pain and the world went black.

When Dave opened his eyes, he was lying on the bar floor, and his favorite bartender, Shari, was leaning over him. She smelled of strawberry shampoo and had obviously been eating breath mints, thank god.

"Dave, are you okay?" She looked worried, but knew not to touch him. She was well-aware of his eccentricities.

"Who won?" Dave sat up and rubbed his head.

"Dave, that jerk just clocked you. We kicked him out, but did you know him?"

"Did I know him? No, people I know don't hit me. Well, not yet anyway."

"Sure you are okay?"

"Yeah. Gin always makes everything a little less painful. So may I have another?"

Shari just shook her head; what else was there to do? Dave got on his barstool and watched Bayern beat Dortmund 3-1.

Most people would have been bothered by what had just happened. Maybe they would have called the police. But not Dave. He rubbed his head and drank his drink, which Shari had said was on the house. Dave didn't care about the large stranger, who was of no significant consequence to him. Dave's mind was still on Ken's silence. Even real physical pain didn't take away the ache in his heart.

He pulled out his phone and texted Peter. "I should have the money to buy the club soon."

Peter texted back immediately, "?"

"That is not a proper question, Peter," Dave texted, smirking. He knew the response would annoy his buddy. Dave could be funny too.

Peter responded, "HOW DO YOU HAVE THE MONEY? IS THAT BETTER?" Dave could imagine Peter's face scrunched up to his phone, wondering. Dave smiled. He would enjoy being in business with him and the many antics, like on a sitcom, that would ensue.

Dave sent him a winky emoji and put his phone back in his pocket. Dave had taken Peter's advice and calculated all the missed tuition his parents hadn't had to pay. He included four years at Hillsdale Prep, where his brother and sisters had gone. Since they had all gone to State school for college, he could only calculate so much for that. His siblings were not Ivy League material, not like his best friend. Dave had gone back and looked at the tuition cost from years ago. He didn't want to overestimate and have his father nickel and dime him. Dave had been so kind as to subtract room and board since he was 18. He researched what renting a bedroom in an apartment, plus utilities, would have cost. He also made a general estimate of how much feeding him had cost. It took time to find the accurate figures, adding them all together and then subtracting all the other statistics. Dave marveled at how much it costs to be a human on the planet, let alone raise one. He would never have four kids. How ridiculous. So much money, and for what? To have persons around that one is responsible for both mentally and fiscally? Jeez, no thanks.

The spreadsheets were down to the most minute detail he could present to his parents. Dave hoped they would be impressed. Though, he more so hoped they would impress Ken. He imagined Ken holding them up to his face and making the little grunting noises he made when he read numbers. He also would bob his head, like, *yes, yes, yes…this is all very good.* Ken wouldn't have said "job well done" or something stupid like that. He would have looked at him, like, *Get on with it then.* And that would have been all the praise Dave would have needed.

But there was also a second set of spreadsheets. One that Dave would not divulge to his parents, but maybe to Peter when the time came. They were in a separate file on his computer marked "PORN" in case his parents wanted to snoop around. Those spreadsheets contained detailed data on every online gambling bet Dave had placed. It had his wins and losses. There were dates, times, teams, and games in one file. Another broke down his ability at Blackjack and Texas Hold-em. He even played Mahjong, the game women tended to play. It was hard to learn at first. The tiles were a mixture of symbols and numbers. But the game intrigued him with its calculating, and naturally, he found money games on the internet. It didn't yield as much as poker, with grannies counting their grocery store money to play. But it was the most enjoyable out of all of them.

The last file in that folder was the link to his online bank account. That was where he could use PayPal to buy into games or deposit his winnings—what had started as fun had now turned into an intense night-time activity over the past few weeks. The goal was to buy the Hillsdale Club and house outright from his parents. Dave had to admit that the whole plan sounded too lofty when he started. But when he pulled out his phone and checked his online account, he saw that the winnings from the soccer game had already been deposited. Because somewhere the gods had blessed the Germans with fast legs (they run an average of 7-10 miles per game) and a love for a game that only lasted 90 minutes, Dave was richer. He forgot all about the dull throb of the lump forming on the back of his head. He tipped Shari nicely and left the bar. He was $20,000 richer, after all. Olé Olé Olé.

Chapter 31

One Last Shot

After Peter got the text from Dave, he knew he had to get up his courage and see his father about the money. No one wants to ask people, especially their parents, for money. It felt demeaning, but there wasn't a bank in the world that would loan him money. His parents had been so distracted by Bob's health that he hesitated to bring it up. But finally, his father was more relaxed around him, or maybe he was just stoned. Peter didn't want to screw up again and piss him off.

Peter didn't call ahead but showed up at his childhood home. Maybe he should have called. He realized you shouldn't barge into people's homes since others had done it to him. Life wasn't some giant frat house with the door open. But here he was, pulling up on his bike the same way he did when he was thirteen and dumping it on the lawn. He liked the feeling that he could go home, and it would be there. He understood Dave's need to have that stability. The one place that felt right, and you felt right in it.

His parents' house had the same trees, bushes, and hide-a-key rock that had been outdated since the '90s. The front door still squeaked, and his father could never fix it. Also, Peter never had to knock.

"Hello? Mom? Dad?" he called.

"Oh, Peter!" Edie came from the kitchen covered in flour. He noticed she had taken to wearing her gray hair down more and less makeup on her face. "Thank goodness, come help me." She shooed him into the kitchen.

The room was a mess. Ingredients and pots covered all the surfaces. Edie explained, "I haven't cooked in years, and I wanted to try out different pie recipes for Thanksgiving. Can you get the trays from the top shelf?" It dawned on Peter that he hadn't told his mother he wouldn't be home for Thanksgiving, less than two weeks away.

He reached for the trays. "Mom, I'm sorry, I won't be here." Peter felt terrible.

She looked at him and smiled. "I know, honey. You have that big tennis tournament! Your father and I can't wait!"

"What? You know about that?" Peter was dumbstruck.

Edie came over and put her hand on his cheek. "I know we have been so distracted lately. I'm sorry about your father's health and all. But it was so impressive when I stopped by the club the other day. That girl Kitty is something!" Peter looked like a dog hearing a high-pitched sound.

Edie continued, "Cami told me all about it. And Hillsdale is rooting for you two! So how could we miss it?"

Peter was happy that his parents wanted to be involved in his life. "So what's with all the baking?"

"I want to have a post-Thanksgiving party after the tournament. I want to get to know Kitty and, of course, her darling sister, Nina. My goodness, she was Bob's nurse. How small a town is it?" Edie said nonchalantly. "I thought, if you win, we could have a soiree." Peter's mind began to reel. Nina in his house, and god, what if Ashley came? Oh shit, he'd have to pretend to be Ashley's boyfriend if the Tinsdales were there.

"Mom, winning is a big if. We can't celebrate yet." Peter didn't want to think that far ahead. "Where's Dad?"

"Oh, don't be such a downer, Peter." Edie giggled. And Peter laughed because his mother had said downer.

Edie sent him to the garage, where he found Bob with an upside-down bicycle and tools spread out over the floor.

"Whatcha doing, Dad?" Peter hadn't seen his dad in the garage since he was a kid. Bob was wearing his Costco sweatpants and an old Supertramp t-shirt. He had let his hair grow a little, and there was some stubble on his face. It was so unlike him to look relaxed. His heart condition had softened him.

"I think I might ride this old thing more. According to the doctor, I need mild exercise. Now, between the kale smoothies your mother is forcing me to drink and this..." he spread his hands out, "I am going to live forever. Maybe we can ride around together?" Peter again was dumbstruck. They never did things together. Or anything that he could remember since soccer practice when he was ten.

"Sure, Dad, sounds good. I came here to ask you something, and I hope you don't get mad."

He had Bob's attention. "You are assuming I will get angry. Is that what you think of me, son?" Uh, oh, Peter didn't like the sound in his voice.

"No, not at all," Peter lied. Here goes. "So, Dad, the Dins are selling the Hillsdale Club, and their son, Dave, and I want to buy it. I want to be more of a coach and be in charge. We have run the numbers, and the club can make a good living for us. I think— No, I know it's what I want to do. It feels right, like the direction I want to go in."

"So why would that make me mad, son?"

"Well, you can assume I don't have any money, and I doubt the bank would give me a loan. I thought, since you didn't have to pay for two years of Yale, and you paid all that money for Charlie to go to school…"

"You think I owe you that money?" Bob now tilted his head. Peter didn't like the tone of his voice.

"No, well, yes, maybe. You were willing to pay for my future back then, so why not now?"

"You think I owe it to you." Bob didn't ask a question this time, but stated it. "And you are here to collect."

"Well, Dad, when you say it like that, you make it sound sinister."

"Like emotional bribery?" Bob raised his eyebrows.

"See, I knew you would get mad."

"Who says I'm mad? Apparently, I owe my son a large sum of money because he dropped out of college." Bob started spinning the wheel on the upside down bike. Peter could read the tension on his face.

"No, Dad, I've asked all wrong. You don't owe me, but since you didn't spend the money on me back then, maybe you would now?"

"Then why didn't you ask me to be an investor? You want me to open my wallet and give you my money because you are my son?"

"Shit, Dad. It's not like that." Peter's heart was racing. This was going south fast. "I mean, would you want to be an investor? Do you want to run a tennis club?" Peter was backpedaling. No, he didn't want his dad to be involved. He wanted it to be his own business.

"What do you want, son? What do you really want?" Bob wouldn't look at him.

Peter held his breath for a second, then blurted, "I want to own it myself. I want a future. I want to build something that is my own."

Bob stared at him, taking a moment. "You know why I would pay for you to go to college?" Peter shook his head, knowing better than to say anything. "That piece of paper would have been proof you did something hard, finished your degree, and saw it through to the end. That degree would show others that you could accomplish that. No matter what you tried for the rest of your life, you proved that you could do something hard. That's why people want to see a degree from Yale. But you walked out, didn't you? You couldn't do it, the first big task of your life."

Peter grasped it now and felt all the disappointment his father had felt. Now he felt it in himself.

"I failed," Peter admitted. "You are right. I didn't work hard, and I failed my classes. They might have kicked me out, so I just left. I took the easy way out."

Bob sighed. "Why didn't you tell me?"

"Because, well, it would disappoint you, and I think I couldn't admit to myself that I wasn't what everyone thought I was. "

Bob continued, "So what's different now? What's going to stop you from walking away? Businesses go under all the time. Hell, you don't even have a business degree. What would you know about running the club?"

"I'd learn," Peter said meekly. He felt childish and stupid. Ashamed. He hadn't done anything in 25 years to prove his father wrong.

"So why now? What makes this different?" Bob asked.

Peter felt tears in his eyes. Why was this such a tricky question? It sounded all fun with Dave. Sure, buy a business! Maybe he was being naive. This wasn't high school anymore. He couldn't just write a term paper last minute and get an A. He couldn't just smoke a bong and forget to show up for work. This now felt surprisingly real.

"Dad, I get it. I'm sorry. You are right. First, you don't owe me anything, and I was stupid to assume you did. I'm sorry about that. And, yeah, I have kind of just been coasting along. I know I haven't shown that I have ever taken things seriously." Peter thought about the pot brownie he had given his dad. Oh god, he was a screw-up.

"But, Dad, remember how I told you I don't know what to do until it is right in front of me? You know, like playing tennis? How, when the ball is coming at me, then I know what to do? Well, this is right in front of me, and I want it. I want to make something of myself. I want to be responsible for myself. But I need help." Peter stared at the floor. He knew there was nothing else to say. His father was immune to any other argument. Bob had seen right through him, but at least now, Peter was being honest. He laughed a little to himself. Kitty would have been proud.

"Okay, let's make a deal." Bob looked at Peter earnestly. He walked over to Peter and put his hands on his son's shoulders.

"You win this tournament. You coach the hell out of this girl your mother told me about. She sounds pretty promising. You win, and you get the money. You follow through, not for the girl's sake but for yours. You get this one last shot."

Peter stared into his father's eyes.

"One last shot," Peter repeated. Bob held out his hand, and Peter looked at it. He put his palm into his father's and felt his firm grip. It was scary and reassuring at the same time. They shook. But then Bob put his arm over Peter's shoulder.

"I'm rooting for you, son."

And Peter could only say, "Thanks, Dad."

Then Bob said, "It's all up to you." And Peter felt the weight of his future finally come crashing down on him.

Chapter 32
Animal Crackers

Nina saw the car again slowly going past their house. A tinted window was slightly down, and a puff of smoke streamed into the cool November air. She didn't like it. This was the third time, and it felt orchestrated. Some people didn't believe in coincidences, and now Nina was starting to think that way too. Was someone following her? Did Kitty get into some trouble?

Nina went upstairs to Oma and Pop's old room, which was now hers. Most of their things had been cleared out except the furniture. Nina's photographs adorned the bureau, and her clothes lay strewn over the old chair in the corner. The closet had nothing left of Oma and Pop except one shoebox. Nina pulled it down and wiped off the dust. Opening the lid, the old revolver lay on a terry cloth towel. Nina had never fired a gun, and she was not sure Pop ever had. Who knew if it worked? She pulled out her phone, googled .38 special, and watched a couple videos about using it. Kitty wasn't a kid anymore, so she didn't worry about her accidentally finding it and shooting the neighbor's head off. The bullets were kept in the back of her underwear drawer. She put the gun and the shells on the bed.

Even just touching the gun sent a shiver through Nina. She had seen a few gunshot wounds in the ER. Hillsdale wasn't immune to the crazed gun nuts in America. Usually, it was some old guy cleaning his pistol or a wife getting vengeance on her bastard husband. She had never once seen proof that a gun was protection from a robbery or home invasion. Most of the time, it was an accident or some wahoo getting revenge. She knew a home was more likely to have a gun incident with a gun, and it was safer to be without one.

But she was a single woman with a teenage girl in the house. Pop had wanted her to keep it just in case. He said he could rest easy knowing she had some protection. So Nina kept it. Never once had she even thought about using it until now.

Carefully, she loaded the bullets, hoping she was overreacting. It was just a strange car, but still, her instinct told her to be prepared. Nina had seen how the world worked once upon a time, and evil can rear its ugly head whether you are a good person or not. The image of sweet Kitty, just a toddler, came to her. Kitty had been a fairly large baby, and as a toddler, she had rolls of fat on her arms and legs. She was always unsteady on her feet, adjusting to her growing limbs. Her hands had little sausage fingers that made Kitty laugh uncontrollably when Nina sucked on them. Kitty had that belly laugh that rocket-fired across the room even at a young age.

But she could never forget finding her little sister squirming in a pool of blood, slipping and unable to get up. Her mother's lifeless body next to her, Kitty was pounding her fists on her mother's back, saying, "Momma, wake up. Momma, I'm hungry." Blood was everywhere coming from her mother's head. Nina had rushed to Kitty and picked up the child, inspecting her for any cuts or bruises. Her arms had bruises, but the blood had been their mother's.

"Shhh, Kitty," Nina had said softly into her blonde locks, scared to make a noise. And Kitty, who always took Nina's direction, quieted down and nestled her head in Nina's neck. "Nima, I'm hungry." Back then, she had been "Nima" until Kitty could say Nina right. They had been in the kitchen, and Nina grabbed a box of animal crackers on the table while tightly holding Kitty. She was frantic but knew to stay calm and trust her instincts.

Kitty's childhood blanket was hanging on the back of the kitchen chair. It was a large green blanket with colorful daisies that she slept with every night. Nina grabbed the blanket and threw it over Kitty's head. It was the only source of protection. Nina rushed the child quietly to her bedroom. Moving her old sneakers out of the way, she put Kitty down on her closet floor and placed a finger over her lips. "Shhh," she whispered. "I'll be right back." Nina placed the box of cookies in Kitty's hand, and the child was immediately distracted. Nina stopped and listened for any movement in the apartment. Hearing none, she tiptoed to her mother's bedroom. Carefully, terrified to make any sound, she lifted the phone receiver and slowly pressed 911. She heard, "What is your emergency?"

Nina held a hand over her mouth and the receiver. "I'm at 1686 Carol Street, Apartment 2. I'm 12 years old, and I have a sister who's three. My mother is dead. Please come now. My grandparents are Sean and Nina O'Connor. They live in Hillsdale, Massachusetts. Please call the O'Conner Auto Repair shop." Then Nina hung up.

Standing there, she listened again for movement, then tiptoed back to Kitty. She wrapped the bloody blanket tighter around her. She closed the closet door and waited. Kitty clutched Nina as if she knew to be quiet. Tears ran down Nina's face, and Kitty wiped each one away with her hand alternating between eating an animal cracker.

Nina shook the memory from her mind. She never wanted to return to that time and had worked hard to erase it. But it would always be there. That fear that someone could hurt them. Or worse, wanted to hurt them.

She put the loaded gun back in the box, but instead of putting it in the closet, she slipped it under her bed. If anything happened, she could grab it. Nina reassured herself it was better if Kitty never knew about the gun at all.

Chapter 33
Death Star

Adam swiveled his chair toward Kitty. He was doing his math homework, and Kitty was doing hers. Hers looked a lot more complicated than his.

"What's calculus?" Adam asked. He was only on fractions.

"It's a pain in my ass, that's what it is," Kitty replied, and Adam laughed.

"Looks hard."

"Nah, math is just like an engine. You must know how to fit all the parts together to make it run. Once my Pop told me that, then it got easier."

Adam tapped his pencil against his forehead. "What if a family was like an engine? We are parts that have to fit together so we can run. But if a part is broken, then it can't. Right?"

"Very astute, little man. Why? What's up?" Kitty asked. Adam liked when he had her attention. Today, her t-shirt read, "Achtung, Baby!" which felt appropriate. Adam explained that how his family was operating would not be very good for the baby. He confessed he had known about his dad cheating on his mom, but didn't say anything. This time, he told Mia about the baby even though he had lost his electronics for the week because he didn't like lying anymore.

"Excellent point. But it's not so much about everyone lying. It's like your parents forget to be honest with each other. They are afraid of how everyone will react to the truth. Like, your aunt Camila probably feels like her sister will resent her more if she has a baby. Your dad probably is chicken because he already hurt your mom badly and doesn't want to do it again. Your mom probably doesn't want to deal with them because they seem to make it about themselves. And then no one talks to you because you're ten, and they don't want to hurt you either. It's a big pickle."

"Broken parts. But, Kitty, how can I fix it?"

"Well, little man, maybe you gotta take charge of the situation. Sometimes pointing out the obvious, whether they like hearing it or not, is the only way to get real. Like Nina, when she is acting all Nina, sitting on the couch in self-pity."

"What's self-pity?"

"Oh, grown-ups love self-pity; it's like their favorite go-to activity. They feel sorry for themselves because they are or aren't in a relationship, are out of shape, or don't make enough money… Stuff like that. Nina does that and stews about her life a lot. It's like a total waste of time. If you don't like something, then change it, duh. I'll tell you a secret. Do you know why I started playing tennis?"

"It's fun?"

"Yeah, that, but I didn't like not being somebody. I make okay grades. Let's face it, my looks are extraordinary—as in, extra ordinary. I'm not going to win any beauty contests, and my body was built for something. I didn't come out this way for nothing. So I thought, how could I harness my power? I heard that on an infomercial one night. I had to harness my power. It was tennis or boxing, and I didn't want to have someone punch me. So there I am, thinking about harnessing my power, and *boom*, I see Serena Williams modeling tennis clothes in an ad. I liked the skirts and the idea of hitting something, just not some*one*. And it turned out I was right. I'm good, and I get to buy new outfits. Win-Win."

"What if you don't win the tournament? Will you be sad?"

"Well, that could happen. But at least I tried. Then maybe I'll find something else to try. But right now, it's awesome having everyone realize I am good at something. Like, you know, I am proud of myself. That's a good feeling."

"So maybe I can do something about my family?"

"Go for it, kiddo. No one can fault you for trying."

"Can I borrow your phone?"

Adam spent a few moments texting, then handed the phone back to Kitty. "I'm sorry, Kitty, but I had to get their attention. Don't worry. I will tell them it wasn't you."

Kitty looked down at the text and started laughing. "Really threw a grenade at them, didn't you?"

Twenty minutes later, a Prius roared up the driveway, followed by Mia's station wagon.

Adam watched from his bedroom window as his parents, including Camila, charged into the house, screaming his name.

"Adam, honey, ARE YOU OKAY?" his mom was shouting.

His dad yelled, "ADAM! Adam, where are you?!"

He walked down the stairs with Kitty.

"He's fine," Kitty said.

"Why did you text us? What is wrong with you?" Eric yelled at Kitty.

"Don't yell at Kitty," Mia interjected. "What's going on?"

"Adam asked me to mediate the situation. So let me explain.

Have a seat." Kitty spread her arms toward the living room couches.

"Who are you to tell us what to do, young lady!" Camila piped in. "This isn't your family!"

"Camila, calm down," Mia said. "This wasn't exactly *your* family to begin with." Camila's head jerked, and she looked at Eric to defend her.

"Everyone, please," Kitty said calmly. "Adam sent you the text to get your attention. I'm sorry, I wouldn't have allowed it, but that's not the point." (The text from Kitty's phone read, "Come now. It's Adam!") "The point is, he's upset with how everything is going with you. Yes, you too, Camila. He hacked your email again. Adam knows he was wrong, but he found out you are pregnant. Mia knows too. So let's just put all the cards on the table, shall we?"

Mia stepped in. "Okay, Kitty, I think I know what is going on. We will take it from here."

Kitty nodded, but she waited until everyone had sat down, then asked, "Adam, you got this?"

Adam, still standing, gave her a thumbs-up, and Kitty left.

Adam started, "Mom, Dad, Aunt Camila. First, I apologize for invading your privacy. I promise I will stop."

"You are in big trouble, young man." Eric sat fuming.

"Eric, give it rest..." Mia said, rolling her eyes. "Go on, Adam."

"Dad, I knew about your affair with Camila. I saw you guys kissing a long time ago. Mom, I didn't know how to tell you." Everyone gasped, and Camila went beet red.

"Oh, Adam, I'm so sorry," Mia said.

"Mom, it's okay. That's old news. But now, all this not telling each other stuff has to stop. We can't do that to my new baby brother or sister."

Adam continued, "I think maybe we all have a bad conscious about something, so let's just tell each other."

The adults fidgeted in their seats and looked away.

"Okay, I'll start..." Mia said. She didn't want to let Adam down. "Eric, maybe we shouldn't have gotten married. I don't think we were properly in love, and when I caught you with Camila, it was pretty easy to end our marriage. I'm sorry, Adam. I hope that didn't hurt your feelings."

"Nope, Mom, that's good." Adam nodded his head like a priest absolving her. "Dad?"

"So you admit it's your fault..." Eric said.

Camila shouted, "Eric! Stop that! We all knew you two shouldn't have gotten married!" Eric looked surprised at her defending Mia. "I shouldn't have lied to Mia like that, but, Mia," Camila looked at her sister, "you always hated me. You never thought I was good enough to be your sister. I wasn't smart enough or proper like you."

"I never hated you," Mia said defensively. "We are just so different. How could you think I hated you? We just didn't see eye to eye."

"Well, I never felt good enough," Camila whined.

"I never felt good enough either," Eric echoed. Mia sat there with hurt on her face. Adam knew that face. "Mia, you tend to be patronizing."

"Patronizing!" Mia shouted.

"Yeah. Remember how controlling you were when Adam was a baby? Do this, do that, always on me about how I was doing things wrong." Eric made a dumb face.

"Yeah, I didn't want our kid to die because you thought the laundry detergent was baby formula!"

"See! Right there, you never thought I was good enough. I could have figured it out if you had given me the space. But always nagging..."

"Really, Eric? Again, it was our child's life. You can't just go out for a run while a toddler is asleep!"

"Okay, that was only once, maybe twice…"

"Hey!" Adam cried. "Stop this shit right now!" The adults immediately went silent. "Dad, Mom is just Mom. She tries hard, and that's not a crime against you guys."

"Thanks, Adam, but, honey, you don't have to defend me. I'm sorry you two feel that way. I didn't mean to make you feel that way," Mia said meekly.

"We are getting married," Camila announced.

"When?" That was all Mia could say.

"New Year's Day," Eric responded.

Silence.

"Anything else?" Mia asked.

"I'm having twins again."

"Really?" Adam almost shouted. His excitement was palpable and made the grown-ups laugh. "I get two for the price of one!"

Camila looked at him. "So you are excited about this?"

"Aunt Camila, I get a bigger family. But please, can you have boys this time? I don't know much about Barbie dolls. I mean, Luna and Aria don't play with Legos and watch *Frozen* on repeat." Adam rolled his eyes.

Eric looked perplexed. "Adam, you're okay with all this?"

"Dad, yeah, I am. But, Dad, you know that means you must spend time with all of us." Eric turned a shade of purple.

Mia said softly, "I think, Eric, that Adam wants to spend more time with you. I know he doesn't say it because he's ten. But I think he also feels a pull between you and me. How about we try to make an effort to put this past us? As he said, it's old news."

"You guys have to stop with the self-pity," Adam said abruptly. It made Mia laugh, and Eric's mouth dropped open, but he didn't say anything.

"That's right, Adam, that's completely right," Mia agreed.

"Mom, maybe Matthew can hang out with us too!"

Now it was Mia's turn to be embarrassed.

Camila looked at her sister. "Matthew? That wouldn't be that dreamy doctor at the hospital?" Camila looked excited.

"Yes." Mia couldn't help but smile too.

"Good for you, big sis. Well done."

Mia laughed at how easily her sister was impressed. Or was it that Mia was trying to move on, which meant Camila could get out of the doghouse? But Mia felt too tired to point that out and have another argument. They all looked at Adam, almost pleading that they didn't have to continue the at-home therapy session.

Adam wasn't stupid, and this was only a start for all of them. His mother and father may never get along, but at least he tried. He had done something about his problems and felt proud of himself.

But he pushed it a little too far. "Hey, anybody want to go to the Lego store and get the new Star Wars Death Star? It's really cool."

Eric looked at him and smiled. "Nice try, kiddo, but you are still grounded."

So then he asked for pizza instead, and Mia said yes. She didn't offer for Eric and Camila stick around, but Adam took the pizza as a win.

Chapter 34
I Dissent

"Mr. Baxter, always a pleasure," Mia said, entering her office.

"Not today, Mrs. Golding."

"Why?" Mia put down her coffee mug and started rearranging her papers. She was in a good mood. Mia felt lighter after Adam's impromptu intervention. Eric, Camila, and she vowed to be on better terms, and she even congratulated them on the wedding, which she thought was very big of herself. Camila had told her it would take place in the local Buddhist Zen garden, and Mia managed not to laugh out loud. What was lingering in her mind was how Eric had called her patronizing. She knew she had been uptight about Adam as a baby; she could admit that. But what new mother wasn't? It was justified, right? Or could she have been a little more forgiving of Eric's faults? Yeah, that could have been true too. What do they say about actors? That they get notes about their performances? These were her notes. And she made Camila feel like she wasn't good enough. Mia once told her people went to Bali because they couldn't go to college. Ouch. Okay, maybe she could see that too. Damn.

Mia never considered herself a snob, but maybe she was, just a little. Admittedly, she thought she was on morally higher ground, but it didn't mean she didn't weirdly love them. She wouldn't have been so annoyed by them if there wasn't love. But now, if she thought about it, they weren't exactly her problem anymore. They could be each other's problems. Oh, she would always have to tolerate their shallowness. She was sure Camila would have her girls on vegan diets in a couple years. But maybe if Eric had another baby—well, two babies—he might get the ass-kicking he needed. No way was Camila going to be able to handle all of them alone. In fact, Mia thought this was going to be fun to watch. And how proud of Adam she was. He saw this as an opportunity, not a hindrance. Adam didn't have a speck of jealousy, just excitement. How long had it been since he was excited, especially with his new two-family situation?

Of course, she hadn't come to all this on her own. She and Matthew had talked into the night about the possibility of change. Who they were in their first marriages and when they were younger wasn't necessarily who they had to remain. She liked that. They could become better versions of themselves, and be better versions of themselves with different people. This was his not-so-subtle way of telling her he liked her. He was smooth, she had to admit. Maybe there *was* a Mr. Darcy out there for her? Probably not, but hey, she could be open to it. She and the doctor could take things slow and see where it went. Maybe it was best to live in the present for a while.

"Mrs. Golding, I hate to be the bearer of bad news, but are you listening?"

"Yes, Mr. Baxter, sorry. What is it?" Mia turned her attention to him.

"There will be an all-parent school meeting about the English department the night before vacation."

"What? Who approved that?"

"Our very own King Lear, Principal Jenkins."

"Now, Mr. Baxter, play nice."

"He approved Mr. Dunning holding a forum."

"That's in just a few days! Lord, I feel like my life is whack-a-mole." Mia sat down hard in her chair. One problem goes away, another pops up. "What are we going to do? Will the parents have pitchforks? You're the one who has been doing this for forty years."

"Mrs. Golding, you know why I love teaching Shakespeare? Because it has survived generations. It has misogyny, bigotry, race, sexism, and violence—all the things people are talking about nowadays. But the one resolute, incontrovertible fact old Willie reminds us is that all those awful, terrible topics existed hundreds of years ago. Being rotten is in the DNA of our humanity. Even the Bible tells us that. Works of literature over time, cultures, and countries have the same resounding theme: how terrible we are. We are shit human beings. But somehow it's wrong to write about it now? In our century? Horseshit. Because Shakespeare's language is so off-putting for today's zealots, most haven't read *King Lear* or *Othello*. Oh, they want to say I'm a white, old man teaching white, old man literature; thus, I exclude people. But we all are just writers' muses. No one is excluded from derision unless you are a perfect human being who has never lied, cheated, stolen, had sex, acted greedy, jealous, gluttonous, and so on. No matter who you are, somewhere there is a seed of yourself in that weird Elizabethan language. Just dare to argue with me otherwise."

"That's rather grim, teaching kids we are horrible."

"Yes, but it's like Aesop and, again, the Bible. By pointing out our defects, maybe we can avoid them. They are cautionary fables...as is your dear *Handmaid's Tale*."

"Fair point. But is it greedy or narcissistic or irresponsible to teach what we want to teach?"

"Mrs. Golding, we wouldn't be teachers otherwise."

"Then that would mean Mr. Dunning can teach what he wants."

"Yes, the same would hold for him—freedom of speech, blah blah blah." Mr. Baxter waved his wrinkled hand like Merlin. "But, Mrs. Golding, what if no one wants to learn what he is teaching?"

"Touché, Mr. Baxter." And Mia smiled with hope.

A while later, Kitty entered her office and plopped down like it was her living room. They had undoubtedly crossed all lines of teacher/student, grownup/child at this point. Mia gave in. It was Kitty, after all. She was wearing a t-shirt that said "I Dissent" with a picture of Ruth Bader Ginsburg. Mia was happy Hillsdale Prep didn't have a dress code.

"What's up, Kitty?"

"Adam said everything went pretty well with you guys." Kitty was picking something out of her teeth and inspecting it in her fingernail.

"Yes, it did. I suppose, again, I owe you a big thank you. I hate that you have become embroiled in our family drama. It's not exactly a place you should be in."

"Don't sweat it, Mrs. G. It's boring with just me and Nina, so I look at this like practice. Someday, who knows, I might have my own weirdo family."

Mia chuckled.

Kitty asked, "So what's up with this Mr. Dunning crap? There's a meeting? He told Gavin Hicks that he shouldn't wear rainbows on his clothing because it was too suggestive. He didn't, you know, outright say 'gay,' but Gavin knew what he meant. Is he trying to make us all conservative or something?"

"I think the best way to put it is Mr. Dunning is trying to control the narrative."

"Control the narrative, huh? Do you mean to get us to think the way he does? All conservative and small-minded?"

"I am not at liberty to discuss with a student the nature of my colleague's actions. It would be frowned upon and disrespectful."

"I gotcha, Mrs. G. You can't go stirring up trouble. Respect. But that can't stop me." Kitty winked at Mia.

"Go to class, Kitty. Be good, learn things, and stay out of trouble." Mia smiled at her with appreciation, not admonishment.

"You know the saying 'Curiosity killed the cat'?" Kitty grinned.

"Yes, Kitty," Mia replied, waiting for the point.

"And satisfaction brought her back," Kitty bellowed loudly and left.

Oh boy, Mia thought and rubbed her eyebrows.

Chapter 35
Them Apples

Dave's leg bounced up and down like some men's did when they sat. He had observed that more men seemed to have this tick than women. What brain nerve short-circuited in a man that went directly to his leg? Dave didn't know how to label it, but his left leg bounced uncontrollably as he sat at his dining room table.

He presented his parents with labeled and color-coded folders. First was the club's business, its yearly gains and losses, expenses, and profits. The second was their home's estimated value and also estimated repair. In the process, Dave discovered the roof was outdated, according to Hillsdale code. The third folder contained Dave's meticulous effort to show how much he had cost them as a child and how much they had saved. It was all there, in numbers.

His parents arrived at the table with their martinis and cheap reader glasses from the local Costco. His father's glasses sat askew on his head because he didn't bother to get proper readers from the optometrist that would accommodate the fact that one ear was higher than the other.

Dave made his case, but not before having two rum and Cokes beforehand. He was no dummy.

His parents, Donna and Derek, passed the papers between them. He watched them silently, pointing to lines and charts that Dave had made like an artist. They sipped their drinks, and he realized they would have made fantastic poker players. He had no idea what they were thinking. Donna would tap Derek on the shoulder and use a finger to show Derek a line, and vice versa. They had a harmony Dave had never noticed before. They *mmmm*'d and *oooh*'d their way through each sheet like it was the original copy of the Declaration of Independence. After a while, Dave just watched and was impressed by their attention to detail. Maybe they were like him after all? When Dave was a child, he fantasized that they weren't his parents—with his mother's aggressive neediness and his father's complete and total lack of reality—but they hadn't built the club as idiots. Dave could see that now.

He did not reveal his online gambling habit. Instead, he had "projected" his income, a term he learned from Ken. He showed them his profits so far, a total of $212,180. 31 in his bank account, and, hopefully, an added windfall of $150,000 from Peter. That was still up in the air, but Dave would bluff on that point. He projected another $75,000 could be subtracted from the total because his parents didn't pay for his education, minus the room and board. He knew it wasn't enough, but he wanted his parents to know he was serious.

He also presented them with a rental agreement for the house. First and foremost, he wanted the business, and if he could work his way toward the house, that would be great. If he kept gambling and winning online, he might pay them back in two years.

"Dave, I have to say, we are pretty impressed with your diligence."

"Thanks, Dad."

"Where did you come up with all this? We didn't know you had such economic savvy. And here we thought you just color-coded rackets!" It was a little demeaning, but Dave let it slide.

"You know, we asked Deborah, Dina, and Douglas if they wanted the business, and they all said no. I guess we never thought to ask you," his father continued. *Seriously?* Dave thought. They asked his siblings and not him?

His mother chimed in, "I mean, you don't even play tennis. You seem so uninterested in all of us. (*Fair point,* Dave thought.) The last thing we thought was that you wanted to run the business. And we didn't know you and Peter were so close. I mean, David, dear, you never tell us anything. So how were we to know?" If his mother was trying to make him feel guilty for something, it wasn't working.

"It's an awful lot to handle for someone like you." His dad had to put the knife in, didn't he?

"Someone like me?" Dave cocked his head and wanted an answer to that question.

"Well, you know, dear, you are a bit different, and you only went to public high school. This may be a little out of your element. You don't even like people. You don't even buy your own food." His mother picked at her sweater and smiled over her martini at him.

"You know, I spent years," his father was about to pile it on, "building this business. It's my legacy in Hillsdale. It provides for the family, but also, Hillsdale relies on it. I don't know if you are the right fit."

Dave took in a deep breath. *Oh, what the hell,* he thought. What did he have to lose if they had already written him off?

"Mom, Dad, you guys haven't even been a part of the club this past year. Who do you think has been keeping up the shop? The books? The payroll? Me. And, Mother, I am not an idiot. I am autistic. I'm also gay, so there's that, and I have a boyfriend—or had, I'm not sure right now. But I am capable of love. I can be around people. I have friends like Peter and Kitty. Kitty Kittrick, by the way, is going to be a tennis prodigy coming from your club. Did you guys even know that? Peter is starting her on the junior circuit, and all of Hillsdale is talking about it. Peter and I will find more prodigies and make the club a mecca for them. Did you guys ever dream of that? Furthermore, did you happen to notice the $200,000 I have? How do you think I got that?"

"Well, dear, I didn't want to ask. I thought maybe you had done something illegal..." His mother turned away.

"Seriously, now you think I am a criminal? Strike that, a dumb, uneducated criminal. No, I earned that money." Dave's voice was rising. It felt so good to stand up for himself. "I earned it because I am smart and an excellent gambler. And I'm not ashamed. In fact, all of this," Dave spread his arms, "has inspired me to get a business degree, or at least take some classes. Yep, I can do that. I am capable of doing that and running a business. What do you think of them apples?"

Dave didn't know when he had pushed back his chair and stood up. His leg was no longer shaking. His parents stared wide-eyed at him from their seats.

"You're gay?" his mother said. "Well, that certainly explains a lot." She shook her head like she had been missing a puzzle piece on the floor.

His father took off his glasses and stared at Dave. Dave made every effort to look him back in the eye. He could only make contact for a few seconds, but he did it.

"David Dins," his dad said slowly. "Okay."

"Okay, what?" Dave was confused.

"Okay, the business is yours. I want to go to Boca Raton, and you have the money. Okay, I agree. Why the hell not? At least it will go to one of my children; not the one I expected, but sure. What the hell." Mrs. Dins looked at her husband and shrugged her shoulders.

"Well, David, if you and Peter think you can do it, I agree."

Elation spread through his body. It was like a standoff in one of his old movies. He wished he had cards in his hand to throw down, like a straight flush or something to be dramatic. He had won and couldn't believe it.

"But, David." His mother faltered.

Then his father picked up where she had left off. "There's one thing." Dave held his breath. What? What could that "one thing" be?

"We already sold the house, dear."

Oh shit.

Chapter 36
Milkshake

The black Corolla slowly moved behind the minivan. Jimmy had been charting Kitty's movements for weeks. It was easy. She went from school to tennis or to the home of the kid she watched. She wasn't often alone, which annoyed the man. The kid with curly black hair who smoked in her car seemed to be getting free rides everywhere. And the little red-headed boy was around too much. Jimmy was waiting to get her alone.

He cruised the streets and hung around the cheap hotel in his spare time. He didn't mind. It was nice to have his freedom again. No one knew where he was, and no one had a say in where he was going. That was the part of prison he hated the most, not the food or the cells, but the fact that people were everywhere. And people created noise. Constant grating noise. His cellmate was an idiot who talked too much. He babbled about his girlfriends and how robbing banks was the coolest thing ever. Jimmy rarely spoke back to him. He preferred whatever solitude he could find. But always in his mind, he concocted a plan for when he got out.

Broke, there was hardly anyone left to turn to. Jimmy had been mainly doing grift work the past couple weeks, nicking credit cards and hitting stupid old ladies in expensive cars for money. It wasn't hard, but he needed day-to-day cash. He was looking for a big payout so he could take off. The plan was to go to Mexico and find topless women on the beach. There he could make bank robbing drunk tourists on holiday. He could live for cheap and get out of the cold for good.

Jimmy had never once dreamed of a life in a place like Hillsdale. It wasn't a life for him, even when Lily tried to convince him. She always thought she could change him, make him a decent husband or father, but she never understood. Jimmy didn't want any of that. As his father had told him, a family wasn't worth the trouble. Besides, his father only spoke to him with his belt out, and his mother, a weak woman, took off when he was twelve. Born and raised in Boston, he learned to fend for himself on the streets. People were gullible and easy to manipulate. Once you tasted using them, it was hard to think about an honest day's work.

Jimmy just needed one more hit before he could split. Adios, amigos. Maybe find a decent-looking woman to take care of him. It'd be nice to come home to a hot meal. Jesus, American women were so full of themselves. Anytime he saw a news story about their rights, he cringed. Fuck, they were all whores who wanted their cake and to eat it too. Some of them were pretty—a pretty good fuck or a pretty good pain in his ass. Yeah, he was done with life here.

The minivan pulled into a Dairy Queen, and remarkably the girl was alone. It was midday, and she was skipping school for lunch. Jimmy had had enough of following her and decided that now was the time to make his move. He rolled up next to the van and got out with ease. This was just another con, he reminded himself. Jimmy had done it a million times and had to play it right. The girl didn't look too bright anyway. She wore hot pink pants and a sweatshirt that said, "Jesus Said So." He didn't think she was religious, but maybe she was being funny. Teenagers could be real assholes.

Jimmy stood behind her in line and waited for her to get her milkshake. When she turned, she barely noticed him while enjoying the first sip of her drink. She was pulling out her phone, a glittery contraption, and about to stare at it.

Jimmy said, "Kitty? Kitty Kittrick?"

She pushed her glasses up to get a good look at him.

He smiled at her and said, "Long time, no see."

And Kitty dropped her milkshake.

Chapter 37
$19.95

"You're dead," Kitty said to her father.

"Who told you that? Your grandparents? No, my little Kitten, I'm right here. Your dear old dad, Jimmy! Surprise!"

Kitty scratched her arms, confused. Stunned, she forgot about her milkshake and walked outside. He followed.

She stammered, "You died with Mom… Someone broke into the apartment and tried to rob us. He hurt you both, and you didn't survive."

Kitty's head was swimming, and she felt dizzy. This wasn't right. Oma, Pop, and Nina said both her parents had died. Kitty's brain searched for the headstone she visited once a year. Lily O'Conner Kittrick–loving daughter and mother. It never said wife, but Kitty didn't ask why. Jimmy had no headstone because he had been cremated and spread in the ocean. But that was a lie? Who had lied to her, and why? Did Nina know Jimmy was alive? Why hadn't they seen their father in all these years?

Her whole life, Kitty had tried to search her memory for anything with them. She longed for one image of them that was hers and only hers, not just a photograph. She had only seen her father through pictures, the one or two of him they had. He looked older now, worn. But the gray eyes and large shoulders were the same. His face loomed more enormous in person. But Kitty could see all of herself in him except the blonde hair; that had been her mother's.

"Let's sit down," he said nicely, pointing to a picnic table. Kitty didn't know what else to do but obey. "What did Sean and Nina tell you about me? Where I went?"

"They just said you were dead." Kitty searched his face for some familiarity. He looked much older than the photographs she had seen.

"Am I right that they are no longer alive?" he asked, and Kitty just nodded. "Well, no wonder they didn't tell you about me. Your mother died because of an accident, and they blamed me. I didn't do it. I told everyone, but they just had to blame someone, so they blamed me. A real shame they didn't have compassion for me. I had just lost my wife. And they took you girls from me because they didn't like me. They were spiteful because Lily never got her singing career when she had you. They said it was all my fault."

Kitty could barely take this in. Her grandparents had never been hateful toward anyone.

But Jimmy continued, "So the police didn't know what to do. I explained that your mother had tripped and hit her head. It was all an accident. But some female prosecutor—always the women— had to blame me for being the man. Said I struck Lily and called it manslaughter. Total bullshit. Some women, baby girl, and I hope you aren't one of them, love to blame the men all the time."

"Did you go to jail?" Kitty asked.

"Yep, but I did my time and got out. I'm a free man. Justice is served."

"Did you kill my mother?" Kitty pushed her glasses up and stared hard at him. She wanted to get a read on him.

"As I said, it was all an accident. Huge misunderstanding, and everyone just wanted someone to blame." Kitty sat there numbly.

"Why are you here?"

"To see my baby girls! I bet Nina is all grown up now like you!"

"Yeah, but why did you stop me here? Why didn't you go to the house? You've been there before." Nothing was adding up for Kitty.

"Well, I wasn't sure how Nina would react, and I was scared I wouldn't get to see you, my little Kitten."

"Why? How would Nina react?"

"Well, as you said, your grandparents blamed me, and well, Nina was a lot older than you, so maybe she is mad at me too. Listen, you gotta know I'm really sorry about the whole mess."

Kitty didn't believe him.

"You could have tried to call us, write us letters," she said.

"Again, Sean and Nina wouldn't let me. Now, here I am to catch up with my girls!" He was watching her reactions closely. Kitty could tell. She forced herself to remain calm and still. Whenever something got overwhelming for her, Kitty could always stay quiet. She prided herself on not reacting when others did. And right now, her composure was comforting to her.

"I have to go," she said. She didn't know where to go, but just wanted to leave.

"How about I stop by the house? Give the three of us a chance to catch up?"

"Okay," was all Kitty could say, and she got up and walked to her car. She felt him watch her, and she slowed her gait. Kitty wanted to scream. Something deep inside her wanted to shout... but she didn't know what words would come out. If her father were still alive, then Nina would know. If Nina knew, then Nina had lied to her. All these years, the one person she thought had never lied to her, never betrayed her, never in a million years would she have felt she couldn't trust with her life, but now all of that was gone.

Kitty wanted to call Nina, but then she didn't. She didn't want to talk to anyone. She drove until she reached the park on the edge of Hillsdale. It was flat and green, with a white stage in the middle where the town gathered for Fourth of July and Christmas parades. There were the swing sets Oma and Pop had pushed her on. And the jungle gym where Scottie Roust had tried to push her off, but she had kicked him instead. Her whole world had been Hillsdale, her grandparents, and Nina. Never was it about her parents. They were just photographs fraying on her desk.

When Kitty was young, she would pepper Oma with questions about her parents. They had described Jimmy as an entrepreneur who didn't make much money. He was a "go-getter," they had called him. Kitty had liked the idea that her father was a man of action. They said he ran a couple small businesses and had tried to help their mother get a singing career. That was how they met. It had never sounded bad to Kitty. In her mind, they were young lovers who died too soon. Oma didn't like to talk about Lily's death, she just repeated that it was tragic.

Pop at least gave her more details. He had said Lily had been home with her, and Nina had been at school. They didn't live in the best part of town, and a man had busted into their apartment and tried to steal money or something. He had hit Lily when she protected Kitty; she had fallen against the counter and died almost instantly. Pop said her father had tried to save her, but the intruder had knifed him in the heart. Nina had come home and found Kitty and called the police.

Pop had lied.

Jimmy was alive and never stabbed. So how much of that

story was true? What could she believe? Kitty sat very still in her minivan as the thoughts turned over in her mind.

Knock, knock. There was tapping on her window. It was Bunny Ryan.

Kitty wound down the window. "Mrs. Ryan?"

"Hi, dear, are you okay?" Mrs. Ryan had a dog on a leash and stared at her worriedly.

"Yes, I'm fine. Why?"

"Well, you are sitting alone and crying." Kitty hadn't realized it until she put her hands on her face and wiped the tears. She looked at her fingers, surprised. She rarely cried.

"My dear, is there anything I can do? Did someone do something to you? Can I call someone?" Kitty looked at Mrs. Ryan's face and saw the years a woman gains. The wrinkles around the eyes and the sag of the jawline that no makeup can hide. Her hair had been colored to cover the gray. It was too bright and washed out. Mrs. Ryan wore big diamond earrings, the symbol of time served in marriage. Her hand, slightly aged and wrinkled, came through the window and rested on Kitty's shoulder.

"I'm okay, Mrs. Ryan. Something did happen, but I don't want to talk about it. I need a moment." Kitty could have lied and said something stupid like she had failed a class or gotten into a fight with a friend. Adults believed the most trivial information about children. But Kitty hated even white lies.

The dog began pulling the leash, wanting to chase a duck.

"Well, are you sure you're okay? I don't want to leave you if you aren't." Mrs. Ryan wrangled with the dog's leash. It had more control of her than she of him.

"I'll be fine. Again, I just needed a moment."

"Well, all of us do need that sometimes. Take care, sweetie." And Mrs. Ryan was pulled away by a large yellow Labrador. Kitty laughed a little. They had the same hair color.

That's why Kitty loved Hillsdale so much. Even in your worst moments, you really couldn't be alone.

She shifted the car into gear and went where she could hide. Like her sister, she didn't like surprises or being unprepared. She wanted to know more about her mother's death and her father. She needed the internet.

No one knew Kitty loved the library. The stacks of books created a protective barrier around her. Someday she wanted to grow up and have an actual library in her house, and maybe it would be in her bedroom. She had never seen that. Kitty had a favorite desk in the back, an old-fashioned wooden cubicle. The library had Wi-Fi, and Kitty set up her laptop. It was time to do some research on her family. The date April 23, 2009, was etched in her mind, because it was also engraved on her mother's tombstone. Robbery or murder would have had to show up somewhere in a newspaper. For the price of $19.95, she could also look up the criminal record of Mr. James Kittrick.

Like Oma said, if you don't know where to start, you start at the beginning.

Chapter 38
Such Damn Fools

Nina came home from the night shift. A married couple had gotten into a nasty argument, and the wife had thrown boiling water on her husband. He had been standing over her, correcting her on how to make dinner. They had been together twenty years, and the wife had had it. Twenty years of her husband inspecting the kitchen as she cooked and commenting on the pasta or the meat. Twenty years of being told she wasn't doing it right. They had made it to the hospital only to continue the fight. Searing bubbles were forming on his arm, but they took the opportunity to list all their grievances with each other. Alley cats howling were quieter. He was emotionally distant. She was frigid. He hated her sister. She had always hated his mother. She smoked too much. He drank too much. He snored. She watched TV too loudly. And on and on they went. Nina had to separate them. Was this really how marriages turned out, full of palpable resentment? Even Stan intervened, slipping both of them a valium. He, of course, agreed with the husband on all accounts.

They had to threaten to bring in the psychiatrist so the couple would calm down. But weirdly, after a few hours of sitting under the bright fluorescent lights and some warming blankets, they mellowed. They agreed to marriage counseling, and Nina watched the wife lovingly help the husband to the car through the ER doors. Maybe they just had to have a good argument and air all their pent-up grievances to move on.

Nina suggested they order more take-out quietly to the wife, and she laughed at her joke.

Now Nina was back at home, her feet aching. She hadn't seen Kitty yesterday and assumed she had been out late studying. Her bed was disheveled, and the minivan was gone, so Kitty must be at school.

Nina was surprised to hear the knock at the door. It was only 10 am. It could be the UPS guy with another package for Kitty. She reminded herself to check the credit cards and see how much all these tennis outfits cost.

When Nina opened their door, her glasses were off, and she had trouble focusing. But it was the voice that struck her. She knew that voice. It would occasionally haunt her dreams, forcing her to wake up before she screamed.

"Hey, kiddo. I'm out!" The large man held up his arms, motioning in surprise.

Nina stood holding the doorknob in shock.

"Don't you have something to say to your dear old dad? Or did you think I was dead too? No, my baby girl knew I wasn't." He winked at her. "Aren't you going to let me in?"

Nina pulled back the door and reached for her glasses in her scrub pocket. Her heart started pounding uncontrollably, and her blood pressure rose. Fear, disbelief, and shock ran through her.

She spotted the Toyota with the tinted windows parked in

front of her house. Shit, she had been right to be paranoid.

"Dad? Jimmy?" She honestly didn't know what to call him anymore. He wasn't a father to her.

Jimmy strode through the door heavy-footed. "Wow, this place hasn't changed." He was inspecting the framed photos on the walls and furniture. "I remember when Lily first brought me here. Your grandfather wasn't nice to me."

He went to the fridge and opened it. "No beer? That's a shame. This is a celebration! I wanted to toast to our reunion." He stared down at her, daring her to ruin the moment.

Nina tried to regroup. "I thought you were in jail in New Jersey."

"I was, but time served! You didn't think manslaughter was a life sentence? And thanks to all that pandemic nonsense, I got out on time. They said I wasn't eligible for good behavior, but the cafeteria incident wasn't my fault." Jimmy winked. "So, woohoo, here I am."

"You can't be here," Nina said. She was holding her arms together with her hands. Clutching her elbows, she wanted protection.

"Why, because my little Kitten thinks I'm dead? Tsk tsk, your grandparents knew better than to start a lie like that."

"No, I told Kitty that lie. Wait, have you seen Kitty?" Nina started panicking.

"Of course, my little tennis star and I had ice cream. Kitty certainly is something. I see you look more like Lily, but Kitty, she's all mine. Chip off the old block." He held up his finger and wagged it. Nina was repulsed.

"Where is Kitty?" Nina almost screamed. She was afraid he had her locked up, or worse.

"I dunno, school maybe?" he said casually. "I thought Lily had stepped out on me to have Kitty. Didn't think she was mine at first, but I see it now!"

"She is not yours, Jimmy. You lost us when you killed Mom."

"Oh, that old story? I didn't kill your mother. Did you see me kill your mother? It was an accident." He looked down at his nails casually, a sure tell for lying.

"There were bruises on Kitty and Mom, on their arms and backs, like someone had punched them. I had those bruises too, and they were from you."

"Oh, Nina. Nina, Nina. So I grabbed you a couple times, don't be so dramatic. You were never hurt that bad. I'm too strong and don't know my strength." He kept wandering around the house, touching the knick-knacks and furniture. She wanted a baseball bat to swat away his hand. These were her things, and how dare he handle them.

Nina continued calmly, "You hit Mom, and she had a brain hemorrhage. You went to jail. You did it." Like if Nina kept repeating the truth, he would go away.

"Again, no absolute proof." Jimmy chuckled in the eerie way people prone to lying do. Most drug addicts who came through the ER acted the same way when denying they were there to get a fix. "It was all hearsay. Your grandparents had a thing against me. They made up that story to take you girls from me."

"I testified to you beating us. You beat Mom for years, and then you started going after Kitty. I was there, Jimmy."

"So you told everyone I died?" He cackled. "Thought I was the boogie man and could scare me away?" He walked over to Nina and put his hand on her shoulder. She tensed. "It would take more than that to get rid of me, baby girl. You should know that. I never left Lily, did I? All those years, I always came home."

"What do you want?" Nina was cold. She wanted to knock his hand off her. How dare he touch her again.

"Well, I thought we could be amicable about it. I was Lily's husband, and you and Kitty were my children. I guess I am owed a little something. Right?" He said it so casually.

Nina was scared, but now she was angry. Anger was good. It helped her compartmentalize. If Kitty was at school, she was safe. She would deal with Kitty finding out about Jimmy later. But now she had to get him to leave. The gun was upstairs, but she was afraid to turn her back. She was scared of the strength he had over her.

All these years, Nina had fooled herself into thinking the problem with her father had gone away. When she was a kid, she dreamt about getting rid of him. She had watched him smack her mother whenever he was angry or drunk. Jimmy never did it in a way that resulted in broken bones or sent her to the hospital. Sometimes Nina wished he had, so that doctors would have noticed and saved her, saved them all. But Lily put up with it, and Nina never knew why.

Occasionally her mother talked about leaving him. But then Jimmy would be friendly for a while. He promised to get her singing career back once they were more on their feet. Lily made Nina swear never to tell her grandparents about the abuse. Lily was embarrassed and ashamed, and she kept getting pregnant. She had lost two babies, maybe more. But Nina was young, and no one told her what was happening. Now, she considered it a miracle Kitty was even here at all.

Jimmy never hit Nina; she was a small girl, and it would have significantly damaged her. He was smart like that. Instead, he would grab her by the arm, under the armpit, and lift her forcefully if he didn't want her in the room. It hurt every time. How he hadn't dislocated her shoulder was another miracle. Then her mother would intercede and bear the brunt of more abuse.

The night before her mother died, Jimmy was drunk. Lily had made Nina and Kitty a box of macaroni and cheese and some hot dogs for dinner.

"What's with all the food?" Jimmy demanded. He was leaning on the counter, a sign he had been drinking all afternoon. Nina learned to pick up on these little clues. The slight slur in his speech, sweat on his brow, or his hand wasn't shaking. It shook when he hadn't had anything to drink. Nina pointed at Kitty's plate of food so the girl wouldn't notice their parents, but would focus on dinner, which Kitty obediently did.

"What, Jimmy? What is it now?" His mother wiped her hand on a dishtowel and, with her body language, ignored Jimmy.

"This means you went to the store. This food wasn't here this morning. You can't spend my money any way you want."

"Kids need to eat," she said dully.

"Christ, woman, they have food." He threw open the cabinet doors to minimal supplies. "I gotta pay Marco's." Nina knew Marco's meant a seedy joint where Jimmy spent most of his afternoons.

Nina hung her head and started eating faster, afraid he would throw them out of the room before she finished.

"I don't care anymore," Lily said quietly. Nina watched her mother hold herself against the sink and swing her head.

"What did you say?!" And Jimmy charged her. He struck a fierce blow to Lily's shoulder, and she cried out.

With full force, Nina grabbed Kitty from her seat and ran to her bedroom closet.

As Nina left the room, she heard her mother laugh and say, "Jimmy, I don't care if you hurt me because I don't feel anything at all." Those were the last words she remembered her mother saying.

One day, Nina came home from school and saw marks on Kitty's toddler arms. Little purplish spots blossomed around Kitty's wrists and upper arms. She began hiding her little sister in her closet, and Nina cried relentlessly, hating Jimmy. She fantasized about pushing him down the stairs and killing him. These reveries were the only things that got her to sleep at night. And then, when the opportunity came to kill him figuratively, it felt so satisfying. Telling herself he was dead, gone forever, washed away all those years. Nina could move on. Thankfully, Kitty was too young to remember. It was a perfect lie at the time. But now Nina was back where she had started.

Was she that naive to think Jimmy would be in jail forever? But Oma and Pop reassured her that they would never see him again. They must have believed it too. Fools, they were all such damn fools.

"Now, Nina. I was never that bad, honey. Your mother and I loved each other." His voice sounded slippery. "We had you girls. Money was tight, and that was hard on me, you know? Your mother didn't work. She could be lazy."

"You kept knocking her up so she couldn't. You beat her so she couldn't." Nina stood her ground. "Then all it took was one good hit, Jimmy, and she was gone."

"Well, agree to disagree. But look how it turned out for you girls. You have a nice house now, and Kitty goes to a private school. That must cost a pretty penny, huh, baby girl?" Nina cringed. No one should ever call another person baby or girl.

"You want money, Jimmy? Is that it?"

"Well, I never saw any of your mother's life insurance, and by the looks of it, you girls didn't do too badly when your grandparents kicked it. All this," Jimmy spread his arms for effect, "isn't on a nurse's salary. I know that much."

He picked up a picture from the mantel of Kitty's tenth birthday. "See, look how happy she ended up. You want her to stay happy?"

"Are you threatening me?" Nina's anger was now encompassing her. It felt good.

"Baby girl. A daddy doesn't have to threaten his daughters.

No, no, no, I just thought maybe you would like to help me out a little. You know, give me a piece of the pie? I got my hopes on a hammock in Mexico. Doesn't that sound nice, your dear old dad living on a beach in another country? I'd be about as far away from you and your sister as possible." He looked at her and grinned. "Like I was dead."

"So it's money, like it's always been with you. I remember the cons. When you used me to lie to store clerks that they hadn't given me the right change so I could get more. Or when you made me pretend to get hit on my bike so the driver would pay up. All those shitty little tricks you used me for."

"We had to eat, baby girl."

"Oma and Pop always sent Mom money, but we never had enough to eat."

"I had debts to pay. Those came first."

"You used Mom and tortured her, and then you killed her. Say it, Jimmy." Now she had dared him.

"Okay, Nina. I'm sick of this talk." He was getting angry now. Nina calculated running up the stairs two by two to get the gun. Maybe she would kill him this time. She could claim self-defense. Jimmy continued, "You want to make it easy on yourself? Get me some cash, and I'll get out of here. The more you give, the bigger the promise I stay away. You gotta pay to play, baby girl." He licked his lips and grinned, raising his eyebrows.

Nina said sternly, "Get out, Jimmy."

"Well, I'm not leaving Hillsdale. Let's see, at three o'clock tomorrow, isn't that when Kitty heads to her fancy tennis club? Maybe I'll pop over there and watch her for a while." When he brushed his greasy grey hair back, Nina couldn't believe this was her father. This vile human created her and Kitty, and the world did not feel right. She never wanted Oma and Pop more than at that moment.

"Stay away from Kitty."

"Well, girlie, you know how to make that happen. I'll be back, and cash would be preferable. And get some beer. Pathetic that you girls don't know how to welcome your dad back home."

He started whistling while walking out. Nina hated whistling. It was arrogant and obnoxious. It only fueled her long-hidden rage. The last time she felt that enraged was when she put her mother in the ground. Oma had held her tightly to her side at the gravesite as Nina threw clumps of dirt into the hole. Only they were at the funeral. Lily didn't have any friends after being with Jimmy. "Let it out, Nina, let it out," Oma had whispered to her, and Nina screamed louder that day than ever in her life.

After she watched the black car pull away, Nina put her hands on the kitchen counter to calm her blood pressure. Deep breaths are what she would have told a patient at the ER. *Compartmentalize*, she told herself. This was a crisis. First, she had to find Kitty. Kitty was the most critical priority. Nina called Kitty's cell phone relentlessly, but no answer. She texted. Of course, Kitty was in class. Her phone would have been turned off. Nina grabbed her car keys and thought she would get her at school.

She went to the campus office. Strange to be back at her high school as a grownup. Those same halls hadn't changed. Nina slowed down. She didn't want to appear panicky with the secretary. But then the secretary told Nina Kitty had checked out for lunch but hadn't returned. *What?* Where was Kitty?

Mia, she thought. Nina knew where Mia's office would have been, and she was sitting at her desk.

"Nina! What is it? You look like something has happened." Mia had registered the alarm on her friend's face.

"Have you seen Kitty?"

"Yesterday she came in here, but that was the last time. Is she okay? Are you okay?"

"Yeah, fine," Nina stammered. "I need to find her. Can you call me immediately if you see her or hear from her?"

"Sure, Nina, but what is it?" Mia said. But Nina turned and fled. She couldn't explain, because if she did, she would have to explain everything about how their lives were built on lies, lies, and more lies. It would be like unraveling a sweater yarn by yarn.

Having just come off work, Nina hadn't slept yet, but her adrenaline pumped. She drove around Hillsdale checking everywhere. She thought the minivan had to be somewhere, but she couldn't find it.

Eventually, she went home. Nina took the gun out from under her bed and placed it strategically by the front door. Under a pile of winter jackets on the bench seemed like a good spot.

Tennis wouldn't start for another 30 minutes, so Nina sat trying to go over the litany of problems. How had Jimmy gotten out of jail and found Kitty? How long had he been stalking them? What had he told Kitty?

Staring at the clock, Nina would go to the tennis club, hoping Kitty would be there. That made her think of Peter, and Peter made her think of Ashley. Ashley was a lawyer, or would be, and could help her.

Picking up the phone, she cleared her throat—*calm, calm, calm* —called the Tinsdale Law firm, and asked for Ashley Tinsdale.

"One moment, please," said a bright secretary.

"Hi, Nina! This is a surprise. What's up?"

"Hey, I don't know if I can ask you a favor. I would pay for your time, but I need you to do a little background digging on someone. Law firms can get criminal records, right? Like, you can do a background check?" Nina nervously tapped her nails against her leg.

"Sure, I can do that. Kind of the fun part of my job, sleuthing around. Dad has this thing about checking every client. Especially with the divorce cases, talk about skeletons in the closet!"

"So you could look someone up?"

"Yeah, what do you need? Is it a new boyfriend or something? What to find out his deep dark secrets?"

"His name is Jimmy or James Kittrick."

"A cousin, uncle, or something? You and Kitty okay?"

Nina had never uttered these words in all her life in Hillsdale.

"He's our father, and no, he is not dead. And no, Ashley, we are not okay."

Nina could hear Ashley's breath inhale sharply, but she recovered and responded. "I'm on it. I need the date of birth and where to start looking."

Nina told her.

Chapter 39
My Pussycat

Peter found Dave on the floor of the office, surrounded by files. There were bags from Staples office supply store filled with multi-colored file folders, and the best Peter could guess, Dave was re-sorting his father's clients. There were stacks of blue, green, red, and yellow, and Dave was punching names into a label maker. Peter could tell he was agitated by his swearing.

"Shit. I jammed it again." Dave looked close to tears.

"Dave, dude, what's going on?" Peter asked.

"We got the business. Correction, we can buy the business if we have the money. Do you have your money?"

Peter was taken aback. Was this happening? "Really? Whoa, that's... Well, that's fantastic. Your parents agreed? That's a big deal."

"Yes, they agreed, but they sold my house. I can't believe they sold my house." Dave kept punching the label maker and pulling the little slips of typewritten names.

"Okay, so you didn't get everything you wanted. It was a long shot anyway. You can move in with me. But the bright side, we got the business!" Peter was stunned. The Dinses agreed, but now he was panicking over his half of the money.

"Dave, I can only get my half if Kitty wins the tournament. That's what my father said."

"Is that another long shot, Peter?" Dave had annoyance in his voice.

"No, just another hurdle. We must climb the mountain to get to the top, right?" Peter tried to sound upbeat.

"Did you just tell me a platitude to get me to feel better?" Dave grumbled. Sometimes Peter hated it when Dave wouldn't look at him. He wanted that eye contact with his friend to reassure him.

"Yes, yes, I did. But, Dave, stop." Dave's hands stopped moving. "We can do this. Don't spiral into some self-pity thing over a bedroom."

"My bedroom, my house." Dave sounded pissed.

"Easy, cowboy. You gotta handle these curveballs easier. Is it Ken? Is he still not talking to you?"

Dave stopped moving, and Peter took that as a yes. Peter wanted to hug Dave, or do something to show him he cared. But there was nothing to do but let him stew on the office floor and re-organize files.

"Hey, Dave, the tennis skirts are a mess. Can you sort those too?" It was all Peter could do to help his buddy and keep him busy.

Peter noticed Kitty was late when Nina rushed into the office. She was upset.

"Have you seen Kitty? Is she here?" Her voice was shaky and broken.

"Are you okay, Nina? No, she hasn't come in yet. She's late, which is not like her."

"Shit shit shit," Nina practically screamed and slammed her hand on the counter.

Dave stopped sorting. This agitated him as well.

"Is she with that boyfriend, Jerry, maybe? Maybe she just lost track of time?" Peter offered.

Nina looked on the verge of tears.

"1822 Buttonwood Street, the home of Jerry Canelli. He lives with his single mother, who is an accountant. He is 17 years old and goes to Hillsdale Prep with Kitty," Dave said without looking at them. "What are you waiting for, Peter? Take Nina there."

Peter just looked at them and thankfully didn't think about it. "Let's go."

In Nina's old BMW, she raced to Jerry's house. Peter held onto the passenger door as she took the curves screeching.

"Nina, I don't mean to pry, but Kitty is always on her own. Why are you so worried about her?" Tears filled Nina's eyes, but she didn't say anything. Peter accepted the silence and held on.

Nina raced to the front door and rang the doorbell repeatedly. She frantically looked for the minivan, which wasn't there.

Jerry opened the door. "Hey, Coach! Hey, big sis! What's up?" He looked like a disheveled kid in his Bob Marley t-shirt with a Pop-Tart in his hand.

Peter took over for Nina, who was visibly shaking, "Hey, Jerry." He still wanted to call him Cheech, but the moment wasn't appropriate. "Have you seen Kitty? She didn't show up to practice."

"She wasn't at school either," Nina said.

"No, man. Not since yesterday. I was surprised because she usually gives me a lift home."

"You two are dating, right?" Peter asked. "Has there been anything strange about her? Would she leave or not show up for practice for any reason?"

"Oh, dude. We are just friends. Kitty's my girl and all, but not that way."

"Then in what way?" Anger edged her voice, protective of Kitty.

"No, man, like nothing bad. About a year ago, I got into drugs. Fell into a bad crowd at school and started partying way too hard. Those rich kids, man, really score the good stuff, if you know what I mean. My dad had taken off, and I'm on scholarship at the school, so it was a rough time. Kitty, well, she and I were in the same English class, and she kind of woke me up. She told me to stop coming to class fucked up and that I would blow my chances. Kitty was the only one who stepped in and snapped me out of it. You know, bro? Sometimes you have to have that one person strong enough to care. So we hang out, that's all, man. She keeps me company so I don't do stupid shit, like sniff glue or eat a laundry pod or something. She's entertaining to hang out with, and that's it, man."

Peter looked at Nina as her shoulders dropped. It was so Kitty to do something like that.

"Okay," Nina said. "Jerry, listen to me. This is very important. If you see or hear from her, please text or call me immediately. If you talk to her, tell her I need her home as soon as possible."

Peter could see Jerry computing as he asked, "Is my pussycat in danger?"

"Yes, Jerry, she is, and we need to have her home."

Peter didn't like the sound of any of it. But they left their numbers with Jerry, and he promised to go looking for her.

Back in the car, Peter asked where to go. Nina said. "Home," with tears streaming down her cheeks.

Finally, Peter was allowed into their house. The space felt personal and homey, unlike Peter's apartment, which consisted of a futon couch and a TV on milk crates. The wallpaper had dainty flowers, and the sofa was a worn orange velvet that looked incredibly comfortable. He didn't know what to do, so he sat. Nina paced and looked at her phone. He still didn't feel it was the right time to ask questions.

The front door opened, and the red-headed kid from the club came in, along with an older woman Peter guessed was his mom.

"Hey, Adam." Peter gave a little hand wave.

"Oh, hey, Coach. This is Kitty's tennis coach, and he's gonna teach me!" Adam said brightly to his mother. At least a ten-year-old kid was happy to hang out with him.

The woman went straight to Nina. "Is everything okay? You have me worried."

Nina shook her head and started to cry. Peter didn't know whether to stay or go.

An idea occurred to him. "Maybe Kitty would answer a text from Adam? You know, she wouldn't want him to worry."

"Hello, Coach? I'm Mia." The woman held her hand to him with a friendly smile. "Adam is my son, and we live across the street. I think that is an excellent idea. Adam, text Kitty," she commanded.

Adam said while he typed, "Hey, Kitty. What's up? Where are you?"

They all held their breath. Adam stared at his phone, then shouted, "BUBBLES!"

Nina almost collapsed with relief.

"What did she say?" Mia asked.

"Oh, the bubbles went away. Wait, they're back." Adam squinted at the phone. "Okay, here we go… Tell Nina I'm okay, little man."

Nina threw up her hands and let out a grunt.

Adam texted, "She is really worried." But there were no bubbles. He looked at Nina. "Sorry, Nina."

"No, Adam, you did well. I know that she is okay at least." Nina wiped tears from her eyes.

"So, are you going to tell us what's happening?" Mia asked. "I know you like your privacy, but you are not alone, Nina. You have us, so let us help you."

Peter was cemented to the couch. He assumed he was part of the "us" Mia was referring to and thought it best not to leave. He had no idea what was happening, but Kitty was five days away from the tournament. But it wasn't just that. It was Kitty, and for whatever she was on the tennis court, she meant more to him off. For the past two months, Kitty had pushed him in directions he never thought he would go. From the moment that minivan pulled into his life, something had changed. Something about her had changed him. She was a pain in the ass, calling him *Pet-eerrr* and rolling her eyes every time he said not to do it again. But she also snuck Reese's peanut butter cups in his gym bag because they were his favorite and exhausted him emotionally and physically until he had stopped drinking so much at night. She gave him purpose, and dammit, he liked her. With her comical t-shirts and her way of scratching her ass before she served, there was no one like her.

Watching Nina break down was jolting. Peter's only feeling was to help and comfort her, but he didn't know how. Mia was the grown-up in the room and taking charge. Thank goodness for her.

Nina sat down and took deep breaths and, without looking at anyone really, started talking.

"I'm sorry, but I have lied to all of you. I have lied to everyone in my life past the age of twelve. But it has caught up to Kitty and me. And right now, I am just praying what I have done doesn't hurt Kitty."

Peter got up, grabbed a blanket off the side chair, and gave it to Nina. Not that she looked cold, but she looked like she needed comfort.

"Thanks, Peter. Sorry you are wrapped up in this, but you need to know because it might affect everything with Kitty." Again, Peter's mind went to the stakes of the tournament, but it wasn't the time or the place. He knew something real was happening here and wanted to help the sisters.

Nina took a deep breath like she was weighing her words. She closed her eyes and blurted, "When I was twelve, my father killed my mother." The silence became the oxygen in the room. No one moved. "He was a terrible man. He abused us physically—I mean, he hit us, and emotionally, he was a real..." Nina paused and looked at Adam.

"It's okay," Adam said, "you can say asshole." Nina chuckled a little and smiled at him.

"Okay, he was a real asshole. He was a con artist and never treated Mom or us right. One day, I was at school and came home to find my mother on the floor. She had a gash on her head. Jimmy, my dad, had struck her so that her head came down on the corner of the countertop. And when I got home..." Nina started choking up.

"It's okay, honey." Mia went and put her arm around Nina. Peter wanted to do that.

"I found Kitty sitting in the pool of blood next to Mom. He wasn't there, but we all knew Jimmy did it. Mom, Kitty, and I had bruises, and the police believed us. Pop and Oma came and got us, and we moved here. They arrested Jimmy and put him in jail for involuntary manslaughter. I haven't heard from him since. It's been thirteen years."

"Until now, Nina?" Peter guessed.

Nina nodded.

"So back then, we all just wanted to put it behind us, and since Kitty was only three, we thought if we told her he was dead, what would be the harm? We thought we were protecting her, giving her a normal childhood."

"Kitty hates lying," Adam said.

"I know, Adam, and that's why this is so hard. This morning Jimmy showed up, and he hasn't changed. Maybe he is even worse. He promises to go away again if I give him money."

"Over my dead body," said Mia.

"But worse, before Jimmy came to me, he found Kitty. Kitty knows he's alive, but I don't know what he told her. At first, I was afraid he had kidnapped her or done something to her. But I guess she is hiding from me right now." Nina looked regretful.

"Is Jimmy coming back?" Peter asked.

"Yeah, but I don't know when. He wants me to give him cash. I only need to know that Kitty is someplace safe, away from him," Nina said.

"Well, you certainly aren't giving him anything, Nina. Do you hear me?" Mia scolded.

"Should we call the police?" asked Adam.

"We don't have anything on him. He's my father and a damn good liar. They released him from jail because he had finished his time. I know he is driving a black Corolla with tinted windows."

"I saw him!" shouted Adam. "He's been driving past our houses."

"He's been stalking us for a while. He knows Kitty's schedule."

Peter looked at these people who were all but strangers a few moments ago. But they were from Hillsdale, his home, and he wouldn't let anything happen to them.

"Nina, I have no doubt Kitty is okay, wherever she is," reassured Peter. "She is fearless."

"Peter, that's what worries me the most. She *is* fearless, and that is exactly what can get her into trouble."

Peter told Nina he wasn't going to leave her alone. If he could swing a tennis racket, maybe he could be of some use. It was minimally better than a divorcee and a ten-year-old protecting her. Peter didn't mind waiting. He had been waiting his whole life, after all, for something to happen.

Chapter 40
Lentils

That morning, Lois Clark made a decision. She and Stevie were going to eat better. The night before, she fell down the internet rabbit hole reading all about the male prostate. Lois wouldn't say it was fascinating, but it was informative. Stevie only had stage one cancer, which by any account could be manageable. There was hormone therapy, radiation therapy, chemotherapy, and surgery. But by the end, they might need psychotherapy for all the previous therapies. The doctor suggested starting with his hormone levels and working from there. He had reassured them it was common for men Stevie's age, 68, to be going through this, and a year from now, it might all be behind them. Well, Lois thought, we shall see about that. Her menopause was hormonal, and that took ten bloody years.

But Lois didn't like the idea of cancer being in one of their bodies. She had been adamant about her mammogram for almost thirty years and forced them to get colonoscopies. Cancer felt like a predator stalking them, and the hunter in Lois didn't like it one bit. She wanted to be on the offensive, not the defensive. But the only thing Lois could do at home for Stevie was change his diet.

As much as they bickered—and granted, she hated watching *American Idol* with him, stupid show—she wouldn't trade him for any other man on the planet. He was a kind, loving, and very dedicated husband for 40 years and was excellent in the sack. He never minded that her belly grew and her boobs sagged over the years. Her hair had gone gray, but she still rolled and curled it so it bounced on her head. She applied makeup and made herself desirable with what she had left. On the other hand, Stevie had stopped wearing pants that required belts. But she couldn't imagine life without him when he took her hand as they sat in front of that incessant show.

The internet had said Stevie needed a diet rich in natural fiber. This would include fruits, vegetables, legumes, and whole grains, which Stevie actively avoided. Admittedly, Lois also did because she liked meat and potatoes. But as of today, their diets were going to change.

She was overwhelmed by the online recipe choices. Back in the day, you bought a single cookbook and exhausted its contents until you bought another. She was of the Julia Child generation who added mounds of butter to everything, including a pat on her steak. So there she was, rifling through recipes for lentil soup, lentil salad, lentil casseroles, lentil curry, and on and on…trying to find a way to make legumes appealing to Stevie. She made a tentative list and headed to the Stop n' Shop, hoping organic food wouldn't be too expensive.

At the checkout, Lois organized her items on the belt and wasn't paying much attention to the large man talking to the petite girl until she heard him say, "Missy, you gave me the wrong change. I gave you a fifty, and you think I gave you a ten? Maybe you work in this dump because you can't count."

It was Jimmy.

Lois perked up. The tone in his voice was rude and menacing, and the girl whose name tag said "Veronica" looked nervous. Immediately, Lois felt defensive of her. Old age had afforded her some long-overdue bravado when it came to asserting herself.

"But, sir," the girl said shakily. "You did give me a ten. And if I gave you the wrong change, I lose a shift. So I pay extra attention." Veronica looked like a Powerpuff Girl next to Hulk Hogan.

"You saying I'm wrong?" The large man puffed up to an even larger size. He waved his arm with a dragon tattoo over the conveyor belt. Lois, who was of good size, didn't appreciate his attitude.

"Sir, may I?" she interrupted. He looked at her fiercely. "Dear, what bill did he hand you?" And Veronica held up the ten. "Are you sure, dear?"

"Yes, ma'am."

"Well, there you go. I believe you owe him only $2.88 in change." Lois smiled at the man, daring him to refute her.

"Listen, lady, mind your own damn business," Jimmy shouted at her.

Lois continued to smile and folded her hands neatly across her stomach. "Oh, it's not my business. It's theirs. See the cameras?" Lois swung her hand around for effect. "We can call the manager, and he can double-check. I used to work here," Lois lied, "and nowadays they have these high-resolution cameras because of all the damn grocery store shootings. So if there is any question, the manager can check his computer and zoom in on the bill. It's all quite easy and only takes a few minutes."

Jimmy huffed and licked his lips, thinking. Lois continued smiling, glad she had chosen her cherry blossom lipstick. Always good to look your best in these situations.

"Fine." He grabbed the change out of poor Veronica's hand and stormed off. Lois heard him mutter, "Dumb bitches." Bullies didn't scare her. She had three older brothers who all went into the Navy.

Lois looked at Veronica, who was now greatly relieved.

"We have cameras?" she asked.

"Dear, I have no idea. He lied, so I lied. I just had to call his bluff." Lois winked at her, and Veronica started bagging her groceries.

Lois had hunted with her brothers in Michigan. They taught her to heighten her awareness in public, scan her surroundings, and be alert. Nowadays, a grocery store parking lot could be just as dangerous as a bear charging. What was the difference between the bear and people? People have guns. Lois always liked to shoot. She was a natural, her father had exclaimed, and she shot her first deer at age 15. But Lois liked it for sport, in the woods, not at post offices and schools. She thought most people shouldn't own guns because they were too stupid or emotional. But that didn't stop them, so when Lois saw Jimmy, she profiled him as precisely the type to have a gun, putting her on edge.

She loaded her groceries in her Kia, a sensible car, and pulled out. Lois became aware of a black Toyota Corolla following her. She was no dummy and squinted in her rearview mirror. Jimmy's large hand was on the steering wheel, and his long gray hair outlined his face. Was he going to come after her? "Game on," Lois said to no one, and took a few random turns to verify her mark. It's not hard for an old lady to shake someone. Old ladies have patience, and that bully had none.

Swiftly, she pulled into her favorite diner parking lot. It was packed with the late afternoon crowd and plenty of people coming and going. Lois pulled up to the building to park so patrons in the window would have complete visibility if she were attacked in the lot. She parked adjacent to a maroon minivan and kept her eye on the rearview mirror. The Corolla passed behind her but sped off and down the street. *Huh? That was easy*, she laughed to herself.

Now Lois could smell the grease from the diner, and her appetite kicked in. Since she was there anyway, she might as well treat herself to one last cheeseburger before the legume festival began at home. Walking in, she noticed the blonde hair first. Lois had only seen it in pictures on Stevie's computer, but it was delightful in person. Lois would have killed to have that hair, mounds of blonde curls.

She approached the girl. "Kitty? Hi, I'm Lois, Coach Clark's wife. It's so nice to meet you in person."

Kitty pushed up her glasses and stared at the woman but didn't smile. Her eyes were red-rimmed, and Lois noticed the crumpled napkins used as tissues. Kitty had a large chocolate milkshake in front of her and was dipping french fries in it.

"Hi, Mrs. Clark," the girl said dully. Not precisely what Lois expected from Stevie's description of a loudmouth, jovial girl.

"Everything okay, dear?" Lois sat down without permission. At her age, permission was a thing of the past.

"Just life, I suppose." Kitty shoved another fry in her mouth, and tears blossomed again.

"Sometimes a stranger is easier to talk to than a friend." Lois settled her handbag on the booth and waited. Again, old ladies are very patient at times. "Is it boys? School? The tournament?"

"None of the above. Family."

"Stevie told me you live with your older sister, but your parents and grandparents are gone?"

"My dad was gone, but now he is back." Lois didn't understand. When the waitress came, she ordered not only a cheeseburger but onion rings as well. The day was calling for it.

Then Kitty explained, and Lois sat rapt with attention. The story was unbelievable for someone from Hillsdale.

"I went to the library and found out that my father had been convicted of manslaughter and had previous convictions of fraud and racketeering. I had to look up racketeering." Kitty looked glum.

"It's threatening force to get money. Like the mafia when they say they protect but also hurt people while bribing them for money. I watch a lot of crime shows."

"Yes, so my dad was a real jerk. He stole money. He hurt people. He hurt my mom. And he was accused of child endangerment, so that would be Nina and me. He hurt us."

"That is a lot to process, Kitty. No wonder you feel a little worse for wear."

"It's like this. I'm mad at my sister and my family for lying to me. I trusted them. But also," Kitty looked down, "I wish I never knew. They had been right to lie. I never had to think about the murder. I never had to think about him. I thought my parents were saints. I'm such a fool. And now I know everything, but I don't know what to do."

"I'm sure lying helped them also put the whole thing in the past. Nina had to move on. She must have horrible memories."

"And that's another thing. I don't have any memory. I used to feel jealous she could remember them, and now I feel awful that she does, and I don't have to."

"I'm sure Nina doesn't see it that way. I bet your sister would do anything to protect you."

"I haven't talked to her yet. She's been calling, but I don't know what to say. I don't know if he has seen her or if he's just targeted me."

"Kitty, do you feel safe?"

"Well, not around him. I can tell he wants something. I watch a lot of crime shows too. I want him to go away again. He's not my family, just a regrettable sperm donor."

Lois spat out her coke, laughing. This is what Stevie meant by Kitty being "something."

They continued talking more about the situation, and Lois tried her best to guide Kitty. She even offered a place at the Clarks' for the night. But Kitty declined, saying she had more work to do. And Lois saw that look in Kitty's eye and recognized it. A hunter can always tell another hunter.

Stevie didn't get home from the doctor's until late, and Lois had prepared a lentil soup.

"Woman, this will kill me before cancer." He sniffed over the pot.

"Deal with it, you old fool. And you have a problem with Kitty." Lois recalled the afternoon events, and Coach Clark went pale. They both went into worrying mode.

Peter wasn't upstairs, so Coach Clark called him. "Pissant, your girlfriend needs to talk to you." And Lois told Peter about her conversation with Kitty.

Chapter 41
Boom, Boom, Boom

Nina paced as she listened to Peter say a lot of "Yeses" and "Nos" along with Kitty's name. Jerry's text came through on her phone; Kitty was at his house. Peter got off the phone and relayed everything Mrs. Clark had told him.

"Kitty had lunch with Mrs. Clark? God, that girl!" Nina exclaimed. "Well, now we know what she knows. That's good."

Nina texted Jerry. "Please tell Kitty I'm sorry I lied, and I love her more than anything else. She needs to stay away from Jimmy. Lock your doors and keep an eye out for him. I will give her space tonight, but I want her home tomorrow. Tell her not to do anything without talking to me first." Nina showed Peter the text. "Is that okay?"

"Tell her not to drive anywhere alone," Peter added.

"That's good, and Jerry will stay with her." Nina finished the text and waited for bubbles.

Then it came. "She loves you too. She just needs a moment."

Nina sighed with relief, then more bubbles. "Also, she says this is why it's time for you to find a boyfriend."

Nina rolled her eyes but didn't tell Peter what the last text said. They had sent Mia and Adam back to their house to sleep. Peter would stay with her.

Nina finally sat down, and Peter did as well. They were alone.

Peter fumbled for words. "You know, I always thought you were pretty smart in high school."

"Thought you never noticed me." Nina had showered and put on her favorite sweatpants. She honestly didn't care that Peter Wise was there. She was too exhausted and forgot all her embarrassing high school fantasies. She was just grateful someone was there.

"Not true. I was a teenage boy and noticed every girl. It is what we do, but I was terrible at acting on it." Nina got a little fluttery. Would he have ever acted on it with her? No, she was 100% sure about that. Nina was glad she was stone-cold sober, or else she might have confessed her crush on him. Big mistake. "I'm sorry no one ever knew about your family," Peter added.

"Don't be. It was better that way. I was just a normal, insecure Hillsdale Prep girl instead of the daughter of a goon. After starting like that, I wanted to be anonymous. I wanted to feel normal."

"I was the epitome of normal, and I hated it," Peter confessed.

"You were never an asshole, if that's some consolation. I thought you were nice. Remember those idiots, TJ Barnes and his crew, who started the Young Republicans Club? They were assholes. They used to slap my ass when they walked past me in the halls. Real jerks."

"TJ Barnes got a podcast gig a few years ago. He dropped out of college thinking he was going to be a millionaire. He was pro-life, pro-Trump, and pro-white supremacist, but his mom was embarrassed by him and took away his trust fund. Now he's selling Kias out by Route One."

Nina smiled and laughed. "Okay, that feels poetic."

"So, do you wish, you know, your parents were different? That it didn't happen?" Peter asked.

"I used to, but that's how a kid would think. I accepted it better when I grew up because I could be grateful for what I had. My grandparents were incredible people, and I lived with them for ten years. I now have this amazing life with Kitty, and I wouldn't change it, for the most part. I mean, I love being a nurse and living in Hillsdale, so no, I wouldn't change any of it."

"Do you think you are a nurse because of what happened to your mother?"

"Totally. Living with my dad, I learned how to handle trauma. I found a part of myself that reacts in difficult situations. I mean, when I found my mother that day, it triggered me to be calm and help Kitty. You don't know who you are until you face that test. And now, it's like I can harness that power at work and help people. I have to admit, it's an awesome feeling." Nina had never had such an honest conversation like this. Because she had never told anyone about her parents, she had never told anyone about herself. The honesty felt euphoric.

"Do you think it had any effect on Kitty?" Peter asked, and Nina nodded.

"You know her weird food obsession? She eats like a truck driver, and honestly, it's my fault because I don't stop her. I can't. When Kitty was little, sometimes I could only find crackers for dinner, or dry cereal. Then I would have to tell her to stop eating so that I could save it for later. There still is a part of me that cannot deny her food. And I think, deep in her memory, that her body remembers being hungry. So yeah, I give her too much leeway with the fries and candy. I'm not perfect."

"No one's perfect, but you're amazing."

Nina felt herself blush and turned away. She would never get used to compliments.

She switched back to Peter. "What about you? What's been your moment?"

"Honestly, Kitty. Dave and I are going to buy the Hillsdale Tennis Club and start a proper school for kid athletes. I mean, if I can handle your sister..." They both laughed.

"I haven't told anyone this," Nina said, "but I want to become a midwife. It takes too long to be a doctor, and the ER gets depressing. Don't get me wrong, I love the action, but car accidents rarely turn out positive. But a woman giving birth is an amazing, gory, crazy event. The adrenaline is so natural. Then there is this great moment of holding a new baby and seeing the relief and joy on the parents' faces. I could do that all day long."

Peter looked at her, and Nina could tell he was seeing her. Finally, she was able to look back at him.

"So, you dating anyone?" Peter asked.

Nina didn't have the energy to lie. "No, I work mostly and take care of Kitty." Nina did not want to return the question. She didn't want to hear how Peter was with Ashley, even though she was curious about why. His being here felt so nice, and the idea that he was someone else's would take away all her good feelings.

She sang, "I'm a loser, baby."

Peter responded, "So why don't you kill me? Forces of evil in a bozo nightmare..."

"You like Beck?" Nina was surprised.

"'90s music is my jam." Peter smiled. He was pretty cute sitting in her house wearing an old Adidas sweatshirt. *No, Nina, don't fall for him,* she warned herself. With everything going on, she was surprised she could feel something other than fear or dread. She wished she could curl up beside him and relax. Nina wanted to put her head on his shoulder and let him hold her.

Snap out of it!

"Hey, I haven't slept since yesterday, so I'm just going to close my eyes." Nina lay down on the couch, and Peter rested her ankles on his legs. He gently covered her with a blanket and rested his hands on her shins.

"Don't worry, I'll be on the lookout," he reassured. And Nina was gone.

Nina woke sometime in the middle of the night. Her body was alert when she heard the click of a lock. Immediately she opened her eyes and listened in the dark, heart pounding. She swore she had heard something.

Then a doorknob rattled, but it was upstairs. Kitty's old crystal doorknob was loose, she reminded herself, and sometimes Kitty left her window cracked, so the wind shook the door. It was a familiar sound, she told herself.

Nina hadn't felt this agitated in a long time. It took her back to the apartment in Boston. She would sneak around listening, hoping her father would leave them alone. Sometimes Jimmy left in a fury, only to return a few minutes later to scare them. Her anxiety caused rashes on her arms that she would scratch until she bled. Now, in her own home, she scratched her arms again. Wide awake, Nina walked around the house, checking to be sure he wasn't there.

Peter was snoring slightly on the couch, and she tip-toed to the jackets, checking that the gun was still there. Her hand pulled it out from under the coats. It had a weighty feel. Holding the weapon surprisingly didn't make Nina feel any better. It increased her anxiety, not her sense of security. She had seen blood flow from chest wounds looking like Rorschach tests. Heads that were missing eyes and ephemeral arteries spouting red liquid-like geysers. Those were the images that came to her mind. Bullets did more damage than people could imagine unless they had seen it firsthand. Guns couldn't decipher people. What if Jimmy was able to use it against her or Kitty?

And this gun was old. Would it even shoot? All Nina knew was to aim and pull the trigger. She was unprepared, and that did nothing to reassure her.

"Nina?" Peter's voice came through the dark and startled her.

"I'm okay, just checking the front door." Nina slipped the gun back under the coats and put her hand on the door's deadbolt. "I thought I heard something, but it was nothing." The house was almost black except for the streetlamp outside. It did little to illuminate the room, but Nina found her way back to the couch.

A warm hand reached for her, and she took it with her own. Peter pulled her back onto the couch, but close to him this time. He let go of her hand and wrapped his arms around her as they sat side by side. They said nothing. Peter held her tightly until she relaxed and finally put her head on his chest. Nina breathed in the faint laundry detergent smell of his sweatshirt. His body was relaxed but muscular. The hardness of his biceps didn't make her feel trapped, but protected. Tears came to her eyes as his hand gently smoothed her hair.

Nina hadn't been held like that since Oma and Pop had comforted her as a child. Those days when she first arrived in Hillsdale, they would find her hiding in the closet. Pop would slowly pull her out and wrap his arms around her. He had to reassure her she wasn't back in Boston with her parents, back in their apartment, back in hell.

The simplicity of Peter's gesture was all she wanted, all she needed at that moment. Nina concentrated on the pulse of his heart, *boom, boom, boom*, and drifted away.

Chapter 42

Sneetches

Mia was distracted when she got to work. Frankly, she had forgotten about the trouble at school. Mr. Dunning and his assembly felt trite and stupid compared to what was happening with Nina and Kitty.

Mr. Baxter came in and sat down in a huff. "Yes, Mr. Baxter, what now?" She was curt. Mia knew it had to be something she didn't want to hear. All she wanted was to be knee-deep in a bottle of wine with Doctor Matthew rubbing her feet.

"Sensitivity training." He tilted his elongated face and wiggled his bushy eyebrows at her.

"What?"

"Check your email. Mr. Jenkins is now requiring teachers to take sensitivity training."

"What the hell is that?" Mia was out of patience.

"So we can learn to tip-toe around these cotton ball students we have. Apparently, we can't piss the little shits off anymore. They don't like anything negative or conflict in the classroom."

"They do realize these are teenagers we are talking about? They are the ones who are negative and causing conflict, not us." Mia pushed back her red hair with both hands.

"Right? Senator Crawley's kid practically cried when I assigned a ten-page essay on *Romeo and Juliet*. He called me overbearing because I had assigned too much homework. That's my job! He's seventeen! Good luck to them if he can't read or write by now. Asshat will probably go to Harvard anyway."

"What are we supposed to be sensitive about?' Mia asked. "We are English teachers. All we are is sensitive." She was getting worked up along with Mr. Baxter. "Our department's entire curriculum is based on race, bigotry, genocide, misogyny, sexuality —he, she, it, them, no matter what color, origin, or culture! All we do is address it, and now they want us to be *more* sensitive?" Mia was infuriated. "How much can we pander to every side of every argument? I am not running for congress. I am teaching kids how to read a fucking book and have independent thought!" Mia paced, liking the sound of her heels hitting the old wooden floor.

"Say it, sister!" Mr. Baxter shouted. "I've had two US senators come from my classroom, one award-winning author who wrote an excellent book about the AIDS epidemic, and one actress nominated for an Oscar for playing a teacher in inner-city schools. Don't tell me I need to be more sensitive." Mr. Baxter threw down his newspaper for effect.

"But we have a meeting to rule out sensitive material? None of this makes sense. Who exactly are we being sensitive to? I don't get it anymore. Should we be more sensitive to the kids who are different and having a hard time, or to the kids who are perfectly fine but don't want anything 'bad' to happen to them? Which is it? Do we have to be sensitive to the religious parents who want their kids to read the Bible and tote guns for protection? Or sensitive to the girl who wants the right to control her body? What about the African American kids who want to go to McDonald's without getting shot by the police? Are we supposed to be the arbiters of this sensitivity? Or the puppets?"

"*Sneetches*," Mr. Baxter said.

"What?"

"Classic book by Dr. Suess. Where some Sneetches have stars upon thars, but some don't. So a little con artist fellow comes and sells stars for those without those upon thars. Then removes the stars with those upon thars because they don't want to be part of the second group with stars upon thars. So basically, both sets of Sneetches get hoodwinked out of money trying to outdo each other because half want to be different and better and don't want the other half to be different or better. Then the other half want to be like the first half because they think they are better. Then nobody knows who had stars upon thars anymore, and it's all very disconcerting and futile. Our society is full of Sneetches. The old Doc was brilliant. It was his finest work, as far as I'm concerned." Mr. Baxter gave a mischievous grin.

"I'm not sure if these little chats are helpful or disconcerting, Mr. Baxter." Mia looked at him with a lowered chin.

"Don't be so sensitive, Mia."

She couldn't help but laugh.

Mr. Baxter left, and Mia saw a fluff of blonde hair and a purple skirt go by. She nearly fell over her desk, shouting, "Kitty!"

Kitty came in and sat with a thump. "I'm okay, Mrs. G, really." Kitty pre-empted anything Mia was going to say; such a teenager.

"Are you? Nina is distraught. She is worried about you with your father in Hillsdale."

"I'm not mad at her anymore. I was, but I figured out why she lied to me. It was just a shock, you know?" Mia didn't know because her father milked cows on a farm in Vermont, but she nodded anyway.

"From what I know, your father is dangerous," Mia warned her. "You must be very careful. He wants Nina to give him money to leave town."

"No! She can't pay him!"

"That's what I said, but Nina can't figure out how to get him to leave. I want you to go straight home after school. If he got to you before, he could get to you again. You are safe at school for now. Thanks to all this school-shooter business, this place is like a fortress."

"Okay, Mrs. G, I promise." Kitty nodded, and Mia believed her. Mia could still see the innocent girl behind those eyes, as tough as Kitty was. She was at that strange stage where she could trust anyone and no one at the same time.

"As a teacher, I recommend you visit the school psychologist to discuss this situation."

Kitty grinned and looked at her over the rim of her glasses. Mia chuckled. "But as your neighbor and friend, I know that's a bunch of horseshit. Also, it's a grey area if I should inform Principal Jenkins. You may be in danger. But also, it's Nina's duty as your guardian to decide whether your family business becomes public. So just for now, I am giving you a little leeway."

"Thank you, Mrs. G. Don't worry, there is only one person who can help me: my sister. She and I can work it out together. We always have and always will."

"But I only say this knowing I live across the street. So I will be seeing you later tonight. You guys are not alone."

"Thanks, Mrs. G." Kitty got up but went around Mia's desk. Catching her off guard, Kitty's large arms enveloped her. Curls and the faint smell of coconut engulfed Mia's face. They hugged, and Mia imagined what it would have been like to have a daughter. Wonderful.

Kitty left, and Mia put her forehead down on her desk. The hard surface was smooth and comforting. Then she could hear her phone ping and she checked it. There were ten messages from Camila.

The nature of a sister relationship is strange and hard to define. There is loyalty and jealousy and hurt feelings and love. The strangest thing had happened since the intervention at her house. Camila started texting her all the time. It was like thirty years had disappeared, and they were kids again. Camila asked her things like what was better, oat or almond milk? Mia had no idea. Should Eric take a parenting class? That might be helpful. If the twins were boys, should they have family names or names from the list of top ten popular names? What? Would Adam like a bouncy house on his birthday? God no.

Mia was gaining insight into her sister's world and realized how straightforward Camila was. Mia used to label it shallow, but it was something less villainous. Sure, Camila was unaware. She never asked how Mia was doing or how Mia was feeling. But Mia oddly didn't mind because she was not obligated to share her feelings. It was rather liberating to have a relationship like that. Instead, she saw Camila as that insecure girl again, who changed her Barbie's clothes ten times a day. Mia tried to grasp Camila's one-track mind and settled on "simple." Camila was actually very sweet and worried about how Adam would react after the twins were born. (Does he need a class? No.) Camila exemplified sensitivity because she thought about everything and everyone's opinion. Her insecurity fueled thoughts about others, albeit sometimes missing the mark.

Mia didn't always respond immediately to Camila's texts because then Camila would write more texts with more questions, which would never end. Sometimes Mia sent her a heart emoji or waited until later to call her. She finally accepted that Eric would probably do better around someone more insecure like him, and she would do better around someone more secure like Matthew. *Progress*, she thought. Mia patted herself on the back at her emotional awareness. But if Camila asked her to be her maid of honor, that would be a hard pass. She had accepted her new family situation, but let's not go overboard.

"Mrs. Golding?" It was Jules Hamel, her least dynamic English teacher. Her pretty brunette hair swayed around her face, but her eyes darted around the office. Mia could tell the poor girl was nervous and wondered what was wrong now.

"Yes, Jules, how can I help you?" Mia was resigned to the next disaster.

"Do you have a minute? It's about this parent assembly." Mia motioned to Mr. Baxter's chair and waited.

Jules looked a little lost and stammered, "I've started receiving emails from parents, and they are a little aggressive." Jules twisted her hands. Mia felt bad for her, but parents and their unsolicited opinions came with the job.

"Well, when you start a fire, something will burn." Mia shrugged. She had little sympathy for what Jules and Mr. Dunning had started by trying to ban books.

Exhausted, Mia shouted, "Let me guess, the Crawleys threatened to rescind school endowments if we go ahead with the curriculum, and the Oswalds threatened to remove Katrina if we did."

"Pretty much, yeah? How did you know?" Jules looked surprised at Mia's accuracy.

"I've taught all their kids, and they all survived under my tutelage. But these families have had the same agenda for years. Senator Crawley is up for Republican re-election and will use any opportunity to make a stink. He could care less what his kid is reading, but if he can garner a few votes at school, he will."

"That's awful, using his kid like that." Jules' hair waved again as she shook her head. Mia wondered what shampoo she used to make it so shiny.

Mia tried not to think about Jules' beauty products and continued, "And the Oswalds made their money the old-fashioned way. They inherited it. The only thing that separates them from the rest of the world is their snobbery which is born from education. Darling Katrina must be well-read to carry on a dinner conversation with her future in-laws and whatever family they come from."

"I never thought of it like that. Katrina is so bright." Jules sat closer to the edge of her seat, listening intently.

"She is, and I have no worries for her, because darling Katrina will go to some costly liberal arts college, get a tattoo, swear off gluten, and hook up with girls. Eventually, she will start her own company or get a PhD to spite her mother and the old money they come from."

Jules looked dismayed and shocked.

"Jules, I know you have the best intentions for your students." Mia tried to take the cynicism out of her voice. "And that's good. We should all have good intentions. But lately, I have learned a pretty important lesson. Something I hadn't realized about myself..." Mia's voice trailed off a bit. She didn't intend to confide in Jules, the glossy, young version of what she had maybe once been. "I have had to learn not to hold so tightly to things. I have had to loosen my grip on what I think is right and the way things should be, or how I think they should be. I expected myself to always do the right thing, and then expected everyone around me to do the right thing. It doesn't work like that, and people, well, are fuck-ups. And I have to permit myself to fuck up now and again too."

Jules nodded, and Mia knew she wouldn't get what she was saying until someday when she had kids, a marriage, maybe a divorce, a career, all the big-ticket items women juggle. But now, Mia was seeing it for herself. She couldn't wrap Adam in bubble wrap, safeguarding him from the world, and Eric and Camila were going to be themselves regardless of her anger or admonishments. But Mia could find a less stringent version of herself, give herself a little more room to let go and have some fun. What did Kitty tell her once? "Fun is the glue that keeps your shit together."

Jules nodded again, and her hair made a sweeping motion. How did it do that? Mia got back on track. Enough with the diatribes already, she told herself. "But I have a question. I thought you were in on the curriculum change with Mr. Dunning?"

Jules turned apple-red. Mia recognized that look. It was an embarrassment all women felt when they had done something with the wrong person.

"Jules, was there something going on between you and Tyler?"

"Well, nothing official. We hooked up just once, maybe twice. I had a romantic notion that we made sense since we worked together and were both teachers. And he is okay-looking, but..." Jules made a face like she had smelled rotten broccoli.

"Then you got to know him better?" Mia offered, dying to know the truth.

"Well, he—" Jules hesitated. Then she leaned forward and whispered, "Please don't repeat this...but he was horrible in bed." Jules made a face again. "Like really bad, and his...you know..." and she pointed down, "was really small. All I could think about was a lifetime of bad sex. I'm sorry, but I'd rather be single."

Mia used her fingernails to dig into her leg, desperate not to laugh. That would have been unprofessional. She pressed her lips together and tried as hard as she could not to imagine how small Mr. Dunning's penis could be.

"Well, dear, I don't think there is a woman who would disagree with you."

Jules let out a little laugh. "I'm almost thirty and thought I would be married by now, but I guess I just have to wait for at least something better…or bigger."

Mia couldn't help it and let out a long laugh. And the fact that it was at Mr. Dunning's expense felt even better.

"Jules, we should catch a drink after work sometime. I think you can be an excellent teacher. You have to trust yourself more. Forget the parents, forget the voices in your head, and start trusting your gut, okay? That will get you further than worrying about what everyone thinks."

"Thanks, Mrs. Golding. I appreciate the advice." Jules smiled brightly at her as if Mia had taken a weight off her shoulders. Mia chuckled. This listening and accepting of people was working out for her lately. See, she wasn't such a snob!

She texted Matthew, "How do you feel about rubbing someone else's feet?"

"I'm a doctor," he texted back.

"So that's a yes?"

"Let me put it to you this way…wanna play doctor with me? :)" Now Mia turned red.

Chapter 43
PandaCam

Dave didn't know what to think. The world was falling more out of place than into it. Yesterday, Kitty didn't show up, and Nina was frantic to find her. Then Peter took off and didn't return. Ken sent a cryptic text saying, "We will talk tomorrow. I promise." Whatever the hell that meant. Then late last night, Peter texted that he wouldn't be at the club today. What was going on? Also, his parents asked when they could close the deal. "Soon would be great, David, because I know you want to get rid of us," his mother had said.

Dave responded, confused, "It was your idea to move to the rat's mouth, wasn't it?"

"We wouldn't have had to go if you appreciated us more."

"We are out of orange juice," Dave responded and left for work.

After an hour of rescheduling Peter's appointments and reassigning classes to other coaches, Dave didn't want to be in the pro shop either. He wanted to know what was going on.

Dave biked to Peter's apartment and found Coach Clark yelling at his trash cans.

"Goddam raccoons!" Coach kicked the can that was already lying on the grass.

"Hello, Coach. Where is Peter?" Dave, being Dave, did not offer help of any kind to the older man.

"Try the Kittricks'!" a female voice yelled through the window.

Coach looked at Dave and explained, "There's a problem with Kitty and her family."

Dave was perplexed. "Will she be playing in the tournament? It's imperative she plays in the tournament." He started to panic.

"I don't know, son. We are just hoping for the best right now." Dave noted it was so unlike Coach to be calm and friendly. It was unsettling. Coach offered, "Why don't you go check on them? I think Peter and Kitty might need a close friend right now."

No one had ever told Dave they needed him as a close friend. It was odd, but he recognized the feeling. It was satisfaction. Yes, if his friend needed him, he shall be there. Dave thanked Coach and went to Kitty's house.

Biking up to the Kittrick house, Dave saw Peter's bike by a tree, but the curtains were drawn and the place was quiet. He marched up to the front door and banged loudly to be heard. What if someone was upstairs in the shower? He knocked louder, wanting them to hear him.

The curtain drew back a little from the window next to the door, but Dave couldn't tell who was looking out. The front door swung open, and Peter shouted, "JESUS CHRIST, Dave! You scared the shit out of us!"

Dave noted his friend's disheveled hair and that he was wearing the same clothes as the day before.

"Why did I scare the shit out of you?" Dave asked, confused. "I wanted to ensure you heard me. Were you having sexual relations here? I am assuming that you have spent the night. Therefore sexual relations may have happened."

"Jesus, Dave, I was not having sexual relations! Kitty and Nina are in trouble. Get your ass in here." Peter slammed the door behind Dave.

Nina came from the kitchen. "Coffee, Dave? Sorry, we just woke up. It was a long night." Dave noted that Nina looked tired.

"Where is Kitty?" he asked.

Nina said, "She's at school." She looked at Peter. "Jerry made sure to text me."

"May I know what is going on?" Dave looked between them. Peter sat down, motioned for Dave to do the same, and explained the whole story.

"What does Jimmy look like? Does he have a deformed dragon tattoo on his left arm?" Dave asked, considering the only violent man in Hillsdale he had interacted with was the stranger from the bar.

Nina went pale. "Yes? How did you know?" And Dave told them about Jimmy clocking him at the bar.

"Dave, I am so sorry. Are you okay?" Nina looked worriedly at him.

"Why are you sorry, Nina? You didn't hit me. Yes, I am fine. But I agree, your father is dangerous, and I won't be leaving here either." Dave grabbed a chair and put it by the front window. "I believe we need a lookout." And he sat. "Would you, perchance, have any orange juice?"

Dave's head was full of thoughts now. He had never felt protective of anyone before, but something about Nina and Kitty yanked at his internal emotions. He had been experiencing so many new feelings lately that he wished he had something to organize. Dave knew well enough that it would have been rude to start sorting Nina's knits or reorganizing the spice rack (alphabetically, of course.) Some people don't appreciate it when you go through their things. Like when Dave organized his mother's antidepressants by color. So he took out his phone and made a list: anxiety, sadness, love, want, needs, fear. They had always just been words before, but now he felt like he understood their context better. Humans are complicated individuals.

A text came, and Dave's heart leaped when he saw the name: Ken. "I will see you later today." Now that was finally some good news. Unless Ken wanted to end things in person to see the look on Dave's face. That would be cruel, Dave thought. Ken wasn't cruel. He knew that for sure. He once looked at Ken's iPad and found Ken had been watching a "PandaCam." The Washington Zoo had two baby pandas, and Ken was watching them roll around on their cage floor. Dave joined Ken watching black and white balls of fur roll down logs and jump on each other in bliss. The pandas were joyful. Someone who watched a PandaCam absolutely could not dump him.

Chapter 44
Places, Everyone

Kitty arrived home promptly after school with Jerry. Charging into the house, she went directly to her sister. Nina stood there and waited for whatever was coming. If Kitty wanted to yell, she would have let her. If she wanted to cry, which Nina doubted because Kitty rarely cried, she would have let her. But Kitty, being Kitty, did what Kitty did and surprised her.

Kitty wrapped her sister's more petite frame in her arms and squeezed as tightly as she could, whispering in her ear, "I am so sorry, Nina."

Nina held her back and said, "No, I'm the one who is sorry. I should have told you. I should have prepared you. I had fooled myself into thinking we would never see him again." Tears welled in the sisters' eyes.

Kitty put her face close to Nina's. "You didn't know. What he did to you and Mom was so cruel." The force in Kitty's voice was palpable.

Nina nodded. "He hurt you too, Kitty. I never wanted you to know, but maybe I was wrong."

Kitty pushed her glasses up on her nose and pushed her shoulders back. "No, you did what you thought was right." With absolute certainty, she said, "I can't say I regret not knowing; it made my life easier."

Nina crumbled. "But now your life is harder, and you won't trust me again."

"That's not true! I trust you with my life. No one has protected me more than you." Kitty shook her tousled hair emphatically.

"But Jimmy's back, and he wants to hurt us again. Says he won't go away until he gets the money." Nina scratched her arms.

"Then we fucking get rid of him. I'm not a kid anymore, Nina. We are not victims, and we are not weak. Oma and Pop made us strong. You made me strong, and you are strong too, Nina. The strongest person I will ever know." Kitty could have led an army with her conviction. Talking rapidly, they resolved their issues in no time. It was a sister thing.

"Kitty, what do we do? Should I go to the bank? We have money in our savings," Nina asked.

"Jimmy doesn't get a dime, Nina. If he comes back... Look," Kitty waved her arms, "we have people to help us."

Jerry, Peter, and Dave were standing there dumbly, nodding. They had just watched the girls rocket out years' worth of words in seconds.

"Should we get weapons?" Jerry asked a little too excitedly.

'This isn't *Games of Thrones*, Jerry." Kitty shoved her glasses up to her eyes. "There are no dragons."

"Actually," Dave interrupted, "Jimmy does have a hideous dragon tattoo. Great, now I can never watch *Game of Thrones* again without thinking of his stupid tattoo."

"Dave, stay focused here." Peter shook his head at him.

"Okay, we'll think of something," Nina said, but before she could finish the sentence, there was a knock at the door. They all turned, startled. Dave ran to the window and cried, "Places, everyone!"

Peter looked at Nina, and she nodded. Jerry stood beside Peter as he slowly opened the door.

"Jimmy? I presume?" Peter said sternly.

"Who the fuck are you? The cavalry?" Jimmy didn't wait to get an answer and barged into the house. He looked at them and said, "Oh, hey, the Scooby gang is here. Aren't you the moron I clocked at the bar?" He focused on Dave.

Dave stood his ground. "Sir, I am not a moron."

"Yeah, okay, moron. Think you can take me now?" Jimmy puffed himself up.

"I have no wish to take you," Dave said without looking at him. "I don't prefer men like you." The sarcasm was apparent, but luckily Jimmy didn't catch it.

"So, girls, who wants to give Daddy a hug?"

Kitty took a protective step in front of Nina.

Nina scratched her arms nervously and said slowly, "You gotta go, Jimmy. Kitty and I don't want to see you. You aren't a part of our lives anymore."

"That right, Kitten?" Jimmy questioned Kitty. He looked hopeful that she would disagree.

Nina sneered at him. "Nice try, Jimmy, but here's the thing. You have no idea who Kitty is. You think she's just some dumb kid. The toddler you used to toss about the apartment like a dog. No, Kitty is a helluva lot smarter than that. And she knows exactly who you are and what you are." Nina stood her ground.

"That so, Kitten? Do you think your daddy is some monster, baby girl? It seems like your sister is just as bitchy as she used to be.

All she ever did was lie about me to people. Nina, you are just like Lily, playing the victim to get attention. That's a sad way to live, baby girl."

Kitty rested her weight on one hip and pushed up her glasses. "Don't talk to Nina like that. Ever. I don't *think* anything, Jimmy, because I know you are a monster. And you will get in that shitty car and drive away."

"Who's going to make me do that?" Jimmy threatened, pointing at the guys. "These morons standing there with their mouths open? This town is full of pussies, and now you girls are a bunch of pussies too. Thought I had better genes than that."

"Hey, the women asked you to leave. Get the fuck out," Peter said in a low voice.

"Yeah, get the fuck out, man," echoed Jerry, holding up his fist. Jimmy lunged at Jerry and punched him in the stomach. He crumpled like tissue. "Umph." He could barely breathe. Kitty went to Jerry, but he got up, "I'm fine. I'm fine," and he held his stomach.

Jimmy was angry and disgustingly licked his lips. "I'll shut all you up, so watch it. Now, Nina, I told you what I wanted. Bank's still open, so why don't you get one of these assholes to drive you there and get your father what he is rightfully owed."

"We owe you nothing!" Nina screamed. Kitty stepped toward Jimmy, but Nina's arm shot out and held her back.

"One hour," Jimmy said, pointing a finger at Nina, and turned to leave.

Nina watched Jimmy go down the front steps, and she ran to the front door. Her hand slipped under the coats and pulled the gun out.

No one saw it at first until Nina was standing on the porch, aiming at Jimmy.

"Hey, Dad!" she yelled to get his attention.

Jimmy turned and was surprised to see the gun pointing at him. Nina slowly walked into the yard holding the piece high and steady. "I can end this right now, Jimmy. I believe they call it trespassing." Nina stood with her legs apart, eyes narrowed.

"Ahh, I see you have some fight after all. That's my girl." He laughed. "But you won't kill me."

"I've only dreamed about it for 25 years. Why not?" Nina's voice was calm, as if this moment had parted time just for her to step in and seize it.

Kitty stepped off the porch toward her sister. "No, Nina," she begged. "This isn't you. You save lives. You saved my life. It won't do any good to take his. You don't need any more blood on your hands." Kitty sounded scared.

Then Mia and Adam pulled into their driveway, got out of their car, and stared at the scene in shock. Mia put a protective hand on Adam's shoulder. Everyone was watching.

Kitty went over and gently put her hand on the gun. "Give it to me, Nina. This isn't you. It's not your fight anymore. Don't let him change who you are."

Kitty gently untangled the gun from Nina's hand, and Nina took a step away.

Jimmy started humming. His head swayed from side to side, and his face was jubilant. He was smug and irreverent. Like his whistling, it was intended to convey that he was carefree. Nothing was going to happen to him. He was a man, he was Jimmy, and his daughters were nothing. They got the message.

The sisters looked at each other, and Kitty raised the gun and pointed it back at Jimmy.

"No, no, no, Kitty!" Nina shouted desperately. She instinctively knew he triggered the one thing Kitty couldn't back down from: justice.

Another car pulled onto the street, and Ashley got out. Eyeing the situation, she pulled out her cell phone and made a call. "Oakland Drive, yes, there is a wanted fugitive by the name of James Kittrick threatening the lives of his children. Please, hurry!"

Everyone heard Mia scream, "ADAM!" He was running toward Kitty at a full sprint with Mia after him.

"Kitty!" he shouted. "Karma! Karma, not revenge. You told me revenge doesn't make anyone feel better!" Adam was waving his hands so Kitty would see him.

He kept shouting, "It's Hammurabi's code. You told me that an eye for an eye wasn't justifiable, then everyone gets hurt. Kitty," Adam took a deep breath and shouted, "did you lie to me?" The words landed with Kitty. She looked at Adam.

Kitty pushed her glasses up, and her hand holding the gun shook slightly. Both the sisters wanted Jimmy gone. They wanted to avenge all the pain and sorrow he had caused their family and put it behind them. It was normal to want, but getting there had two paths—one that would scar them further, and another that would free them.

Nina started talking. "Kitty, you belong here with me. You belong on the right side of things too. You always have. Here, come with me. Kitty, don't let him take anything more from us. You don't want to be like him, a murderer, for the rest of your life. You save lives too. You saved mine long ago by being kind, smart, and loving. Don't destroy that part of yourself. Then you wouldn't be you anymore."

Everyone was silent. Distant sirens echoed in the trees.

"Here, Kitty." Nina held out her hand for the gun.

But then, without much forethought because that was what he was known for, Peter charged Jimmy.

Running full speed, Peter body-checked the large man with his shoulder. Everyone gasped as Peter bounced off him. His body was no match for Jimmy's. Like a tennis ball, he hit and ricocheted off. Jimmy only stumbled.

"Peter!" Dave shouted from the porch. "You aren't the goddamn hero!"

Peter just rolled on the ground clutching his arm, moaning into the grass.

But Kitty had already handed Nina the gun. The sisters were looking at each other and nodding silently the way sisters do.

The sirens were getting closer, and Jimmy looked visibly nervous.

"I'll be back for you bitches!" he shouted, running to his car.

Adam went to Kitty and held her tightly. "I knew you were the best person I ever met," he said, crying. "I knew you would never lie to me."

"No, little man." Kitty pulled him closer. "That's the god's honest truth."

Jimmy put the black Corolla into gear and hit the gas pedal.

No one saw the yellow Porsche turn onto the street, and as Jimmy gunned the gas, both cars collided.

The crash was loud; metal compacted and split the afternoon air.

No one moved. But when Peter looked up from the ground and saw the car, he shouted, "CHARLIE!"

When Dave saw the car, he shouted, "KEN!"

Peter pulled himself up and ran to his brother shouting, "Charlie!"

Dave jumped from the porch, shouting, "Ken!"

Peter struggled with the driver's side door to the Porsche. The airbag had deployed, and Charlie's face was bruised and scratched. "Ugh," he moaned. "What the fuck happened?" He saw Peter. "Numbnuts? Why are you here?"

Dave pushed Peter out of the way. "Ken, are you hurt? I will get you an ambulance! Get Ken an ambulance!"

Peter stared bewildered at Dave, and then at Charlie.

"Dave, this is my brother Charlie," Peter said stupidly.

"Peter, this is Ken," Dave said. They both looked down at Charlie/Ken, stunned.

"Yeah, about that…" Charlie looked at them both.

Nina raced over and pushed both men out of the way to examine Charlie. The sirens were close, and everyone was on edge. No one wanted to check on Jimmy in his car.

They could hear him groaning in pain, so they knew he was alive. The old Toyota didn't have an airbag, and a line of blood was going down his face.

Nina assured Dave and Peter that Charlie would be fine, but should go to the hospital to be checked. Ashley was already calling for ambulances.

Nina walked over to Jimmy without saying a word. Father and daughter stared at each other. His eyes narrowed at her. The Porsche had pushed the Toyota's wheel into the driver's side. Nina guessed his foot was crushed, so he couldn't run this time. His head had hit the steering wheel. Maybe there *was* justice.

Ashley appeared at Nina's side.

"Nina, I found out your father is a fugitive. The New Jersey police want him for violating parole and robbing a convenience store. He also stabbed the clerk, who is on life support. If the clerk dies, he will return to jail for murder, hopefully for good."

"Are you sure?"

"Also, he was never supposed to see you and Kitty again. I found an affidavit in his file signed by a judge. Your grandparents created a restraining order that Jimmy would never physically see either you or Kitty for the rest of your lives. That's why your grandparents thought you would be okay."

The police arrived and ran Jimmy's plates. Even the Toyota Corolla was stolen. Jimmy would go back to jail for a very long time.

Nina looked at her father. "Like the kid said, Dad. Karma." And she turned and walked away.

Nina walked slowly back to the house and hugged Kitty for a long time. This was the end and a beginning of a new life for them —one without secrets, lies, or Jimmy. But also life without Oma, Pop, or their mother, just the two of them, and Nina was okay with that. She was okay if it meant the rest of her life doing Kitty's dishes and watching old movies on Saturday nights. Their friends had come to help them, and Nina was grateful for the life they had built from the ashes of her childhood. Bruises can heal, memories can fade, and time will march on with Kitty still able to be Kitty. That was all Nina wanted for herself and her sister.

Ashley came over. "Are you okay, Nina?" Nina nodded and wiped some tears from her eyes. She was exhausted, but yes, she was okay.

"Can't believe Farmer Ted went after your dad like that," Ashley mused. "I mean, who knew Peter had it in him?"

Nina smiled at the thought of Peter doing that for her and Kitty. He tried to protect or save them in a stupid, stupid way. But then, Nina thought that Ashley would be proud of her boyfriend, and a twinge of sadness washed over her.

"He must really like you," Ashley said, confusing Nina.

"Oh, Ashley, I'm so sorry. Nothing happened last night. He just stayed over to make sure I was safe," Nina stammered, realizing how bad it looked.

"He did? How cool," Ashley said.

"But you know, I totally respect him as your boyfriend. I mean, I would never... And all that information you got on Jimmy. I am so grateful," Nina said softly..

Ashley stared at Nina. "Peter, my boyfriend? Ohhhhh." Ashley's hand went up to her forehead like, duh. "Nina, he pretended to be my boyfriend so my mom would leave me alone.

I'm dating this other guy, Ravi. Peter's single. And by the looks of it, he may be into you…" Ashley gave Nina a little shoulder-to-shoulder bump.

Peter was off to the side, watching Charlie being loaded into the ambulance. He looked at the women and gave a goofy thumbs-up.

"He's a good guy, Nina. Sometimes a little slow on the uptake, but there are worse things." Nina felt the rash start on her neck as she flushed. But somewhere down inside of her, she recognized a feeling she hadn't had in a long time: excitement.

It's like when Kitty quotes *The Sound of Music*, in her best Julie Andrews voice, "When God closes a door, somewhere he opens a window." The hills (dale) are alive.

Chapter 45
A Really Great Deal

Sitting awkwardly in the hospital waiting room, Peter didn't quite know what to say, nor did Dave. Peter was trying to process all the information that had just been downloaded into his brain at warp speed. Of course, there was everything with Kitty and Nina, but now there was Charlie. His brother was gay, or supposedly, because he hadn't officially told Peter that. And if he was gay, he was in love with Dave, his best friend and new business partner.

Ashley had given them a ride to the hospital. "So let me get this straight?" Ashley asked. "Your brother has been secretly dating Dave? And you two idiots couldn't figure it out?"

"How was I supposed to know my brother was gay?" Peter whined.

"Yes, if Ken, I mean Charlie, had not told Peter, how was he supposed to know?" Dave agreed.

"Dave," Peter asked, "why was Charlie on your street? How did he know where you live?"

"It was on my spreadsheets, Peter. He said he was coming to see me today."

"Was he going to make up with you?"

"I don't know." Dave looked confused.

Before Ashley let them off at the ER, she turned to Peter. "Nina thought we were dating. Isn't that funny how small a town this is?" Ashley winked at Peter. "Good Luck, Farmer Ted. A little advice, maybe it's time to be a Jake Ryan." And she sped off.

Edie and Bob arrived shortly after and only knew Charlie had been in a car accident. They were nervous, as parents should be when their child was hurt. Edie played with her purse straps, watching the ER door like a hawk for someone to tell her how her son was doing. And Bob had regained the stoicism he had been hiding of late. This was the time for him to play the commander of the family.

"Edie, dear, he will be all right." Bob placed his hands on her leg and rubbed it. It was those sweet interchanges Peter liked to see.

Peter did not want to be the one who outed Charlie. That was up to Charlie, not him. He and Dave said nothing to the Wises about the present situation.

"So, Dave, you are the one going into business with Peter?" Edie tried to fill the silence of waiting. "I think it's all exhilarating. Right, Bob?"

"Yes, yes. Do you guys think you are up to the task? It's an enormous undertaking, and I must admit you both seem a little young for such an operation."

"My dad was 26 when he started the operation, so we are on schedule," Dave announced.

Did Dave have a schedule? Probably, Peter thought. Nothing surprised him anymore. His shoulder hurt from slamming into Jimmy, but he didn't feel like it was the time to start whining about himself.

"Dave, tell us a little about yourself. Do you play tennis?" Edie asked.

"Do I play tennis? No. Hate it. But that will be Peter's job. I will handle the business and finances." Bob perked up in his seat at the word *finances*. It was like a dog whistle.

Dave answered politely, "Yes, sir. I like numbers. I made all the spreadsheets concerning the business and figured out its profitability. I may even get my business degree soon."

Bob made an impressed face. Peter assumed his father thought that all his friends would be idiots. "Well, Peter, where have you been hiding this boy? Can I take a look at your numbers? Would it be too much to go over the business portfolio?"

Dave's head uncharacteristically whipped around, and he looked at Bob.

"Mr. Wise, that would make me very happy indeed. I think you will appreciate all the work I put into it."

"Now, can I ask how you came up with your down payment? Are your parents helping you?" *Oh shit*, Peter thought. *Please don't say it, Dave*, he wanted to shout. *It's a trap!*

"Sort of. First, I will be honest: I like to gamble online. It's my hobby. I wouldn't say I am addicted, but my mind works differently than others. I have a range of autism. I am one of the fortunate ones with exceptional cognitive skills in math. But really, I find counting soothing and with definitive answers. Math lacks the emotional pitfalls that humans get wrapped up in. It lacks sentimentality, which I prefer."

Bob was now on the edge of his seat, nodding vigorously.

"In the past month, I have made a couple hundred thousand dollars by playing blackjack, poker, Mahjong, and betting on sports events."

"What?" Peter cried. He had no idea.

"Yes, Peter. I gamble. But I also asked for money from my

parents because they never paid for college. I figured they owed me." Peter's hand slapped his forehead.

Edie chimed in, "You play Mahjong? I love Mahjong. You should join our group on Saturdays. We have so much fun."

Bob looked at both boys and said, "I see." He smirked at Peter. "You two concocted this plan?"

"Dad, you know, it just…" Peter stammered. Bob held up his hand for Peter to stop talking.

"So your parents have agreed to all this?" Bob questioned.

"Yes, they want to live in a rat's mouth," deadpanned Dave.

"Rat's mouth?" Edie looked confused.

"Mom, they are retiring to Boca Raton," Peter explained. Edie nodded like she understood and didn't say anything further.

Bob continued staring at the two boys, back and forth. Peter thought, *Re-verify our range to target...one ping only.*

Peter waited for his father to say something to admonish them both for bribing their parents. But Bob rubbed his face in an exhausted way. He sighed as if he should just let this one go.

"Dave, you know, I like this. You are an interesting boy." Bob was nodding again with his thoughts. "Now, let me ask you. Have you ever thought about day trading? That sounds up your alley. You can do it from home."

Oh my god, Peter thought. His mother would start playing Mahjong with Dave, and his father would teach Dave about the stock market. But they still didn't know he was dating Ken/Charlie, their son. Oh, Jesus.

A nurse came in and asked only for Peter. Edie, Bob, and Dave looked disappointed, but Peter understood why Charlie wanted to talk to him first.

"Hey, Chuck!" Peter said brightly, tossing back the ER curtain.

"Peter, are Mom and Dad out there?" Charlie looked grim.

"Yep." Peter had a little grin on his face.

"Did you tell them?"

"Tell them what?" Peter shrugged his shoulders and tilted his head. He wanted Charlie to say it.

"You know."

"Know what?" Charlie glared at him. Peter would have stretched the torture out if Charlie didn't look so fragile in a hospital johnny with two black eyes from the airbag. "That you have a secret identity called Ken and have been seeing my friend without telling anyone?"

"Yes," Charlie said glumly.

"First, I need to know. Are you serious about Dave? I mean, you aren't stringing him along? In the last couple weeks, you ghosted him. He's been distraught. Dave is not as immune to emotions as he might let on."

Charlie explained, "When he sent me the spreadsheets for the business, that's when I found out who he was. I didn't know you worked with him, and I freaked out a little. It's not his fault. I was the one lying to him. I thought he was Dave, a beautiful math genius."

"But why? Why have you been lying to all of us?"

"C'mon, isn't it obvious? I was Dad's good kid. While you acted like an imbecile, taking off from Yale and biking around town like a teenager, I was making VP at my firm. Did you see how Dad was so proud of me? You were the golden boy in high school, and I rose in the ranks when you tanked. I wasn't neurotic, pudgy Charlie anymore, but the responsible adult making six figures. I was everything you were not, and it was glorious. I couldn't throw him a curveball like that. I mean, has Dad ever met a gay man? He's from a different generation."

"Dad is not that bad. I don't think you gave him a chance. You just wanted him to see the version of you that you thought he wanted. Let him get to know the real you. Trust me, Dad can handle it. I mean, it's not like you are quitting your 'six-figure' job." Peter made air quotes to annoy Charlie.

"But I like it better when you have all the problems. Takes the heat off me."

"Being gay isn't a problem, bro. It's the twenty-first century."

"I know, but every time I wanted to say something, I felt like a teenager telling them I wasn't a virgin. Who wants to talk about sex with your parents? I mean, you explain to Mom how Tinder works." Peter couldn't help but laugh. So true.

"Hey, Charlie, I failed my classes at Yale. They were going kick me out." Peter let that hang in the air.

Charlie's face brightened. "What? What did you say? I didn't quite hear you." Charlie's spreading smile outshone his two black eyes.

"You heard me. Merry Christmas." Peter smiled back.

"Well, well, well… Dad know?"

"Yup. And he is okay with it."

"Damn," said Charlie, "that's no fun."

"So I know he will be okay with you and Dave."

Charlie sat and stewed a little, thinking. Peter continued, "If this thing with Dave is real, isn't it worth telling them?"

"I want to, but how do I explain Dave? I mean, he's not exactly normal."

"Jesus, Charlie, are you normal? Am I? Mom? Dad? Stop labeling and start living, numbnuts." Peter looked at him. He wanted his brother to get past his insecurities and trust their family. He continued, "Let me tell you what's going on out there. Dave offered to show Dad all his spreadsheets, and Dad practically adopted him. Mom's probably going to make him a casserole later. Listen to me. They like him. I can tell."

"Thanks, Peter. You know, you aren't such a loser all the time.

But I need you to do one thing for me." Peter looked at his brother, and it came to him.

"No way, Chuck. I'm not going to tell them! Hell no."

"Aww, c'mon, Petey... You do this for me, and I'll convince Dad to give you the money whether Kitty wins or not."

Shit, Peter thought. That was a really good deal.

Charlie smiled at his brother. "C'mon, you can't tell me it isn't your wet dream to out your brother. Also, I went over Dave's numbers. You can make the business work."

Peter swooshed the curtains dramatically, yelled, "Fine!" and returned to the waiting room.

Peter marched up to his parents and took the Dave approach. "Mom, Dad, Charlie is fine and...also he is gay. He wanted me to tell you that Dave is his boyfriend."

Peter waited for their reactions. They stared at him for a minute. Then Bob turned to Edie and smiled. "Pay up," he said. Edie looked down at her purse in her lap. She gently zipped it open and withdrew her pink leather wallet. Unclasping it, she withdrew a crisp $20 bill and handed it to Bob.

"You won this one." His mother rolled her eyes.

"Mom, Dad?" Peter looked between them. "Did you have a wager on Charlie being gay or not?" He was flabbergasted.

"I called it in high school, son. I was waiting it out." Bob's grin was more for winning the bet than caring about whom his son fell in love with.

"Well, I suspected," sighed Edie. "But we had already made a bet, so I lost." And it was apparent his mother only cared about losing.

Peter narrowed his eyes. "What other bets do you two have?"

Edie looked away. "Well, that wouldn't be any fun to tell you, darling."

Dave hadn't said anything but was smiling. "Peter, did Charlie say boyfriend? So it's official?"

Peter sat down with a thud. As Kitty said, they were all weirdos.

Chapter 46
Single Best Day

Bob, Edie, and Dave went in together to see Charlie. They did exactly what good upper-middle-class WASPs do—they ignored the situation. While Edie fussed over Charlie and his bruises like a doting mother, Bob excitedly talked about the club's profitability, and Dave stood quietly. He was still unsure of his situation with Charlie/Ken/Charlie and felt they needed a private conversation.

Eventually, Charlie's parents got bored, and the new season of *Better Call Saul* had come out on Netflix. Bob explained there was a pot gummy with his name on it, and Edie was making homemade pizza tonight.

Before they left, Dave watched Bob lean a little closer to his son and whisper something.

Dave couldn't hear it, but Charlie looked at his dad and smiled fondly. "Thanks, Dad." Dave guessed that whatever Bob had said had put the whole gay issue to rest.

Dave liked them. Unlike his parents, he didn't feel uncomfortable around them or find anything particularly annoying about them. He could see himself getting high with ol' Bob and rewatching the movie *Big Country*. Why had Peter never told him what a cool dad he had? And Edie seemed like the type who would have fresh orange juice for him. Yes, Dave wouldn't mind spending more time with them.

Finally, he and Charlie were alone.

"You must have questions," said Charlie sheepishly.

"Yes, I have questions. Your name is not Ken, correct?"

"Correct."

"Am I your boyfriend?"

"Correct." Charlie nodded. Dave felt an immense relief flood through his body. Without thinking, he put his hand on Charlie's for a brief second. It was so uncharacteristic of him that he even shocked himself.

"Why were you going to my house? We usually meet at the hotel." This one detail had particularly bothered him for the past couple hours.

"Dave, it will be my house soon. I was going to sign the paperwork with your parents."

"Excuse me? How is my house going to be your house?" Dave was too stunned to understand. How could Charlie steal his house? It was his house.

"I looked at the comps you gave me, and it's an excellent investment, even with the new roof. So I called your parents and made an offer. It saved us both real estate agent fees, and we are happy with the deal."

"It's my house." Dave started to get worried.

"Yes, Dave, I know. But I was afraid that your parents would sell it to someone else first, then you would lose it completely."

"I hadn't thought of that," Dave said, but he wanted to own

his house, not his boyfriend.

"I drew up a payment plan for you to buy it from me, with interest, of course, when you are ready. That way, you can live in it and pay me off while focusing on the club. You won't lose it to a stranger. Your parents are very anxious to leave town."

Slowly, Dave began to understand. Charlie didn't want it for himself, but saved it so Dave wouldn't lose it. It was the nicest gift anyone had ever given him. And for the second time, Dave uncharacteristically did something. He choked up.

"You bought my house for me?" Dave smiled at Charlie.

Charlie smiled back. "At five percent interest, of course."

"Of course," Dave agreed.

"Also," Charlie continued, "instead of going to a hotel all the time, maybe I can come to stay at your house? Like on the weekends and when I need to check in with my parents. I can't trust them not to be idiots."

"No," Dave agreed, "you can't trust any of us not to be idiots."

"Maybe my mom can do the shopping for you?" Charlie continued. "She likes caring for people, and it would give her something useful to do."

Dave almost fainted. This was the single best day of his life.

Charlie looked at him. "And one other thing. I deleted all my dating apps."

Chapter 47
Extra

Peter took a cab from the hospital, leaving Dave and his family with Charlie. They didn't need him. Also, he was starving and craved Sal's pizza. Sitting in a cold, plastic booth, he ate, but it wasn't as satisfying as he thought it would be. The pizza was delicious, but he felt lonely after being around so many people the past few days. He admittedly missed the chaos. The thought of going back to his apartment by himself didn't sound appealing.

He was startled to see Mrs. Ryan standing over his booth. "Peter, my goodness, are you all right?" She had genuine concern all over her face. "We can't believe what happened to Nina and Kitty today!"

"Mrs. Ryan, how did you know?" Peter was too tired to guess. Again, news like this would certainly go around Hillsdale like wildfire.

"Oh, you are such a lamb. Of course we all know. Ashley told Cami everything, even that you tried to tackle that awful man. You know, I met him at the club one day. Chased him off myself. Those girls should not have a father like that in their life." Mrs. Ryan looked quite confident about that. "And your mother thinks he bumped into her car one day and scammed money out of her!"

"Mom?" Peter was confused. "Is she okay?"

"Oh, Peter, don't worry about us old birds. We still have some bite in us. We protect our own." Mrs. Ryan gleefully smiled. Peter gathered she liked the feeling of a little danger around town.

"Now, us ladies are getting together at your mother's tonight, you know, to chew this thing to the bone. We certainly haven't had this kind of excitement in ages. Probably organize some food for Nina and Kitty, and let them know we are there for them. Your mother explicitly told me to get pizza, I don't know why, but she said she had a special treat for us."

Peter laughed and thought of the gummies. "I'm sure you ladies will have fun."

"Oh, and congrats on the club! Your parents are so pleased." And that struck Peter. They were proud of him. The fact that his mother had turned it into town gossip weirdly validated him. He smiled again. Bless this crazy little town.

"Oh, Mrs. Ryan, you know who you should call? Mrs. Clark. She was a part of it, and I bet she would love to chat about it." He thought about Lois needing some time away from Stevie.

"Ooh, sounds juicy. Will do! Take care, Peter." Armed with three pizzas and a bag of garlic breadsticks in her mouth, Bunny Ryan appeared young again.

Peter remembered his bike was still at Nina and Kitty's and thought that it wasn't a bad idea to take them a pizza and get his bike. He knew it was only an excuse to see them...or maybe it was to see *her* again.

When Ashley winked at him, something struck him, and he was just now putting it into thought. Nina Kittrick was a possibility.

That's what he had never felt before until now. It was a possibility with Dave, with Kitty, with the club, and maybe now with Nina. It turned out he hadn't done anything to her in high school except not notice her. Now he saw her not only for her beauty, but her strength. Peter felt lucky to know her. It was a new feeling that made him nervous. He ordered a pizza with extra pepperoni because Kitty would appreciate the gesture. He liked when he made Kitty happy; she almost felt like a little sister to him.

Peter walked to their house, taking in the brisk night air. The stars were shining in the cold, and he could smell fireplaces filling the night air with burning oak and hickory. He loved that smell. Winter would be coming soon, but for now, the fall leaves crunched below his feet, and he wanted nothing more.

Peter gently knocked on the front door. Kitty opened it with a smile. "Peee...teeerr, long time, no see," she joked and eyed the pizza. "There better be pepperoni on that thing."

"Extra," he said.

"I have taught you well." She grabbed the box and turned away. Nina came to the door.

"Hi, Peter. That was nice of you."

"Well, you know, Kitty loves pizza." They both laughed nervously.

"I wanted to thank you for last night and today. How's your shoulder?"

Nina stood there, slightly scratching her arms. She was in her old sweatpants, and her hair was piled in a messy bun. The streetlight reflected on the gold rim of her glasses, but Peter could look into her bright blue eyes.

"It's fine. I just wanted to see if you guys needed anything, and, you know, grab my bike."

"Oh, yes, your bike. But do you want to come in?" She was smiling at him.

"I don't want to bother you guys. You must be tired. I'll get my bike and go."

"Oh, okay. Well, thanks, guess we will see you later." Peter wasn't sure what he detected in her voice. But he turned to go. The front door was closing when he got to the bottom of the porch steps.

"Nina!" he turned and shouted. The door reopened, and she stood there. Without any forethought, Peter climbed the steps as fast as he could, put his hands on her shoulders, and kissed her. It lasted seconds or years, Peter would never remember, only that it was the greatest shot he ever took.

"ABOUT DAMN TIME!" Kitty yelled from the hallway, pizza grease dripping down her face.

Chapter 48
Oedipal Thing

Mia was startled when she walked into the school library. The room was packed with adults and children alike. She stopped for a second and looked around. The irony was to have the meeting in a library of all places. This could be Principal Jenkins' subtle way of making a joke. Libraries were notoriously against banning literature. They acquiesced to censure by putting a warning note on some books, but otherwise, librarians were subversive operatives saving the written word—no matter how old or outdated. They were education's secret army. Maybe they had a password? Fitzgerald or Twain?

Mia tried not to make eye contact with anyone. She knew there were people who either were pro or con or just there to create a whole new argument, like banning football because of concussions, or implementing a dress code. Maybe doing away with health education, which was just a code word for sex ed. Mia knew how these meetings worked. They opened a window, and just about anyone and their agenda would jump through it.

Mr. Baxter had saved her a seat between him and Mrs. Wills. She nodded happily to Jules, who was also seated with them. Mr. Baxter had the crossword out and was adept at ignoring the crowd. Mrs. Wills showed Jules pictures of her new oven and explained that spicy Italian sausage was her lasagna's secret ingredient. Mia liked their little huddle until she noticed Tyler pacing on the opposite side of the room. He had worn an expensive suit, and his black hair was slicked back with some form of gel.

"More vampire than statesman," Mr. Baxter chuckled in her ear. Mia repressed a smile. She noticed Tyler had index cards and was cueing up for a battle. Mia had done some reading, but Matthew had advised her to wing it. *Don't sound prepared*, he said, *sound passionate*. That was good advice, she thought, as long as she didn't come off like a ranting middle-aged woman.

Principal Jenkins had gone so far as to hook the microphone to the library's rickety old podium. He obsessively tapped it, and two pimply-faced students were fussing with the wires. Who didn't love the audio-visual club nerds who would someday rule Hollywood with indie films?

"Can't get a read on him. Is he judge or jury tonight?" Baxter again said in a low voice.

"Jenkins is walking the line. Hard to placate everyone, Mr. Baxter. I don't envy him," said Mia. If being head of one department was this complicated, how about dealing with a whole school?

"Thank you, everyone, for coming," the principal began. Mia noted that he had not changed his usual dark blue blazer for the occasion, or his stained Burberry oxford. He had a habit of rubbing his balding head when he spoke and swayed in his worn loafers. Near retirement, Jenkins was just there to make it through the night unscathed and keep the endowments intact.

"As you know, there are concerns about the curriculum regarding the English Department. I understand everyone has an opinion, but let's be respectful of whoever is talking, and one at a time. Let me clarify: no decisions will be made tonight about what literature will or won't be taught at Hillsdale Prep. We are a private institution that promises the highest education to your children. We are committed to what benefits the Hillsdale community, and we value the input all of you have to offer. First, we will begin with Mr. Tyler Dunning, who brought the issue to our community's attention, and then we shall hear from Mrs. Golding, the head of the department." Jenkins did a little sidestep so Tyler could start.

"How exceedingly diplomatic," Mrs. Wills whispered to Mia and rolled her eyes.

Honestly, Mia heard nothing Tyler said. The gist was that certain LGBTQ books were grooming kids to explore sexuality. Other books contained too much sex, violence, glorified foul language, and drug use. It was the same rhetoric Mia heard from politicians; frankly, the sound bites were old and overused.

Mia twisted in her seat, not about what he said, but more about what she would say. Mr. Baxter didn't help by muttering "Horseshit" and "Christ almighty" several times. It took Tyler ten minutes to finish his diatribe, and Mia could see the room had waned on his platitudes. When he said, "I believe the children are our future," Mia almost shouted, "Teach them well and let them lead the way!" But she doubted Tyler would find the Whitney Houston reference funny.

Mia was called to the podium. And when she looked up at a sea of eyes waiting for her impassioned plea to teach kids, to let them understand stories and literature, to allow them to decide how to handle sensitive material, all the things she believed in—she saw Adam giving her the thumbs-up sign. Mia caught her breath. Nina was next to him waving as well, and Mia assumed Adam had convinced her to bring him. Her son had wanted to come because he believed in her and loved her. Mia smiled so proudly that she didn't even care what came out of her mouth.

"Hello, every——" But before she could speak, the library doors slammed open. It was Kitty, pushing her glasses up as she surveyed the room. Mia thought she looked glorious in a bright neon yellow tracksuit and her hair bedecked with rainbow ribbons.

Even Mr. Baxter set down his crossword to watch the scene. Principal Jenkins took a step forward, but Mia waved her hand at him and roared into the microphone. "I think it would be great to hear from a student. It's their education, after all."

Kitty stepped toward the microphone without hesitation. She commanded the room. Being so tall came in her favor, with broad shoulders and wavy hair that were hard to look away from.

Kitty tilted her head, smiled, and stated, "This week, I learned the most horrific thing in my life, and it wasn't from a book. My father murdered my mother. I had been made to believe he was dead, but he wasn't. He had been in jail and returned to threaten my sister and me. We are okay now, and my father is returning to jail." She expertly paused, waiting for the information to roll throughout the room. Kitty was well aware she and Nina had been branded orphans by the Hillsdale community, and this would certainly be news to them.

"My point is, bad things happen, and they happen all the time. You can't shelter us from it. You can't censor life. Books are a reflection of life. They are stories, and our lives are stories too. If you tell us not to read other people's stories, we will stop writing ours. We will stop finding our commonalities, learning about the hero or heroine and how they overcame obstacles and found brave new worlds. You will be muting us with your fear that, what? We will grow up? That bad things will happen? That we will experiment with drugs and alcohol? That we will have sex?

Because only one in five teenagers are not having sex, by the way."

"Okay, that's enough, young lady," Tyler interjected loudly across the room.

Mia almost said something, but Mr. Jenkins stood up. "No, she can continue. Go on, Kitty. I think we all need to hear what you have to say."

Tyler shook his head with disgust. Kitty pushed up her glasses.

"Speaking of sex, which is your point, Mr. Dunning, correct? You think some books are too sexually explicit? Too graphic? Talk about, god forbid, masturbation or rape?"

He stared coldly at her.

"You think we, as teenagers, can't handle it? Is that your point?"

"Yes," he replied. "It's inappropriate to talk about in an academic setting."

"Wanker," Mr. Baxter said a little too loudly, and some parents snickered.

"Does anyone here know who Dr. Susan is?" Kitty asked with a grin on her face.

Dr. Susan was a nationwide sex therapist who rocketed to fame on the radio, discussing how to achieve orgasms with or without a partner. After being heralded by Oprah and Ellen, she became a household name and wrote the bestseller, *The Perfect O*, which by 2010, almost every American woman had a copy of.

Mia watched Tyler, whose anger was palpable. His hands began to ball into fists, and Mia closely watched him. Would he punch Kitty?

"Come now, a show of hands, Dr. Susan?" Kitty lifted her hand, and ninety percent of the room did as well.

Satisfied with the outcome, Kitty continued, "We all know that Dr. Susan talks about one thing and one thing only: sex.

According to Forbes, she's worth about 50 million dollars for helping people with what's clearly an essential subject matter. Something that people are eager to read about."

"Kitty Kittrick, stop right now, or I will have you thrown out of Hillsdale," Tyler shouted.

Kitty patiently looked over at Mr. Jenkins, who was rubbing his bald head, weighing his options. Mia could tell he was as curious as the rest about where this was going.

"Kitty," Jenkins said, "please get to your point?"

"Yes, Mr. Jenkins. For a mere $19.95 and the internet, it's amazing what you can find out about people. Dr. Susan dated a tantric yoga instructor in Boston named Swami in the late nineties. His original name was Kevin Schlepper, and he was from Pittsburgh. Together they made sex tapes to buy, which helped contribute to Dr. Susan's fame. Again, the public wants to know how to have good sex. The Pope even admitted online porn is a vice for nuns and priests."

"Kitty!" Tyler screamed.

"Okay!" Kitty screamed back. "In 1994, Dr. Susan and Swami had a baby boy. Since the Swami had no last name and had thrown out Schlepper, the boy took his mother's surname. According to Boston records, the boy's original name was Bhakti Dunning, but it was officially changed to Tyler on his eighteenth birthday."

"Fucktrumpet," said Mr. Baxter, having moved to the edge of his seat.

Mia's mouth fell open, and she heard gasping around the room. Mrs. Wills turned to Jules and said, "*The Perfect O* changed my marriage. Do you have a copy, dear?" Jules sheepishly nodded.

The color drained from Tyler's already abnormally pale skin. Mia noted that he had almost gone catatonic with rage.

Kitty used the silence of everyone's shock to continue. "Also,

Dr. Susan Dunning published a smaller, lesser-known book called *His Wet Dream*, documenting her teenage son's puberty and sexuality. It can be purchased on Amazon for $9.99 in paperback or Kindle."

Mr. Jenkins now had his head almost between his knees. Senator Crawley got up and stormed out of the room.

Kitty turned to Tyler and couldn't help herself. "So, Mr. Dunning, what's this really about? Getting back at your mother? Some sort of Oedipal thing? It's not about us at all, is it? Are you just embarrassed by your mother?"

"Okay! That's enough, Kitty!" Principal Jenkins got up and grabbed the podium. Mia heard chants of, "Here, Here, Kitty! Here, Here!" A group of kids in rainbow colors jumped up and down in the back of the room. Several parents started making their way toward the exit like rats on a ship going down.

Mia caught Nina's gaze. She was laughing so hard that tears were running down her face. Adam was fist-pumping for Kitty. Some moments are just too good to describe.

Principal Jenkins said slowly, "This meeting ends right here. For now, the curriculum will stay the same, and if any parents have any concerns about it, they may come directly to me, not to my staff. Hillsdale Prep is committed to giving your kids the finest education as we see fit. And I'd like to add that personal opinions or agendas will not sway us." With that, he swung his head around toward Tyler, who appeared to be hyperventilating. Kitty handed him a paper bag.

Mia stared in awe at Kitty. That girl was going to do great things someday, she thought. Kitty looked at her and winked.

"Atta girl, Kitty, atta girl," Mia said to no one.

Chapter 49
The Stanley Cup

Small towns are filled with characters, both ordinary and extraordinary. Places like Hillsdale function year after year, generation after generation, with merciless charm if one chooses to find it. There live the people who realize there is no secret to happiness except hope, and no formula for change except will. Bad things happen, but also good things too. The past will always be present, but the present creates opportunities for the future. The important part is to remember the moments that change everything. Duh.

Coach Clark was pacing and digging his thick fingers around in a zip-lock bag of baby carrots. One by one, he was loading them into his mouth and chomping noisily. Little bits of orange gathered on his chin and spewed from his mouth.

Kitty sat there calmly. She was adjusting her new rainbow-colored headband, trying to stuff stray blonde hairs into it.

"This is it," he said. Kitty laughed because Coach was acting like it was the locker room of USA v. Russia.

"Yes, Coach." She smiled warmly. Strangely, she wasn't nervous but excited to get back on the court. Playing felt good to her. This was the tournament's final match, and she had done it. For five days, Kitty was undefeated and had taken out the first-seeded player. This was it. If Kitty won, she would be the champion.

But she didn't feel any pressure. In the back of her mind was the week before, when she held a gun for the first time. Everything with Jimmy happened so fast, and her reaction scared even her. Kitty didn't think she was capable of killing anyone. The idea had never occurred to her—not once. But the anger and hatred she felt toward her father were overwhelming. Like when people say you have an out-of-body experience. For an instant, Kitty thought killing Jimmy would solve her problems. But she understood that nothing that violent ever would. It was Kitty's first life-altering choice, and she stared it down. She had harnessed her power, as the infomercial said.

Now? Winning a junior tennis tournament felt like a piece of cake. Every second she was on the court, she felt stronger and faster. The ball came at her, and Kitty had to think, strategize, and hit it the best way she knew. Nothing more and nothing less existed on the tennis court except her ability to play. She wasn't the daughter of a criminal. She wasn't an orphan of tragedy. Her body wasn't overly large, nor her hair too wild. The crowd cheering also helped. Kitty loved the attention and being seen for exactly how strong she was.

This was what it was all about for her, making the right choices.

"One fair shot, that's all any of us want, Kitty. One fair shot at life. It's up to you, and only you, what you do with it. Are you going to take it?"

"Yeah, Coach. And, Coach?" Kitty said, looking into the older man's eager eyes. "Don't worry about cancer. You're going to be fine. We can beat that too."

Coach Clark stopped chewing and smiled down at Kitty with love.

"You know, if you win or lose, we love you, Kitty. Everyone out there won't give a damn if you lose, so you don't think about them. You don't think about pissant here." Coach thumped Peter on his bad shoulder.

"Owww, Coach."

"Pet...errr, man up." Kitty laughed.

Coach continued, "You think about yourself and what you can do for yourself. You got the ability, do you hear me?"

"Yes, Coach." Kitty rolled her eyes a little.

Dave had made sure the Hillsdale Tennis Club was represented by color-coding the fans. He purchased Peter and Coach Clark matching red and white tracksuits with *Hillsdale* embroidered on the back. Kitty wore a bright red tennis dress, but he had allowed the rainbow headband and socks. It was Kitty, after all. She would have done it anyway.

Bunny Ryan and Cami Tinsdale sported new pink jackets with the red embroidered Hillsdale logo. He had made a special limited edition for the ladies of the club. Charlie had been right; they paid more for the clothing because of the word "limited."

The Wises, Dave, Ashley, Jerry, Mia and Adam, Mrs. Clark, and Nina all had chosen the white and red t-shirts, the *un*limited version. Dave was proud of how neat and concise their section on the bleachers looked. Everyone was in order, unlike the hodgepodge of other clubs. Charlie couldn't come because of a business meeting, but Dave videotaped the match. Depending on Kitty's outcome, they would watch it later at Edie's Thanksgiving and/or celebration party. Everything was in place.

Kitty won the first set 6-3. Then she lost three games in the second set but came back 5- 4. If she won the last game, she would win her first tournament. It was 40-30, advantage Kitty. If she aced this serve, Kitty would win.

One fair shot, she thought to herself, *that's all any of us ever want.*

Kitty threw the ball in the air and slammed down her arm with everything she had.

Everyone from Hillsdale screamed.

Bob Wise turned to his wife and smiled sweetly. He raised the palm of his hand and said, "Pay up, darling."

Edie smiled brightly and pulled a crisp $20 from her pink leather wallet. Sometimes you have to lose a little to win everything.

The End

BOOKS BY
HAYS BLINCKMANN

In The Salt

Where I Can Breathe

Yell Out Loud

Here, Kitty

Hays Blinckmann

ABOUT THE AUTHOR

Hays Trott Blinckmann is a writer, journalist, teacher, and recovering painter. She has a Bachelor of Arts from Tufts University and a Bachelor of Fine Arts from the School of the Museum of Fine Arts, Boston. Hays Blinckmann lives in Key West, Florida, with her husband and two sons. Her other novels, *In the Salt, Where I Can Breathe,* and the young adult novel, *Yell Out Loud,* are available on Amazon and at Key West bookstores.

If you enjoyed this book, please review it on Amazon.com. This is a self-published novel, and with your help reviewing and recommending it on social media, *Here, Kitty* can reach a larger audience. Places, people. Places! Thank you.

Get more information at
www.authorhaysblinckmann.com.

ACKNOWLEDGEMENTS

My editor, Emma Borges-Scott, thank you for knowing my voice and relentlessly finding the better story.

My graphic designer and loyal friend, Irene de Bruijn, whose creativity and humor make this writing life way more fun.

To those who keep me sane daily: Kerry Gallagher, Alisa King, Leslie Johnson, Raquel and Pepe Gonzalez, although no one should listen to Pepe.

To those who have been in my life for the long haul, near and far, thank you for knowing all along who I was supposed to be... and pointing it out.

My ride or die family: Tricia Brown (The Knowles Clan: Harvey, Drew and Katie), and lastly, Forgan McIntosh, my brother Fred.

To my German family: Julia & Birger, Sanya, Kaya, Stella, Tina, Oma, and Opa, thank you for your never-ending support.

To the city of Key West and all its wonderful inhabitants who support their own.

My sister, Buffy, who taught me how to laugh and still causes me to lose it with a single phrase from a movie. Love you always. Nellliieee... Celieeee...

Lastly, to my true loves, my husband, Jan-Marten, and my sons, Hugo, and Max—may I always find new ways to tell you how much I hate loading and unloading the dishwasher. And that I love you most of all.